PRAISE FOR *THE FARMHOUSE*

"A fresh start becomes the stuff of nightmares for a husband and wife on a rural Nebraskan farm in Chelsea Conradt's twisty debut. Whispering cornfields, a restless barn, and a truly terrifying number of teeth abound in this **slippery slow burn of a haunted tale**."

—Christa Carmen,
award-winning author of *The Daughters of Block Island*

"*The Farmhouse* is a **thought-provoking, action-packed thriller**... Conradt has a knack for building tension and creating fierce, unapologetic women... A must-read for anyone who enjoys a thrilling journey that champions women's strength and agency."

—Lisa M. Matlin, author of *The Stranger Up*

"Haunting and atmospheric, **Chelsea Conradt's debut th** **led me on a chilling ride to a deadly crescendo**. I did not s end coming!"

—Nalini Singh, *New York Times* bestselling auth

"**An unputdownable novel**. Emily's quickening spiral into paranoia feels both terrifying and relatable, a woman's cry to be heard, to be acknowledged, while those she trusts the most attempt to placate her into silence. **A smart, chilling, ferociously feminist thriller**."

—Kristen Simmons,
Bram Stoker Award nominee

"**A deviously twisty thriller** that kept me turning the pages, eager to see what happened next."

—Kelley Armstrong, *New York Times* bestselling author

"*The Farmhouse* will leave you looking over your shoulder for stalker barns. The story is a **satisfyingly layered** narrative that explores both the isolation of small towns and the loneliness one can feel within their closest relationships. **I expect big things for Conradt.**"

—Jaye Wells, *USA Today* bestselling author of
High Lonesome Sound

"*The Farmhouse* twists together the threads of rustic dreams and pastoral nightmares, creating **an atmospheric read that will haunt you long after the story is done. Conradt's thrilling debut is not to be missed.**"

—Lish McBride, author of *Red in Tooth and Claw*

"Wholly **gripping, chilling, and compulsively addictive...** Conradt masterfully crafts a fast-paced, eerie thriller."

—Rachel Fikes, author of *Keeper of Sorrows*

THE FARM HOUSE

A NOVEL

CHELSEA CONRADT

Poisoned Pen
PRESS

For Lish and Kristen,
who should both live much closer to me.

Published by Poisoned Pen Press, an imprint of Sourcebooks
P.O. Box 4410, Naperville, Illinois 60567-4410
(630) 961-3900
sourcebooks.com

Cataloging-in-Publication Data is on file with the Library of Congress.

Printed and bound in Canada.
MBP 10 9 8 7 6 5 4 3 2 1

CHAPTER 1

THEY'D TOLD ME THE CORNFIELDS CARRIED A CURRENT IN the summer, but no one said it could pull me under. No one told me I could drown here. In the middle of a field. Alone in a sea of green stalks.

It'd started beneath the summer sunshine, warmth and welcome washing over me. My husband Josh and I were three days in and eighty-seven miles out from our destination: mile marker 116 on Route 136.

The address read like a clue in one of those murder mystery delivery boxes. We'd tackled one early on in our perpetually at-home life, but the grisly nature unnerved Josh. Or maybe he didn't like that I was *really* good at solving crime. Probably intimidating to have a potential crime-fighting hero in your home. The destination, though, had zero death, ghosts, or sickly memories for us: a farmhouse.

Our farmhouse.

Even with speed-limit signs that read more as a challenge than a limit, the drive from California to Nebraska was into day three. We'd researched ahead of time, of course, but I wasn't certain knowing the state was No. 2 in cybersecurity and also the home of Kool-Aid counted as prepared.

My mother would never have let me live down this move, but if she were still alive, I might not have needed the clean slate it provided. I'd grown up between the brightly painted Victorian homes and the sticky punk rock shops of Haight-Ashbury—San Francisco's best neighborhood, if you had asked my mother.

But then Penelope Wagers had been a paid arbiter of cool for decades. Her voice, sweet and salty, with too little sleep and two sips of liquor, enveloped me.

"Emily, the Bay is in your blood," she'd say, probably flinging her arms wide like the drama could encompass everything she loved about my hometown. "I raised you with far too much style to waste in a field somewhere."

Mom had a way of delivering compliments that snuck a jab around back afterward. *Style* had never been my area. *Aesthetic*, yes. It's what made me land in graphic design and not fashion. Even imagining her distaste for my decision didn't make me miss her less. It'd been six months since she passed—the nice way the hospice workers described the quick decline from thriving fifty-eight-year-old to gone.

She'd liked Josh, but I suspected she would have blamed this move on him. When he'd crashed out after two cups of Mom's signature eggnog, she'd teased, "He wouldn't have made it a night on the Haight in the seventies."

"Good." I'd lifted a glass in salute to her. "I want a man who thinks I look hot in lounge pants and is happy to snuggle on the couch with me."

She'd tapped her glass to mine, but her attention flitted to everything in the room that wasn't me. "All I want is your happiness."

I needed to quit letting my thoughts, my heart linger in her memory, but all attempts had failed. There was value—and hope—in this journey. I had to cling to that, to the future. I had Josh, a job I could do from anywhere, and a new life waiting for me whenever our GPS led us to the turn toward the farm. Our new mailbox's little flag waved hello. This was my path back to happiness, and I was determined not to get lost.

The land here was beautiful. Yellow fields waved from either side of the moving truck, welcoming us to the Heartland. Water towers stretching white or blue in the distance, marking other small towns. Not that I could see much in the way of buildings. The last half dozen towns we'd passed through had populations less than three hundred. There were more people who took 6 a.m. workout classes at Lifetime with me than lived in those entire communities. Nebraska was nothing but glorious space and freedom, and Josh and I deserved them both.

Loose pebbles pelted the underside of the U-Haul. I'd already tapped Josh's arm a half dozen times to slow down. I'd expected dirt roads, but there was more gravel than anything else on this last stretch to our new home.

Our new home.

Hope bubbled bright beneath my breastbone. Nebraska was the

start of something big. This bumpy road was the kind of precipice that lifted your belly with flashes of future freedom. I'd felt it when I'd left for college. When I'd found a creative job that was distinctly corporate. If you needed graphics for a white paper about accounting or human resources software, or a style guide for your attorney's website, I was your girl. Going corporate had given me that same tinge of fear, but it turned out health benefits were rad. Being the reliable graphic designer at a behemoth agency meant people only cared enough to tap the party horn icon on Zoom when you announced you were buying a farmhouse in the middle of nowhere. The specter of my mom tried to resurrect, all effervescence fizzling. Six months wasn't long enough to dull the pain of losing her. Would six years? Six decades? Would I be alive in sixty years if my mother died at fifty-eight? Those other moves had been leaping to new adventures, but if I was honest with myself, this time I was fleeing the past.

Plink. Pli-pli-pli-plink. "Those rocks are going to wreck something."

"It's a rental." Josh thrummed his fingers against the steering wheel like the jostling was more massage chair than a puke-over-the-edge boat ride.

My stomach was less convinced.

"Our car is hitched to the back." Had memory swallowed him too? Or was he simply drinking in the expansive scenery?

Josh swore and slowed the moving truck. "We're here though."

A simple white mailbox marked the driveway. We turned onto a dirt road. Dust whirling behind us in the side mirrors. Fields stretched on either side of the path. Green and thick and structured. The road arced hard to the right, revealing our farm.

The house's exterior was picture-perfect, which made sense since we'd toured over FaceTime. Good to know our Realtor wasn't working camera angles on us. It was a single-story ranch painted white. Two steps led up to a porch nearly as long as the house. A wooden bench swing hung at one end. Like, the Waltons would be jealous of this style. Not that the house was big enough for a TV family like that. It was only Josh and me, making the three-bedroom setup perfect. One room for us, one for a home office, and one to set up for guests, because eventually people might visit. (Okay, we were putting gym equipment in next to a pull-out couch. But *if* someone decided to visit, we'd move it.)

"This is good." Josh slipped his arm around me, my constant home. "Everything you thought?"

"Even better." My gaze skipped from the daylilies blooming in the front garden to the endless blue sky surrounding us to the barn. "Did they show us the barn?"

While the house was ready to be submitted to some home and garden magazine, the run-down barn would not be allowed in the background of a two-page spread. The walls were a mishmash of peeling gray and red paint. Darkness speckled the corners and eaves. The window over what I expected was the loft had only one of the four panes of glass still intact. At least the eyesore was a healthy distance from the house.

"There were pictures. Remember, it's part of the farm?" Josh's attention locked solely on me. Seven years in, and he could still make me feel like the center of the universe.

"Right. The farmers have access to it." We weren't trying to change careers here. I knew exactly shit about gardening or grains or working a tractor. The folks who had sold us the house wanted to keep the fields and tend to them. So we got the house and leased the farmland back to the people who actually knew how to use it.

Josh rolled his shoulders. I pressed my palm to the center of his back and slowly rubbed. We both would feel that car ride tomorrow.

"We can use the barn too, for storage or to park the car when storms hit."

I squinted at the barn, and my stomach lurched. When had we last eaten? "It's far from the house."

"That's why we're parking up here, Em." Josh leaned over and kissed my forehead.

I clambered out of the moving truck and took in a noseful of country air. "You smell that?"

"Clean air?" A dimple flashed in his right cheek.

"I totally thought it was bullshit."

"You thought people made up fresh air?" He wasn't even bothering to hold back his laughter.

"I understand air pollution and smog, and that some days it's gloomy because of selfish, climate-change denying assholes driving big SUVs in rush hour, but I didn't think it actually *smelled* different." I inhaled, saturating myself in the fresh euphoria.

"You're ridiculous and I love you." Josh pressed his lips against my forehead once more and then offered me a proper kiss.

I surely smelled like fourteen hours in a moving truck, but Josh wrapped his arms around my back and lifted me. And everything was freedom during that kiss. His body supporting mine—which, God, I'd let him do so much the last year while I tried not to fall apart in grief—but now he held me with only excitement behind his eyes. I slipped my hands up the back of his neck, letting my nails graze him. His smile forced my own. All I cared about now was the clean air in my lungs, the man before me, and our fresh start.

When he finally released me, we were both breathless. A fresh start indeed.

Our Realtor had left the key out front. A heavy black rubber mat with the bold red *N* of the University of Nebraska's Cornhuskers—a logo I'd seen on billboards, in store windows, and on T-shirts at every stop within the state—had been placed before our front door. Its center hid the brass key. The mat was crisp on the white wood of the porch, but the big yellow sunflowers and "Welcome" in looping script on the coir mat I'd brought were far homier. I could move this one to the back entrance. The grooves would be good for cleaning mud off running shoes.

Josh unlocked the door and stepped through first. "It looks huge without furniture."

"It's bigger on the inside!" I couldn't resist the joke.

Josh groaned, continuing to pretend he hated *Doctor Who*— even if I caught him watching it every time he was sick.

He was right though. Not about the Doctor, but about our new home.

Our apartment in Mission Bay had two bedrooms, eight hundred square feet, and zero space. This house tripled our living area.

We had an extra bedroom and a kitchen with counters for days. And the mortgage cost less than half our monthly rent.

"We're going to have to buy more stuff," I said, stalking across the oak floors into the empty living room.

"Or we could enjoy the extra white space."

"White space is useful on a website, but in a home, it just makes it feel cold."

Josh leaned against the counter marking the entrance to the kitchen. "We don't need to fill every corner..."

He was talking about my mom's place. There was a difference between a collector and a hoarder, but where that line landed depended on your personal sensibilities. Josh and I had different barometers. My mom had loved vibrant fabrics and killer music. Decades of producing music will do that to you. Signed music memorabilia covered the walls of her home. Silk screen prints and concert posters and drumheads. She'd repurposed the utensil pot from the kitchen to hold drumsticks from visiting friends. You came, you signed your stick, and dropped it in. It really was a wonder that I didn't become a drummer.

"I'm not trying to cover our walls immediately," I muttered.

Josh's tone softened, as it always did when the memory of my mother or the rawness of my grief clawed its way into our conversations. "They are awful stark though. These walls."

"I might have already considered that." The paint swatches had been on my desk for weeks. Cornflower blues and sunflower yellows. A summer palette to steep our sweet new home in.

"We can get paint tomorrow after I knock out those UK calls."

Right. We'd taken our time trekking across the Rockies, and Josh had pushed off some sales meetings until tomorrow. Unfortunately, with the time difference, he'd be up before the sun tomorrow. I swiped a hand over my face, like I could clear the sweat of future anxiety. "We need to set up your desk first. Where did we put it in the truck?"

"Calm down, Em. That's why we have virtual backgrounds."

"I thought we had them because people wanted to cover up those piles of unfolded laundry when they worked from their bedrooms."

"Or maybe it's weird to know you're *in* your coworker's bedroom?"

I snorted. "Now I'm picturing your boss lounging on his bed while talking about a software update."

"Why did you have to say that? Now I'm going to be thinking of Dennis in his boxers when I talk to him tomorrow."

"I'm sure he'll wear a shirt." My company didn't have a camera-always-on policy, but I still wore work-y tops in case we had to show our faces. Workwear was now in mullet form. Business on the top, nap-ready on the bottom.

My phone vibrated in my back pocket. "Weather app says it's going to rain in thirty-four minutes."

"That's precise," Josh deadpanned.

"How much do you think we can move in here before then?" My body was achy from sitting all day and my stomach sour from drinking gas station coffee, but I also did not want to sleep on the floor tonight.

"Bed, at least." This man read my mind. "And the priority stuff out of the car."

"You mean everything in the car," I corrected. We'd put the items we'd need immediately, like the coffee maker and our shower essentials, into the sedan we'd towed behind the U-Haul. I'd also put my mom's turntable and the most prized records from her collection there. You did not risk those kinds of precious belongings in the black hole that was a twenty-two-foot moving truck.

"Yes, that's exactly what I meant." No, he had not.

Someday I'd find the record that converted him into a vinyl enthusiast.

It took us a solid ten minutes to get our bed into the house. The sky darkening by degrees each minute. We didn't know this house yet. Where to turn, where to step. Moving it was an exercise in Josh smacking his back into doorframes, me getting a mattress plowed against my sternum, and the kind of swearing that would have had the neighbor in 2D doing her damn lean-into-the-hallway judging move. At least we got to fight the fucking thing without an audience. Josh brought in the toiletries and the quickly packed clothes. I'd just carried the last box of records into the house when lightning split the sky.

My stomach rumbled moments before thunder cracked hard enough to rattle our new windows. "Are they supposed to shake like that?"

My even-keeled husband didn't even flinch. "I think so? I could call Realtor Rita, but we're in a 'you bought it' situation, babe."

I shook my head and stalked toward our kitchen. The shush of rain cocooning us in our new haven. I yanked open the fridge out of habit. It was empty save a bottle of champagne, two flutes, and a note card.

"Who leaves a note in the refrigerator?"

I lifted the chilled bottle and smiled at its orange label. "Don't care if they leave the note duct-taped to the door, if they leave Veuve Clicquot."

I passed the bottle and flutes to Josh and opened the envelope. "It's Rita's 'welcome to Nebraska' note. She says she hopes the farm fills our hearts with love and..."

"Hmm?"

"She thought she should remind us the back bedroom would make a perfect nursery."

"Do women usually have baby fever for other women?"

"Not in my circle." Not that I'd had more than a forty-five-minute Zoom happy hour with my friends in...God, years.

"It's the thought that counts?" Josh was already uncorking the fizzy deliciousness.

I didn't need anyone thinking about tiny humans for me. This place was supposed to free me from pressures. I shook away the slight and focused on the immediate issue. "You know we have no food here."

"We have the cooler out in the truck."

Ah, yes, our road food. "That's not a meal."

"Snack now. When the storm dies down, we can figure out real food."

As if to prove his point, my stomach whined and the thunder rumbled in unison. "Fine, but you're going out there for the cooler."

Celebratory champagne fizzed in the filled flutes on our new counter, as if effervescence could match the anticipation of all of this. Josh ran to the U-Haul and returned with our half-full cooler and a soaked shirt. Shucking his shoes and divesting his T-shirt at the door, he brought me the minimal container of food.

I began pulling the options out. Three varieties of chips (shared), beef jerky (shared), sunflower seeds (his), grapes (mine), protein bars (mine, but would share upon request), one apple (mine), and candied pecans (his).

"Give me five minutes, and I'll see what I can do."

Josh shook his head like a puppy, splattering me with frigid drops. "I'm going to grab a towel."

With the bubbly in the background, I pulled together the most absurd charcuterie board of my life. My husband beamed at the sight though. "Only my Emily could take filling station finds and make a spread like this."

We snacked, drank the entire bottle of champagne, and rechristened our bed. We did not go back into the rain. We did not walk our property that night at all. We didn't even lock our doors.

Was this my life now? Carefree sex and fancy booze? Not bad, Nebraska. Not bad.

CHAPTER 2

THE NEXT FEW WEEKS FOUND JOSH AND ME ACCLIMATING TO
our new rural life and reacquainting with one another. Our open-
spaces freedom allowed us both to breathe and really settle into our
quirks in a way that could only come with no neighbors for miles.
It wasn't merely me getting high on smogless wonder air; it was the
lack of pressure this place put upon us. I painted the living room
the color of a morning sunrise and the kitchen Pantone 16–4031
TPG (Cornflower Blue), which I'm putting my money on being the
next color of the year. Josh mounted floating shelves in the hallway
and loaded them up with Lego brick models of spaceships from
Star Wars. We hung abstract art from our favorite Bay Area artists
in the living room.

Our secrets, our thoughts, our lives belonged solely to us here.
No nosy neighbors listened through thin walls or rifled through
deliveries piled out front to get another voyeuristic peek into our
lives. Every time a sympathy plant arrived—why had everyone sent
succulents instead of flowers? Had they thought I couldn't cultivate

a single rose?—2D would find an excuse to repeat her condolences. If I never had to hear "I'm so sorry for your loss" again, I'd die a happy woman. Then they could be sorry for someone else's loss. My mom would have hated the grief fest. She'd requested we play "Bohemian Rhapsody" at her funeral. The confusion on the pastor's face would have had her in stitches for days. I'd picked Jeff Buckley's version of "Hallelujah." His sandpaper vocals buffered my heart that day more than any "we're thinking of you" cactus ever would.

Memories swirled in my mind as I lay in the diffused darkness next to Josh. The ceiling fan whirred softly overhead. Wetness collected in the corners of my eyes. Attempting to go back to sleep was pointless. Thinking of the funeral meant I'd fuel nightmares now. I tapped my phone screen. Only four minutes until the alarm. *Not bad.* Josh snored by my side. Swiping tears from my face, I snuck out of bed.

Ozone and earth tangled in the air. Even inside the house. The farm came alive in the rain. The storms were primarily an afternoon event, with purple skies and big fat drops that plinked with satisfaction against the porch. But this time, the shushing of water over our roof had lulled me to sleep. I yanked on my leggings and a neon pink sports bra. The high-visibility outfit had been useful in the city—necessary to not get knocked over or flattened—but here I realized I actually just thought it was cute. How funny was that? The cows a couple miles west seemed to moo more when I wore pink. Not that I was doing it for the cow calls.

Laced up, activity tracking on, I sprinted out the front door. *Clapclapclap.* The screen door's goodbye was so satisfying. Like it applauded my escape. The green tops of the cornfield swayed a hello too. *God, how is this mine?* I started across our yard. The dirt path that was our driveway was sticky, making me really lift my feet with every step. A little extra quad action today wasn't a bad thing. I savored the musky soil with every breath and focused on my feet hitting the ground, planting myself with one step after another.

I would be sown in the soils too. I would grow here again.

The estate's lawyer would call again today. Persistence paid in his profession. I needed to decide about Mom's house. We were out of probate. Did we want to liquidate? Did we want to keep everything? Josh and I had moved here saying we were selling the house, but I hadn't done shit about making that happen. The house I could part with. Its creaky fourth step, its drafty window in the dining room, the drops of emerald paint on the carpet in the living room from the time Mom and I painted the whole downstairs in jewel tones to make it feel like a 1920s speakeasy—it could all go. My eyes burned. I ran faster. I'd outrun the memories before. If my body worked hard enough to hurt, it could burn right on through grief.

My watch buzzed on my wrist. I glanced down, confirming I was already moving into the orange heart rate zone. It was too soon to be there, but I couldn't care about that today. I charged toward the runner's abyss. That chasm where my heart and lungs collided, and lactic acid seared my legs and my ass. It was easier to reach that point on our farm, where I didn't have to look at the city my mother had loved or her house or her things. That was the piece that killed me. Those possessions. I exhaled hard, forcing myself to breathe deeply. The house could go. We couldn't afford to keep it. We'd bought this new life instead. The Madonna, Sabbath, and Queen records were with me, but what treasures she'd stored in her room, in the attic, I didn't know. Would it matter? Would I want to keep them? Would I be happier if I never knew they existed, and some random person purchased them at a sale while I sprinted past cornstalks?

I swiped the wetness from my cheeks. Pumped my arms. Ran faster. I neared the barn and slowed. How was I only now getting here? My legs were hot. I looked at my watch. Eleven minutes? Our barn was a three-minute run from the house. I turned back. My cute farmhouse was there, with its white wood siding and two-seat porch swing and fuchsia pansies cuddled up by the yellow daylilies in their flower bed. It was far though, too far. Like I was looking through a paper towel tube, pretending it was a telescope. I shook myself. A protein shake or at least a latte this morning might have been wise. I lowered my head, wiggled my shoes in the squishy soil. When I looked up again, the house was bigger.

Closer.

Where it should be.

I trudged forward, the mud suddenly turning to sludge and clinging to me, slowing me. Maybe that was why it had taken me so long to get to the barn? Fire licked my calves, but only the fields mattered. Once I was on the path between two crops, I could be lost. The good kind of lost. I could run, sear away these thoughts, and be as alone as if I were adrift on the Pacific. No people. No land. Just endless waves of green. Those plants didn't judge me; they didn't watch me; they didn't give me a "How are you doing today,

Em? No, really. You can tell me." They swayed with soft comforting nonsense and left me alone.

Only I wasn't alone.

I ran harder and faster. The soil was better packed here from frequent passes by the farmers' trucks and tractors, and my footfalls clapped again. I needed to order some new trail shoes but, first, to stop my brain. I ran until my lungs hurt, until my legs wobbled, and, finally, my stomach flipped. The berm marking the side of the road acted as a rest area. If I'd taken the other path, my reprieve would have included cows. I hoped they didn't miss me too badly. When I thought I'd avoided another upchuck, I began the journey back home.

Thirteen point three miles. Not terrible. I logged it in my journal along with the time—slower than my usual, but not enough to mean much. I showered, ate a bagel, and got ready for work. (Let's be real. I just put on a cute sweater and turned on the "touch up my appearance" filter on Zoom. They didn't need to know I'd switched from running leggings to workday leggings.)

Josh brought me a latte around nine thirty. I was on a daily stand-up call for a big launch, but my work on the project was already complete. I toggled off my camera and kissed him thank-you.

"Your meetings back-to-back today?" he asked. His hair was still damp from the shower. I couldn't remember the last time I'd been capable of sleeping in.

I tapped down the volume from the meeting. "It's not bad. Want to have lunch today?"

"A date with my wife? Absolutely. I know this alfresco place nearby." Josh leaned against the doorframe like he'd seen a TikTok of the ideal way a man should linger.

"I hope they have sandwiches." Had his arms always been so stacked? My husband was hot. This was not news, but also *hello*.

"They also have leftover pasta for any lucky customers who are sick of sandwiches." The knowing smirk on his face did not take away from the appeal. "See you at noon?"

Delight bubbled bright beneath my breastbone. The barn, the meeting, the probate, it all fell away. "Yep, and you can have the leftovers. I'll sandwich it up."

Uber Eats did not deliver to farms—well, not to ours, anyway. In fact, nothing delivered here. No pizza. No biryani. No sushi. But they made up for it with "holy shit" fresh ingredients at the market. Besides, if I could become a mixologist in the last few years at home, I could also become a chef. Or Josh could. We were still figuring out who was going to be the next Food Network star, but if they wanted to hand out cooking shows for people who make really stellar sandwiches, I was 45 percent their lady.

No one had noticed my off-camera foray, and I kept it that way for the remainder of the morning. Even the office Slack was quiet. I dropped a couple of links into our #now-playing channel. My boss loved to tell me what she liked about every song I shared. She never admitted she used to read my mom's music column in the *SF Bay*, but my performance reviews were nonexistent, and she fell over herself to tell me about concerts she attended. I'd put it together.

I toggled my status to "lunch nom nom nom" and followed the

whir of the microwave to find Josh. He'd set the makings of a BLT out on the counter, but had his nose pressed to the glass, watching his pasta reheat.

"Didn't your mom tell you that would give you cancer?" I teased.

"My mom thinks everything gives you cancer."

"WebMD also thinks everything could be cancer. Does your mom moonlight for them?"

Tension jacked his shoulders up. His mom was a touchy subject, depending on the day. "She's doing better about it now. Retirement suits her."

"I'm really glad to hear that." I meant it. "That job was running her ragged."

"They didn't deserve her..." Josh chattered on about his mom's old job, her former boss, and the time he worked at the office when he was fourteen. They'd made him run to the coffee shop sixteen blocks away for a special roast.

Josh's mom stayed busy, which was fine as long as she did those busy things far from us. I loved her and, obviously, so did he, but the woman couldn't sit still. She pried into every corner of our life, and that wasn't just giving her "I'm not a doctor but..." medical advice; it was also looking under the couch to see if we'd dusted there (literally never) and doing a full survey of the expiration dates of the canned goods in the pantry.

I began preparing my epic sandwich. Zero canned goods required.

"I still can't believe we can just walk outside and there's food," I said, holding up a ripe tomato.

"That is where it grows. You knew that before we moved here, right?" Josh could fake serious like no one else.

I clapped my hand to my mouth, aghast, but broke out laughing before I could even speak. Zero poker face here. "I meant this gorgeous fruit was straight-up outside the door."

"Just remember, the corn doesn't belong to us." It was a tease, but his jaw hardened.

"I know how leases work." We weren't built to be farmers. I had no idea about cultivating the land or driving a combine, but I did know about sharing the load. Also, the leaseback amount bought me more time to decide about Mom's estate. And thanks for that.

"How many tomatoes are still out there?" Josh gathered silverware and napkins.

"There's only the one plant, but it's still producing." I had no idea how long it'd keep giving me tomatoes, but I'd been watering it daily because Google told me to.

"Do you still want to plant more out there?"

I did. Every day I loved being outside more. "I need to learn more about when to plant, but if I could get salad ingredients to grow there, I'd be happy. You, of course, could still eat leftovers."

"Of course," he said, head in the refrigerator. When he stood, he held two cans toward me. "Coke Zero or lime fizzy water?"

"Caffeine me."

He passed me the soda. Did I need to call it *pop* if I lived here?

"What Midwest terms do we need to learn?"

Josh quirked a brow. "Midwest terms. Like what? *Hoedown?*"

"Don't stereotype."

"You just said, 'Midwest terms.'"

"That's not stereotyping. Have you heard a single thing about a hoedown since we moved here?"

"I don't talk to people here other than you. I mean, I say hi to Ray and his farmhands, but they aren't inviting me out for beers."

Ray Clausen was the head farmer, and Josh had quickly gotten on a first-name basis with him. Would Josh want to go out for beers with the farmers?

"There are two bars in town," I announced, like he hadn't been to our nearby town of Deshler with me for groceries and gas.

"I don't need to hit the local bars, babe."

"That so?"

"Oh yeah. Why would I go to there when I have the hottest bartender in the USA right here at home?"

"I'm also a sandwich artist." I waggled the BLT between us, mayo plopping down onto my plate.

"You angling for a job at Subway, Em?"

Sticking your tongue out at your spouse was a right.

A few breaths and a couple bites later, I asked, "How'd your pitch meetings go this morning?"

"Fine." That automatic reply shoved distance between us. It always had. Josh must have seen my flinch because his face softened. "Ellen can't resist telling every client about our move."

"Why is that a bad thing?" I loved our change. Did he not?

"Other than talking about *me* instead of *her* or *the offering*?"

Talons of trepidation tugged at my arms, trying to yank me into a defensive position. I straightened my spine instead. "Yes, other than that."

"It's silly. Let's go back to talking about your future in artisanal lunches."

Fuck the sandwich. "No, tell me what's going on."

"It really is nothing. I'm just feeling the pinch of new hires in my territory."

I sipped my soda—pop—and waited both for him to open up to me and for the needle of unease to release me.

His tongue darted over his lips, his gaze turning to the bees tasting the petunias. "She's turned our life into an icebreaker joke."

My stomach couldn't have sunk faster if the tomato had turned to coal. "A joke?"

He shook his head, still watching the bees. "Yeah. 'If you could live anywhere, where would you?' She talks about how so many people in tech have taken to island-hopping. They move to Key West..."

We'd talked about islands in Florida too. "And have to evacuate and rebuild after hurricanes?"

He plowed ahead. "And then she's like, 'Josh here could have moved to a private island, but he packed up for a farm.'"

I didn't get the joke. "Our farm is better than the islands. They're both tranquil, but ours comes without tourists or politics and at a price tag that doesn't make me feel like some one-percent asshole."

Josh reeled back like I'd hit him. People who grew up rich wanted to align themselves with the truly wealthy. We would never be billionaires. We couldn't even afford to own a house in the city I grew up in. And yet there was a part of my husband that wanted to believe it was achievable. That moving here meant saving, investing, securing a comfortable future. All of that was true, but divesting the trappings of *perceived* wealth was hard.

Harder than it should be, at any rate. Hard for my husband right now.

"You know what I mean." I was garbage at walking back my words. Josh merely sipped his seltzer. I tried to explain. "We picked this place to bring us joy and security. I love this life. I love this view, this farm, and you."

"I know all that, Em. I wanted this—want this—but she's just gotten under my skin."

I nodded. Technology sales was a battlefield. Josh had to learn about every industry, every potential client, and then tailor offerings for them. It was a game of both knowledge and bluffing, and he was very good at it. He was also very competitive. Fear clawed my chest. Was I the reason he was losing?

The barn's dilapidated walls, its bent boards stabbing into the muck, rose in my mind. I'd lost time there. *Lost my shit.* I'd meant to tell Josh about it, about the way my body ached after I'd showered, about the way I almost thought I could still sense the barn slipping farther down the path now. But if his heart had already been roughened by work and a challenging colleague, I wasn't going to add my one-off ridiculousness to the pile.

Maybe I should have said something then. If I'd spoken sooner, would it have changed everything?

Emily's Running Log:

5:30 a.m. farm run! 13.1 miles—Ran through the east cornfields, then headed straight back. Longer route open with a path to the south when I hit the end of our field there. Barn looked closer to me than the house from way out there!

Barn should have been 3 minutes or so from the house. Took 11 minutes to get there—1,980 steps—how can that be right?

CHAPTER 3

SWEAT SLICKED MY SKIN AND STUNG MY EYES WHEN I WOKE.
My jerk of a phone screen said it was three in the morning. Josh was
snoring. The viscous pool of regret saturated only *my* side of the
bed. My nightmares rarely touched him. My grief had thickened
the darkness, filling the room. I could paint the walls yellow, but in
the night, memories of hospice, of neglect, of all the shit I should
have done had a way of seeping from my pores, soaking the sheets
and turning our room into a sauna of sorrow.

I carefully toed out of bed. The oak was warm and solid beneath
my feet. No oil slicked the surface, no matter how sticky my dreams
had become. The fan whirred overhead, but the air pressed against
me, stagnant. I was going to have to build a sacrificial altar to our
AC unit at this point. The seventy-six degrees we'd set it at was
a bridge too far, apparently. Some days it'd chug along fine, but
at night it stalled out on us. Always on the nights that memories
pierced my dreams.

Every night these days.

Perhaps that was the problem with all this quiet. Too much space to think.

I started a pot of coffee. At 3 a.m., I wasn't about to make the effort to tamp espresso shots. I slipped back into the bedroom to switch into a dry tank top.

I never thought I'd be back to so-early-in-the-morning-it's-night coffees after twenty-five. But maybe this didn't count? I wasn't in some hipster diner ordering the greasiest thing on the menu and trying to sober myself after dancing my ass off at a concert. I was on my couch, in my pj's, with fresh coffee filling my Rose Apothecary mug. Hell. Maybe that was worse? My mother's roughened alto still lingered in my ears. From the dream, I supposed.

Who starts their day that early? She'd said that very thing when she found out I was running before dawn. *At least run for the sunsets, baby. The view is better.*

This wasn't an intentional early morning though. She'd woken me or, I guess, our fickle air-conditioning unit had.

The magic bean juice burned my throat. I sipped again immediately. Heat made glass resist shattering; it could work for me too.

Some memories, I was learning, refused to be cauterized. You'd think six months after her death, I'd at least be dreaming of birthdays or hibachi nights or small precious moments. But each night I shifted back to her in hospice. Her cheeks swollen, her hair gone, chunky rings constantly slipping off rail-thin fingers. Her words were slower in those final days, but every bit as sharp. Cancer couldn't change who my mother had been, but it claimed her nonetheless.

A fresh wave of guilt sloshed in my belly. I poured more coffee down my throat like the acid could cut through the roiling regrets. The dream, memory, nightmare, the bullshit that had me waking up swimming in my sweat, hadn't been from those last days. It was the kind of memory I'd been waiting for, and it'd wrecked me all the same.

Fucking unfair.

"There are two things you have to promise me." Mom folded her legs beneath her on the couch, perched like a kindergarten teacher needing to survey the entire room.

Oh, this would be good. "Hit me."

"One, never date a drummer." Candlelight pooled in the depressed curve of the wide gold ring on the index finger she held aloft.

I eased back against the chartreuse chaise, a prize Mom had won in a poker game with some indie band in the early aughts. It'd been my reading spot as a teen. At twenty-two, I'd still loved it. "You married two drummers, Mom."

She tilted the lowball glass in her other hand toward me. "Which means I'm speaking from lived experience."

"My dad was a drummer."

"And he fucked right off, didn't he?"

I shrugged it away, like I always did. He'd drop in when the tour stopped nearby. In high school, he'd get tickets for all my friends. It was fine. Like some cool uncle. But he was never a dad.

"Right," I sighed. I'd just started dating Josh, and he was a movie nerd who had zero musical talent. "So I should never date a drummer. Or I guess marry one. What's number two?"

Mom rose from her perch, a hawk primed to tackle its prey below. "The best things happen after midnight. Or the worst."

"How is that a promise I could make? Am I promising to never have a mediocre night?"

She cackled and lowered herself back to lounge on her couch. After a long sip of her vodka soda, she explained, "You have to promise to make the most of those hours. When the moon is hanging heavy and sound carries brighter. You gotta promise me you'll embrace it, even if it ends up being a total shitstorm of a night. Take the adventure. Never just sit and wait for life, baby girl, because even when the night is a wreck, it makes for the best story in the morning."

Even then my heart had ached. My mom had the best stories. "I'm not going to embrace the night like a vampire."

"But wouldn't it be more fun if you did?"

I groaned like I was still a teenager with too much eye makeup and even more disdain for my mother. "I can do adventure though."

"Oh, baby girl, you were built for adventure."

We'd lived in the same narrow three-story house at the top of a hill together my whole life. Well, until I left for college and then moved in with Josh. Mom had bought the place when she was pregnant with me; a deal with my dad, I gathered. It was one of the few topics that were verboten. It had the view that people who only knew SF from *Full House* reruns expected we all had. Inside though, Mom had sheathed the walls in velvet. Golden cords pulled the drapes aside to reveal memorabilia tacked or framed, like we were some roadside attraction and not merely a collection of fire code violations.

It had been our labyrinthine home base. My mom had meant it about the adventures. We'd trekked all over the U.S. Impromptu excursions to Joshua Tree. Short jaunts as tour tagalongs for bands Mom was producing albums for. And once I was old enough, the occasional overnight haul in Reno because "Vegas is expensive excess; Reno is reasonable chaos."

Had she sustained herself on chaos all those years? Was that why the cancer caught up to her? Her cells finally giving themselves over to anarchy in rapid succession? She was Stage Four before we'd even known she was sick. Mom had been going going going until she simply wasn't.

"Maybe you would have liked this adventure for me?" I said aloud to the empty room and to my ghosts.

The night sweats did not meet Mom's idea of leaning into bonkers nighttime events. But the willingness to ditch the hills and the trolleys and the bad corner jam bands and the fantastic food, and try a whole other way of life?

This *was* an adventure. The stress of San Francisco, the memories, the responsibilities, they were distractions. But there was rebellion in sitting on your couch in your pajamas at 3 a.m. drinking decent drip coffee.

I pulled my laptop out, because if I was going to be up this early, I might as well get shit done. A flurry of activity lit my work Slack. Not from my regular colleagues, but the Budapest office was online. Apparently, the software developers were prepping for an office marathon. Not the building a website kind of sprint, but like a "don't forget to lube up to avoid chafing" kind. I'd never paid attention to their water cooler conversations before.

The coffee kicked in, and I started asking questions. *When is the marathon? Is it a full or a half? How much of your office is participating? Where is it? When is it?*

We worked for the same company on opposite sides of the globe. I'd never talked with them. If you weren't a project manager or on the creative team, you didn't need to talk with the graphic designer. I usually liked it that way.

Dimu: Where do you live? USA?
Emily: Yep. Nebraska.

I waited for the joke about corn. The creative team always dropped one. I usually replied with a picture of the sunrise outside my door, and it shut them up.

Oana: It is very early for you!
Dimu: I don't know where that is. Sorry!

I thought about explaining geography or talking about how it

differed from San Francisco, but I didn't need to do that. No need
to justify my adventure.

Emily: It's a good place to run.

The #coffee-talk-marathon chat continued. I leaned into the
vicarious adventure of it. I had only become a runner for sanity's
sake when I started working from home. The idea of doing it in a
group or—God forbid—as an organized activity had never crossed
my mind. But this almost sounded fun.

Emily: How many of you have done this before?

A flurry of responses hit my screen, but it was Oana's that caught
my attention.

Oana: There's a virtual option.

I'd rather be sleeping, but perhaps this was part of the adventure
I'd promised to take?

Emily: Send me the sign-up link?

I'd scrolled through the photos on their marathon page of the
blue-green waters and the intricate architecture runners would
zoom past. Though the virtual option was more of a "share your
GPS data" variety. The Budapest team was kind and eagerly sent me

so many extra links to suggest ways I could pretend I was in their country while I ran the marathon that I might have hit my browser's capacity for open tabs.

So I guess I had to add Hungary to my travel bucket list. Josh and I had made two international excursions a year for the first five years of our marriage. My passport probably wondered why it was perpetually stuffed into a drawer instead of in my pocket now. I still wanted to go places and see things. The people less so. The last few years, we'd settled into being *home*, and I hadn't realized how much I really loved solitude until it had been imposed on me. Turns out if you marry your best friend, seeing only them for days on end is actually pretty great.

I poured myself another cup of coffee in the kitchen. Josh had painted the cabinets a pristine white a few weeks ago. He'd gone full *Property Brothers* since moving in. When he wasn't decked in a sport coat for a pitch session, he had a hammer in his hand or paint smudged on his knuckles. Rugged fixer looked *good* on him. I lingered in the kitchen, admiring the way his latest update brightened the room against the warm blue walls we'd painted on our third day at the farm. It had become the kitchen you'd see in a Hallmark movie but updated with shiny stainless-steel appliances.

The windows were dark. We didn't need to bother with curtains out here, but I'd tucked sheer white ones on either side of the panes over the sink. Decorations could be just that sometimes. Not everything had to be functional. The nights here could slip to pitch-black. Tonight a deep darkness enfolded the farm on a new moon. We had a flood lamp over the back door. It lit up when our car pulled in. We'd yet to actually drive home after the sun had set, but if we ever did, I hadn't wanted to rely on moonlight to keep me from face-planting in my yard because of a wayward stone or root.

I took a step toward the living room—and my voyeuristic vacation of Budapest's Castle District—and stopped cold. Outside, in that distant darkness, in the sea of night that surrounded my farmhouse chic island, was a light. One small square glowing honey yellow.

One small square of light hovering.

One lit window that wasn't mine.

One light shining in the barn's loft.

I glowered down at my coffee like a good cup of java could make a woman hallucinate. But when I returned my gaze to the kitchen window, that yellow square was still there. Closer? Maybe? The longer I stared, the better I could make out the divisions of the four panes of glass. The once-white shutters on either side, now sallow in the glow and stripped in age. A chill curled around my spine, corkscrewing up to my skull until my whole body shook.

There were plausible reasons for the light to be on, right? Farmers worked early. Maybe Ray needed to get an early start? The clock we'd mounted on the wall was beefy and analog and had big bold roman numerals. Three thirty-seven. Okay, that was early, even for the farmers. The earliest I'd seen any of them on the property was—maybe—four thirty? But what did I know? I wasn't a farmer.

I tried to stare down the barn as if, with proper countenance, I could cut the light and kill my anxiety. Only the longer I stared outside, the tighter my chest became.

I tried to sip my coffee. My stomach bit back at the acid. I edged toward the back door, which offered a direct line of sight to the both the barn and the drive up to it. The door, like the cabinets, was that stark white. I'd placed a lightweight white curtain over the glass in the top half. The curtain had little blue and pink flowers embroidered at the bottom. I shoved the blossoms aside.

No vehicles, save the outline of ours.

No lights on in the barn proper. Just the constant glow from the hayloft window.

The floodlights hadn't kicked on. There were two installed on the barn's eaves too. They were damningly dark.

Mom, this is not an adventure I can embrace.

My calves twitched, and a dull roar built in my ears. Did I go out there? My fingers glanced the knob. The cold metal rattled against my shaking palm.

I dropped my hand.

Josh? Yes, I should get him. I started back toward our bedroom, toward the steady snore. With every step, his snores sliced through the panicked hum in my ears. By the time I'd made it to the bed, I questioned everything. He was there, tangled in the sheets, arm draped over his face. Blissfully unaware of the malevolent light outside.

Lord, who the hell am I? Malevolent? It's light, *Emily.*

Should I wake him? I was scared, so he should be here to comfort me. I think that was in our vows in more eloquent terms. "To have and to hold, especially when she is freaking the fuck out." Only what was I going to say? He'd already been teasing me about my "adjustment period" to rural life, as if that negated his frustration with his colleagues' jokes at our expense. I'd embraced everything here, but I didn't think I would ever stop lamenting the lack of takeout. Eventually, I'd probably stop getting "seasick" in the car.

My gut, though, wouldn't let this go. I pressed my palm against Josh's shoulder and nudged him. "Babe?"

He grumbled but flopped an arm out toward me.

"Babe?" I tried again. "There's something happening in the barn."

"Barn? Don't worry about the barn. Go back to sleep."

Oh, to be able to fall back asleep. "No, really. I need you to come look."

When he didn't get up, I tried again. "I think someone is in our barn. It's too early for the farmers."

My eight thousand scenarios for why that light tripped my fear had landed on trespassers or thieves. The most plausible. I'd already woken Josh so many nights with tears from my nightmares. I didn't want to become *that* woman. The needles of being watched pricked my skin, but I pretended my fear was merely that we might get robbed. It was the flavor of fear that got my husband out of bed.

And so he stumbled his way to the kitchen, groggy and grumbling. When we got to the window, the light in the barn was out.

"It was probably Ray coming to get something before they start out on the far field today."

It was my turn to mutter noncommittally. Why would the head farmer be here now?

"I'll talk with him later. Let's go back to bed," Josh grumbled.

"I'm too amped-up to sleep."

"You gotta stop making coffee in the middle of the night, Em."
His smile was kind and the kiss he pressed to my cheek gentle. "I'll
see you in a few hours then."

I set up my laptop at the kitchen counter and watched that
window until the sun ignited the horizon. The light never turned
back on.

Not that night anyway.

Emily's Running Log:

4 minutes, 3 seconds to the barn—723 steps—Yesterday was clearly a fluke.

12.9 miles—Protein shake before running clearly sharpens my mind. Hit orange heart rate early again.

CHAPTER 4

I WANTED NOTHING MORE THAN TO NOT CARE ABOUT THAT barn light, but three days had passed, and I still checked the window nightly. Before bed. When I inevitably woke up too damn early and too exhausted to fall back asleep. I needed distractions, and I found them: training for the marathon, which turned out to not be so different from my current running routine. I didn't tell my colleagues about sprinting until stopped by a sour stomach, but I did start keeping a running log in their format. Dates, distances, times. I logged in miles, because (don't tell my new European friends) converting to kilometers was more math than I was willing to do.

But I also needed a hobby that better embraced our new life. An endeavor only for me.

"Are you sure you're up for this?" I asked, even though we were forty minutes into the drive already.

"I said I was." Josh's hands tightened on the wheel. "Don't worry, Em, we'll have everything ready."

Not that I doubted my husband's abilities. Josh had firmly

proven himself worthy of an HGTV show. I only questioned how committed he was to my new project.

Chickens.

"Do we have enough time to build it?" I had asked this already too. Idling was not my forte. Sitting still, waiting, *anticipating*? Hard pass. I was the girl who could love roller coasters if I were blindfolded. But if you wanted me to *c r e e p* into the sky, watching the ground fall away slowly, and sit with that impending dread of what could happen? Hell, no. There is no joy in that.

Not sure how I'd equated becoming a chicken mama with riding roller coasters, but I honestly hoped it would not be an apt analogy. I would not be blindfolded around the hens. *Could your chickens blind you?* I would not Google that later. Probably.

"The coop will be up and habitable today." Josh was laying it on thick, but his dimple made an appearance.

"Seems like a big task. Building multifamily housing," I teased.

"Well, it helps that they're all living together. It's more commune than apartments, Em."

The anxiety static in my belly smoothed. "I would one hundred percent watch a reality show called *Chicken Commune*."

"Now you've done it." He lowered his head, mock worry pulling his features taut.

"What?" I played along. Even when watching the road, Josh's attention was on me. Every time those hazel eyes flitted to me, the delight that this was my partner hit me all over again.

"You said it, and now when we get home the 'Recommended for You' is going to be all chicken shows."

"That was going to happen anyway."

"Have you been watching chicken shows?" He was serious. What did he think I did in the middle of the night while he was crashed out?

"No, I've been watching serial killer documentaries and reality dating shows."

"Okay. Good."

"But I will definitely search for chicken shows tonight. How many episodes are you in for?"

"After building this luxury villa for hens we don't even have yet, I think I should probably command the Netflix queue tonight."

"They'll be here in two days!" I announced in my biggest voice, which I hoped meant he would forget this idea that he'd select our nighttime viewing. I didn't think I could do another episode of *Ancient Aliens*.

Josh tapped the Next button on the steering wheel. See? The man was power hungry to make media decisions. A Baroness song thumped its way through our speakers.

"I still can't believe you ordered chickens online," he said.

"I guess it's how it's done?" My copious late-night Googling said the easiest and quickest way to get hens for your at-home coop was via the United States Postal Service. Shipping chickens sounded dangerous, but the sites assured me it was not only safe but the standard.

Josh hiked a thumb back in the direction we'd come from. Hastings had a Menards—perfect for home improvements—but we'd passed several feed and supply shops on the way back to our dot of nowhere.

"They have baby chicks at the Farm Equipment and Supply," he said.

They did, and they were the cutest little chirping babies, but I had five egg-ready hens on the way. "Did you ever imagine yourself casually saying shit like that?"

He laughed. "If my parents could see me now."

Josh's parents were both tech developers. The kind of IT people who'd built Silicon Valley and who were immensely disappointed that their son sold tech instead of building it. They also were the most literal people I knew, and I loved that about them. You always knew where you stood—which I guess worked for me because they liked me. It worked less as their kid because there was no filter and no mask for him.

"Have you told your mom about the farm yet?" They knew we'd moved, but Josh didn't talk to them all that often.

"I sent pictures of the house." He shrugged. "She liked the blue you put in the kitchen."

"Did you tell her about the shelving you built?" There was practically a library in the office now. If I could get Josh to pretend he was a bear, I'm pretty sure I could live out a full *Beauty and the Beast* fantasy.

"I told Dad." He focused on the asphalt in front of us, the speed limit a solid sixty-five miles per hour.

"And?"

"He asked for the specs to model out how many books we could fit if you only purchased hardcovers in the future."

"He knows I read mostly thriller and romance, right?"

"Like that matters."

"It's like Paperback City in there," I said, as though he hadn't had to heft in twelve boxes of books from our moving truck. And that was after I'd downsized.

"He does not understand that. His books are hardback; yours should be hardback."

"Well, at least he's supporting creatives with his dollar then, I guess."

The fact that everyone thought my job was a hobby because it involved Photoshop was *a thing*.

We were quiet long enough for the Baroness song to finish and a newer Miley Cyrus track to kick in. "Disney kid or no, that girl has pipes."

Josh nodded, which meant he wasn't really listening. He would never forgive her for saying she wanted to hear a Britney song in "Party in the USA." My husband might not have been a music nerd, but man, if my mom hadn't rubbed some elitism off on him too. She had that effect on people. Not making them snobs, but making them seek the most "real" music, to look for the art.

She never got to hear "Flowers," but she'd have loved that track.

The other night and the light that unnerved me seeped back into my thoughts. "Did you ever talk to Ray?"

"Hmm?"

"About the barn. Was he out there in the morning?" I'd asked the last two nights, but my husband said he kept missing the farmer.

Josh flattened his lips. "Wasn't him."

"So who was in the barn?"

Josh flattened his palms against the steering wheel, but his voice remained even. "Probably no one. Their everyday equipment is stored on the other side of the acreage, but Ray said he'd ask his guys if anyone was in there. And he'll poke around the loft."

"I can do that when we get home," I muttered. I hadn't because I was trying not to be the paranoid city woman who freaked out in the quiet and the dark and the *s p a c e.*

"He'll do it. I'm sure."

I nodded, unconvinced.

"Besides, he said the stairs were tricky there, and the loft needs repair." His tension ebbed with each word. Josh's hands relaxed back to a light grip. "It isn't safe to walk around up there if you don't know what you're doing."

"I know how to walk." So much for a light conversation.

Josh hadn't caught my tone. "I think it's more about knowing where to step."

It was a loft, not land mines, but I dropped it. That barn was haggard. The last thing I needed was to poke around and fall through the floor.

We hit a bump, and the coop supplies clunked in the back. I'd cleared out the back seat and flipped it down to open it to the trunk. I hadn't opened that space since the move. From a record collection to lumber and chicken wire.

Unreal.

"What do you think my mom would say about all this?" I asked.

"All of what? The chickens or us living on a farm or the fact I'm really good at construction? Because I think she would tell you the benefits of having a strong man around the house." He couldn't keep a straight face. His laughter spilled in the car first, but then I was the one who couldn't stop cackling.

"She said I shouldn't marry a drummer." The memory was still so fresh.

"Wait, is that why you balked when I said I liked Travis Barker all those years ago?"

I'd certainly made a face because of *how* he knew of the Blink-182 drummer—from a guest track with an obnoxious guy who I'd definitely dated a decade ago.

"Liking Travis Barker doesn't mean you're a drummer. It means you're a person who listens to popular music."

Josh glanced toward me, eyebrow arched like a disapproving principal.

"Don't use the sexy professor look now. You're supposed to be driving."

"I got you. Ten and two, babe." He slapped his palms against the steering wheel, blissfully out of time with the song playing. "I can be sexy and safe at the same time. Very un-drummer-like, apparently."

I focused on the scruff on his chin. He let it linger a few days at a time now between shaves. *Not bad, Mr. Hauk.* "While I'm sure you're right, she would have had commentary on your newfound handyman skills—and would have put you to work at her house. I meant more about the fact we're leaning into this whole new life?"

"Your mom was like a cat. All the lives."

My chest squeezed, eyes burning instantly. I turned my attention out the window. The grain waved at me, no judgment at my sudden tears.

"She had one life, but a lot of stories. I dreamed about her last night." I tried to continue the conversation. Continue like I wasn't being swallowed whole in the passenger seat.

Grief was a tsunami on the bad days. A swell I didn't see coming. It fell over me too fast and held me there long long long longer than I expected to survive. When I finally breathed, it was merely a reprieve.

"Another from hospice?" Josh was next to me but might as well have been across a cavern.

Cold sweat clung to my palms. I wiped them on my leggings.

"No." My voice went breathy. "It was about adventure. Her hopes for them. For me. For doing something memorable."

"I miss her too." He meant it. He'd loved her like his own mother, and she'd cared for him thusly, but right now his sorrow and mine were separate silos. His filled with bittersweet cocoa and mine sloshing with acid.

"Emily." Josh's hand was on my leg. The heat a tether, pulling me back. The endless green beyond the window slid, sloshed. There was no anchor on the horizon. Josh tried to be one here. I focused on that connection. The water tower in the distance hopped from one field to the next. It swayed with the stalks, with my stomach.

"Pulloverpulloverpullover." The plea pulled from me. I'd like to say it wasn't common, but I hadn't quite developed my middle-of-the-country sea legs yet.

Josh pulled the car to the edge of the two-lane road. There

was no traffic, but he still tucked the passenger tires in the dirt. I popped the door open, stepped out, and dropped my head between my knees. Hurling on the side of the road was embarrassing and gross. It was also, sadly, cathartic. Though I didn't quite know why. This wasn't a food poisoning scenario where I needed to expel an invader.

Afterward my body was reset. The tears tracking my cheeks weren't from the cut of loss or unfair hurt at misplaced words. They were born of a physical act. Out of my control. Out of Josh's. I'd started running in the city to get this mental and physical reset. I'd expected to need it less in Nebraska, but my overanalyzing last night—my panic that felt silly in the daylight—had my tenderest parts exposed.

Josh rubbed slow circles on my back. He never talked about the puke. He never questioned why I still let him drive the car when it was infinitely better when I was behind the wheel. He just held me, which how could I want more than that?

"You ready to go home and build a house for chickens?" he said when we were finally back in the car.

I forced a laugh, but he didn't call me on it. "I'm ready to go home and watch *you* build a house for chickens."

"How much work are these chickens going to be for me?"

"You're the muscle. I'm the chicken mama."

"Lord, Em, we don't even have them yet and you're already in full mom mode?"

"It was chickens or kittens, and you're allergic to the latter."

"They're going to lay eggs, right?"

"They're chickens, Josh. Yes, they will lay eggs. And before you ask, yes, we can eat the eggs."

"We're going to have to get some of that venison sausage at the meat market next time then."

I snickered. We had a meat market, and it wasn't the name of a club. Josh shot me a glare. "I can't help it. *Meat market.*"

"You're twelve."

"You know you love it."

Josh nodded resolutely. "I do love you."

And we continued on like that—like my mother's ghost hadn't sat up in the back seat earlier, like I hadn't booted outside the car like a college kid who made poor choices—the rest of the way home. The drive involved zero upchuck and lots of decent tunes. We didn't talk about my mom or adventures. Josh had compiled a list of names for the chickens, which I promptly vetoed. No one wanted to eat eggs laid by Plucky Percher.

The barn faded into the background. Another benign element of our picturesque life—although nowhere near as styling as the coop Josh built in record time. A streaky pink sunset warmed the fields when Josh declared "Chez Egg" complete. I didn't have the heart to tell him I'd already ordered a little wooden sign for the coop. He'd find out it was Cluckingham Palace soon enough. Might as well let him have the joy for a day or two.

Mine wouldn't last that long.

Emily's Running Log:

5 minutes, 52 seconds to the barn—1,056 steps—Am I slow today?
12.7-mile run—Average heart rate still high. 70% orange zone.

CHAPTER 5

WHEN I TURNED TWENTY-SIX, I STARTED TAKING SPIN classes. There was a gym one block from my house, and my best friend had already been a member. The instructor had the energy of twelve Red Bulls and cranked the pop music loud enough I often questioned if I needed to be wearing earplugs. It'd felt great to sweat, to use my muscles, but also the constant shoulder shimmies and the talking of the teacher never gave me the escape I'd wanted.

Running outdoors gave me that release though. I'd researched the best shoes, the best paths, the best of everything when I'd figured out morning jogging could turn on my mind's white noise machine. Competitive running hadn't even been a thought for me. Unless you count a couple of Turkey Trots on Thanksgiving. I'd never cared for how I performed against others because that wasn't what running was about, but the virtual marathon thrilled me. I could help a team, and I could be alone. An introvert's dream.

My regular run was a few miles short of a half-marathon distance. If I wanted to get my body prepared for 26.2 miles in one go,

I needed to stay on the daily push and focus on my heart rate. Easier said than done when I couldn't help but monitor the barn on every run. No matter which direction I left my house, there was a sense of the barn at my back.

I took off this morning toward the eastern field. There was a path there that would let me loop past a pasture with baby cows and their mamas, and would put the sun behind me when I was full-out sweaty. It'd been a good plan. The truck paths between the crops were packed well, and my trail-running shoes gripped them just right.

The last several weeks my heart rate had been high earlier than usual. That wouldn't prepare me for endurance at all. So today's plan was slow and steady. No intervals. No sprints. Just a leisurely jog alone with blue skies and sunshine.

Five miles in, sharp voices broke my reverie. I slowed my pace, instinct tightening my core.

Every step forward though, the men's conversation grew more heated. What was I running toward? A lecture? A brawl?

A metal hinge groaned; a door slammed.

The nose of a truck poked around the upcoming curve. How long until they saw me? Were they coming this way? Would their fight spill over me? Panic lit my chest. Mom's advice to always "step out of the path of dumb, mad men" ignited instinct, and I bolted into the field.

Corn is not soft. The stalks slapped me, every blade roughing my body, slowing me down. Silk poked from the husks, tickling my shoulders. The voices only grew louder. One truck moved closer, parking where I had stood moments earlier.

Once I was three rows deep, I stopped and crouched down. Though the field was taller than me, a person standing on the back of a pickup could have spied me. Maybe. But not when my fingertips could graze the cocoa-colored dirt.

"Put that garbage away." The man's demand was punctuated with a throaty hawk and spit.

"Not hurting you," a younger guy snapped back.

Peering between the stalks did me no good. I could make out a flash of red through the rough green leaves. The truck?

The deeper voice said something beneath his breath. The intonation was a swear, but there was more to it.

Another car door slammed.

"I'll do what I need to. Like I always do." The younger man's threat settled over the crops for so long that I thought even the plants were about to lie down.

"We're not doing this," the other man said.

What was *this*? Why were they so mad, and who fought in the middle of a field?

"You need to stop," the older one said, more resolute.

"I don't think that's up to you."

"This is my farm, kid."

"No. This is the Belkin farm."

"*Was*, kid."

"Take it back." The scrabble of feet on the ground suddenly stopped with a hard *thunk* against metal.

"Take your hands off me." Menace oozed from the older voice, but there was no inflection.

Another hard slam resounded, like metal on metal. I leapt backward, crashing into the corn and planting my ass in the soil. Fiery scrapes licked my elbows.

Heavy footsteps fell nearby. I didn't move. Didn't flinch. Didn't breathe.

"Go check the center pivots." The older voice must have been Ray. He was the boss.

The other guy groaned. "I did that yesterday. Sprinklers are working fine."

There was no room for discussion in Ray's reply. "Go check them again then. Make sure the heads are clear."

Whatever grunt work went with this task, the farmhand hated it. He swore, slammed the truck door, and revved the engine before leaving. Dust plumed overhead. I remained in my cornfield hideout.

Minutes passed. Then another door slammed closed. Another truck drove onward. I counted to one hundred like I'd just been mugged and the guy had ordered ample time for a getaway. Only these men hadn't known I was here. It was me and the corn. Alone.

This wasn't the city. There wasn't a fight about to spill from a bar and knock me into the road. This wasn't the corner fentanyl addict trying to push into my apartment building. But the constant vigilance I grew up with didn't evaporate simply because I'd moved to the center of the country.

The men throwing fists back in the city didn't care if I was hurt, and I doubted the ones arguing here cared much about my safety either. Perhaps being the landlord would have bought me some kindness, but anger has a way of narrowing one's gaze. My hands were shaking—damn adrenaline dump. I squeezed them into the soft, tilled soil.

My knuckle nudged something hard and plastic. I turned around and dug in the dirt. A sparkly teal hair clip jutted from the base of a cornstalk. I pulled it free, half coming with me. The spring had snapped.

Why was there a glittery claw clip five miles out from the house? Why would there be one in the field at all? I hadn't seen a single farmhand with hair long enough to use one, even if they weren't all wearing ball caps.

The dirt here had been tended to not long ago. It was that fluffy texture that made the ground soft and squishy without caking your shoes. This couldn't be old. Who had been in this field? How had she lost her hair clip?

Why did these questions scare me more than the angry voices earlier?

I shook out the rest of the adrenaline as I best I could. My mind wasn't going to blank today anyway. I edged back out of the field and onto the path, and turned back the way I came.

I took the claw clip with me, which was probably silly.

Emily's Running Log:

9.2 miles total today. Derailed by farmer drama. Road route next
time? Heart rate in yellow for first half.
4 minutes, 27 seconds to the barn—801 steps

CHAPTER 6

SLEEP REMAINED ELUSIVE. CATCHING DREAMS BETWEEN MY fingers was never an option, but I wondered if someone had kidnapped the sandman. I'd read a book where that happened, and it was bad news for all involved. I'd flopped in the bed enough that Josh had muttered pleas for my rest. He said them kindly, if poorly enunciated, but at 1:47, I called it.

Better to watch several episodes of *Love Island* on the couch than make both of us miserable.

The AC was churning out the good stuff, but my clammy skin couldn't appreciate it. Could you go through menopause in your thirties? I wasn't ready to Google that one. Three episodes and nearly a dozen "hot new bombshells" and my eyelids were heavy.

A Stevie Nicks song was playing on a dating show? I opened my eyes.

My vision slowly adjusted to catch judgment from Netflix.

"Are you still watching?" filled the center of the screen.

More than three episodes had played then. I checked the time.

Edging up on four in the morning. The song kept playing. A raspy voice so packed with soul and heart and determination filled the living room, filled my chest. Where? How? My phone remained locked, but a tap showed my music app wasn't open. I checked every tab on my laptop. Not a one was offering audio, and especially not "I Will Run to You."

It had been one of Mom's all-time favorites before her second husband left her. After that, it had become the albatross in our house. Some people burned pictures; my mom had banished songs. I didn't think I'd heard this track since I was eight. But here, earlier than the sun, Stevie Nicks was singing to me.

That pulsing bass line sent my heart skittering. Needles of awareness nibbled at my fingers. I rubbed my palms together like I'd lost the feeling in my hands. Better than acknowledging the shaking overdose of every anxiety chemical my body could manifest.

The song's chorus slithered into my conscious. Folding myself smaller, wanting to hide, I pressed my fingers against my ears. The sound quieted. So *not* in my head? Any dregs of sleep had evaporated, but the music still played. Coffee. Coffee could cure this. I started toward the kitchen but stilled at the front door. The melody was louder here.

Clear.

Beautiful.

Unnerving.

The screen door whined open and then clapped behind me. On the porch in the sticky air, "I Will Run to You" cocooned me. I wanted nothing more than to close my eyes and let the song fill me with calm. To be seven years old again and have my mom wrap an arm around me. But that was decades ago, thousands of miles away. This wasn't California. My mother's ashes were in the Pacific. The empty night offered no comfort. Dread bubbled beneath longing, a charging geyser waiting for the perfect pressure to explode.

The music commanded the air. Louder. Still louder. This wasn't a dream. This wasn't my brain tricking me. The wooden slats of our porch creaked beneath my steps. I paused. Another creak. Whirling revealed...nothing. Empty space behind me. My nightmares, my thoughts couldn't do that. The bridge surged, guitar soaring in the emptiness. Each note plucking a hair from the back of my neck. I turned toward the sound, lifted my gaze.

The hayloft light was on again.

Someone was in the barn.

Someone playing my mom's former favorite song.

Someone who knew it'd bring me out here.

Impossible. No one knew me here.

Josh? Bands of panic slapped around my chest. *No, he's asleep.* Did he even know about this song? I'd shared so much with him, but I hadn't spoken of "I Will Run to You." Had I?

I didn't think, just ran. Soft grass gave way to the painful bite of gravel against my bare soles. The impact didn't register. Or didn't matter. The music was coming from the barn. How loud did it have to be that I could hear it inside my house? The sprint burned my thighs. I ignored that too.

Closer. Closer. Closer.

The light went out.

The music cut.

And I was alone in the dark. Pain shot through my ankle, and I pitched forward. Pebbles digging into my hands and knees. Cutting me, collecting penance. For what?

"Who's there?" My voice was a sobbing mess.

Tears fell onto my hands, onto the ground. The earth swallowed every drop. An eerie stillness settled around me.

"Who are you?" My throat thickened with *everything*. "Where are you?"

No one replied. An oppressive melancholy rose around me, as though the soil itself sought to drown me in its sadness.

My legs refused to heed my command to march into the barn, but my stubborn self wouldn't let me retreat. And so I sat there, bleeding in the gravel.

"What do you want from me?" I shouted. The barn remained mired in darkness, unaffected by my cries.

Eventually, the diesel grumble of the farmers' arrival broke the silence. Their truck headlights bounced against the corn and then the barn. I stalked back toward the house then, avoiding the back door and its floodlight.

I showered and bandaged my knees before Josh even woke up.

I checked the turntable. We didn't even have a record mounted. I thumbed through the record collection. No copy of *The Wild Heart* by Stevie Nicks. Had we brought it from San Francisco? I didn't remember seeing it, but maybe I'd overlooked it. Had a person crept into our home while we'd been in town? Was it my stolen album playing outside?

I flipped the dead bolt on the front door for the first time since moving to the farm.

When the sun was up, I was going to look in the hayloft. I wouldn't stomp about—I'd hurt myself plenty today, thanks—but someone had been up there. Someone who wanted my attention. Well, they had it.

I should have been conserving my energy for chicken prep and marathon training, but I was glaring out the kitchen window every thirty seconds like whoever had fucked with me last night would suddenly appear and I could kick them in the shins. I'd had enough random people in my house growing up to know some men thought mean jokes were funny. Mom never invited them back. Same.

————

By the time Josh woke, I'd downed three lattes. All in the same mug, so he wouldn't know. Still I remained quietly stewing for another half hour. My husband had eaten a bagel and poured a second cup of coffee before I said anything about the night before. I told myself I was waiting for him to be fully awake because there was no urgency. I'm a shitty liar though. My nerves were like the sleep shirt I'd had since I was sixteen, threadbare and ragged. My knees yelped whenever I stood.

"Did you hear anything last night?" I tested the water. The song had been so loud.

"You got up early again?" Josh cocked his head to the side, like he was trying to see me better. "I didn't hear you get up. Another nightmare?"

Maybe? "Not exactly."

"That's ominous, babe. Do I want to know?" No matter how playful his tone, Josh cared.

"You really didn't hear anything?" How could the music that had drawn me from our house—that had set me sprinting over rocks in bare feet—not have even disturbed him? I guess I was disturbed enough for us both.

He shook his head, but his eyes were narrow. Watching me. I hadn't seen that look in six months—since the funeral—but that blend of pity and responsibility was memorable.

And it got under my skin.

"Someone was out in the barn again last night." My folded arms became a fortress. Coffee mug tight in my grip, archers at the ready.

Josh eased back in his chair. No longer looking like he was going to leap across the table to protect me from myself. "I talked with Ray about that—"

"We should talk to him again." Because this wasn't the farmers. Not that farmers couldn't jam to Stevie Nicks.

Josh nudged a banana toward me. "Even if one of his guys is out there early, how is it hurting anything?"

I ignored the fruit offering. "I don't want strangers walking around outside our house in the middle of the night."

"We had strangers walking by our front door at all hours back in the city," he countered.

"That was different. We expected them." And we had locks and peepholes and keycard access into the building. "There aren't *supposed* to be people walking around our house here."

"I get it." He clearly did not. His next words only proved as much. "But none of these people are bothering us."

Thwack.

The crash of my oversized mug against the table reverberated in the suddenly silent room. Coffee sloshed over the side. A worthy sacrifice. "Do I look unbothered?"

Josh pushed back from the table. He scrubbed at the nape of his neck, like he could rub away his embarrassment. I only stared at him harder.

"Sorry, not trying to discount your feelings," he said finally. "I only meant they aren't up by our house. We don't keep our belongings out there. Honestly, if it should bother anyone, it would be Ray or the other farmers."

I blinked at him. "How do you know they're not up here?"

"I just don't think anything nefarious is happening." He extended a hand toward me. Left it palm up on the table when I ignored it. "How do you know anyone was in the barn, babe? A light? Maybe there is one on a timer."

"They were playing 'I Will Run to You' by Stevie Nicks."

That gave him pause. Finally. "And you could hear it up here?"

I accepted his hand. "Exactly. That's why I was shocked you didn't hear it."

When Josh looked toward the kitchen window, the same way I had over and over in the night, I wished he could have seen the same thing I had. I should have woken him.

"Was there like some barn party happening?" he asked.

"I swear to God if you make a hoedown joke now..."

"No no no, I only meant, for it to be loud enough to hear up here, wouldn't they have needed amps and giant speakers?"

A fresh coat of dread dripped down my insides. Renovating me from determined to uneasy.

"I guess so. I didn't go down there to see their setup." I was already losing steam.

I needed Josh to rail on my behalf, but he paused to calculate all the variables like this was some logic problem. We had a good balance most of the time, but I hated that his words made me doubt everything I'd experienced last night.

"I can talk to him again, but it might be worth taking a sleeping pill tonight." Not a new *gentle* suggestion.

"Are you taking them?" My fingertips grazed one abrasion beneath my lounge pants. Honing myself on the sharp bite.

Josh laughed fully and freely. "I think we both know I've been sleeping like the dead lately."

"When are you heading in for that sales enablement session again?" Pretending not to know was a good way to divert this conversation.

"Wednesday." Two days from now. "Which is why you need to get some good rest."

"Oh, there are like ninety episodes of *Love Island* for me to watch."

He squeezed my hand. "Please promise me you're not going to watch trash reality shows the entire time I'm gone."

I was also going to investigate the hell out of that barn and lock all the doors at night. "I thought I might bond with our new hens over couples' drama on the show."

"Shit. That's right. The chickens get here soon." When Josh smiled, his eyes crinkled. Even after seven years, that look still gave me the tummy flutters.

"I assume the mail carrier will come to the door." It'd be nice to meet them too. Have a local connection.

Josh placed his coffee mug in the sink—much better at the two-cups-a-day deal than I was. Probably because of all the sleep. "Good thing we work from home. Not like we'll miss him."

The hens were scheduled for arrival Tuesday. At some point. We hadn't quite parsed out the mail delivery times. One, the box was a two-minute drive from the house. Two, we didn't get that much mail.

"What time do you need to be online today?" he asked, already looking down the hallway to his office setup.

I glanced at the clock like I hadn't counted every minute since I'd flipped the lock on our door. "I've got an hour and a half."

"If you want to do a shorter run, I could come with you." Josh would not be signing up for a marathon with me, but we used to do quicker cardio together. This was nice. A peace offering.

"How short?" Even with him at my side, I was going to need for my legs to get that good burn.

"How far do I have to go to see the cows?"

I brightened. "About four miles to the cows."

"I'm in, but I have a favor to ask."

If he brought up the chill-out or sleeping pills again, he could run alone. I bravely inclined my head for him to continue.

"Can I name one of the chickens?"

My guffaw knocked loose every band of tension in my body in a way that made me think it should be part of my warm-up. Stretch, laugh, sprint. "Sure, you can name a hen, but I get to pick which one."

"That's fine. The name will be the same no matter what."

Our run included seventeen cows (I'd named two of them, and Bertha and Genevieve totally moo-approved my outfit), one dodged cow patty (a first!), and three minutes and twelve seconds to run to the barn. Yes, I timed it. No, I didn't mention it to Josh. The windows were dark, the farmers out in the fields. Josh had promised to talk to them again. I told myself I'd investigate that hayloft as soon as Josh was out of town. If it was nothing, I'd rather be embarrassed solo. If I was right, though I'd drive my ass into Hastings and get some help.

Emily's Running Log:

3 minutes, 12 seconds to the barn—576 steps—This feels like the accurate time. Maybe my pedometer was off before? We didn't run into the farmers at all. Eastern field for the win!

9.8 miles—Josh joined me. Longer time, but lower heart rate. Not bad.

CHAPTER 7

THE CHICKENS HAD ARRIVED IN A PALLET—LIKE THE POSTAL worker was delivering cargo to the back of the Farm Equipment & Supply Co. instead of my home. Though, I supposed living on a farm added a touch of Farm Supply to your vibe. Not *my* vibe, but the overall farm's, sure.

Most of the farms in town were known by the name of the family that lived there. Because acreages and homes like ours were property that passed down like the good dinnerware in some families or one of June Carter Cash's dresses in my family. My mom had seven different stories detailing how *her* mother had acquired the gown—everything from working backstage at the Grand Ole Opry to a wardrobe malfunction rescue to a royal flush in a greenroom. The truth lay somewhere in those stories, just as it would one day when people spoke about our farmstead.

I couldn't ask Josh to name our estate after any of my mother's heirlooms. Besides, this place was a new beginning. *Our* new beginning. So no music history and no carrying on the burdens our parents had placed upon us.

I knelt on the lawn, my back to the barn—because if I didn't look directly at it, that creeping sense of being watched, the anticipation of an attack couldn't claim me. Right? I told myself no one was looming, but even as I freed the first beautiful hen from the wooden shipping container, my pulse quickened. Since I'd stumbled in the dark, I'd sensed a sadness in the soil. I glanced toward the barn, knowing better. The chill of death skated over my skin, the wind bringing the scent of sulfur to my nose. I coughed into my elbow, cradling the chicken on the other side. This hen did not need to look at the barn to have foreboding knock her back.

"Don't worry, Sophia," I said to the chicken, placing her inside the pen around the coop. "Your house faces mine. You're going to be just fine."

Sophia ruffled her burnished red feathers and then tottered forward to the chicken feed I'd scattered toward the back of the pen and up the ramp into the coop.

Josh had done a marvelous job on the home for our hens and only muttered a little about putting the "Cluckingham Palace" sign up. It really added a homey quality I was certain the birds would love.

I moved each chicken into the henhouse with a proper hello and introduction. I won't say the girls all understood their names yet, but it's not like humans know their names right away either. Blanche and Rose nestled inside, quickly finding the roost very much to their liking. Sophia, Dorothy, and Mother Clucker (Josh really earned naming a hen by building their house, didn't he?) pecked about. Only Blanche looked toward the barn. Could chickens sense evil? Probably. My Golden Girls (and guest star Mother Clucker) hadn't pecked me once. Clearly, they had a good sense about people.

I was a first-time chicken owner, but I wasn't completely unfamiliar with animals. Josh had grown up with a sweet—and a little dopey—boxer mix. Sandy was the kind of dog you invited into your bed. And, honestly, it was good I felt that way because Josh always brought her into the bed with us when we stayed at his parents'.

If only one out of five hens was giving the barn any notice, that had to be a good sign, right?

I latched the gate. Josh needed to come out here and see my new babies. His efforts had made them so comfy, and he deserved to get proper accolades. The office door had been closed all morning—not even a five-minute bio break in hours. It was as though he was being penalized for working from home. Silly, given that 90 percent of his company's workforce was remote or traveling.

The hens were settled, but plastic, nails, chicken wire, and wood littered the lawn. If I was going to brag about how great this was, it needed to be perfect. Details mattered. Josh had a way of seeing an object or two and putting together a whole story. He was usually right. It's why I had to make sure my coffee mug wasn't only washed but dried and put away if I didn't want him to know about my increasingly common middle-of-the-night caffeine intake. Same with the coffeepot.

It was also why I'd ordered some under-eye gels to stave off the worst of the dark circles but scheduled their delivery on a day I knew he'd be in Omaha. He cared about me. He'd told me over and over just last night how important it was to him that I took care of myself, that I was resting and "coping."

God, I hated that word. I'd told him as much, but in the brightness of day, I could see his point. He was alone here as well. Demonstrating I could be his steady rock, too, mattered.

I tossed the wrapping materials from the chickens' delivery into the trash bin near the house. The wooden pallets though, I loaded onto our wheelbarrow.

"Be good, girls. I'm going to pitch this stuff and then find your dad, and then we'll finish getting you all settled in," I told the chickens like they were nervous instead of clearly making themselves at home. Though I suppose anything was an upgrade from the squished situation in the back of a USPS truck.

The big bin for all the industrial farm refuse was on the other side of the barn. *Of course it is.* Ray and the guys stacked empty pallets, bags, and such there until they had a good enough collection to haul it off-site. Leaving the wooden bits up by the house would make it Josh's problem, and every heavy sigh he'd dropped last night said I was already bringing him enough of those. The weight of the wheelbarrow wasn't enough of a distraction for me to miss that it took four minutes and twenty-two seconds for me to get to the barn. At least my activity tracker was happy about my heart rate.

I hustled around the path curving behind the barn and over a soggy patch of soil. Tension twisted behind my breastbone. *So much for heart rate goals.* The sooner I was back with my chickens and my house, the better. A steady *thumpa thumpa thump thump* of an unfamiliar bass line pulsed against my arms. Damp earth and anise clogged my sinuses. I sputtered for breath. Melody overlaid the beat. Country music. Not the edgy rap country that slipped into my workout playlist rotation or the Patsy Cline Mom so often played when it rained. This tune was about dudes and their trucks. If someone was trying to unnerve me, this track wasn't it. I sent a silent thank-you to the empty sky.

Around the curve, next to the trash bins, were two of the men who worked on the farm.

Men was perhaps a stretch. These weren't the rugged adults who had been lifting bales and driving combines for twenty years. These were just-out-of-high-school kids with baseball caps, fuzzy attempts at mustaches, and an indefatigable determination. One stood at the barn's back entrance, lifting huge forty-pound bags of something that only reminded me of potting soil, but smelled far from earthy. He tossed the bag as though it were light as a bed pillow to a second boy standing in the back of the truck. He caught it with ease and dropped it onto a stack. The labels read, BLOOD MEAL. I flinched away from the words. If these boys weren't scared, neither was I.

"What are you listening to?" I asked, in the hopes of not startling anyone. Okay, it also bothered me a little that I didn't recognize the band they were listening to. Like I was somehow letting down my mother's legacy by not picking up on a jam.

The boy on the truck straightened like I'd slapped him. Dark brown hair curled out beneath his baseball hat, and an echo of sunburn lit the back of his neck. He turned toward me, his pupils blown beneath the brim of his hat, making his gaze darker than it was.

"Oh, hey," he said, clearly trying to make sense of a thirtysomething in neon showing up at the barn and attempting conversation about music.

The other guy recovered more quickly and rattled off a band name that filtered into the ether.

Before I could register his answer, the man on the ground hustled toward me.

"You want us to take that for you, Mrs. Hauk?" he asked.

The only person who ever called me Mrs. Hauk was the receptionist at my doctor's office. Ugh. I needed to find a new one of those. Add it to the list of adulting tasks I didn't want to take on. This guy said my name like I was a substitute teacher and he was reminding me of the required formality that carried no respect. It instantly made me feel both old and off-kilter, and I hated every second.

"No," I said more harshly than I'd intended. "You have actual jobs. I can toss a few bits of wood into a pile."

"It's no trouble." The guy on the truck jumped down, dirt caking his boots.

That voice. He'd been in the field the other day, the one arguing with Ray. Whatever he'd been up to had pissed off his boss, but he'd also talked like he had a claim to the farm.

"It's fine," I stuttered. Anxiety drizzled down my throat.

Up close he looked familiar, which was ridiculous because I knew literally no one here.

The farmhand ignored my dismissal, grabbed wood from the wheelbarrow, and threw it on a larger pile. A treacly watermelon scent clung to him. The vape pen poked from his front pocket.

"We haven't actually met." He dipped over my wheelbarrow, brushing against my arm. Not a shove by any stretch, but his wide elbows practically screamed I wasn't supposed to be there. "We see you in the fields sometimes."

Had he seen me that day?

"Don't make it weird, Tyler," his friend said. He was back to throwing bags of whatever into the truck.

"It's not like we're watching you. I just meant Ray told us to leave you alone, and we do. But this farm...." He shrugged like there was some obvious ending to that statement.

I huffed a fake laugh. "This farm?"

"It takes good men to run a farm. That's all." His one-shoulder shrug fooled no one. It wasn't that he was a bad liar. He wasn't even trying.

"If you need anything else carried down here, just holler, Mrs. Hauk," the one still focused on his job said. The heavy bag thwacked into the truck.

The music switched to another song. I stared at the black oval Bluetooth speaker. Small enough to carry with one hand, loud enough that I'd heard it from around the other side of the barn. Why hadn't I considered portable speakers in the barn? The music came and went, just like this truck, just like these guys. Teenagers playing music in the barn at night made a whole lot more sense than anyone actively messing with me.

"Ma'am? Are you okay?" The one who had cleared my wheelbarrow narrowed his gaze on me.

I was not okay, but there were certain facts about me that these boys had no business knowing. In fact, none of them. Maybe Ray had been right to tell them to avoid me.

I nodded, thanked the guys, and trekked back toward the hens and my husband.

I'd forgotten to ask the farmhands' names. This is why they liked Josh more than me. Not that I needed anyone to like me.

Emily's Running Log:

5 minutes, 13 seconds to the barn—939 steps
4 minutes, 22 seconds to the barn with wheelbarrow
14.7 mile run—25% green today. Yay heart!

CHAPTER 8

ADULTHOOD MEANT DOING SHIT YOU DIDN'T WANT TO DO,
but it also meant you had significant practice at avoiding said shit.
Josh and I were living proof. He didn't talk to the farmers. I avoided
calls from the lawyer handling my mom's estate. We pretended I
slept peacefully through the night.

The vibration of an incoming call would regularly *frrrrrpt*
through our whole house. Winston Lanford, Esquire. Each time, I
silenced the ringer. You'd think it'd be easy to run from my responsibilities with all the open space. Turns out it merely opened a chasm
for me to dwell in. To think about what might be stored in my
mother's house that I didn't want to see. To think about why my
dad hadn't reached out since the funeral. To wonder if the music
the other night was my heart—and a lack of sleep—telling me this
wasn't my home.

When Wednesday arrived, my husband left.

That sounds so dramatic. It'd never bothered me when he traveled
in the past. In fact, I used to love having the entire bed to myself. I'd

flop in the middle, stretch out like a starfish for a few minutes. I'd bring popcorn into the room and snack and watch television. Look, yes, I can do that on the couch. But there was something relaxing about reveling in my annoying habits when they didn't harm anyone. Josh would never know about my in-the-sheets snacking.

This time, though, I wasn't thinking about snack foods. He rolled out before the sun had stretched above the stalks. I gave my best impression of grogginess, and Josh pretended I was a decent actor. Farmer Ray Clausen waited on the porch while Josh kissed me goodbye. Soft, perfunctory, still a bit sleep mussed.

We'd loaded up both the fridge and the pantry earlier this week, but Josh didn't want to leave me without a car, so Ray had agreed to drive Josh to the regional airport up in Grand Island. Somehow, the hour-and-a-half jaunt was "on the way." Josh didn't suss out what other errands the man could have that far out, but then he only pried when it impacted business. Never in his personal life. Perhaps that's why he wasn't pushing me now? Did he expect me to come to him in my own time about the estate? About how I felt after what had happened the other night? Any time I caught him glancing at my scraped knees, he'd distract me by putting his hands on my hips. All was forgotten. Perhaps that was a gift. Bitterness pooled in the back of my throat, but I swallowed it.

Dirt plumed behind Ray's truck, the halogen of the floodlights allowing me to watch Josh's departure longer than I would have at the airport drop-off lane. I moved into the kitchen, made my fourth cup of coffee (shh!), and watched the sunrise through the window.

The barn remained dormant the entire time.

I yanked on leggings and a chartreuse tank top like I was going to get in my morning run. I even carried my training journal into the kitchen. The corners curled up on the small black Moleskine notebook, despite it being new. Those edges lied about their age. I'd folded the cover between my hands, squeezed, twisted, and basically mangled the notebook with my anxiety. The fact it showed so little wear was really a testament to quality manufacturing.

But both my notebook and I were lying. Beyond the kitchen window, past the coop and my new hens, beyond the dirt driveway, the barn waited.

The light hadn't turned on since the night I'd run out there. I hadn't heard music in days. If I didn't count background audio on the TV or the occasional bump of EDM from Josh's office. (I didn't.) Yet the pressure between my shoulder blades increased the longer I stared at the roughened walls, like a hand was pressing me forward. Or down.

Goldenrod light warmed the verdant tips of the cornstalks. Waiting for light was a child's move, but I'd been toppled in the darkness last time. Not doing that again. That barn was mine. It was on our property. It was nothing to be afraid of. If I could only survey the interior, I could let go of this dread. My hand slipped from the doorknob. A shoulder shimmy and a sweaty palm swiped clean on my moisture-wicking legging later, I opened the door. The running notebook discarded on the countertop.

I want to say I didn't count the steps to the barn, but the morning had already been filled with so many lies. Keeping a mental tally of each of those 586 steps had to be healthier than letting the apprehension coalescing beneath my breastbone overwhelm me. My steady pace and bright attire weren't for the cows today (sorry, Bertha and Genevieve), but if Ray's crew was nearby, it would look to them like I was exercising.

More like exorcising my own bullshit. The barn doors gaped before me. I stalled there, worn trail shoes planted against the packed earth. Awareness prickled behind my right ear and pinched its way down and around my neck. Glancing over my shoulder only tightened the invisible noose. I pressed the heels of my hands against my eyes, forgetting to feign confidence for whoever was watching. Red, yellow, green flashed before me like streetlight shots of Roman candles. I righted myself and let my vision clear again. God, I hoped no one had seen that.

Aging flecks of red paint still clung to the graying wood on the barn door to my right. In daylight the building was more elderly woman than haunted house. It was the wood-and-nail version of frail. Not teetering from a too-full grocery bag, but from eroding support soil. I rapped my knuckles against the wood. Warm and solid, it made a soft thump.

"Ray? Anyone?" I called, knowing the farmer was well on his way to the airport with Josh and the others should be in the fields. "Anyone here today?"

Seconds ticked by with only the gentle shushing of a breeze atop the crops. Three chips of red paint clung to my hand. I brushed them off and listened for one more moment. I was alone and out of excuses.

I'm not sure what I expected upon stepping inside. I'd been past these doors day after day. I'd seen the spare tractor tires, the equipment covered with beige tarps, the hooks and handles and brooms stored neatly on a pegboard along the far wall. Sunlight slipped through the open doors and the windows on the far end of the space. Dust motes danced in the honeyed air. Earth and age mingled around me as if a reminder that this was a place of work—and had been for far longer than I'd owned the place.

Stretching my neck from side to side didn't negate the simmer of fear in my belly. *It's a barn, Em. A building. A glorified storage shed. Let it go.* My heartbeat tripped. Were the words mine? Josh's? I couldn't untangle the ones he'd offered as assurances from my own chiding. Clenching my teeth sent a bolt of ice up to my temples. I just needed to go upstairs. I'd see the loft was empty, like Ray had told Josh, and I'd move past this. And then, I guess, I'd call the lawyer, because clearly the stress of releasing my mother's possessions had me hallucinating her favorite jams played in an old equipment barn in the middle of nowhere.

The ladder to the hayloft was tucked in the back corner of the barn. Simple wooden rungs bracketed on either side by two-by-fours affixed to the wall. It had likely been a light wood once, but years of use had darkened the steps. Wood on the side rails had splintered in several spots. I gripped a smooth section and gave it a yank. The wood whined, but nothing moved.

Good enough.

I planted my foot on the bottom rung and climbed. The ladder groaned. I stilled, then hopped once, twice. If I was going to bust my ass on the floor, it would be from one step up, not ten. Steadiness confirmed, I kept moving. The top rung was darker than the rest. I reached for it, slime meeting my grip. It was as though the wood writhed beneath my palm. A full-body shiver overtook me, and it was everything I could do to not let go. I scrambled over the top step and flopped face-first onto the hayloft floor. I was too busy scrubbing my hands against my legs as hard as I could to even look around. My hands were clean, but the slimy sensation clung to me.

The stagnant scent of years' worth of cardboard and the acrid bite of rotting hay settled in the space. Exposed beams stretched far overhead. I'd need another ladder to reach the ceiling. Good thing I just needed to confirm no one was hiding out here. Light trickled in through the far window, spearing its way onto rusted shovels, rolls of chicken wire and chain link, and a random smattering of sagging boxes.

The floor creaked with every step I took. The farmer's warning—by way of my husband—about the rickety structure echoed with each pop and groan. Was I going to drop through at any moment? What was beneath me now? Could I die landing on a combine? There's an epitaph no one would want to write. "Here lies Emily Hauk, who ran from her problems, ignored good advice, and died sprawled out on farm equipment. Her husband loved her stupid ass."

I tiptoed my way across the room, stepping only where I could see the floorboards peeking from beneath the straw. If someone had stepped there before, it had to be safe. Right? Humidity tightened the room; I would have been sweating anyway though. I'd built this place into a boogeyman. I'd anthropomorphized a barn.

Humor tickled my sternum. In the hazy light, the barn seemed far from sentient.

Old, disregarded, and gross? Yes. Out to get me? Probably not.

I plucked my way across the room. There was freedom in realizing I was simply spinning myself up over nonsense. Josh hadn't used those words, but he'd thought them real loudly. He'd been right. I shook myself and spun to survey the rest of the room quickly.

No record player.

No amps.

No giant speakers ready to blare Fleetwood Mac or Tom Petty or any other Mom jam at me in the middle of the night.

Because that shit was in your head, Emily.

Behind me I expected someone to be laughing, someone to cackle that I'd fallen for this, someone to tell me that the last year had been a dream. But I was alone. Still. Always.

I trudged forward. Hay had been piled in front of two large cardboard boxes. Their lids sagged and the sides bulged, possibly due to the moisture in the air or overfilling. Again that needling sensation speared my neck. I turned again, but only earned more pressure at my back. An urge to look.

And I wanted to.

I'd come here for answers, and I had them. There were no people up here currently. This hay, though, said maybe someone had been? Maybe they'd been here to pry into these boxes. I lifted the lid off the closest one. Green fabric poured out. The smell of mildew punched me in the nose. I lifted the dress out of the box and tossed it near the wall. The next three below it were the same. Bold colors, reeking of disgusting growth. I was about to disregard the box altogether, but the delicate white fringe of an old photo peeked up from the bottom. A pile of four black-and-white images had been left beneath the rotting clothing. I thumbed through them. A family posed in front of a sleek sedan. Children eating Popsicles on a curb. A wedding photo, both participants way too young from what I could tell. Black mold had commandeered part of the image, blotting the woman's face.

The next photo had mold crusting it too. Again the woman's face and her right hand were covered with the black sludge. I wiped at the offending growth with the hem of my shirt, but the mold wouldn't budge. I angled the photo into the light more fully. The black smudges darkened, but it was the same man, two young children, and a woman all standing in front of a barn.

This barn.

My barn.

A heavy crash rumbled from the roof. *Squawk!* I jerked back a step, the floor groaned, split. I leapt forward, landing in a pile of old straw, dropping the picture. Overhead hung the light fixture. It began to sway slowly, taunting me. I was ten feet from the window that faced my house. Ten feet from the source of my recent fears. Anxiety swelled, consuming my heart, my lungs, my mind. The chaotic cocoon cloistered me in sickly sweetness. Darkness tried to cloud my vision, but all I could see was the cord dangling above me.

No lightbulb.

The white wire knotted in a noose. Black mold growing on the light socket.

CHAPTER 9

THE THREAT DANGLED OVERHEAD, SWAYING, WAVING HELLO. As if that mold were ready to plop down onto my face. Blight my mind. Obscure me.

Blood, hot and wet, sluiced down my shin. My foot was still caught in the new jagged hole in the loft flooring. If anyone had been below, my scream would have sent them running. Instead my wound was adding to the rust stains on the old farm equipment on the ground level. I stared at the empty light socket and hovered with half breaths on the floor. The treacly air unable to escape my lungs. Mildewy hay clung to my hair and cloyed the room with the sweetness of decay.

And I was lying in it.

Under it.

That braided cord and the black growth within it shouted, "*You're next*," in a way that only my lizard brain could process. Josh would tell me it was nothing. The socket's emptiness was proof *nothing* was happening here. And yet, sprawled on the rotted wood,

I felt the weight of foreboding only pressed more firmly onto my chest.

The sun was streaky through the bare and broken windows at the end of the loft, but at night there was no way for a glow to emit. No lightbulb above or shattered on the floor nearby. Even if a farmhand had been up here—staying warm or napping or screwing with me— they wouldn't have snatched the bulb when they left.

The black mold stared back at me, mottled and accusatory. As if its presence confirmed the lights and music had been delusions. That light wasn't *capable* of working.

I shifted, and the floor creaked. Scrabbling backward, I ripped my leg from the hole, staining more straw a vicious red. I hissed at the burn of fraying wood digging in, and then I got the eff out of there. I tiptoed back through my previous steps like I was the living embodiment of a Nintendo hero. I'd spent countless hours playing Zelda when I was ten. If Link could sidle up the exterior of a castle with half a heart after dying two dozen times, I could get out of a goddamned hayloft I wasn't even supposed to be in.

Josh was going to freak out. He'd thrust the prescriptions at me again, tell me to journal or sleep or whatever great tip he'd heard about on some grief podcast. But then he had no idea where I was. That was the point, right? I was alone on the farm and in need of answers. The barn, however, had only provided more questions and a bloody leg. I hurried over the gravel back to the house, careful not to go for round two with the rocks against my legs. The barn loomed behind me like a creeper at a coffee shop who swore they weren't reading over my shoulder.

The first aid kit was under Josh's side of the vanity. I hobbled my way into our bathroom and shoved his shaving supplies to the side. He hadn't used that beard trimmer in weeks. The bright orange box stuffed with bandages peered from behind the U bend in the pipe. I yanked it onto the floor next to me. A small pill bottle clacked to the floor. Valium. With my name on it. Filled two weeks ago at a Walgreens an hour away. I didn't even have a doctor here, but he'd managed to get the nice pharmacist in Hastings to transfer the prescription. I flung the container against the wall. Nothing happened—the childproof cap stealing any satisfying spill.

The Valium bottle lay where I'd thrown it. Josh might be right that I should take one. Calm down. Think this through. The barn's loft had been a storage space. Old pictures and clothes. No amps. No way to emit light. *Unless they brought a lantern,* my mind immediately countered.

I carefully peeled off my pants. *Those are going into the trash.* The possibilities of who had been in the barn and why churned and redoubled while I flushed the gash on the outside of my calf with hydrogen peroxide. The wound was the deepest I'd had since a hiking trip when I was twenty. I'd been real ambitious, determined to get a great picture from the top of a waterfall. If that rock-meet-thigh incident didn't need stitches, this sucker didn't either. The more I thought about it, the clearer it was that Josh didn't need to know about any of this. It wasn't like he was going to go up into the loft—he was the one who had warned me against it. And he talked to the farmers far more than I did.

Was that why they were messing with me? I waved whenever

I saw *anyone*, but were Midwestern women supposed to be more homey? I didn't really *bake*, but all the home decor magazines showed pies on the counter in the shabby chic photoshoots. Would a cupcake cure this? But how could I have offended them? I jogged and I worked and I watched garbage television in the middle of the night.

Or maybe no one was doing *anything* to me. The barn was creepy. It was moving—I was certain—but were those lights real? The mold and the now-broken floor sure were. The tarnished photos were the closest thing to evidence that anyone had been up there, and they were decades old.

What was it about the barn that unnerved me so much? It didn't match our farmhouse; it didn't belong here.

Or maybe I didn't? Mom would have hated it here, hated my being here. No matter the *adventure* level. My opinion kept changing as I sat on the bathroom floor beneath the vanity lights. If my mom were going to send a message to GTFO, would she use Stevie Nicks or drop a Type O Negative track?

I scrubbed my hands against my face, the faint tinge of astringent lingering on my skin.

I needed to get off this farm right now. Away from the barn. Away from Mom's records. Just...gone.

Three gauze patches, a butterfly bandage, and a fresh pair of leggings later, I grabbed my keys for the first time since we'd moved here. Josh always drove whenever we went out. Not today.

The filmy window at the top of the barn was empty. I refused to drop it from my view until I had the car doors locked. I put the sedan in drive. In the rearview, I almost thought I saw the light socket swinging. My vision wasn't that great though. The noose in my mind kept ratcheting tighter.

I wriggled my fingers and jammed my foot on the gas pedal. A farmer's truck rolled past the barn. *All yours, guys.*

I needed coffee. That was it. A strong espresso solved everything. LTE data kicked in at the end of our exceedingly long driveway. I paused before turning out onto the state highway and checked to see that the best coffee within twenty miles was open.

The closest town—population 723—offered only a truck stop for breakfast, lunch, and dinner. The Diamond R was open twenty-four hours a day. *Good to know.*

It was my first time visiting the truck stop, but I arrived to a packed parking lot. Was everyone in town at this place? A bright chime sounded when I stepped inside. The hostess stand was also the cash wrap. Multicolored lighters, novelty toys, and a small carousel of hair accessories swallowed the counter. The shimmer of a blue claw clip caught my attention, but the woman who greeted me had a perfectly tousled topknot with two Bic pens pierced through it. Her rounded cheeks and bright eyes put her at nineteen or twenty, but she called me "sweetheart" like I was the one who was practically a child. She ushered me to an empty booth—the red sparkly vinyl on the seats creased from use—and placed a laminated menu in front of me.

"Pies today are coconut cream, cherry, and lemon meringue, but we might have an apple streusel ready in the next half hour," the waitress announced in that perfunctory way that made it clear that, despite the early hour, she'd already run through the dessert specials a couple dozen times.

"It's not even nine." I blurted, immediately knowing this was not the way to win friends.

"There's no wrong time to have pie." She sucked her teeth and then continued. "I'll give you a minute with the menu. Coffee first?"

I nodded emphatically. She tilted a carafe over the white ceramic mug already on my table.

"Oh, could I get a latte? It's been a morning." I added the latter hoping for sympathy and not questions.

I got neither. She pointed to the sugar and creamer packets at the back of the table and wished me luck.

"No problem," I said, immediately feeling like my whole life— and complete lack of luck—was on display in this gas station restaurant.

I ordered the American breakfast because I overheard people at four other tables select it. In fact, it was the only option anyone ordered despite a bevy of omelets and French toast. The food arrived hot and fresh, and came with a giant bowl of berries. That much fruit would have cost me half a month's rent back in the city. My bill here was twelve bucks.

The coffee was acidic and heavy, and my stomach ached after the first gulp.

"Everything good, sweetheart?" The waitress slid into the seat across from me and placed a steaming pot of coffee on the table between us.

"Oh, yeah. Food is delicious." I fumbled. Small talk at a party?

I got that. Random teenager joining me at a truck stop? Zero experience.

"Of course it is. You said you were having a morning though. Me too." She kicked her feet out and crossed her ankles. Clearly getting comfortable then. "My daughter got into my makeup. Whole bathroom was smeared with foundation. You might think a bottle wouldn't go that far, but in the hands of a five-year-old, it can really stretch."

I laughed despite myself. "Sorry."

"Why? It's funny. Want to see the pictures?" She brought out her phone before I could reply and started swiping through a series of images of a little girl practically camouflaged in beige paint.

After I gave her an appropriate amount of sympathy and praise for her precocious child, she leaned both arms on the table and met my gaze with a gravity I was not prepared for. "You just passing through? Where are you headed?"

My leg ached, my head was muddy, and now this woman was watching me like she saw all of it. "Nope. I'm a local."

The waitress's laughter drew the attention of two elderly men sitting two tables over. They wore matching black VFW ball caps.

"You okay, Hattie?" the one in a maroon jacket asked.

"Sure thing, Ernie." She inclined her head toward me. "This one says she's local."

Now the men were laughing too. My insides tried to shrivel, like I could straight-up *poof* into the upholstery. Something was happening with my barn, my leg was oozing blood beneath my patchwork bandages, and now these strangers were laughing at me. Really a banner day. Wasn't the perk of living a rural life supposed to be zero people?

"A *new* local, but I still live here," I clarified. As if it helped. Heat slapped my cheeks, and I pretended none of us noticed the shame surely rising on the sides of my neck.

Both older gentlemen straightened. One coughed as he covered his smile.

They asked where I moved from, each wearing a newfound wariness around me. Like everyone had put on their coats to leave and I was just sitting down. Late to the party. Or uninvited.

"Frank's just messing you with, darlin'," maroon jacket, Ernie, said to me, as if we were in on the same joke. I was decidedly not in on this one. "She's the one who moved into the Belkin place."

The other war vet nodded as if this was all he needed to understand me.

Hattie, though, asked, "How I am just now meeting you? Didn't you move in like weeks ago?"

It had taken nearly three years before I met the man who lived in the adjacent apartment back in San Francisco. Neither of us had thought anything of it. The UPS guy had caught me walking into the building, and I'd signed for the neighbor's package. Our leasing office was terrible. I'd passed the box off to the next-door neighbor, and that was the limit of our interaction. I don't think I spoke to him again before we moved, come to think of it.

I cradled my mostly full coffee mug. "A couple months, actually."

Her brow furrowed as if I'd dismissed the pie again, which I was quickly gathering was a grave offense.

"We've been settling in on the farm. What's the point of moving to someplace this beautiful if you don't stay put and enjoy it?" I mostly meant it. The sunrises lit my chest with joy, but I'd fled this morning. Maybe I was running from my own problems though.

My phone buzzed on the table. "Winston Lanford, Esquire" lit the screen. I silenced it.

"Where are you from that *this* is the upgrade?" Hattie asked like every teenager in the history of ever. In high school, I'd been convinced New York would be a million times better than living on the Haight. Because parents. Even cool parents were oppressive when you were seventeen.

Winston Lanford rang again. *Proving my point, man.* Dismissed.

I tried to give the waitress the short "I don't know you" overview, but Hattie and the two men asked a lot of questions. The VFW twosome were Ernest—"call me Ernie"—and Frank.

"California to Nebraska." Ernie shook his head like I'd somehow dumbfounded him. "Smart call, girl. It's called the Good Life for a reason. There's a brewery—"

"In every city with at least five thousand people," Hattie ended for him. Her smirk suggested she'd been to a brewery or three. I mentally bumped her age up a few years.

Ernie flattened his lips. "You know, coffee's getting a little cold over here."

She slipped out from the booth and moved to freshen mugs all around. Even mine, which had approximately two sips gone.

Without the young woman to connect us, I wasn't sure what to do. Was this my chance to escape? I'd already dropped a twenty on the twelve-dollar tab, but what waited at home echoed in the back of my mind. Closing my eyes only flung me supine on that loft floor again, staring at the small white noose, the rotting black mold stretching over the light socket's mouth like it intended to choke me. Had I truly seen that? Who would even do such a thing? A noose in an attic no one visited? What was the point?

Unless I was right, and that attic wasn't empty at night. The overhead bulb might not be an option, but that didn't mean the barn was empty after sunset. Darkness dripped into my stomach, souring the eggs-and-bacon combo. I'd been eager for Josh to leave to prove...something. Had I succeeded? He'd say no, but he would have said that anyway. He didn't believe in anything he couldn't touch. Hell, he didn't even believe that he was the most Aries to ever Aries.

I'd found photos in that loft. Ones where I couldn't see the woman's face. Those were tangible. You couldn't tell mold where to grow, but c'mon, that was suspicious.

"You're thinking real hard over there, California girl," Frank teased. He'd nearly finished a slice of coconut cream pie.

Busted. "I don't know anything about the people who used to live on our farm." It hadn't been a concern before. But if there was a noose in the attic of our barn—one that very much lit up at night for no reason—perhaps I should care.

Frank and Ernie shared a long look. When wizened old men look worried, I pay attention.

"How do I become a local without learning the lore?" I nudged playfully.

"You spend time with people. You come into town," Frank mumbled, but didn't bother pitching his voice low.

"Sorry," I replied like the people pleaser I didn't want to be anymore. One my mom never had been. She'd have kept this crowd on their toes.

"You don't need to apologize to these grumps." Hattie returned with a fresh glass of water for me. "The Belkin family had a rough time after Bridget went missing."

"That family was cursed. Little Bridget wasn't the first problem. But I'm not here to dig up ghosts. Bad luck." The temptation to gossip speckled Ernie's cheeks with red spots; his nostrils flared. He'd caught the scent of being the most knowledgeable in the room and was tempted.

The stay-at-home-mom set from my old spin gym wore that same look every Thursday morning.

"I didn't hear anything about a little girl..." A missing girl had to be something a Realtor disclosed, right?

"Bridget was fifteen," Hattie corrected.

That didn't make it better.

"How long ago did she...die?" That last word was a guess, and as soon as it was out of my mouth, I wanted to flee the conversation. I clearly had not peopled in too long.

"She's not dead," Frank snapped.

"Bridget has been missing for three years," Hattie said softly. "Presumed dead" was underscored in her heavily lined eyes.

I apologized again, if only to have something to do while I forged a path out of this increasingly uncomfortable conversation. I'd fled my home to regain my sense of, well, everything. Instead I had more questions. How long had that noose been dangling there? Had a woman died in the barn? Did Bridget spend her nights rocking out to my mom's favorite jams while hiding in the hayloft?

Hattie patted my hand. That's right, she's a mom. "You didn't know, sweetheart."

"I'm sorry," I said again, softer this time.

Hattie sighed. She lowered her voice to a near whisper. "You should know about Alice too."

Frank's harrumph cut into the conversation.

"She should know," Hattie said to him.

"Aye," Ernie agreed. His attention turned to me. "We don't want to run you off. You seem like a nice girl—though quit holing up on the farm. Eat some pie."

"I'll have pie next time," I replied automatically.

Appeased, Ernie continued. "Alice Belkin was a good woman. Her girl's disappearance ruined her."

I quirked a brow but kept my mouth shut.

Hattie leaned over the table toward me. "She killed herself."

"It was an accident, Hattie Mae. Don't spread those lies," Ernie snapped.

The waitress blanched.

They were talking about tragedy on my farm, at my house. "What happened to Alice?" My voice wavered.

"Poor thing fell from the barn's loft."

"Drunk as a skunk," Frank muttered.

"It was ruled an accident," Ernie said firmly.

I gripped the seat beneath me. "How long ago was this?"

Ernie waved a hand. "Couple years back. When they gave up searching for Bridget."

I wanted to ask more, to know everything about these people who had lived in my house and suffered such tragedy. But Hattie quickly stood from my table.

"You sure you don't want pie?" was the strangest conversation ender, but I shook my head no.

Awkwardness billowed from my pores until it was a thick cloud looming over my table. Ernie and Frank returned to a conversation about a pothole in front of the grocery store. I'd been chucked from my seat when Josh had driven over it, but I'd already proven I wasn't yet ready for locals-only discussions. Knowing my luck, I'd joke about concrete and get a story about how the last time they poured concrete, it killed someone's grandma, and I'd have to feel like the asshole outsider yet again.

I slipped from the truck stop with half-hearted waves and clung to what I'd learned. The Belkin family had lived on my farm. Ernie said they'd been cursed. People back home threw that word around casually. A war vet wouldn't. Not about a dead woman and her maybe dead daughter. And that's what the Belkin's girl was. Bridget had been missing for three years.

Our Realtor had mentioned none of this on our countless Zoom calls. But then did she have to disclose whether anyone had died on the farm? Had we even asked?

Emily's Running Log:

3 minutes, 15 seconds to the barn—586 steps

CHAPTER 10

I TEXTED JOSH FROM THE CAR.

Me: Ate at a truck stop. Met locals.

A few moments later his reply pinged through.

Josh: Making friends?
Me: You'll love Ernie and Frank.

He would. My husband was built for absorbing gossip about people he didn't know. Sales guy instincts ran deep with him. Small talk grated on my sensibilities, but Josh could file away tidbits about strangers for ages. And he liked it.

Josh: I'm gone a few hours and you're already
    replacing me?
Me: Two for one deal.

He sent a middle finger emoji.

Me: Do you know anything about the people who lived on our farm before us?

The triple dots of typing appeared and vanished four times before he finally replied.

Josh: One of the farmers was related to them. That's how we could lease the land back to them.

Not an answer. I waited for Josh to ask what I'd learned; that's what a normal person would do. Clearly I'd learned *key information*. His reply dismissed me. Again.

Maybe it was the throbbing leg or the emptiness of the fields beyond my car windows, but I needed my husband to hear me. I called him.

It took him four rings to pick up, as if he hadn't just been holding his phone, texting me.

"Babe?" His irritation licked his pet name for me.

"Got a minute?" I asked.

He hesitated. He'd had time to message me cutesy GIFs. He could make time for this. "Always, gorgeous."

"What else do you know about the people who owned the farm before us?" I asked, knowing his need for details would have ensured he'd asked about the sellers. I'd been more focused on the pictures and how to get out of California as fast as possible.

His sigh slapped through the line. "I have a meeting in a few minutes. I've told you what I know, but we can talk more about that when I get home."

"There's a darkness in that barn, Josh."

"Not the barn," he muttered.

"That light has been on again, and today—"

"No, Emily. The barn isn't turning on lights randomly. No one is out there playing boho lady rock jams in the middle of the night either."

I choked on my next breath, anger and hurt billowing down my throat in tandem. He wouldn't even hear me out. I would have told him the truth about going into the barn, but now—how could I?

"Just—I'm trying to tell you—" I sputtered.

"Shh, babe." He said like I was still grief-stricken and crumpled on our couch beneath a tear-soaked blanket. "I know it's freaking you out, but you need to focus on taking care of your body. Drink water today instead of coffee."

"Water isn't going to fix this."

"No, but rest will. I left your meds on the nightstand. Take them."

"Josh," I groaned.

"Please, Em. I need you to take care of yourself." In the background another male voice called for him. "I have to go. I'll check on you tonight. Love you, babe."

Click.

My fingers tingled with unspent rage. What did Josh know? I could handle whatever he'd learned from the farmer or the Realtor, but he wouldn't tell me anything if he believed I was delusional.

Going home now was not an option. I couldn't bear the haggard view of the barn, its weathered walls, knowing my husband wouldn't simply take my word that something was wrong on our farm. I posted in the company Slack server that I'd been felled by a stomach bug. I mean, the urge to puke was real. I didn't mention how my leg had developed its own pulse. Instead, I went toward Hastings and the hope of finding answers that would make my husband listen long enough to understand I wasn't speaking from grief or fatigue but from knowledge. That's all he would trust now.

CHAPTER 11

THE TOWN OF HASTINGS, NEBRASKA, IS ADORABLE. CUTE, quaint, and packed with people who wave at me. They could reboot a show like *Gilmore Girls* here on vibes alone. Not that I would describe it that way to the people at the truck stop. The town was the equivalent of a metropolis within the county. Four-lane roads. A mall. And, blessedly, a Starbucks.

The green sign welcoming me to town proclaimed a population of slightly more than twenty-five thousand. Five digits were significant around here. Would it be enough of an escape for me to shake the outsider ick on my back and forget the fear the morning had settled in my bones for the last hour?

The "city," as I would eventually have to learn to call it, had this gorgeous Industrial Revolution vibe. Redbrick buildings with stone ornamentation where one shop blended into the next. Nothing stretched higher than three stories, but the detail here was far more interesting than the view of Salesforce Tower. (Don't tell Josh I said that.) The edge of the community had newer buildings with enormous windows and bland wood, but as I drove to the bastion of better coffee, I cut through the center of town. The richness in simple beauty was part of the appeal of moving here.

Nebraska came with history. And honesty. Hastings was up front about what it was. A small town that had grown over time. A town built on the backs of people who worked with their hands. A town that understood people like me were going to drive into town to eat and drink and shop. Had the Belkin family driven these same roads? Was I repeating the same drive the people who had lived on my farm before me had? *Now who's getting themselves worked up over nothing?* Josh would have called me out for spinning up stories. I dismissed the thought and started counting the breweries and bars. The waitress's comment echoed in the back of my mind. There were so many locally made options.

The corner of my mouth quirked. I could almost picture *the* Penelope Wagers walking down one of these streets with a growler in one hand and a basket of veggies in the other. Mom couldn't have hated the regional sourcing. The scene in San Francisco had lived in my mom's heart. The creativity and the music and the pulse of it, but more than anything she bragged that we could get food sourced from a garden at all our favorite haunts.

Nebraska probably had everyone beat there. The OG farm-to-table. With real farms within view. Nebraska Beef was proudly labeled in the grocery stores, but the logo peered from windows of restaurants too.

The garden next to my farmhouse had once been loved. Planting tomatoes and herbs weren't exactly adventuresome tasks—they did fine in apartments too—but I was happy to be cultivating my own food. Like a local. Even if my journey to earning a "Nebraskan" title was in progress.

How could I even earn that label? Why did it matter?

The tilled earth beside my kitchen was mine now. Had it belonged to Alice Belkin before me? Her missing daughter? It shouldn't matter who had lived in my house previously. People moved all the time. Worst case, you'd find those little hash marks in a doorway logging a kid's height. I tried not to think about what the VFW duo had told me. Alice died by the barn, but what history had been painted over in our home? My belly twisted. Surely that acid brew I drank at the Diamond R fighting back. Probably heard I was upgrading to espresso.

The familiar green coffee shop awnings rose before me just in time. I parked and waited behind a trio of tweens ordering cake pops. I scrolled on my phone, trying to ignore the red bubble counting voicemails from the estate attorney.

Listening to them would require making choices. Talking about mom's possessions, her exes, when I was coming back to finalize paperwork. That last one was the stinger. I could scribble on a PDF from Nebraska just fine, but what he really wanted was to look at me when I signed his forms. Like he'd unravel the enigma of my mother in a single sit-down. I didn't have those kinds of answers for him. I didn't know why she hadn't set up a trust. He hadn't been happy to hear she'd used most of her savings investing in a new soundboard for her favorite concert venue. Well, that isn't true. His eyes had lit up like there were more assets. She'd *gifted* a soundboard. That's different.

Loss flicked its meaty finger against my heart. A jump start and a reminder of the wound I refused to let close. What would my mom have done here? Bands cut through Nebraska on tour. Stops in Lincoln and Omaha were standard. There had to be a rock culture here too. It didn't matter. Mom wouldn't ever visit me here. Or anywhere else.

When I was thirteen, we'd packed into the back of a tour bus with an indie rock band she was producing. The stop in Omaha was a weird one. I hadn't thought of that night in decades. We'd rolled into town around two in the afternoon. The sun had been oppressive when we'd stepped outside in the parking lot of a bowling alley.

The lead guitarist had clapped me on the back and let me know we had two lanes comped for the day. "And shoes."

Not a standard ask on the tour rider, but one he'd clearly expected at this location.

I had never bowled before, but the concert venue was attached to the alley. I spent the hours through setup and sound check getting a series of bowling lessons from rocker men with swooping bangs and very tight pants. It was the late nineties. Bowling while bands played was normal at the Ranch Bowl, I guess. The four-hundred-seater was sold out that night, and I managed my first, and only, strike.

"Next," the barista called in a way that made it clear I was holding up the line.

I buffed the heel of my palm against my sternum, but the movement never relieved the anguish there. Grief was every bit as stubborn as that black mold I'd seen in the barn.

I ordered a hot venti vanilla latte. Usually I skipped the whip, but today I needed a swirl of extra sweetness. Frazzled, I forgot to use my stars. *They don't expire, do they?* Whatever. The seven bucks and seventy-mile jaunt were worth it for the handcrafted coffee. I lingered at the end of the counter while beans were ground, tamped, and such. Phone still in my hand, I swiped past the estate attorney's voicemails and directly to my browser. Paranoia made me toggle to incognito mode.

I entered Bridget Belkin's name.

News articles upon articles appeared. Most dated two or three years ago.

LOCAL WOMAN GOES MISSING

DESHLER TEEN STILL MISSING; REWARD OFFERED

SHERIFF: NO LEADS IN BELKIN CASE

ONE YEAR LATER—WHAT HAPPENED TO BRIDGET BELKIN?

Sorrow looped around my neck like a borrowed scarf. My throat constricted, itched. I'd only heard of the Belkin family tragedies this morning, but my soul ached for them. Losing a family member severed a part of you, but how did you process anything if you didn't know what happened to them? Did that broken bit dangle until it developed gangrene? I'd clung to the fragment of my mom in my heart for weeks, months, but the tighter I squeezed, the more tarnished my insides became. I wasn't over her loss by a long shot. A solid playlist could have me weeping in seconds, but I'd tried to let that piece of her crumble. I had to; it didn't belong to me any longer.

Had grief been what claimed Bridget's mother? I knew all too well how it could swallow one whole.

The barista called my name. I accepted the white cup and sipped without hesitation. You'd think scalding my tongue would pull me to the present. But I'd tapped on the most recent article. Bridget's bright face stared at me. Long cocoa-brown hair framed a heart-shaped face. Her eyelashes were long, her brown eyes lit with humor. Her mouth a bow. A small gold cross rested on her clavicle. The image was cropped close to her face, but the peeling paint over her right shoulder was more than familiar. It was home.

Bridget stood by my barn. *Her* barn.

What happened to Bridget Belkin, and why had no one mentioned her to us?

CHAPTER 12

DRIVING HOME WAS NOT SOME BEHEMOTH ACT OF BRAVERY.
I'd dawdled in Hastings for a few hours, but I still bumped my way down our winding drive in full daylight. The summer sun was oppressively huge here. Maybe it was the lack of topography to block it? Driving along the two-lane highway toward our mile-marker turnoff felt the same as floating adrift in the Pacific. Once you got far enough out to not see land, it became this lesson in how unimportant you were. The universe was huge, the ocean was huge, and holy shit these fields were huge.

Our neighbors grew more than corn, but whatever crop swayed on either side of me, it was ready to swallow a person. The light glinted off the plants, every bit as bright as the sea. Focusing on the familiarity, as unnerving as it was, helped, but didn't stop me from muttering. "One sixteen," over and over. I would not miss our mile marker. Not that there was anyone on the road to notice if I had to flip back. Part of me felt like Josh would just know.

"You missed the turn, didn't you, babe?" His voice had that playful "Oh, Em" tone to it. Even in my head.

I thumbed down the volume on my "Confident" playlist. Hearing Demi Lovato and Metallica on the drive had not, in fact, made me feel more in control.

I made the turn with minimal skidding on the gravel. Figuring out the speeds for driving on this stuff was not a technique anyone had taught me. Curving around the swaying green stalks of the edge of the corn, my house came into sight. It still hitched my breath. Picture-perfect serenity. The flowers out front bloomed in welcome, the gauzy curtains added a quaintness from the outside, and all was still and quiet. This was like the picture of a luxe Airbnb listing. Not that I was renting out my house.

I parked close—almost on top of our oak tree out front—and did my damnedest to not look toward the barn. The ugly building was a distraction from what my home was supposed to be. It was a nuisance at my refuge. Nothing more.

I hated lying to myself, but it was easier to do during the day. I tutted at the chickens when I passed Cluckingham Palace. They mostly ignored me, but knowing they were there settled my focus toward the house.

I made it almost an hour before I peered from the kitchen window toward the peeling paint and the broken window of the barn and its loft. It stood there. Silent. Decrepit. I wasn't about to personify a barn—again—but foreboding filled my chest until my breath was strangled into a gasp. When I looked away, it all eased.

Josh was wrong. This wasn't in my head.

I shifted my weight and winced. The pain pills I'd taken for my leg were clearly wearing off. I'd rebandaged the sucker and popped a double dose of Advil when I'd gotten home. How could I have already bled so much? I texted Josh to check in. I'd forgotten to tell him I took the day off, but then he hadn't asked why I'd go into town for coffee. He had shut me down when I called. Why bother opening that door? I sent him a meme featuring that weird towheaded kid from *Children of the Corn*.

Emily: I'm acclimating while you're gone.

He didn't immediately reply, but then he could have been in another meeting. Traveling for work turned his schedule into chaos. I might hear back in minutes or not until midnight. That distance was normal, and yet it hit me with a twinge of loss today. Like I hadn't been looking forward to being alone for the last few days.

Not that I was entirely. Outside the window, one of the younger farmworkers walked into the barn. It was the friendly one who had helped me the day the hens arrived. I wished I knew his name, but I wasn't about to hobble down there again to ask for it. I'd had enough of the barn for today.

At least it was staying put. Hell. It was thoughts like that one that made Josh worry about me. I stepped back from the counter. It was a building. Old and falling down, yeah. In need of demolition. But an inanimate object nonetheless. I turned on the coffeepot. Chugged a glass of water while it brewed.

"See? I'm taking good care of myself," I muttered like my loved ones were standing here too.

I could ask the Realtor about the barn. She'd said if we had any questions we could call her. Granted, that was when we were talking about dropping serious cash on a property and her getting a percentage. But a person who left champagne in our refrigerator probably wanted to maintain a relationship with us. Right? I pulled up her contact card on my phone but couldn't make myself tap her number. What was I supposed to say? It's not like it was appropriate to ask if our property had deep dark secrets she'd failed to share. Like had someone *died* inside my house or out in that barn? *Good Lord, Em, get it together*, I chided myself. Tragedy struck everywhere. Mom had been stolen from me in hospice, but that wasn't the facility's fault. Cancer was the asshole there. That barn was not cancer. It was not eroding anyone's body. There was no reason to think it was the home of anything nefarious.

But everything inside those walls had been old, run-down, filthy. That tracked with it being disregarded. Except farmhands entered it. Someone was in there now. What would he need from there? Hadn't Josh told me it was storage for the equipment they *didn't* use regularly? It was like the junk drawer for them. So did the kid who'd walked in there store things in that barn? Was he leaving a lamp or a speaker for later? Was he the one screwing with me?

Shit, was he related to the Belkin family? One farmer had to be, but what about the farmhands? I'd heard the way one had spoken to Ray—like this farm should be theirs. I pushed away from the sink, as if a few steps would somehow settle my mind. My stomach agitated like the off-kilter load of laundry I needed to go shuffle. Josh's tennis shoes were in there. I'd heard them thunking away last night. I should ask about Alice Belkin too. Maybe she didn't even die on my farm. It could just be gossip. That's why no one disclosed it to us, right? I lifted my phone and stared at the Realtor's name on the screen. Josh would know how to ask this question. He also would 100 percent *not* ask.

The VFW members this morning had rattled me though. Not only with their comments about the missing girl and the accidental death of her mother, but with the way they looked at me. Sorrow and hope tangling like they could see the echo of grief on me, like they wanted to help but didn't know how.

Everyone surrounding me—the people at the truck stop, the farm crew, our Realtor, and maybe even Josh—was in on something. I was decidedly outside. Well, as outside as one could be watching from her kitchen window.

Being sandwiched among truths others knew scrubbed my skin. Being the last to know sandblasted my nerves, leaving me raw and angry. Or maybe my Advil was already wearing off. Josh might have some leftover low-dose hydrocodone in his cabinet, but the last thing I needed was a drug that would knock me out. Not when I needed to see what happened when that man left the barn.

That was it. I'd watch until he came out. If he drove out of there or was carrying some tool, I'd be able to rest. I flipped the switch on the coffee maker and let it brew another pot. How was I already due for another pot?

The minutes ticked by, and each sip of coffee heated my core another degree. The farmhand remained inside the barn. He could have left through another door, I supposed, but then I should have still seen him going back out to the truck. Unless he'd disappeared into the corn, which despite many a joke, people did not do.

A shadow passed behind one of the windows. *He's in there.*

I set my mug in the wide basin beneath the kitchen window. I needed to get closer. The hens were between us, and since when did chickens not love food? Fresh feed in hand, I edged out the back door and walked toward the henhouse like I always fed the girls this time of day. From a distance no one could see the food still scattered in the pan. Sophia clucked at me, eager to take from my hand. I stooped low, letting her gather the good stuff from my palm, her beak skimming the skin but never breaking it.

Settled low, my hens close by, my gaze never strayed from the barn.

The farmhand emerged at the other end of the building. He cradled a phone to his ear and loped toward my house—like the motion was aimless. He kicked dirt, sending little plumes up and dusting his jeans.

His voice carried on the thick summer air. "No, you picked her. She's your problem."

I sidled out of the coop, closing the latch as softly as I could. The farmhand's back was to me, but he was close enough that I could sprint to him in moments if I needed.

He tilted his chin up, as though the person on the phone could read the visual defiance. "We have to move her. You should know better." There was a haughtiness to the demand, like this conversation was beneath him. Frustration pulled his shoulders forward, but there was more. A malevolence clung to air around him.

He shoved his phone into his pocket, swearing under his breath, and ambled back into the barn. I pretended to pull weeds from my garden for another five minutes. When he emerged from the barn, his hands were full. A large black nylon duffel bag big enough for a long weekend was slung over one shoulder, and a worn metal shovel was gripped in the opposing hand. He threw both in the truck's bed and headed off in the truck—not toward the highway but into the fields.

I remained in my garden for the next hour. No one came back to the barn. What were these guys doing on my farm, and why did I know Josh wouldn't care?

The whole scene had unnerved me. Why did that guy need to rush off with tools? Who was he talking to, and more importantly what "*she*" was their problem? Did they meet up with girls in the fields? I'd found that broken hair clip among the stalks and soil. Worry speared through me, pushing me to my feet.

I ambled closer to the barn. Not that I was going inside again today. I didn't need to see my blood on the wood, the moldy light socket, any of it. But I also needed to know what that farmhand had been doing. When I was close enough to disappear in the barn's shadow, determination galvanized my gut. I scuttled faster toward the building. My quick glances toward the paths out into the fields were anything but covert, but there were no telltale dust plumes to indicate trucks coming my way.

Humidity glued my shirt to my back, the gentle shushing of a breeze over the crops not touching me on this side of the barn. I slipped beneath its shadow, a chill skating down my spine and sending a shock wave of goose bumps down my arms.

Just one peek. I'd look in the doors. Everything would be normal, and then I could haul ass back to my hens and my house.

Because this was no big deal, right?

The farmhand had left the main barn door open wide. Sunlight splashed the dusty floor deep into the barn. My legs locked at the threshold.

"Anyone around?" I called out.

Silence seethed around me. The tingle at the tips of my fingers feeling more and more like a warning than mere anxiety.

I leaned forward, gripping the doorway like holding the barn would keep it from moving, from anything terrible happening. Beige tarps were still draped over equipment. The wall had tools on it, though there were open spaces like items were missing. Had they been gone earlier too? I didn't think to catalog the room.

A few buckets were knocked over beside the ladder stretching to the hayloft. They were the five-gallon kind. Bright orange and bold blue. Had I knocked those over fleeing the other day? Wouldn't the farmhand have put them away? A heavy stone settled in my belly. It rolled when I stepped inside the barn. Just one peek at the buckets.

Five quick steps, and I stood beside them. Each was empty. Heat slapped my cheeks. *They're buckets. What did you expect?* I stacked the empties like it was penance for my foolish thoughts.

Beneath the last one, a flimsy white corner peeked out. I pulled the paper out.

Not paper. A photo. Unlike the ones I'd discovered in the loft, this was fresh. The new kind of Polaroid that was narrow, as if even using old-school technology needed to mimic the selfie mode on your phone.

There was no mold marring this image. A wide-eyed blond girl. Definitely in her teens. She had three multicolored beaded necklaces on, glitter dappling her cheeks. Red ringed her eyes, like she'd been crying, but in the image, she was blowing a kiss to the camera. I had no idea who she was, but behind her shoulder was the pegboard on the far wall. Someone had snapped this picture here. In my barn.

She looked nothing like Bridget Belkin. So who was this girl, and when had she been crying in my barn?

CHAPTER 13

STARING OUT THE WINDOW FOR HOURS MIGHT HAVE BEEN A selling point of moving to the Midwest. The view beyond my front porch was everything I'd wanted it to be. Swaying green fronds, crisp blue skies, and the honeyed glow of unfiltered sunlight. Half the photos I'd taken on my running loop were the types of images friends back home would put up in their office or their home gym. Aspirational. Hopeful. Peaceful.

Only I was looking through the kitchen window, fixated on warped wood and fractured windowpanes. Age and sorrow pressed down on the barn even in the warmth of the setting sun. The miasma of red and gray flaking from its walls absorbed none of the sky-blue-pink hues of the setting sun. Its shadows stretched gooey black across the hard-packed soil leading to the fields. It couldn't reach the crops though. Those were safe. Still alive. Still beautiful.

I drank more coffee than I kept track of but witnessed a whole lot of nothing happening at the barn. The one farmhand who had entered had come back out with a short handheld shovel and a bag, and had driven into the field.

Maybe he'd taken stuff earlier too? He hadn't returned the gear that night, nor had whomever he'd been speaking with on the phone. If people were coming and going from the building, then it was plausible the light in the barn—what I knew I'd seen—was real. But there was nothing to see this night.

I crashed on the couch, still in my favorite pair of running shoes. The laces were double knotted too. If I had to run outside to catch whoever was playing music in my barn, I was going to be ready to sprint. No gravel scraping my soles; no face-planting. No more injuries. I propped Josh's softball bat next to the back door. The first agency he'd worked for had a softball league. It was the kind of office sport that was more about drinking beer after the game than flexing actual skills. This suited Josh fine—and me, honestly. Really cut down on the time I spent sitting in the stands and meant I could invite my friends to the bar for the after-party. That was before lockdown, obviously, and long before I got used to Zoom hangouts. Now I got the ick every time I entered a bar.

Josh and I had done the "invite our friends to a bar to mourn" thing after my mom died. I'd seen it in so many movies, and a celebration of life with shots was a million percent on-brand for Penelope Wagers. My mom had been the life of the party down to her very bones. And the wake was everything it was supposed to be for the first hour or so. Then the bar began to fill with people I didn't know. It was like my brain had forgotten how to filter out background noise. I couldn't understand the words my friends hollered in my ear. The musk of bodies I didn't know filled the air, pressed against my skin, into my clothes. I should have invited everyone to Mom's house. I could have filled my trunk with Costco booze and it would've been fine.

Other than having to look at my mom's possessions. There was no ghost of her in that bar, but there was an overwhelming presence of everyone who wasn't her.

My chest burned. I sipped from my water bottle, but it cooled nothing.

I locked the doors when the sun had set. We shouldn't have needed to bolt doors on the farm. The whole point was we were alone. *I* was alone.

Only that barn was out there. Watching me. Watching my house. Whatever or whoever was inside was waiting, and I was ready now. I mean, as ready as a woman armed with a bat she'd never held could be.

I woke with a jerk just before 4 a.m. Dolly Parton's voice cut through my house with the earnestness and "I'll own you" confidence that I'd grown up with. Mom's life goal was to work on a Dolly record, but she never got the chance.

Awareness rattled my ribs. It was happening. Again. Mom's favorites blasting in my house. I should have been the only one here. I rolled off the couch like I was one of the commandos in Josh's video games. The remote control clattered on the hardwood next to me.

I popped to my feet, trainers not letting me slip. I was halfway to the kitchen when the music tapered. A high-pitched voice chirped from the TV, "It was disrespectful. Every other guy kissed the girl they were coupled with..."

I stilled. My sneaker squeaked against the floor. Adrenaline lit my veins, but doubt rolled gauze over my head. The patches on my leg were fused and saturated. This was like pale tulle. Just enough to disorient. I swallowed and turned toward the kitchen window. A heavy darkness had settled outside. Charcoal sketched the outline of the barn in the distance—more than the few minutes away it should be. No lights. Only darkness.

The dating show contestants prattled on from my living room. No more Dolly anywhere.

I edged closer to the sink. The faucet plinked a drip against the deep basin. I wet the kitchen cloth I found on the counter and pressed it to my face. Cold water centered me but did nothing to ease my doubt. The barn wasn't doing shit. No one was out there. I let the water drip from my chin to my chest. Anxiety spiraled in my center, spooling tightly. This is what Josh was worried about. Me getting spun up over nothing. Clearly, he was *right* to worry.

I could hear him in my head, sadness and frustration tightening his voice. *"Your mom worked in the music industry for decades. Every song has a tie to her."*

The dismissal rocked me. As though my connection was ephemeral. Or my mother's had been meaningless. If every tune resonated with us, did any of them? Were we the G chord that centered every song?

I squeezed my hands into fists until my fingernails dug into my palms. *Not every song*, I would argue. Our family history had a soundtrack. Holidays had their own playlists, the years on the road had whole albums, and the dance party tracks my mother used when I had the mean-girls era at school and needed a joy boost after yet another garbage day rocked me back to comfort mode like no other.

But some songs carried more power, more emotional resonance than others. I knew them all.

I eventually stumbled back to the couch, guzzled half the bottle of water I found there, and tapped down the volume on the latest episode of *Love Island*. How was this dating show playing Dolly Parton though? They usually had covers of great tracks from the nineties and the aughts. I backed the video up. The contestants played a game where the men were businessmen, and apparently that meant using "9 to 5." Bad choice, music director. Dolly is a good pick, but not for the dudes. And also not to wake me up...for reasons I now don't want to discuss.

———

Four a.m. was practically real morning. Plenty of people blended their protein shakes before sunrise. I opted to craft a pretty latte. The espresso maker was usually too slow and finicky for me. Josh was the consistent barista in the house; I was built for craft cocktails and makeshift charcuterie. Today though, I needed the busywork of hands-on coffee making. I ground the beans, flinching at the first whir of the device and hoping that Josh had left it at the ideal setting. Not like I could text him now without him putting together that I hadn't slept. I could lie and say I was up early for a longer run, but I didn't want to have to fake a reason for being awake. Not with Josh. He loved me and my flaws. I wasn't supposed to have to hide parts of myself—but grief was a singular emotion. People thought they could relate. They'd lost people too. But their people aren't my people. My memories are different. My loss lingers in new recesses even now. The hesitation when I drop the needle on a record isn't about track selection. It's that echo of my childhood, my mom's breath on the back of my neck.

I tamped the grounds, locked the little metal basket in place, and pressed the button to start the brew. If only processing my mom's death was so routine. I filled a little metal pitcher with whole milk from another farm in Thayer County. Blasting the beverage with steam warmed my fingers, but the cold spot in my chest never eased. That's what Josh didn't get. I loved him, but he thought the grief process was literal. Like a step-by-step thing. I couldn't tick off checkboxes though, and apparently my failure to do so explained why I didn't sleep, why the barn loomed ominously beyond the window.

"It's ugly, but that's only dangerous if we're sending photos to my mom," he'd said Sunday morning, which had only proved he didn't understand the threat. Or maybe he didn't understand me?

As much as aesthetics brought me joy, my objection had little to do with the barn being an eyesore. I finished pouring my latte and checked the windows in both the kitchen and living room. Darkness lingered heavy outside. The thin white curtains no match for the shadows keeping me inside.

I set up camp on the couch with my laptop and a big

sunshine-yellow mug filled with all the caffeine. Back scrolling through the company Slack server helped me shake the dregs of dread from my mind, especially the #coffee-talk-marathon channel. The Budapest team was *hyped* about the marathon. They'd done a group run that morning, and the times had been excellent.

> **Oana**: They will rename the marathon after us.
>
> **Dimu**: Whoever wins get to name it.
>
> **Dimu**: I will make it the Wild Boar Run.

The reaction emojis were plentiful and varied from pigs and bacon to confetti, champagne, and cake.

> **Emily**: You have to post your times if you're going to brag like that.

Eight colleagues posted their times immediately, and they were impressive.

> **Emily**: I don't think I'm going to get to name this marathon if those are your times!

Not if I didn't focus on actually training. The running was good to clear my mind, but my calf had its own heartbeat today. Rest day was warranted.

> **Oana**: This is your first marathon. Correct?

Emily: Yeah but I've been running for a long time.

They wouldn't know that meant I used the physical push to reset my brain.

Oana: Marathons are a wild beast.
Dimu: Focus on your own marathon.
Emily: Thought we were a team, Dimu!
Dimu: Running is only about you and your body. Putting
in the kilometers together pushes everyone, but you
can only focus on yourself and the road.

Part of me wanted to send them a picture of the roads I'd been running, but the wave of encouragement that flooded the screen was too kind to ruin it with my "I'm so alone" pity party.

I'd wanted this. Solitude. Serenity. Orange light shot streaks along the horizon outside the big front windows. The fields were waking; the farmers would move out soon; the adorable cows would meander into their pastures in the next hour.

I was still wearing my favorite pair of Brooks. They were navy blue and neon pink, and I was pretty sure that Genevieve the cow thought they were cute too.

Oana: It is morning there, yes? How many kilometers are
you going to run today?

The temptation to switch into running gear and get in the

mileage was this omnipresent itch between my shoulder blades. The kind that made me squirm.

> **Emily**: Hurt my calf yesterday. The adult thing to do is rest.
>
> **Oana**: Noooooooooooo.
>
> **Oana**: No to hurting yourself. Yes to resting.
>
> **Dimu**: I'd walk a kilometer or two. Good to keep the blood flow going.
>
> **Alex**: Dimu is not a doctor.
>
> **Dimu**: I was a medic.
>
> **Alex**: No medical advice in the marathon thread.

Was human resources monitoring us? I didn't know the HR team in Europe, but they had way stricter privacy protections over there. So probably saying anything about our bodies or doctors or whatever was going to send the write-up version of the Bat-Signal.

I toed off my shoes, still laced. I'd worn wide-legged yoga pants for my lazy couch foray last night, trying to give my beaten body a little reprieve. Tugging the pant leg up, I could tell the bandages needed an update. The skin around the white gauze was a mottled purple and warm to the touch. *You don't actually need a doctor,* I told myself and hoped that wasn't wishful thinking.

I fetched the first aid kit and went to work freshening up. The gash was ugly, but not bleeding. I slathered it in Aquaphor—which my mother had believed cured everything—and replaced the bandages, feeling more confident in my body's ability to heal.

The Slack channel had filled with advice from no less than thirteen people. I tried not to feel like that number was ominous, but given the amount of WTF happening around me lately, I had to narrow my gaze.

Emily: A girl steps away for minute...

Oana: Are you running today? Because I don't think you should.

Emily: No running today. Leg is decidedly swollen. Rest day for sure.

Dimu: Elevate it.

Dimu: Not medical advice. Just practical rest advice. 👀

Emily: Got it. Foot up. I've got to get two "have you thought about preparing for Black Friday?" white papers formatted for the sales team today anyway.

The fact that our agency had to help people plan for Christmas retail in the middle of summer always grossed me out, but then I remembered we had great health insurance and they let me work from home on my own schedule. Comfort helped assuage my morals, which was shitty but true.

I made a fresh pot of coffee and let it massage my brain into action. I toggled into the folders shared with the marketing team and reviewed the materials for the first project. Charts, pictures, and text were all there. A first. This team always forgot something. Maybe we'd hired someone new. I started laying out the pages for this mini ebook they'd send to prospective clients.

I made it about forty-five minutes before an antsy-ness needled my legs. It had nothing to do with my injury. I hit the bathroom, refilled my water bottle, and paced a circuit around the room.

The barn stood, slanted but resolute, outside. There was no sign of the farm crew. Sunlight dappled the green stalks in the field, looking every bit like some B-roll from *Field of Dreams*.

My attention flitted back to the barn.

I swore I could see the light socket swinging. The white loop taunting me from its recess in the hazy glow of morning.

Icy breath kissed the shell of my ear. *"I see you."*

CHAPTER 14

I WHIRLED AROUND ONLY TO MEET AN EMPTY KITCHEN. A full carafe of coffee sat on the maker. No steam. The mug on the counter held only dregs. Ice clunked into the bin inside the fridge. I skittered against the counter.

"Who said that?" My demand eked out in a child's squeak.

No one answered. Skimming my fingers over the edge of my ear didn't replicate the voice, but the skin was cool. As if I'd dunked my head in cold water. I snatched the bat from its super safe spot next to the back door and tiptoed forward.

"Not sure who you're looking for, but it's not me," I said, the bat bolstering my confidence so that I could at least fake like I was in charge.

Again, I was greeted with only stillness. Hustling to the front door proved it was still locked. My fingers hovered on the latch. Only two people had the keys for that dead bolt. Josh and me. He was hundreds of miles away.

I scoured the house with the methodology of a woman who'd had a distinct *Law & Order* era.

Empty.

Well, save for a stack of dirty laundry on Josh's side of the bed where there'd been another bottle of Valium. How many times had he filled my script? I only did it one time. And I hated it. It made me slow, sleepy. I wasn't built to be dull, and I didn't think doing so changed the hurt in my chest.

Although, I wasn't exactly at peak performance with zero sleep if I was imagining eerie voices saying they *see me*.

It wasn't fair that my mind could hold these facts: I'd felt that breath, the words were real, and it made no logical sense. No one else was in my house.

By the time I returned to the living room, the sun had crested the horizon and chased every shadow from the great room. The specter of night clung to my veins regardless. I poured yet another cup of coffee to chase it off with caffeine.

I drank it on the front porch. I'd let the frigid fear that had curled around my spine go. Except dread still pooled between my hips while I kicked back on the porch swing. And perhaps that's why I stared down the barn during the first cup of coffee. From this angle the window was harder to see. There was no light socket taunting me. *Or maybe there never had been.* When was the last time I'd actually slept more than an hour or two?

I sat there, leg propped up and throbbing less than I thought it would today, daring the world to come at me again. But unless you counted a pair of blue jays dive-bombing the flowers in the bed below, there were zero attacks.

Not that I was complaining.

Another cup of coffee, and I might have the focus to work or exercise. Jogging a little today might be good for me. I'd take it easy, but my body needed a daily endorphin boost. Jump scares in the predawn hours hit fight-or-flight, but that was all the feel-like-shit chemicals. Cortisol made you fast, but that stress hangover hit harder than any tequila I'd tasted.

But a fitness high wasn't in the cards today. One of the younger guys who worked for Ray was exiting the barn. The same one who'd taken the shovel last time. *When had he gone back inside?* His attention flitted from the black satchel tucked under his arm to the path leading to the east fields. Another black bag. Did he know I was watching? Had he looked for the picture of the girl? The quick-develop image sat on my kitchen counter. Was he the one who knew her? Who had made her cry?

I practically tumbled out of the porch swing. I left my mug on the ground and headed toward the barn. The smile I plastered on my face and the over-the-top wave I offered got no attention. I hurried down the gravel road toward him and the barn.

The farmhand's boots kicked up dust as he scuttled toward the corn or perhaps a truck. They used a few pickups and often parked them on the paths. Maybe I just couldn't see it. Maybe Ray or one of the other guys had brought him over here.

But why did they need small tools? Why were they in that decrepit barn again right after I'd been there? After—apparently—a teenage girl had been there.

Moving faster spiked pain through my calf, but I couldn't slow. Not when I needed to see this guy up close. To know what he was doing. To see the truth in broad daylight.

"Hey…" I called out, fumbling for a name or anything that didn't make me feel like some *Downton Abbey* type calling to her staff.

The guy's shoulders hiked up. If it offended him that I'd called out, it'd remain a mystery. He remained focused and plowed ahead and out of sight.

Determination urged my feet faster, but my inner "don't be a crazy lady" and "maybe don't scare the teenager" flicked the back of my neck.

Was I really going to stalk after some just-out-of-high-school kid? And do what? Question why he was getting tools from a place they stored tools? Ask what he knew about the noose dangling in the window? There was no question I could ask that wouldn't make me sound like the paranoid woman Josh was more consistently implying I was.

"This is my house. My land. My farm. It's beautiful and vibrant and mine." I repeated the mantra until sunshine shimmered against my sternum.

I'd left my fitness tracker watch *somewhere*, but I'd counted the steps to the barn myself. Mentally logged the count: 612 steps. The teenager's lanky form was long gone by the time I reached the fields. I followed the path I thought he'd taken and tried not to feel like one of those people on the street corner shouting about the end of days. *Do they still do that?* COVID had killed a lot of industries, but likely not the soapbox damnation set.

The dusty layer on the path carried tire tracks, which meant exactly zilch. There was no blood here. No mold. No tiny twig people set roadside to make me think I was in some horror move from the early aughts.

The gash on my leg grumbled with every right footfall, but not so much to make me think it was bleeding again. Not enough to stop me. There was more than one way to blank my brain. I could push myself as hard as possible, which admittedly was my go-to method. My leg wouldn't support that today, and I needed to be able to get back home. I had work and a life, and I sure as shit was not going to be stuck in the middle of a field right now.

Not until I knew what was really happening on my farm.

The balmy air clung to my skin. Even at this early hour, moisture swaddled the heat against my every pore. My water bottle must be watching the field like a forlorn widow. The pang of regret that rang in my chest had nothing to do with grief and everything to do with impending dehydration cramps. Coffee wasn't great fuel for workouts, despite what every weight lifter in the gym in our old building swore.

The cornstalks crinkled on my left. I jumped like the plants had gotten up and flounced onto the road. My back brushed the other side of the pathway, more hearty green plants grazing my skin by the time I realized wind was causing the crisp leaves to collide. I pushed the heel of my hand against my sternum hard. Not that smooth rub people do when they are winding back anxiety. I pressed harder and harder. Like I could compress my heart into submission.

What *was* I doing out here? In the fields. Was I in my head? Maybe. Josh could be right about the music. There was Dolly on my current trash television obsession, but the light, the cord tangled into a noose, the pictures, the missing girl. That was too much to be a coincidence.

Now there were people I didn't know coming and going from the barn I'd been warned to stay away from? Not just people who worked here, despite what Josh claimed. *Someone* was up to something. Trepidation and terror knotted in my chest. If a woman had died here, if the barn was a tool to threaten me—or was threatening me—I should have been hauling my ass back to the house to pack, booking a flight to California, and getting the eff out of here.

But at the center of each of those knots, like a shimmery tinsel thread amid the roughened twine, was a big ol' middle finger. There were three things I'd unquestionably inherited from my mother: the auburn undertones in my light brown hair that only showed themselves in the summer sunshine, killer music taste (if I do say so myself), and a "good luck with that" attitude when told what to do.

I'd claimed this farm. Bought it. Made it mine. Well, the house, but still. This was my home, Josh's home. He might not be here now, but since he was consistently unconcerned when it came to creepy shit, I was going to assume he'd also refuse to leave.

I needed to make sure everyone knew Josh and I were Nebraskans now. We were rural folk too. No matter the little laughs at breakfast the other day. Those people were friendly. So why wouldn't someone want us on this farm? Why would a *barn* have a history?

It was time to learn. I trudged back toward my picturesque home. Shoulders back, limited limp, and gaze focused on the perfect white wood. Ice skated down my spine when I walked past the barn, and I fought the shiver. The chill lingered on my skin just like the whisper this morning. A ghost, a kiss, a ghastly promise. But only my sharp breath filled the air. Almost like it hadn't happened.

That's what I told myself.

I had eleven hours in the workday to get projects done for my job. A deadline. Expectations. I made sure my little dot on Slack stayed green so people knew I was online and working. I shook the cobweb of hurt from my mind, cranked some Green Day, and began searching for everything I could on the Belkin family.

And I'd meant to work *at some point*. Really. But my search history revealed Bridget Belkin's name the moment I clicked in. One search turned into two, and my heart wrenched with the need to know more. To connect. To keep feeling this rush of sympathy instead of wallowing in stagnant grief.

SHERIFF: WE NEED YOUR HELP TO FIND BRIDGET BELKIN

There are conflicting reports of where Bridget Belkin was last seen. Her mother, Alice Belkin, told sheriff deputies her daughter was home the night of May 8. All of the daughter's belongings are still in her home, including her phone and house keys.

However, two local teenagers—names withheld due to their age—report seeing Bridget Belkin in the early hours of May 9 with a male teenager at the track field in Deshler. The Thayer County Sheriff's Office is investigating both angles and requests that any person with information about the girl's whereabouts call the nonemergency line...

In the middle of countless headlines about the fruitless search for Bridget was an article that made me smile. I hadn't thought it was possible to smile when reading about this girl.

BELKIN BRINGS THE HEAT IN FOURTH STRAIGHT JV VICTORY

Every article I'd read so far had the same cropped photo of the teenager. This beautiful face that everyone was meant to immediately recognize before calling the number below. But this article? Bridget's whole body made the photo. She was in profile, jumping, her right arm stretched high as she spiked a volleyball over a net. Determination sharpened her features in the picture.

Seven hours later, I hadn't eaten anything or opened a single work email, but I'd read newspaper article after newspaper article on the family who used to live on my farm. There was more than the stories about the missing daughter. There were articles about her brothers winning wrestling competitions for the local county high school and the car accident they died in ten years back. There were agriculture articles that featured Herb Belkin, Bridget's dad, talking about the business of farming. Pressures from regulations, pest problems, and a general "we do what we have to" tone. I had to respect that. The work ethic required to make the farm work was wild. I used to think of myself as self-motivated, but here I was researching a family I wouldn't ever meet during my work hours while farmers were out there putting in fourteen-hour days. Almost made me feel like a voyeur looking into the lives of those who had lived here first.

But then I remembered the way the barn moved. The loft was creepy. People were skulking around our property when I should be alone. It wasn't spying if it was at your own house.

Emily's Running Log:

3 minutes, 24 seconds to the barn—612 steps—It's staying closer now. Why?
Recovery day, I guess.

CHAPTER 15

THE FRONT PAGE OF THE LOCAL NEWSPAPER'S ONLINE EDItion was a mishmash of national news from the wire and local "interest" pieces. The stories would not cut it in a Sunday magazine section of SFGate—but honestly, maybe should have had a place there. The huge photo at the top of the home page of the *Hebron Journal-Register* featured a septuagenarian holding up a quilt, her smile bumping the brightness on my monitor by at least four ticks. She'd gathered T-shirts from every location her grandsons and nephews had been stationed for military service and made a quilt. Six boys all in branches of the military—three Army, two Navy, and one Air Force. The local VFW chapter was auctioning the blanket to raise money for the USO.

I, not surprisingly, did not come from a military family. I think my grandfather served in a war, but it wasn't voluntary, and he hadn't ever talked about it. The little puff piece talked about the town, about its people, and made me think of the old guys from the truck stop restaurant. They'd know this family. My news feed could have used more random old ladies making crafts while Josh and I were wallowing in our tiny apartment in the city.

A peal of laughter bubbled from my chest. *In the city.* Even my vernacular had claimed the rural life.

I quashed the giggle fit by typing Alice Belkin's name into the search bar. Her obituary came up first but had no details. Loving wife and mother. Preceded in death by her parents, who had both lived and died in Deshler, Nebraska, and her sons, Bryan and Tobias. Below that link, though, was the article about her death. I clicked it, ready for the full story.

LOCAL WOMAN DIES FROM ACCIDENTAL FALL

Alice Belkin (née Meints), 47, of Thayer County, was found dead on her property early yesterday morning. Authorities have ruled the death accidental. Her husband...

Subscribe to keep reading! Only $10/month!

Usually a paywall of ten dollars to read an article would have me shutting the browser so hard. But ten bucks to know what happened to Alice? I keyed in my credit card information like I needed to bail my best friend out of jail.

My paltry reward for memorizing those sixteen digits was a sum total of three paragraphs including the freebie I'd already read. One paragraph, though, had what I needed.

Belkin's body was found by her husband, Herb Belkin, 52, also of Thayer County. Sheriff Randy Wilson confirmed that investigation showed Belkin had tripped while retrieving stored items in the upper level of the family's barn and fallen from a window. Her blood alcohol level was above legal limits.

She'd died by the barn. Falling from the window that kept illuminating when I was alone at night. I'd been in that musty loft. I'd fallen in there too. But how could one—even drunk—tumble out the window? My stomach pitched hard enough I tasted bile in the back of my throat. The cops had to know more than I did, but either way a woman had died on my farm. One who had lived in this very house.

I searched for more articles about Alice's death, but even with my new status as a subscriber, there simply wasn't much detail about the family. The problem was everything written about the people who had lived in my home previously was of the "lead with kindness" journalism variety, which I suspected was necessary when you knew everyone who lived in a fifty-mile radius. I was about to cave and work on tasks people actually paid me to do when I noticed a label on the *Journal-Register*'s navigation: "Smoke & Sirens."

One click, and I tumbled into a well of gossip fodder. Every paragraph was another fact that would stir conversation and be the kind of thing my friends would DM one another. Back when I hadn't muted the group thread. Someone at this paper, probably an intern, had punched up the details of a police scanner. Every visit to a house—including the block and street—was listed and why.

Speeding tickets didn't seem to be listed (because everyone speeds here, like *everyone*—no way there were zero tickets), but the DUI details were there.

I leaned over my laptop like the words were spilling tea all over the place and I was trying to lap up the gossip as fast as possible. And I didn't even know these people. Marc Paddingston, though, had been pulled over for this third DUI after crashing his car into a fence along Highway 136. *Do we need to reinforce our fences?* How common was this?

They didn't include mug shots. In that way, it was less garish than when an arrest record pops up on Facebook. A former coworker's husband had posted her mug shot—tagging her like it was the best way to initiate a divorce—when she'd been driving drunk. It was a targeted attack to shame her among the people who knew her, but this was almost worse. Back home, I wouldn't know about the mistakes or crimes of my neighbors unless I was directly impacted. A few minutes into this section, and I already recognized the recurring names. The people who had police visits on the regular. I'd never met them but already had an image in my mind. That line of thinking was unfair, but also might keep me from trusting the wrong person.

I tugged my hair tie free from my ponytail and reaffixed it higher. My fingers needed something to do other than itch for news about people I didn't know.

Or wait.

Tap tap tap. There was an advanced search. I plugged the name "Belkin" in and told it to look at "Smoke & Sirens." *Why was this excluded by default?*

Results flooded the page. My farm was clearly the location of calls to the sheriff. Over and over. *Domestic* littered the limited descriptions. Herb Belkin was taken into custody on more than one occasion.

Alice Belkin had been picked up for driving while intoxicated. There was a flag for minor in possession, but also on the same date Alice and Herb were charged with providing alcohol to minors. There were flags for safety checks at the house. For Bridget or Alice? Both? Police had known all of this and still called Alice's death accidental? Did that mean the accident was obvious or they were keeping a secret? The three-line missives from the newspaper only gave the top notes of the tea, but there had to be more.

The records only went back five years. Bridget had been missing for three. What had happened in my home? An unnerving sadness settled in my bones when I so much as looked toward the barn. Had sheriff's deputies had to check on children there? Was there a reason the former farm owner's belongings—memories—had been discarded in the hayloft? What kind of trauma was steeped in these walls? Fresh flooring and cheery paint couldn't conceal heartache for long, and no one had even tried with the aging barn.

Every time I stepped in my mother's house, I *felt* her. It sounded very woo-woo even thinking it. When I'd told Josh, he'd nodded solemnly with skepticism slipping across his face. Superstitious vibes aside, that house *was* her. I didn't think she was still inside or a ghost or whatever. But an echo of her resided in the Queen Anne's support beams. As if the entire structure was built on her energy. Which was silly because we sure as hell weren't the first people to

live there. The house I'd grown up inside had character that came
with years of experience. Creaking floorboards that refused to
let either Mom or me sneak in or out late at night. Two trick air
vents that were pinned in an open position with a paper clip. Even
after stripping Mom's room to the bare furniture and rogue picture frames, the home brimmed with character. Mom's clothes had
been immediately donated to charity, one of the few stipulations
my mother had bothered including in her will. She'd also noted I
was to receive her green velvet blazer, her favorite black Docs, and a
specific box of vintage jewelry, which I had still not opened. It had
come to Nebraska with me though. The cloche was in the shallow
drawer of my nightstand.

Even after all that, the room carried her distinctive perfume.
As though she'd walked through moments ago instead of months.
Light florals, musky patchouli, and a gentle warmth that I only asso-
ciated with my mom.

I had no such echoes in this farmhouse. No memories of the
previous owners. Was there a special paint that cured history from
the drywall? Could you expunge the past like it was a fungus on the
bathroom tile?

Mold was in the barn loft. My belly hollowed. Was that about
the past or about age? Wouldn't there be mold somewhere else if
it weren't a sign? But I hadn't seen so much as a spot inside our
house. Josh would have been bleaching the shit out of whatever
we'd found, if there were.

How could I find out what occurred in my home before it was
mine? There had to be a way to know what had happened to the

Belkin family. I searched for a full archive of the paper, but for the gossipy bits, I'd need to look at the real thing. The library in Hastings had copies. I'd need at least a day to dig into that. I closed my eyes, again feeling frigid breath pulsing against the back of my neck. I looked up the library's hours. By the time I drove over there, they'd be closing. I could go Friday. I could make it until Friday.

I'd left myself three hours to get my work project done. The design was simple. No one told me I couldn't use one of my past designs as a template. I cracked open InDesign and tried to focus on the white space ratio, but my hamster wheel of insidious thoughts spun in the background. Who were the Belkins, and what had happened in their barn? Where had their daughter gone?

Josh texted around five.

Josh: Busy day? You were quiet.

Emily: I knew you were in meetings.

Not entirely a lie, but I hadn't thought about him. That made me feel like a shit wife.

Emily: Looking forward to you being back in the office down the hall from me. Could use a lunch date.

My husband sent a selfie. He was smirking, leaned back on the bed in his hotel room.

Josh: Soon, gorgeous.

I snapped a pic of me in grungy clothes, laptop perched on my knee.

Emily: I promise to be more interesting when you get home.

A FaceTime alert dropped on the screen. Delight prickled my cheeks as I tapped to accept. Josh leaned against the headboard in what looked like a Marriott. Honeyed wood mounted to the wall behind him. He'd ditched the sport coat I knew he'd packed and rolled his shirtsleeves up his forearms. I glanced at the clock. I still had two more hours of work to complete today.

"Someone is done early," I said, making sure he heard the teasing lilt in my voice. No jealousy.

"That client on-site was brutal this morning..." Josh recounted the highlights of his day so far. He faked techie so well, even when dropping the SparkNotes version, he had me believing he could write the damn code. Apparently the solutions architects had presented today, and he simply had to ask smart questions and bring home the money slides at the end.

"Looks like you're in the thick of it today, babe. Everything fine on the farm?"

On the farm was our playful joke before moving here. We'd drop it casually into conversations about our futures, our slower lives amid the open skies and the cows. Josh still carried that playfulness. A dimple appeared beneath the beginnings of his five o'clock shadow. My fingers twitched, wanting to feel the scruff. To center myself. For him to actually be here. Because if he were, I wouldn't have to worry about strangers inside our home. The barn might be a problem when he was here, but there was safety in numbers, in my partner, in my marriage.

Except now, when we were merely connected by decent Wi-Fi and a couple MacBooks.

"It's crunch time here. Our sales guys aren't as convincing as you. They need this mini ebook thing polished to get in the door."

His humor dimmed, stealing the dimple and the flash of youth that came with his joy. "I thought you were way ahead on that stuff. Did they drop more on you? They can't load everything on you just because you're out of the office."

Maybe he really didn't want to be back on the road, because holy projection, Batman. "No, it's not new. Just got a late start on it today."

Josh shifted on the bed, making the view tilt and bounce. When he steadied it, his face was closer to the camera and the twin worry lines between his eyebrows were plain. Fucking great. Even with miles between us, he could see straight through me.

"What happened?"

There were a lot of things I loved about my husband. His laugh, his deep sense of right and wrong, and his curiosity. That disappointed dad tone though? Zero stars.

The day had left me raw, but the lie came quickly. "I overslept."

"Really?" He pulled away from the camera, adding distance even with hundreds of miles already between us.

Lying was a skill I had never honed. Had I failed tremendously?

In for a penny... "With how things have been, I hadn't bothered to set an alarm."

His chin dipped, but the worry twisting his face smoothed.

Before he could ask a follow-up, I added, "Maybe PB and J is my magic bullet. Had one around eleven and fell asleep on the couch."

Not making it to the bed was authentic. Even in my pre-grief, pre-farm life, couch naps were standard.

"You've been pushing yourself so hard. Your body probably admitted it needed sleep."

"Or it was the sandwich," I teased with a little shoulder shimmy.

"Good thing the pantry is stocked then. You could eat double sandwiches and get two nights of good sleep." He eased back on the bed and *relaxed*. Josh believed me. He didn't ask about the barn. Had lying about sleep been all it took to quell his concerns?

"I thought you had an extra glow about you today." Heat licked his throat, transforming the simple compliment into something baser.

Part of me preened at the attention. Even when I was sloppy and wounded and exhausted, he saw someone beautiful. Adoration flowed from his every move. The subtle way he lowered his chin but maintained his gaze. The careful words chosen to explain the ways he missed me, my body.

It was enough to ignite the burner beneath my latent guilt. I'd gone in the barn after (probably good) advice not to. I'd busted my leg in a way that would certainly make Josh believe his advice was sound. But if I hadn't gone there, I wouldn't have seen those photos, seen the mold, the noose. I wouldn't have known to watch the barn more closely. To see the farmhands coming and going. To look into the Belkins. Whatever had happened here had tainted the land, and I couldn't let that go. Everyone here had moved on from Alice's death and Bridget's disappearance, but I'd been swept into the sadness. The wrongness was undeniable.

A quick gust cut through my living room. Wind swiping loose strands of hair across my face. The windows were closed. The air-conditioning wasn't running.

Ice bit my earlobe. *"He can't be trusted."*

I stood so fast the laptop clattered to the floor and slammed shut, hanging up on Josh. I spun to look behind me, but the soft light bore only a chunky knit throw and two sunflower pillows. I spun in a circle, whacking my damn injured calf on the coffee table. The picture window carried my reflection. Messy ponytail. Oversized sweatshirt. Exhaustion leeching the color from my skin. Over my shoulder was a halo of black hair, a heart-shaped face, features smudged in black.

My jaw dropped and a keen of agony and terror ripped past my vocal cords. The cry scraped my throat, burned my sinuses, pushed tears from my eyes. As though the sound needed to escape from every path possible. I turned back to face her—the woman from the hayloft photos. I knew it, in my heart, in my gut, in my freaking lizard brain.

But the room was empty. I jerked back toward the window, but the second face was gone. Alone again.

My phone buzzed against the table. Josh. I needed to answer.

Instead I sprinted to the bathroom and puked until my stomach ached as badly as my heart.

CHAPTER 16

HEAVY THUMPS RESOUNDED THROUGH THE FARMHOUSE.
Were the windows rattling? Deep orange poured in through the windows on either side of my and Josh's bed. The warm afternoon glow that was perfect for new love and lazy Sundays filled our bedroom. Neither appropriate now.

The panes clacked again, but the only storm raging now was the one kicking bile against my esophagus. I swallowed, determined to be done heaving.

"Mrs. Hauk? Er, Emily, you in there?" The muffled voice was definitely male and certainly familiar.

I left the comfort of the cool tile and stood on legs more appropriate for a newborn giraffe. They grew no steadier as I wobbled toward the front door. At least I could see Ray on the front porch. Part of me marveled at the fact that I had uncovered panes of glass surrounding my home. That I could let whoever walked up to the door see inside. I'd been raised latch-key style, which of course meant my mother had given me free rein alone in the house since the age of eight, but with the explicit instructions to open the door for no one. I had—for a very long time—been one of those people who hid whenever a person rang the bell. It'd taken living with Josh and months of his sour skeptical face whenever I faked like I wasn't home at the door buzz to get used to *opening* a door to anyone arriving unannounced. The unhindered visual now was a comfort. Yes, those on the outside could see me inside, but no one was in my home who shouldn't be. There were no dark faces looming beyond that door. Just a farmer. Dust faded his blue denim jeans, and navy-blue bandannas hung both from his pocket and around his neck. Fixating on his stagecoach-robber readiness dulled the panic squeezing my skull enough to allow me to pull open the door with steady hands.

Ray swore under his breath. "You okay?"

Sweat slid down my spine, a teasing tendril of cool worry he had no way of seeing. Sinking my teeth into my cheek stilled the impending shiver. I swiped my wrist over my forehead like it, too, was damp. Did that make me look more ill?

Worry darkened this guy's features, but while I trusted my farm with him, I didn't know him. Not really.

I tucked my hands in my pockets to keep from fidgeting. "I'm good. What's up?" Reediness underscored my lie.

Ray's attention skittered around the doorjamb but never landed on my face. "Your husband called me."

Josh? What was going on? "Is this my turn to ask, 'Everything okay?'"

Ray's wrinkles mapped his ability to laugh, but he did not find me funny. He pulled the bandanna from his pocket and made the motions of cleaning his hands. "Your husband said you were on the phone with him, screamed, and the line went dead."

My face cooled as dread pulled all warmth to my gut, as if it my body needed to go into hibernation survival mode.

"Oh," I fumbled. "My stomach—I had to book it to the bathroom. I'll call him..."

Confiding in another person about what truly happened might steady my nerves or help it make sense, but that person wasn't Ray. His right shoulder was already angled back toward the fields. He didn't want to be here, didn't want to deal with my feelings, didn't want to be involved in Josh and my...whatever this was.

He cleared his throat, though it bore no hoarseness. "He tried to call you."

"I'll call him." Shit. How long had it been? Long enough that Josh had phoned his farmer friend. How far into the field had Ray been? How long could a person puke? Ten minutes?

Ray hovered, like he couldn't decide if he'd completed his duty. His mouth had flattened into a thin line, his boot scuffed a soft shush on the porch planks.

"Thank you for checking on me. Really. I'm okay. Just a stomach bug, I'm sure. I didn't mean to scare anyone."

Ray nodded. I'd said the right things, and he had been absolved. Yet his gaze flicked behind me, to the sofa, to the hallway. There was no chill on my neck, but was there an icy breath on his? His Adam's apple bobbed like he was choking on a memory.

"Did you know the people who used to live here?" I shouldn't have asked. I'd just told him I was sick. He had only come here after my husband freaked out. Josh had to be losing his shit right now. How terrified would I be if he'd yelled and then disconnected on me? But, God, that haunted look in Ray's eyes wouldn't let me ignore it.

His chin dipped. "Alice was my cousin. Bright girl. Thoughtful. She wouldn't leave her loved ones wondering if she were okay."

His implication was not subtle. "Of course." I backed into my house, clinging to the edge of the door. "Thank you again. I should call Josh now."

Alice had died where her family could find her. Probably not what Ray had meant.

The number of missed calls on my phone was absurd.

Thirty-seven calls.

Six voicemails.

Texts. Texts. Texts.

The dread weighing my belly barrel rolled into guilt. The thick, sticky sensation was familiar and overwhelming. It'd been an hour.

The phone didn't even ring before Josh answered. His panic was palpable. "I'm on my way home," he said, heat licking through the line and setting a spark to my guilt. As if the emotion could become molten and cauterize my heart.

I babbled half-incoherent for a full minute. I said I was puking, I said I was sorry, I pleaded for forgiveness.

Josh required none of it, continuing to be the epitome of understanding. He wasn't mad or disappointed or anything. "The deal is closed. No reason for me to be away from you."

He did that thing where he stuffed his anxiety into caring for others. It was a move that had made me feel special, sacred, from our early days.

Josh was the kind of man who, when he learned I'd never been to Yosemite despite how close it is to the Bay Area, had planned a "only runs on roads" level adventure for me. Hikes on the trail, both cabin and tent accommodations, signature pictures of me hugging trees, and a metric ton of campfire foods that he crafted over open flames while my only task had been opening the wine.

That was the man who had rented a car and was taking advantage of the high speed limit on I-80 to get home to his wife.

My earlier joy at having the privacy to investigate that damned barn had been replaced with the elation of having a second person in the house. One I knew was real and here, and who could validate what was going on.

I stayed on the line with Josh for forty-five minutes before we agreed I should rest. He believed my stomach was revolting from bad eggs. Like the Golden Girls or Mother Clucker would give us anything subpar. I knew better but tried to accept the lie too.

We hung up, and I rushed around the house to clean up. Coffee mugs rinsed and on the rack. First aid kit shoved back beneath the sink. When I finally made it back to the couch, I'd had enough time to accept that what I'd seen in the window had been an illusion. A trick of the light. The stress I'd been putting my body through. The drama I'd read online. I lifted my laptop to finish the last bit of work.

Under my laptop was a single photograph. The one I'd

dropped in the loft when I'd fallen through the floor. The one of a family standing in front of our barn. Black mold obscuring the mother's face.

Ice filled my veins. There was no face, but that dark hair, that pointed chin, that long elegant body. *It was her.* That was the woman in the reflection.

Was this Alice? What was happening here? And why had I seen her? Why did she tell me not to trust my husband?

Gravel crunched outside. Josh? The farmers? The ghosts of Belkin women? I shoved the photo inside my planner. It might not mean much to Josh, but it made everything more real to me.

CHAPTER 17

MY MOTHER ONCE JOKED THAT MY PHONE WAS TETHERED to my body. She'd gifted me a slim silver flip phone when I was seventeen. Since then I'd kept a phone on my person perpetually. If I wasn't working on carpal tunnel from scrolling through social media, it was wedged in my back pocket. The rectangular outline of an iPhone was my generation's version of cigarettes rolled in a white T-shirt sleeve.

"Why would you want to be accessible *all of the time*, Emily?" My mother's chiding was less due to our age difference and more her free spirit versus a daughter who valued controlled connections. Having the whole internet in my pocket was a freedom my mother didn't understand. But then her cheeks turned rosy in a room full of strangers, delight brightening her eyes and parting her lips. Comfort settled in my bones at whispered secrets.

"Mom, turns out I can lose a device even if it's strapped to my arm," I grumbled as I picked my way across the dirt toward the barn.

Back to the barn.

Back to my watch-slash-fitness-tracker.

It was the only place it could be. I wanted to believe it'd spilled onto the floorboards in the car or wedged itself between the center console and the driver's seat. But no. It wasn't in the house on the charging stand beside my bed. It wasn't in my belt bag—which I checked only because it was the last place I'd ever put the damn watch.

Driving into town to buy a new watch was silly. There was no way I could just drop a few hundred dollars on a new one without Josh asking what happened, without him offering to repair the old one, without questions that I would have to answer with lies. Plus I was garbage about backing it up. I'd lose heart rate logs and activity tracking and... Who was I kidding? I didn't want Josh to know I'd been in that barn, and if my watch was out there, someone would find it, and I'd have to explain everything. My skeptic husband would only double down on demands that I take medication.

So I was going to tiptoe back into the barn, find my watch with its shimmery purple band, and haul ass back to my house. I could lock the door on this whole day once I got the device.

If only it were truly that easy. The back door to the barn was open again, but that's where my luck ended. The sunlight that had filled the interior on my morning exploration had shifted to the windowless side of the building. Spotlights of diffused glow hit the floor like a concert stage before sound check. Muddy shadows ate the room's edges, ready to swallow secrets. My knees wobbled as I tried to lift my newly concrete-encased feet. The shadows weren't out to get me, but they sure weren't helping either. Where the hell was my watch?

I scuttled around the edge of the aging tractor I'd nearly collided with when I'd busted the floor overhead. No spots of red on
the floor that I could see—though, admittedly, my phone was my
usual flashlight, and I wasn't risking *two* devices to this place. Josh
kept a Maglite in the junk drawer, but I hadn't thought to grab it.
Not going back now. The sooner I found my watch, the sooner this
would be over.

The buckets I'd restacked were still up against the wall. No new
pictures littering the ground. When I had sprinted from this building, I told myself I wasn't going back in that hayloft again. It didn't
matter what I wanted, if keeping this secret mattered. I hobbled
over to the ladder. The twinge in my calf dialing up with each step
as if it, too, remembered what happened here. My heart flopped
against my rib cage, also lodging a complaint. I looked toward the
opening overhead, the entrance to the loft. Would I find a light
now? A speaker? A sign I was losing my mind? I rested my foot
on the bottom rung, and a chill skated over my wound. Like an ice
pack pressed too briefly to the flesh. I jerked back, heel not catching
me. For the second time in this place, I landed on my ass. At least
this time there wasn't a tractor for me to crash toward. I pressed my
palms against the dusty floor, my right hand meeting uneven surface. Beneath the crumpled hay was my watch. I lifted it as though
I'd found the Holy Grail. The screen wasn't so much as scratched,
and the battery was still at 29 percent.

"Thank God." I exhaled a rush of worry I'd stockpiled behind
my sternum. Rising from the floor was easy enough, my leg whining
minimally. "Let's get out of here," I whispered to my watch while

I strapped it back onto my wrist. Like I'd performed a true rescue mission.

Frigid air blasted my face, pushing me back into the hazy shadow beside the loft ladder.

"Wait." A strangled voice curled around me.

Nope. I was not staying here. Whatever went down in this barn was not for me.

The heavy creak of the main door echoed. Tight talons of fear pinned me in place.

"Not your place," a masculine voice was saying, clearly mimicking someone else. "Like you'd know anyone's place."

I sidled along the shadow's edge until I could see the door. A smaller truck had backed up to the opening. The young farmhand I'd seen coming and going from the barn a few times stood at the end of the truck bed. A long knife extending from his hand. Even from forty feet away, I could see the serrated edge, the nasty hook on the end. The metal didn't need to glint to carry menace; the teenager's body bore enough. His shoulders were rolled back, but his chin was jutted out and stance wide. The truck groaned when he stepped forward.

"They might think I don't know how to handle you, but I'll show them." He leaned low, wiping his blade on something.

He rose to his full height, putting himself into one of the sunbeam spotlights. Sweat stained the underarms of his shirt, his light brown hair was mussed, and his mouth was pulled in a wide rictus that would make the Joker proud. Red smudged a dimple on his cheek.

He jumped down, leaving the gate open.

A blue tarp lay in the center of the truck's bed. Golden grommets stained with rusted red flashing like an SOS. Was that blood? What—or who—was under that tarp?

I tried to rush forward—for answers, to help, anything—but cold hands gripped my shoulders.

"*Stay. Hid,*" an eerie voice commanded. The pleading tone and *ohmygod* the lack of anyone behind me, glued me to the spot.

The tarp in the truck bed rustled. The corner flap rising and falling with no rhythm.

A whimper cut through the thick air.

"Shut up. This isn't about you," the farmhand snarled from across the room. His back was to me, but he didn't so much as look toward the noise.

Dread sluiced down my body, pooling at my feet and holding me in place. The keening grew louder. The tarp rose at the edge again, slender fingers reaching past the blue plastic. A thin silver ring slipped from above a torn fingernail. Blood smudged the pale skin. The ring dropped to the ground.

What had I walked into? My heart echoed in my ears. I tried to move, but it was as though a barricade of ice had been erected before me. I couldn't budge. Frost could have formed on my bones for how still I stood. A hot tear slipped down my cheek.

The guy sauntered back, and the high-pitched whimper crescendoed.

"You really don't know when to shut up, do you?" He threw a rusted shovel into the bed. The flat metal thumped against whatever was beneath the tarp. Something solid, but it almost sounded wet. The fingers stopped moving.

The farmhand shoved the bared hand back beneath its plastic sheet and latched the gate. The truck was moving before I had a moment to so much as exhale.

There was a dead *something* in that truck. A dead *someone*. Everything in my body said so. I'd been in the same room with a killer.

A killer on my farm. In the barn with a noose. The place Alice had died. Minutes from my bed.

That teenager had been in my barn over and over. What else had happened here? I swallowed and remained hidden until the coldness around me subsided.

I searched the floor for the ring, but never found it.

Emily's Running Log:

2 minutes, 43 seconds to the barn—489 steps

CHAPTER 18

THE WHISPERED WARNINGS ECHOED IN MY BONES, LIKE MY marrow knew good advice when it heard it. There was blood in the barn. In that truck. Whoever that boy had in his pickup wasn't alive. The same voice that'd questioned Josh had also hidden me from the farmhand, had held me in the shadows. It'd wanted me to bear witness to *that*.

Why? I rolled my shoulders, trying to dispel anxiety.

Farms were supposed to be a source of life—growing plants, feeding animals, building a sustainable source of nutrition and necessary food. Every time I looked out my kitchen window now, the overwhelm of grief crumbled the semblance of a life I'd cobbled together. And I didn't understand why.

The farmhand—damn it, why couldn't I remember his name?— had driven away with his shovel and his kill. My stomach tumbled again, but I had nothing left to empty. And I just ran back to my house. I hadn't chased him down. What was wrong with me?

Loathing threatened to turn my legs liquid, to drop me to the living room floor. I snatched my phone and dialed 9-1-1. I waited for dispatch to answer.

"I—I—I—just saw a man with a body in the back of his truck." That was what I'd seen, right?

"Take a breath, miss. Where are you?"

I rattled off the farm's location.

I swore I heard her mutter, "Old Belkin place again." But then, more clearly, she asked, "And you're sure it was a person? Deer season just started, hun."

"Deer don't have fingers," I snapped before recounting exactly what I'd seen. The blood, the ring, the fingers.

I gasped between words like the fear was only now catching up to me, trying to choke me. The dispatcher urged calm and promised deputies were en route.

I paced on the front porch, gripping the phone like it'd keep me safe, for seventeen minutes. The white car that rolled up to my house didn't even have its lights on. *Was a dead body not an emergency?*

That hadn't been the farmhand's first time. I'd hidden in the shadows with the sticky straw. The musty odor of old hay clung to my pores, sweat and God knew what else matted my hair. My clothes were filthy from the barn and saturated with the stench of fear.

The sheriff's deputy held his hat in his hands while he had me recount the same details I'd given the dispatcher. He nodded solemnly.

"And can you point in the direction he left?" he asked finally, with a wary look toward the fields.

"No, I stayed in the barn. Was I supposed to run after a murderer?" My incredulity surpassed fear.

He placed his hat back atop his head. "We don't know that anyone has been killed, Mrs. Hauk. Hunting and trophies can unnerve the best of us."

"Are you kidding me?" It was a miracle I hadn't cursed the man.

He placed a hand on my arm, like a stranger's touch would be calming. I jerked away.

"We'll find him, ma'am. Until then, you need to stay inside. Is your husband home?"

I glanced at the watch—so important earlier. Josh was still driving; he'd be home in thirty minutes. He'd make more sense of this. "He'll be home soon."

"Good." The deputy nodded once with finality. "I'm going to drive around on your property. I've got another deputy out on the highway. We'll find out what's going on."

He left and I dead-bolted the front door.

Josh would arrive soon. This house would no longer be silent. The kid with the pickup wasn't going to roll up on the farmhouse with my husband here. Apparently the deputy thought so too.

But if my husband discovered my lies, would he stay? Our marriage was built on honesty and respect. It was more than those love-and-honor vows; it was a promise we'd made to each other not to keep painful secrets. I'd been hiding my insomnia bouts as best I could, but they were careful lies of omission. Those lies were about easing his guilt. He wanted to fix me, save me, make the pain go away. I mean, the guy had bounced from his big success dinner in the city to come home because he was worried about me. That was love. That was chivalrous.

He'd shut me down earlier. I hadn't told him about Alice. Or Bridget. Not really. But I'd called the cops now. What I'd witnessed... I needed him to believe me. He would back me on this thing with the barn if I had proof. More proof. Tangible evidence. He loved logic and detailed plans and fucking crossword puzzles. Panic was bubbling in my chest with each bump in heartbeats-per-minute flashing on my activity tracker's screen. Twenty-four minutes until he arrived.

The lavender band on my watch was back where it belonged. The color underscored how much of a yellow tinge had seeped beneath my skin. I didn't think I could get jaundice from too much coffee or not enough sleep. Maybe having the shit scared out of me repeatedly would do it though.

I'd said I was sick earlier—which wasn't a lie. I'd absolutely heaved my guts out. Only that wasn't why I'd hung up on Josh. I'd promised I'd slept, I'd promised I was solid, I'd promised he was coming home to his "totally good on her own" wife. But in the time since I'd slammed that laptop shut, since I'd heard the icy warning not to trust my husband, I'd become a disheveled mess.

He'd call this a hallucination if he walked in to find me wrecked like this. Probably run outside and find the deputies just to apologize. I hadn't put on makeup in over a month. (That's why they invented the filters on Zoom.) That'd be a red flag to him. I could be clean and calm though.

I turned on the hot water in our shower. While I waited for it to heat to an acceptable temperature, I pulled a double shot of espresso and threw it back like bottom-shelf liquor. It scalded the roof of my mouth and agitated the acid in my raw stomach, but I kept it down. Stripping as fast I could without smacking the bandages on my leg, I tucked my filthy clothes in the bottom of my hamper and jumped into the shower.

The bathroom mirrors were still fogged over when I dressed. I squeezed the majority of the moisture from my hair and combed the damp strands.

Josh blasted into the house like the summer storm winds we'd been warned about. The door near the kitchen rattled with his slam. He lunged toward me, eyes wide and nostrils flaring.

"You're okay?" His shaking hands skated over my shoulders, down my sides, and eventually held my hands.

Emotion pricked the corners of my eyes and thickened my throat. "I'll be fine."

His hands tightened on mine.

"Really, Josh."

"What did you eat?"

I answered, because it was easier than opening with a bloody hand. "I think the egg salad I made a couple of days ago was not my best lunch choice. That's all."

"We have fresh eggs outside," he said, like that cured food poisoning.

I slipped into his arms, nestling my head beneath his chin. "Everything went to hell after we talked."

Josh held me loosely and kissed the crown of my head. "I'm here now."

"You didn't have to come home for this." I held my belly. Nausea sloshing again.

"Of course I did." A thread of indignation cut through his comfort.

Duh. I'd scared the shit out of him. I'd screamed. Disappeared. *Did he see the deputy on the way in?* This farm had a history, and I had seen enough outside to know it wasn't only entrenched in memory.

"I just feel terrible, babe." The tears I'd tried to hold back fell. "You must have been—"

"Shh." He pulled back, pressing his fingers to my lips. "What matters is that you're okay and I'm here."

I nodded, speaking through sniffles. "There's more."

I told the barn story for the third time. Like with the others, I didn't mention the hands holding me back, the voice in my ear. Only that I'd hidden watching as the farmhand drove away with someone in the bed of the truck.

Josh gripped my arms and held me away so he could meet my gaze. "You what?"

"I called 9-1-1, and the sheriff's guys are out there now looking for him."

"And you didn't think to call me?"

"How were you going to stop a killer, Josh?"

"You waited here? *Showered*? Shit, Em. Do you realize how much danger you put yourself in?"

"The deputy thinks I'm safe in the house." I didn't entirely agree, but it wasn't like I had another place to go. "With you."

Josh released me and pressed his palms over his eyes. Like darkness solved a damned thing.

"I'm really sorry..."

Josh dropped his arms and rushed me. His hug made it hard
to breathe. "Forgiven. You're everything, Emily. I'm so, so sorry I
wasn't here for you. For this."

"You're here now," I said into his shirt.

"I'm going to talk to the deputies. Do you want to come with
me?" It didn't feel like a question.

I nodded but was spared from leaving by a knock on the door.

Josh answered. The person at the door wasn't the same man from
before, but he wore a similar tan uniform.

"Mr. Hauk, ma'am," he said, acknowledging us both, but sepa-
rately. "We found the truck and the boy driving it."

I pushed past Josh, demanding attention. "And?"

"Truck bed was empty, ma'am. There was a tarp, sure, but same
kind I take with me out to the deer blind."

What was it with deer and these people? "There was a hand—"

"Seeing blood or a hunting knife can really trip you up, ma'am.
We didn't find any evidence of a person in the truck."

My jaw dropped. Were they messing with me? I knew what I'd seen.

The deputy shrugged apologetically. "We'll add this farm onto
our regular patrol route for the next while. Drive the perimeter."

It'd taken them nearly twenty minutes to get here for an actual
emergency. I had little faith in their patrols. They'd been to this
farm for years. For domestic calls. Is that what they'd expected this
time? If so, why suggest I was safest with my husband?

"I know what I saw," I said, still staring at the taillights. I managed not to cry while the deputy drove away.

Josh's hand pressed at the center of my back, guiding me to our living room sofa. "There's been so much happening. You can't be blamed for seeing animal blood and thinking it was...more."

So this is what I was supposed to accept? That I couldn't tell fingers when I saw them?

I shook my head and flopped down onto the couch. My leg ached, but my heart hurt far more.

"I can tell you rested." Josh slid down next to me. Slipping his arm around my shoulders. "Even with the egg, ah, food mishap, you look gorgeous, Em."

I wanted to scream. To tell him I was not an idiot. I was not delirious. But I was so exhausted, and he was staring at me with that pitying look. I gave him the out instead of trying to prove myself. "I'm sure I look more peaky than fabulous in my lounge pants."

"Would I lie to you?" He pressed a sweet kiss to my forehead, sealing in my rage.

"I'll take the win. Thanks for coming home." I leaned against him, letting him take my weight. I hoped it felt like a hug, like assurance, and not like hiding. My lower lip trembled. I looked toward the picture window. Our forms echoed in the glass. Just me and Josh. No mystery woman. No threats. No chilly warnings. Just my husband holding me like I was a precious object in the sanctuary of our home.

I tried to absorb that feeling. His heart's steady thump beneath my ear a reminder of his resoluteness. This was his peaceful place. It was supposed to be mine too. How could I regain that?

This farm had secrets. Every day I became more convinced I was being watched. That the barn *moved*. I'd heard the music. I'd seen the light. Moreover the sharpness in my gut said whoever had been in the back of that pickup had been dead. Had I been wrong, or had I let someone drive off with a dead body? Was this how they ended up ruling Alice's death an accident? What about her daughter's disappearance? This place had belonged to the Belkins for so long, everyone called the farm by their name. Had it been more than finances or obligations that made them give up a farm that had been in their family for generations?

I squeezed Josh more tightly.

"Em?" My husband leaned back to meet my gaze but didn't ease up on the hug.

"Hmm?"

"I hope Ray didn't scare you." His hazel eyes glimmered with knowledge. Like he knew more than I'd realized.

Wait. Was my husband baiting me? My brain was too mushy to be evasive. Not that I *wanted* to lie to Josh. We weren't supposed to be the people who did that. Old people who bickered and "stayed together for the kids" did that trash. My love for him was a billowing heat in my breast even when anger threatened to choke me. He deserved every part of me.

I nuzzled in against his firm chest. "I think I scared him more, but yeah, I was not prepared for him to be at the door."

"You scared him?" Josh chuckled. "You're a powerhouse, but that guy is a tough one."

"He kept looking past me into the house." Should I tell him? Would he shut this down too? Hell, this was my Josh. "He stared behind me like he was seeing a ghost."

Josh squirmed. His embrace loosened. "He didn't say—"

"No, no, no, he didn't say anything weird. Just went pale. Maybe my sick face was that bad." I tried for levity.

Josh wasn't having it. "Even sick, you're hot. I bet it was just strange to be at our place."

"Why?" I asked, trying not to show how eager I was for any insight. Josh talked to these people. He'd ridden up to Grand Island side by side with Ray. What had he learned?

Josh let go of me. His mouth quirked in a familiar half smile that said he was trying to be casual but wanted to change the subject. "He knew the people who lived here before us."

I bit the inside of my cheek until the tang of iron lit my tongue. I counted *one two three four five*, and then when I was certain it wasn't too eager, I asked, "Wasn't he related to them? I remember you saying the farmers we're leasing the land back to had worked here for years."

Ray had told me Alice was his cousin when he'd been here. Did Josh know? Would he tell me?

My husband nodded slowly. "Same farm crew for the most part, yeah."

Unexpected relief flashed over me. Josh was being up front with me. We were fine. I would be fine.

He walked to the kitchen and pulled a beer from the fridge. He waggled a bottle in my direction. I shook my head. Even if I hadn't

yakked like a freshman recently, I would not risk being anything
other than sober now. If that frigid voice returned, if the music
played again, if there was so much as a flicker out in that barn, I
needed to know I could trust myself.

"Why would you think they're related?" he asked. He popped
the cap on the IPA and took a sip, his focus centered on me. Was
I reading too much into his attention? Did he know something?
What secrets was he holding? Or had he just hauled ass back home
to make sure I was safe?

"Everyone calls this place 'the old Belkin farm.'" I shrugged. *No
big deal*, I faked, while the back of my mind still whirred through
every police account I'd read featuring Alice Belkin.

Josh sat on one of the kitchen chairs and then pulled me into his
lap. I kept my gaze on him, because if I looked dead ahead, I'd be
facing the sink, the window, the barn.

"Who is 'everyone'?" he teased, with a little tickle on my side.

I groaned and pulled away from his touch. "Hey, remember the
earlier puking? No tickling."

He muttered an apology, looking properly abashed.

It didn't escape me that Josh didn't confirm if Ray was part of
the extended Belkin family. He didn't talk about the Belkins at all.
But then this was meant to be our fresh start. If he'd seen what I
had, he'd understand why I wouldn't drop it. I glanced at my calf.
The bandage wasn't visible beneath my joggers. I sighed and relaxed
into Josh's hold.

"What do you think we should call our farm?" I changed the
subject. Kind of.

"Our farm?"

"When I went to the truck stop, people knew I lived 'at the old Belkin place.'" I used air quotes like one of Josh's company's vice presidents that he made fun of after his Zoom calls.

His lips parted on a slow breath. Hops and Listerine filled the pause. Then he smiled. Like I'd passed some test. One I shouldn't have needed to take.

Josh took a long pull on the bottle and then pretended to be deep in thought. "This house was totally renovated. We can't have *old* in the name."

"I think they meant that it used to belong to them." I didn't hide my bitterness.

He shot me a stabbing look that said I was killing the fun.

"Sorry," I muttered. "I love the brightness of this place. The yellows we've filled the house with."

"You did that, babe. You made this place warm and into a home."

I preened at the praise. Decor I could handle. If only I could do the same for the barn outside. A coat of paint wouldn't solve its problems though. The dilapidated walls weren't under my skin the way that loft and its shadowy horrors were.

"Pretty sure we'd get laughed out of town if we called this the Sunshine Farm," I tried.

"Sounds like hospice." He winced, like he could slurp back the words. My mom's hospice had opted for *hope* in the name, but it didn't change the fresh wave of sickness that slammed into me. I slid from Josh's lap.

He rattled off apologies, and I waved them away.

I filled a glass of water from the tap and kept my attention on the drain. Beneath the stainless steel was darkness. Was there black mold down my drain? Was that rot everywhere? I squeezed my hand tighter on the cup and hoped I wasn't inviting more sludge into my life with every sip.

Emily's Running Log:

6 minutes, 2 seconds to the barn—1,088 steps

CHAPTER 19

I SLEPT IN MY BED THE NEXT TWO NIGHTS. WELL, I LAY QUI-
etly between the sheets. The aches lingering in my muscles said it
didn't count, but Josh reached for me first thing each morning. He'd
set a sunrise alarm.

"You don't have to do the morning run with me," I told him
while I laced my sneakers.

He lumbered toward the espresso machine, sleep holding his lids
at half-mast. "It's good."

I shrugged. Acclimating to this new level of attention was harder
than it should have been. Josh was my best friend. I *loved* doing
things with him. But he hadn't left me alone for a solid seventy-two
hours, and it was feeling more like being babysat than being adored.

How would I behave if I thought I'd lost him? my own thoughts
admonished me. That kind of fear doesn't simply evaporate when
you learn it's a false start. There were worse reactions to panic than
wanting to hang out with me. Hadn't I just complained about being
alone here?

Besides, if I saw any of the farm crew out on the run this morning, I'd like them to see Josh at my side. If I got the chance to peek at the empty pickup truck, having my husband nearby would be smart. Although, he would dissuade me. He'd believed the deputy; I knew better.

I'd tried to watch the barn when I could, but with my husband glued to my side, it was hard to focus on it.

Now, who was I lying to? The blood, the warning, the callousness. Everything about what I'd learned when Josh was away claimed the forefront of my mind. And it was like he knew it.

Every time I lingered at the window over the kitchen sink, he'd slip behind me, hands on my waist. He had no meetings this week, so he planted himself beside me on the couch while I worked. If I stared a second too long out the big window overlooking the fields, he'd bump his shoulder playfully against mine and ask if I needed a break.

Everything about it was perfect on the surface. It *should* have been perfect. This was the life I'd dreamed about. And yet Josh's choice to run with me again this morning sandblasted my nerves. Because today I could see he didn't want to be putting on a ball cap at 4:57 a.m.

He poured two espresso shots into his coffee mug. "Let me get two sips in, and I'm good."

He wasn't. I wasn't. But those words from three days ago, wispy and cold, *"He can't be trusted,"* floated around me, urging me to keep my worries to myself.

"I need to feed the girls. You've got time to drink the whole cup," I said.

Wry humor twisted his mouth. "Such a chicken mama."

At least this part of my life still delighted him. I snatched the bag of feed and went out to Cluckingham Palace.

All my hens aside from Dorothy were awake. She'd climb out of the coop when she wanted. The other chickens flocked to my ankles as I entered the pen. I sprinkled the kernels around the ground—they liked the meandering process. That pecking thing was instinctive. But I still put a portion in a metal bowl for them. Dorothy preferred it that way, and the others would leave her plenty. It's like they knew she'd get surly with them otherwise.

"Josh is going with me on the run today," I told my hens.

They focused on the feed and not my commentary, but that never stopped me from chatting them up. "If he keeps this up, I'm going to need to make him sign up for the marathon too."

I hadn't made the joke to him because then he *would* sign up. I needed this for me, but also he wasn't truly up for putting in those kind of miles.

Mother Clucker ruffled her feathers. I changed out the water, and she settled down.

I dropped my voice to a whisper, which was ridiculous because no one else was out here. Josh was likely still mainlining caffeine inside. But some secrets were just for me and the birds. "Can you watch the barn for me while I'm gone?"

No one objected. Chickens were solid judges of character in my very limited experience—which was to say I just really wanted to believe they were. And whenever I figured out two-way communication with them, it was going to be a game changer.

Until then, I latched their coop. "You girls stay safe in there."

Josh met me on the porch. Grogginess clung to his cheeks and pulled his mouth into a sour pout, but warmth filled his tone. "You might have a hang of this farmer thing, Emily. Who knew you'd be a natural at raising chickens?"

I laughed, a real one, and the sound carried out toward our acreage. "Can you imagine if my mom saw me now?"

There was something wistful about the way he stared at me. Like he was seeing the Emily he met at college. "She'd be proud."

"Maybe," I admitted. "But I think she'd also be really confused."

"She'd still be asleep right now." There was a ruefulness that said *someone* missed his pillow. No need to call him on it though.

"No, she'd just be coming home." My mother had been a last-call kind of woman before she became sick. But even then—and I suppose when I was young, if I let my mind wander back that far—she'd been built for night. Her creative energy kicked in after 10 p.m. I remembered finishing homework my junior year of high school and hearing Mom tapping drumsticks against the kitchen counter along with a guitar track she was experimenting with. Producing albums meant pulling threads together. It was the one area where our minds worked similarly. Only hers had always been audio input. For me, it was visual. Colors, patterns, space between objects, text, images. She'd find balance between instruments and sounds and melodies. I sought peace in a room, on a page, wherever I stood.

Could I do that on our farm? Was "the old Belkin farm" destined for something more beautiful? Our house had a modern serenity. If you didn't count the late-night jump scares.

Josh had been so scared for me. But was that his only fear? He'd been so casual with the farmers and the cops and, hell, every man who came onto the farm. Did none of them scare him? If I'd frightened him with the FaceTime hang-up, did that mean he knew there was a threat here? I stretched my hamstrings and let the pinch of tightness re-center me. No, Josh would never encourage me to run out into the fields if he believed a man on our farm was a killer. Which meant he thought I was just losing it. That was worse.

How could I make him see what was happening? If I couldn't convince my own husband there was something wrong here, how was I supposed to stop anything? How would I convince anyone else to help us?

For once, I appreciated the slow warm-up. My mind spun through how I would broach the barn with Josh again. We ran ten miles. Not as much as I would have done alone, but far more than I typically clocked when Josh joined me. His chest heaved. Beneath the shadow on his jaw, ruddiness rose. Dirt capped the tips of his Nikes. The tl;dr was my husband was tired. My body was in that languid state of well use. Muscles burning, heart pumping, mind clear. I slowed our pace as we approached the house for a cooldown.

Josh muttered, "Oh thank God."

I'd worried I'd pushed him too hard, but if he could make words, he was fine.

"Do we store anything in there?" I asked as the barn doors came into view. "I mean 'you and me' we."

"No," he huffed. "Sorry, that came out shitty."

"Jeez, you don't have to be so mean to me," I added a singsong whine just to amp the teasing.

"What did you want to store out there? We've got an attic and a basement. You thinking about your mom's stuff?"

I hadn't been, but that added one more thing to the Adulting 101 pile. "I haven't even called back the estate guy."

Admitting one truth eased the rest of it. Even if I was *guiding* the path to honesty.

"I can call him, find out what he needs," Josh offered.

"He wants me to make decisions," I grumbled, letting us fall to a pace that was only a jog if you squinted.

"I can still call and get a list. I know how much you hate having to call people on the phone."

I did hate that, and not having to do it was nice. None of that shielded my pride from the nick of needing to be cared for.

"That'd be great." I slowed us to a walk, and then as my breathing evened out, continued. "The younger guys on the crew have been in and out of the barn a lot this last week or two. I didn't think they had regular need of it, but it got me thinking about how we'd divide things up in there if it's in use."

"In and out?" Genuine surprise slowed my husband's pace. His concern was my validation. "Is this about what you saw the other night? I've spoken with the local deputies the last three nights, and they haven't found or seen anything concerning. It really was a misunderstanding."

Whimpering and bleeding a misunderstanding? Was he serious? "There was no mistake on my part."

"Emily." He dropped my name like a hammer on an anvil.

"Joshua," I countered. "I'm not a liar."

"No, but you're tired, and you're grieving, and you just had food poisoning. I truly believe you're safe here."

Yeah, that's why he'd been running with me every day since he'd gotten home.

I stopped and let him catch up to me. "Even if I was wrong, there has been lots of backing that pickup up to our barn and carrying out duffel bags." That was mostly true. I'd only seen the bag twice, but I figured whatever else had been placed in the back of that truck accounted for embellishment.

"I can talk to Ray about it." He reached for my hand and squeezed it. "No wonder it freaked you out when he came to the door. People have been buzzing around the house."

Not the description I would have used. "Ray didn't scare me. I just feel so awful that you had to call him, and he looked wrecked too. I'm sure the whole farm was like, 'That Emily Hauk has lost it.'"

Had Ray told everyone in town too? Would they stare when I walked into the market or went for round two at the truck stop? I needed people to spill secrets *to* me not *about* me.

"I'll talk to him," Josh said more firmly. "I don't mind them using the barn, but we'd agreed it was for storage of the backup equipment."

Josh's eyes widened for a moment, and I thought he was going to ask about the loft or the light or the music. He had to put it together. My husband was *smart*.

Instead he turned his attention toward the house.

"I think the chickens' pen door is open."

"What?" I turned and saw the wooden gate ajar even from this distance. I hauled ass up to the house.

"Em, slow down. It's fine." Josh called after me. He assumed everything was *always* fine. That was the problem.

I ignored him and kept sprinting.

I rattled off the hens' names as I reached the coop. Four chickens remained in Cluckingham Palace.

"Blanche is missing," I yelled down the drive to Josh.

I tried asking the hens where their sister had gone, but—shocker—they provided zero clues.

Luckily the silt was soft enough that I could see a faint track of her little three-toed feet.

Heading right toward the barn.

Emily's Running Log:

8 minutes, 27 seconds to the barn—1,521 steps—Run again later?
This feels wrong.
10.2 mile run—Josh joined. Slower pace. Leg is still store, but heart
zones were good. Baby cow on the north path run.

CHAPTER 20

CHICKENS LOVE BERRIES. THIS HAD LIKELY BEEN ALL OVER the damn internet and chicken mama message boards and I—I don't know—forgot? Or missed it? Or didn't think it would be important because I focused on getting *proper* chicken feed for my hens?

I figured fruit was a special treat for birds. Like ice cream. Well, Blanche apparently wasn't waiting on anyone to bring her a pint of Cherry Garcia.

In lieu of a jaunt to Ben & Jerry's—which, by the way, was at least a hundred miles away, if not more—my feisty chicken had walked her way around the farm to a scraggly raspberry bush next to the barn's rear door.

I wrapped my hands around her middle and lifted. She pecked at my arm, leaving purplish pulp behind.

Josh huffed behind me. "See you found her."

I clucked my tongue at the bird in a way that I hoped was soothing. She squirmed with obvious intention to dive for a second helping of rogue berries. "Yeah. Blanche here is a real self-starter."

"We need more hens with ambition," Josh teased, his hand resting on my lower back.

"The hell we do." Blanche fluttered and puffed enough that I finally set her down by my feet. She immediately sought all scraps lingering on the dirt. "You, my hen friend, need to stay in the coop. This is no place for you."

Josh's shotgun laugh made me stagger. "Em, it's a *barn*. It was probably made for her."

Not this barn. But I couldn't say that to Josh. He was ignoring the danger here. I needed more logic to layer into our conversations before he'd accept what my gut was screaming—that a terrible thing had happened here. A terrible thing was still happening. I wasn't safe on the farm, and deep down, I suspected he knew it. He'd hauled ass back here fast enough to tell me he had to at least halfway believe there'd been a person out in our barn those nights I saw the loft aglow.

"Did you know this bush was here?" I asked as our hen tried to snag a plump berry from the middle of the plant.

"It's a normal plant, Em." The jerk had the audacity to groan like I was exhausting him. Like I was making him retread a painful conversation.

"I didn't say it wasn't," I snapped.

Josh scrubbed his hand over his forehead, as though the heel of his palm could swipe a layer of sanity back into place. "Sorry sorry sorry. I didn't mean…"

He absolutely meant it. He believed I was making things up. He'd told me before that I was "merely finding problems" just like my mom. But I didn't want to fight this morning. Hell, I didn't want to fight with him ever.

So I gave him the out, because I always gave him the out. "I hadn't realized there were raspberries back here. I'd never noticed."

The corner of Josh's mouth quirked, his shoulders dropping and body easing into the post-workout relaxation that I so desperately needed. "Why would you, babe?"

He turned and gestured to the empty expanse. There were cornfields on two sides. The space between the barn and the field on this side was rutted like a tractor had driven through midstorm and slopped mud in all directions. It'd hardened that way. The haul-away garbage pile was up past the next door. The one that would feel like the rear door if I were back inside the barn. Not that I was returning to the scene of the crime. Trepidation trickled down my throat. I swallowed and tried to lock my attention on Blanche's feathers. The ones at the tips of her wings were white. Thick juice dripped from her beak, the tiny seeds in each fruit clearly her real goal. The handle of the door was rusted at the top, but the bolts on the wood remained a flat silver.

"I brought a pallet down here once," I said. Not that Blanche would remember.

"You were pushing a wheelbarrow. I think you're forgiven for not noticing the plant. And even if you forgot about seeing it, it's a plant. You won't hurt its feelings." Josh plucked a berry from the top. It was a rich pink. He pressed it to my lips. "Besides, I rather like us finding it together. Makes it ours."

I accepted the snack—and tried not to think about how the fruit was probably filthy. Josh's fingers brushed my lips, and I kissed them softly. The berry burst in my mouth, sweet and lush.

"Oh my God," I managed around the bite. "This is amazing."

Okay, Blanche was on to something here. Farm life had its perks. Sunshine, beauty, and holy shit deliciously fresh food. Not enough to override the horribleness that happened in the barn though.

Josh's smile widened. "They're good?"

I nodded and pulled one for him. *Focus on the now. On the good*, I told myself.

He took the ripe raspberry from my hand and turned it back toward me. "I don't like berries," he lied. He ate strawberries aplenty.

"Since when?" I played along, eating the fruit because it was goddamned delicious and one of us wasn't about to ruin the moment.

"All the seeds stick in my teeth." He shrugged. "Besides, it means more for you. And you're adorable when you get all farm wife on me."

"Farm wife?" I cackled, his distraction working. "What does that even mean?"

He lifted his eyebrows like some shocked cartoon character. His lips twitched from the pain of keeping a straight face. Josh nodded toward the hen at my feet, seemingly now sated from her berry binge.

Heat rose to my cheeks. I stooped and gathered my chicken. She was happy to be carried now. "I don't know what you're suggesting." I pumped as much faux haughtiness into the words as I could.

I tried to strut off, too, like I imagined Eva Gabor would have on *Green Acres*. Man, I hadn't thought about that show in ages. I'd clocked some hours with Nick at Nite while waiting for Mom to get home decades ago. I'd been old enough that it wasn't dangerous to leave me alone, but young enough to not want to sleep without my mom in the house. She'd blast into the living room, pull her favorite patchwork blanket—a quilt of concert shirts from 1982—off the back of the sofa, and slide in next to me. She'd sing along with the classic TV theme songs. She'd hug me. Those nights she'd promise there was no other place she'd rather be than home with me. And on that couch, I'd believed her.

Now everyone told me time would make me miss my dead mom less. Bonus: Josh told me a bit more sleep would cure the disturbing views beyond the windows—as though they were also linked to my mother.

She wasn't with me anymore. Whatever memories lived on this farm, they didn't belong to me.

I slowed my walk and turned to Josh. Would I rather be back in California?

"Sorry, Em, I didn't mean to make fun," Josh sputtered, misreading my fallen mood.

The specter of Penelope Wagers rose between us, but only I could sense her. "No, it's not that."

He leaned toward me, bumping his shoulder against mine. It was playful and encouraging, and yet it only jostled my sorrow. Josh might spot the dregs in a coffee cup, but he'd also never missed the way my mom's laughter bumped the wattage of even shitty overhead fluorescents.

"It's nothing. Just one of those errant memories." I waved it away, as if I could dispel the longing clinging to my chest so easily.

I'd been married to the man long enough to know he'd drop it. Josh pushed only when it was truly important. That's what I told myself. The river of guilt for ignoring his pleas for rest sloshed against the makeshift dam I'd created in my chest.

"I'm pretty sure I'm cradling a hen like she's a naughty toddler. That seems like a farm wife move." I lifted Blanche. Both proof and protection.

His smile warmed my heart. Those hazel eyes had a way of turning me liquid with a single glance. Like he saw everything important and discarded whatever didn't define me. Had I changed since we'd moved to Nebraska? Could he see I was now the type of person who held secrets from her spouse? I wasn't a liar. I *wanted* to tell Josh everything I'd seen, everything I knew was true. I'd tried before, but he was simply too driven by logic to accept my gut. I needed him and the idea of shunting a wedge between us unnecessarily raked nails down my back. I'd be raw and bloody without my balance. He was that. I just needed more information before I brought him in.

"You're thinking hard over there, gorgeous." He reached for Blanche and eased the hen from my hands.

We'd reached Cluckingham Palace while I was spiraling. If I intended to buy time, I had to focus. Dazed stumbling did not support my whole "healthy, happy, totally chill" front.

"I'm thinking about those raspberries." Quick thinking anyway.

"The chicken will be fine." Humor spiced his tone.

"Of course she will." I latched the coop now that the hen was back home with her sisters. "I just wondered who it belonged to. The bush."

"Well, it is our farm." Josh opened the back door of our house, holding it for me to go through first. He pinched my butt as I passed. I swatted his hand away but scampered inside, amused. We would be fine.

I gestured to the coffee maker. Josh was the kind of person who usually did protein shakes for recovery, but today he nodded for my post-workout coffee regimen.

"If the fields and the barn are for the farmers, then wouldn't the plants around the barn be part of their domain?"

"Domain? Who are you? Magellan?" he teased. I shot him a dirty look. Josh ignored it and began dicing an apple while a pair of frozen waffles did their thing in the toaster. *Guess we're having breakfast.*

"Pretty sure explorers stole land and pretended it was their own."

"So you're about to ford the river on the Oregon Trail instead?" Josh cracked that joke like he didn't own an "At least you didn't die of dysentery" shirt in the back of the closet.

I shifted my weight and tried to focus on the steady stream of black gold pouring into the coffeepot. "I'm trying to avoid stepping on toes."

Josh softened his tone. "I doubt anyone is going to care that your chicken ate a few berries."

"Our chicken," I corrected him but returned my attention to my husband. The coffee would be ready when it was ready.

"She went on the hunt for snacks. Definitely yours, Em." Josh's dimple made an appearance alongside his amusement.

"I don't know what you mean." I folded my arms, pretending this actually riled me.

He pursed his lips, knowing I was faking. "How many times did you think we should find a Circle K at one a.m. so you could get a pint of ice cream?"

"You said you didn't mind!" I threw a dish towel at him.

He caught it, the nimble bastard. "Like I'm going to say no to ice cream?"

"What you're saying is my snack inhibitions improved your life." I sprung toward him and pecked his cheek. "You're welcome."

Josh snaked his arm around my waist before I could move back to the properly percolated coffee. "Thank you," he said, heat adding grit to every syllable. "You know I love everything about you, Emily."

Playfulness tumbled away, replaced by a burgeoning heat. My husband's gaze smoldered. The cloying smell of our sweat-slicked bodies mingled. The air only missing the note of sex to be perfection.

Josh's thumb stroked my jaw.

The toaster popped, but neither of us could break eye contact to acknowledge it.

"*Farm wife* is a compliment, Emily."

That sobered me. I tried to pull back, but Josh's arm locked tight behind me.

"I mean it. This new life—our life—is a start that's only about you and me. You're the bravest woman I know."

I relaxed into him, my chest against his reminding me how thin the sports bra was—and how hard it was going to be to pull it off.

"That so?" I squeaked. My arms wrapped around his neck, needing his steadiness.

"Mhm." Josh spoke against my neck. "Strong and brave. *My* farm wife."

Suddenly the term was the sexiest pet name I'd ever heard. For once, I didn't need a caffeine fix to find energy.

We did not make it to the bedroom. If any of the farm crew drove by the house, seeing my ass in the window was on them.

It was only in the afterglow that I realized I had never weaseled in a question about the rules of ownership with the barn. I should know this, but I'd let Josh handle so much when it came to the property purchase. He was the only one in this marriage with experience reading contracts.

I had a copy though. Amid my inbox chaos. I could find the details of who we leased the crops back to, understand what they could keep in the barn and, if I was lucky, discover why it mattered.

And I could do it without squashing the confidence Josh had in me.

Emily's Running Log:

Solo run in the afternoon. Two-a-day was not terrible! That red truck was parked in the path to the east field. One of the guys stared at me hard enough to make me veer onto the long loop to the south. Teenagers shouldn't unnerve me like that. Am I getting old?

5 minutes, 59 seconds to the barn—1,077 steps

CHAPTER 21

PALE MOONLIGHT CAST A PALLOR ON THE GREEN FIELD
beyond my bedroom window. The bed quaked at regular intervals,
Josh's snoring resetting. Counting sheep was a garbage way to fall
back asleep. Mentally tallying tomorrow's to-do list hadn't helped
either. I stared past the gauzy white fabric I'd placed over the windows, a false sense of privacy. Not that we should need cover here.
No one is out there, I reminded myself.

The gray cast to the world beyond the window turned the
organic beauty of morning into an artificial version. Metallic stalks,
stunning in the way an art installation by someone who had never
seen a real cornstalk was. No movement, no life.

I flopped onto my back. Josh groaned but returned to nasal
kazoo tryouts. Was I trying to make Nebraska into my ideal setting?
Was I being an asshole outsider who expected the farm to be a quiet,
remote sanctuary like in the movies?

My friend Serena had certainly thought so.

"There's a reason it has a low population density," she'd said as we walked out of the spin gym.

"Well, I'd argue it'd be weird to have apartments on a farm." I gestured toward the taqueria at the end of the block, our regular post-workout indulgence. Not that I'd been to an in-person class in two years. I came for Serena today. To see her before we left.

"Won't you miss all of this? The stores? Spin? Really good tacos?"

"Maybe?" I admitted. I had no idea if Nebraska was truly for me, but I needed change. "The point is to get some distance. I'm already shopping online, running solo, and getting mostly okay at making my own tacos."

"Liar. You DoorDash four times a week."

That had been true in early quarantine times, which had made me feel like such an ass. "Not any longer." I lifted my hand like I had been a Girl Scout for more than three weeks. "YouTube can teach you anything. Including how to meal prep and make a chimichurri sauce that turns boring pork tenderloin into something fancy."

"Well, shit. You should have a going-away dinner party so I can experience your culinary prowess." She elbowed me playfully, but worry still tightened her eyes.

I'd scrambled to shut down any hint of an invite. "I still don't want to host anyone. I'm moving to the middle of nowhere because I want to be away from everyone."

"Ouch." Serena blinked rapidly, like she could clear my friendship gaffe.

Yet another reason for the move. I'd become really poor at

people-ing. Even with friends. "I didn't mean it like that," I back-pedaled. "I'm really craving the serenity of it. No rude neighbors stomping around at two a.m."

She let me shift the conversation. Probably because the restaurant was in sight. "Are you really not going to move into your mom's place? I still think about that party we had senior year—"

"You did not experience the fallout from that party," I quickly reminded her.

"Your mom knew how to throw down. She was proud of you for getting a band set up in the house." Serena's chin rose like she'd heard the praise directly from my mother.

I sucked my lips but nodded reluctantly. "She was, except they stole drumsticks signed by Dave Grohl and smashed her Stevie photo."

Serena gasped appropriately. "Not Aunt Stevie."

The memory tugged at the corners of my mouth. "I don't think she'd ever been so livid with me."

"Your mom was chill through and through," Serena said with the experience of a friend who had slept over at my house nearly every weekend in high school.

"My mom railing about how I brought 'some shitty indie band that has so little taste as to touch that photo' into her home was the closest I got to a 'you broke curfew and are clearly drunk' speech."

Serena snickered. "I got that other one."

I remembered. "I didn't see you for a month."

"And now you're moving to another state," she said, like she was about to hug me again. She'd hugged me at least a dozen times that day.

"They have airports. You can come visit," I'd offered, knowing she wouldn't. Serena had leaned into returning to bars and restaurants and spin class in the last year. And she was straight mom-ing the rest of the time. I found I was so much happier without all that. Happier at home. With Josh. In my comfy clothes with no one to impress but myself.

I hadn't talked with Serena since we moved here beyond sharing social media posts that would make the other laugh. I hadn't even told her about the marathon training. She'd probably want to join in. Did it make me a terrible friend that I didn't want her to?

I didn't miss food delivery.

I didn't miss my old apartment.

I didn't even miss Serena the way I probably should.

I did, however, miss seeing my mom's house—with her in it.

The ceiling fan whirred overhead, cutting through shadows with a slow *tick-tick-tick*. I closed my eyes—easier to do without the barn beyond the window. It couldn't be seen from this side of the house.

Eeeeeeeeeeeeeeeeeeeeeeeeeeeeee.

A wail pierced the night. I rocketed upright in bed. When had I fallen asleep? Emptiness grabbed every sound in the room in the wake of the scream. The fan was silent, the crickets paused, even Josh stopped his snoring. Not that he woke.

Had I dreamed the screech? I tapped the screen on my phone, illuminating the whole bedside table in blue light that made me scrunch my nose.

3:56 a.m.

I made it past three. My heart galloped in my chest like it was already thirty minutes into this morning's marathon training. I yanked on a pair of joggers and pointed myself toward the coffee machine.

Eeeee. Eeeee. Eeeeeeeeeeeeeeeeeeee.

The sharp, tinny cries cut through the air. They scraped the glass on the windows, snaring my eardrums and seeking to shake my equilibrium.

I shot forward, unthinking. Those small screams—as though a tiny person were in peril—activated my instincts. A child needed help. Maybe more than one. I didn't have to be a mom like Serena to feel that alarm in my chest. I blasted through the front door, letting the screen slam against the house with no regard for the wood. The slam could scare away any animals.

Or farmhands who shouldn't be here. *Oh, God, what if there was another person in the back of that truck?*

The early morning air wrapped around me like a damp blanket. *Eeee. Eeee. Eeee.* The screams pierced the sky. Erupting from seemingly everywhere. I spun around on the porch, trying to pick a path. Near the chicken coop? I sprinted to check on my girls. The hens were tucked in, beaks down. The door was latched. How were the chickens sleeping through this? The sound shifted locations. No longer emanating from the coop, but from the fields. And behind my car.

I sprinted forward on the dirt path but stalled out when I reached the gravel. I stood in the spot I'd fallen before. Pebbles tinged with the oxidized brown of my blood marred the earth here. Once more, the scream slashed my thoughts. I blinked twice and the barn was before me. Not the three hundred-ish steps away it should be, but directly in front of me. I held my breath, but its foul odor filled my nose regardless. The barn's weathered paint close enough I could reach forward and brush it. I spun. My house was still behind me, close. The chicken coop only two dozen steps away. I skittered backward, toward my house, my chickens.

The keening crescendoed until I had to clap my hands against my ears. Frost nibbled my nape. I glanced back.

The barn was back where it should be. Far away. The moon dangled overhead, a waning crescent. The road between my home and the damned building stretching thin, every cream-colored pebble illuminated by the natural night light.

The screaming quelled. Silence once again backfilled until it pressed into my very pores. The absence of sound thickened the air until I was gasping.

I couldn't leave the path though. Not when I'd heard those cries. I couldn't abandon anyone to a sad end in the back of a pickup truck. In the fields. *My* fields. What if the Belkin girl was out there right now? What if I could save her?

"Is anyone there? Are you okay?" The night absorbed my breathy words.

I tried again, louder. I was shouting into the void.

No one replied.

Damn it. Had the screams come from within the barn or in the field? Both? The ethereal moonlight made walking on the driveway doable, but among the cornstalks, it would be impossible to see. I needed proper shoes and Josh. He'd help with this. Someone was in danger.

Wait. It shouldn't be this dark. We had floodlights on the house. There should be a brilliant halogen light pointed toward the car. Josh had adjusted the angle to make sure the chickens had appropriate darkness for sleep, but my running outside should have triggered the lights on the front and side of the house. Neither had flared.

Not for me. Not for whoever had been yelping moments ago.

I edged toward my house like one wrong step would drop me into a ravine. Shuffle step one foot, then close the gap. Repeat.

"Don't go." The words echoed as if on the wind, but there was no breeze.

Fucking A. If I clenched my jaw any harder, I was going to crack a tooth, but I held fast and kept inching toward my home and my husband. Toward help.

"They know. Watch them." Icy water sluiced through my veins at the message.

"Watch who?" I asked before I remembered I was alone here except for whoever had been screaming in my field or the barn or—wait, no one had been at the chicken coop. Screw cautious steps. I sprinted up the stairs onto my porch and toward the warm glow of the lamps in my living room.

"They know." Urgency laced the woman's voice, though the words shimmered with the echo of being spoken underwater. Frigid air kissed the shell of my ear, burning the skin.

I stepped over the farmhouse's threshold and then reeled around. No one stood there. Picture-perfect white porch, shorn grass lawn, packed gravel driveway, and endless waves of cornstalks.

"Who?" I whispered, both wanting and very much not wanting an answer.

It wasn't fair that I was disappointed to receive only silence. No one was here with me. Had there ever been? Were the screams real? They'd stopped too.

The standard sounds of early morning on the farm resumed. The hum of insects, the whoosh of gentle movement in the tree nearby, and the steady exhale of my fear.

I woke Josh as gently as I could. Panic still blasted my veins, but one of us needed to be steady. I relayed the screams I'd heard, the lack of lights, the need to investigate to him.

My husband nodded, furrowing his brow more deeply with each detail I dropped.

He parted his lips a few times, like some trout mounted on a business bro's office wall. "Babe." The patronizing tone pooled at our feet. "I would have woken to that kind of screaming."

"You would sleep through a tornado." A real worry, to be honest.

"It's not a time for joking." He rested his hand on top of mine. "Are you sure you slept tonight?"

He leaned toward me with those concerned eyes, like he knew what was best.

"What is that supposed to mean?" I fought the urge to yank my hand from his touch.

He shrugged like he was the only sensible one. Like he hadn't just slept through the screaming show. "I only meant maybe you didn't get enough sleep tonight."

I jerked back, getting out of his reach. "Come the fuck on. I slept *right next* to you."

"I know you were here, but were you asleep? Did you take the medicine? It can have side effects."

Did he hear himself? "Are you trying to say I'm not capable of knowing if I'm awake or asleep?"

He cast a look toward the doorway, like if he turned away, I wouldn't catch him rolling his eyes. "This sounds like a waking nightmare, babe. Absolutely normal. You're not getting the rest your body craves; you're dealing with so much. It's normal for you to imagine—"

"I didn't imagine this!"

He muttered under his breath, but I swore I caught the word *barn*.

"Don't do this," I pleaded. "What if there's a little kid out in our field who needs our help?" Or a teenage girl. She wouldn't be the first.

"Why would there be a child out here? How would a little kid even *get* to our farm? It's a hell of a place to accidentally end up." My husband was wearing his professor face. He usually wore it when we ate dinner with his parents. He wanted to win a debate with logic, but this wasn't some thought experiment over dry turkey. This was real.

Don't yell. Don't get mad. Focus him. "I don't have those answers,

Josh. I just know there were *screams* on our farm, and I want to make sure no one is injured."

"If I go out there and there's no one, then what? Are we done with this?"

He looked to the ceiling as if asking the Lord for patience. Rich from a guy who was loudly agnostic.

"Done with what, exactly?" I pushed to my feet before he could reply. "You know, it doesn't matter. The longer we sit here talking about whether there's someone to save, the longer they're stuck in our fields."

I pulled on a pair of sneakers and snatched the flashlight Josh kept in his bedside table.

"I'm coming," my husband said, not hiding that this was a huge pain in his ass.

"Don't bother. You don't want to believe your wife. You can stay in bed." I stormed out while he was still searching for pants.

My blustering confidence waned once was I was outside again. Imminent daybreak warmed the horizon. A few of the chickens were awake, shuffling and clucking.

There were no cries or yelps.

I trudged down the steps and across the path. I pushed into the cornfield. The tacky leaves attempting to cling to my skin. I turned sideways as I ran in an attempt to cut down on the plant groping. I called out, but no one replied. Tilting the beam from the flashlight from side to side, I only saw rich soil and solid stalks. No bodies. No footprints. I must have entered the field at the wrong spot.

I backtracked, ready to find another entry point and try again.

As I approached the house, gravel popped against metal ahead. Dust billowed over the tops of the stalks.

"Down down down," the ghastly voice whispered on the wind.

I crouched instinctively, gaze and flashlight beam pointed at my feet. A slim silver ring, the kind one would stack with other simple bands, peeked from the dirt. One like I'd seen on the fingers poking out from the tarp in the barn.

Gruff conversation rumbled near the farmhouse.

I snagged the jewelry and tucked it in my pocket. Stepping out onto the drive, I found the old red pickup idling in front of my home. My husband stood, pajama pants flapping, arms folded over an old Metallica shirt, looking every bit the city guy vacationing on a farm. Inside the truck's cab were the younger farmhands. The tarp and its contents were no longer in the bed. Nearly a dozen preteen boys in long-sleeved shirts filled it instead. All very much alive, thank God.

"Probably foxes," the driver was saying to Josh.

"Really?" At least my husband had the sense to question that answer.

"They scream in communication," the farmhand replied. "Sounds like agony, but they're just talking."

Josh canted his head in disbelief. Nice to see him skeptical of another person for once. "Seems like we should have heard that before."

"Nah. They roam a pretty good distance," the driver said. He was the one I'd seen coming and going from the barn. How was *this* the person on my side and not the man in the PJ pants?

I stepped close to my husband, letting everyone see me, letting them know I was watching. "It didn't sound like an animal."

"Trust me. Those fox cries trick everyone the first time." The other farmhand chimed in from the other side of the cab. He tilted his ball cap brim toward me. It'd have been a respectful move if his eyes weren't on my braless chest. "You should keep an eye on your chickens."

Josh saw an easy exit from the conversation and leapt on it. "That's probably what brought the fox here in the first place."

It wasn't a fox. Couldn't the icy breath offer some guidance now? Were these the people I should watch? Because I'd already been watching this kid, and he was dangerous. I knew it in my bones.

Josh, clearly, had no such innate knowledge. "Thanks for stopping. We won't keep you. Tell Ray I'm heading to Grand Island again tomorrow, if he's making a run."

"Will do, Mr. Hauk." The farmhand behind the wheel slapped his palm on the outside of the truck and then drove away billowing black exhaust.

I was yet again left looking like the idiot.

It wasn't a fox. That kid knew more than he was saying. He was a part of this.

Josh rubbed slow circles on my back while we walked inside. Must be nice to move on so quickly.

I stepped away from his touch and made coffee without a single look backward. He lingered in the kitchen. We rarely fought, but only because my instinct was to rush with apologies. Not today.

The cut was deeper than Josh not believing anyone was in peril. I could buy the fox excuse as plausible without the other information—the blood I'd seen in the truck, the noose in the hayloft, the tinge of death that lingered beyond these walls, the way people spoke about the family who had lived here before. But to suggest I couldn't be trusted to know if I'd been asleep? Did he see me as so delicate, so breakable that I couldn't be permitted to be an autonomous adult?

He hadn't told me about the trek to Grand Island tomorrow, but now my mind sifted through the possibilities for while he was away. If he was headed to the airport, then he was leaving for longer than an afternoon. I'd wanted my rock here, but he wasn't that when he looked at me with pity.

I topped off my mug, for once happy to be gazing out the kitchen window at that godforsaken barn. I didn't know if the light had been on last night. I'd been too close to look up before, but also focused on other problems. A nervous laugh kicked in my chest.

"Em?" Hesitation pulled my name like taffy on Josh's tongue.

"Hmm?" I stared at the barn, appreciating that it was no longer my greatest worry. Josh could enjoy my back.

"Are you okay?" There was earnestness in the question.

But it was the wrong way to approach me. "Don't you want to decide that for me?"

His arms wrapped around me from behind. I squirmed and shrugged him off.

He slumped into one of the kitchen chairs. Crestfallen. "I'm sorry." I believed him. "I didn't mean to... I had just woken up and..."

"Waking up made you doubt your wife? Call her a liar?" That was a weak excuse.

"I never said—"

"You suggested I didn't know the difference between a dream and reality. That I didn't know if I was awake." Nope. We weren't doing that. He may be the more emotionally stable of our duo currently, but that didn't make me unreliable. And he was not perfect— but I wouldn't throw it in his face. We both deserved better than that. High road and such.

"I know you know what's real." He really wanted to believe what he was saying, but he couldn't hide the hitch in his shoulders. The pinch of his mouth, like the lie was bitter. "You were right about the screams."

"Even though they didn't wake you?"

"Guess we need a plan if there's a tornado watch?" His joke fell flat.

The fractured trust between us littered the tile. Could we decoupage it into a mosaic of what it once was?

I'd been so focused on convincing him to help me. Had I even had a chance? "Why can't you believe me?"

Josh dropped his head into his hands, elbows planted on his knees. "I do, Emily. I swear. These last six months have been hard. Losing Penelope broke a part of you, and I'm sincerely trying to help you."

Angry tears and hurt tears burned my eyelids all the same. "I know that. But there's a difference between helping me work through grief and turning your back on me."

That sobered him. "I would never."

"You did. This morning."

He rushed to hug me. This time I let him. "I'm scared. I only want to protect you. I'm going to be traveling more again, and I hate the idea of you not taking care of yourself."

"But I am."

"I get that. You're doing so much better." He was trying to convince himself, but that was a start. "The farm is busy, and I don't want anyone out there causing you heartache."

Busy was one word for it. Did the farmhand know I'd called the sheriff on him? I sipped my coffee to avoid derailing us. Never stop your husband mid-grovel.

"And I guess there are foxes this time of year?" He sighed. "I'll research natural deterrents and get it set up so they won't get so close to the house."

An idea struck me. "We need cameras."

"We live in rural Nebraska, babe. I'm not sure we need an alarm or security system like that." He was hedging like he didn't want me to panic. Sigh.

"Not for our house. For Cluckingham Palace." I could keep an eye on my chickens in the event this fox thing was real. But if we angled things right, I might get proof of whatever was happening in our barn too.

Josh might not believe me now, but he would.

When I ran the fields at first light, there was no sign of a crime. I found no body. No random accessories. No blood. Even the barn stayed 362 steps from my house both times I counted.

Emily's Running Log:

16 seconds to the barn—47 steps

2 minutes, 1 second to the barn—362 steps

2 minutes, 6 seconds to the barn—362 steps

16.5 miles ran today—Pushed hard out the gate. (Thanks, Josh.) Puked 7 miles in. Glucose chew and box breathing helped. Pace was trash.

CHAPTER 22

I RETURNED TO QUALITY COUCH EVENINGS THE NEXT NIGHT.
I wasn't about to be caught unaware by a scream or a song again. Not
tonight. Hopefully not ever again. Part of me wondered if Josh was
right, if I was losing it. But I could distract myself with the best of
them, and my favorite garbage reality show had copious seasons set
in numerous locations. Josh's only commentary when I'd switched
to the show around 10 p.m. was, "Why do they all have accents?"
Because they're Australian, Josh. Jeez. When the ninth person with
overly white teeth bounced onto the screen in a bathing suit, he
called it quits and crashed out.

Sleep remained elusive on my end. I'd put on a Stephen Sanchez
record—low volume, of course—around 2:30, I think? The singer's
1960s-era vibes mellowed my anxiety and filled the emptiness in
the house. Anything to drown out any potential music from the
barn. The eerie building had been mysteriously dark and silent since
I'd cowered in a corner while a farmhand threw a shovel atop a
bleeding tarp in the back of a pickup. Maybe that shit scared even

the broken-down barn. Or maybe I was supposed to have gotten a message.

Had I? That icy breath hadn't hit me again after I'd found the ring. I'd kept it in my pocket, like holding a touchstone to what was real. But the disembodied words and the dark frame of a woman's hair in the glass? They stuck with me endlessly. Whoever was warning me about the barn, about my husband, about *them*, wasn't a teenage Bridget Belkin. So who was she?

The anticipatory energy of today's plans coursed through my veins. My knee bounced every time I sat down. Because as soon as Josh left for this latest work trip, I was driving into Hastings. I'd already put in for the PTO. It would be "read old newspapers" day for Emily Hauk. Look, did I expect to be excited about reading hyped-up police blotters in the newspaper? No. Was the gossip about people I didn't know *fascinating*? Oh my God, yes. But I needed more than voyeuristic entertainment. I needed to know what had happened at this farm. Who had lived here before, and what exactly was it that no one wanted to tell me about the old Belkin farm? *We really need to rename this place.* Blue Sky Acres? Hauk Haven? Sanctuary Farm? Anything else.

The minutes ticked by. I pulled on an aqua sports bra and matching leggings, laced up my favorite trainers, and waited in my living room for the sun to ignite the horizon. The second it did, I blasted out the front door. I needed all the nervous energy gone before Josh was up. He would hesitate to leave me if I looked scared or, worse, fragile. He'd worry. I didn't want that burden on him, but also it wasn't useful. Worrying about what was happening in our barn, about who had been hurt in this place, about how whatever had happened on our farm would pull us into darkness—that was useful. He continued to pretend it was all normal. The screams. The songs. The mold. The lights.

I'd get him proof. Once he understood what was truly happening here, he'd back me. We could protect ourselves and others in the area from a killer, could save this new life, if we could work together.

I just had to show him the path.

Determination aside, I counted the steps to the barn, as usual—2,115. The farthest distance yet. Was the barn retreating because it knew I was on to something? I sucked in the damp morning air. Josh would shove more pills at me if I suggested the barn was sentient. I couldn't explain it, but the numbers in my notebook didn't lie. The barn shifted around this farm. Closer, farther. Warm and cold. Deadly and broken-down.

I ran until my legs shook, then turned and kept running back to the house. It took me 2,925 steps to get from the barn to my house this time. Farther still.

What was it retreating from?

Mold marred the dirt at the base of the barn, the sticky black oozing on the outside wall and creeping up near the raspberry bush. I plucked a handful, cradling them in my shirt, and brought them back to the house. If I was successful in today's research expedition, I was baking myself a reward pie.

Was it as satisfying as picking up the perfect cheesecake from the tiny Italian bakery down the street from my mom's house? No, but I'd use fruit from my farm and eggs from my hens, and honestly, that made it taste better. Or at least I hoped it would. YouTube assured me making piecrust was easier than sourdough, and I'd become ace at the latter during the early pandemic days.

I hurried back toward the house, leaping a puddle of ichor. Berries dumped in a bowl and chickens mucked and fed, I had time to shower and dress before Josh even shuffled out of bed.

"How long have you been up?" An expletive was buried beneath his muttered grumble. Mornings could be hard for him. Especially mornings after he'd cleared the cache of beer from the back of the refrigerator.

I let the dig slide, poured him a cup of coffee, and added a quick glug of creamer to make it the perfect umber.

"The usual. I like running when the fields are just waking." No need to tell him I didn't *actually* sleep last night.

Josh rasped his fingers over the scruff on his chin. "How did your mom cope with you being such an early riser?"

There was a genuine curiosity in the question. It didn't stop the sting of loss from spearing my heart. It was a tiny needle though. As though I were one of those little tomato cushions seamstresses used to store their unused pins.

"I didn't mean—" He backpedaled before even sipping his coffee.

I waved off his concern. "It's fine. I like talking about her." There was life in memory. Being remembered was the only way we could ever be immortal. Even if it punched my gut every time.

He shook his head with chagrin. "It's hard to imagine Penelope awake before noon."

"She did it when I was a kid. To get me to school. Though I suspect she crashed right into her bed once I was in the building." The images of my mother in satin pajamas and flip-flops staggering in the elementary school drop-off line and, a few years later, staggering toward the bus stop were vivid in my mind. The chartreuse fabric fluttering against her honeyed skin, her hand clutching the button between her breasts as we hustled to the ride, lest she flash a teacher. Our neighbors had long been beyond being scandalized.

"It's true Mom was never a morning person." I filled my favorite water bottle with the filtered H_2O from the refrigerator door. "I'm not sure she even noticed I was purposely up early until high school."

I snickered. At Josh's questioning look, I filled him in. "When I started morning workouts and she realized it? It was like I'd told her boy bands were better than Otis Redding. Abject horror."

"I thought she wasn't judgey about what people listened to." That note of "Hey, you promised she thought I was cool" was a bit much, but Josh was enjoying the levity as much as I was.

"Oh, she was very 'love what you love,' but also 'you don't talk shit about the greats.'"

"So she judged my taste in music?" Josh's eyes remained bleary, but the conversation and caffeine certainly sobered him in the kindest of ways.

"She judged everyone's taste." I patted him on the back. "Don't worry though, I'm pretty sure she thought even Trent Reznor's taste wasn't as good as hers. And he's a literal genius."

"Did you just compare me with the guy from Nine Inch Nails?"

"You're welcome." I slid into the chair next to him, letting our knees brush.

The corner of his mouth quirked up, in that mischievous way that said good distractions were imminent. Why then did I change the subject? What was wrong with me? "I've been thinking about ways we can add greenery to the house."

Josh snorted. Coffee splattered out, mostly into the mug.

Crisis averted. "Are you okay?"

"Are you?" Humor razzed the air; the earlier accusatory tone *poof*-ing out.

I smirked. "I've already run fourteen miles and tended to the hens. I've got plans to bake pie later. I'm peak productive farm wife."

"Babe, I love you, but the farm *is* green."

Oh, that. "The fields are, absolutely. I just think a trellis near the garden would be nice. Maybe grow some herbs in the windowsill."

"We have a garden." He didn't disagree, but his confusion was palpable.

"There's a continuity in life. Carrying that earthy vibrance from outside to inside brings good vibes. It's science."

"Science?" He leaned closer, clearly delighted in the lighter conversation.

"Pretty much." It probably was. My Google searches had been a lot more bad vibes lately. He did not need to know those details just yet.

There were a great many things my husband would debate. Vibes were not one of them. "A little indoor greenery wouldn't hurt us, I suppose."

Why did he tempt fate like that? As long as the seeds are from the store and not randomly plucked from the acreage, it'd be fine.

"I can pick up seeds today," I offered.

"You're venturing into town?"

I tried not to be offended by his surprise.

"We're getting low on chicken feed," I lied.

Josh's hand found my knee under the table. He squeezed. "You can just admit you miss Starbucks."

The heat dappling my cheeks was real, even if his guess was so very wrong. "Got me."

"You probably have rewards languishing on your account. Free coffee is the best coffee." He slipped into a story about a coworker's preferred order on free drink days. Josh shook his head like the guy's work to get every penny out of the megacorporation was pitiful. I liked free things but also was too lazy to craft a special expensive drink just to get the biggest bang for my free buck.

Of course I didn't care about coffee today—well, I always cared about coffee, but today wasn't about a grande flat white. I wished it were. How different our rural life would be if I wasn't stealing off to the library to research a missing girl, her dead mother, and the family who had run this farm long before we moved here. Imagine being able to just enjoy the silence, appreciate the still summer nights, and only venture from the farmstead for a little treat.

"If you're hitting up the feedstore though, can you pick up a couple things for me too?" Josh tossed back the last of his morning brew.

"You could always come with me." I waggled my eyebrows like some B-movie starlet tempting him to a dark fate.

"You forgot?" He pressed a hand over his heart, feigning injury.

"I thought you left tomorrow?" Disgust rippled through my center at how convincing I was. The sadness tightening my mouth was real, but not because my husband was leaving for another work trip, but because somehow I'd become the partner that awaited his departure. We weren't supposed to be those people.

The barn had made us into them. The farm and its secrets wedged between us. Whatever was happening here had settled into our marriage like a third wheel, and until he acknowledged the reality, we couldn't expunge it.

So I lied to him. I faked longing and forgetfulness and shoved the bitterness of self-disgust into the hidden pockets between my ribs. I only felt them every time I breathed. No big deal.

Josh had conscripted lead farmer Ray into acting as his ride to the airport again. An hour later Josh was ready to leave.

"Are you sure you don't want me to drive you? I'm going to Hastings anyway today." It was my guilt offering. Adding the extra four hours in the car would severely cut my library time.

"He'll be here shortly," Josh said, zipping his suitcase closed. It was a compact roll-aboard. Enough room to stash both his gym shoes and the fancy dress shoes that gnawed at his heel but made him look *boss*.

By the time Ray arrived, we looked like an odd couple—or maybe like exactly who we were now. Summertime work-from-home wife and traveling tech bro. He'd trimmed his beard short but hadn't shaved. His hair was slicked back enough to be polished without looking like he was trying. Jeans, a sport jacket, and the casual loafers said, "I'm working, but I'm cool." Honestly, he was hot.

I told him so.

He snagged me by the waist, pressing my body to his. His lips brushed mine as he spoke. "Like you don't know every inch of your skin begs me to stay."

My cutoff shorts weren't booty-level, but they made sure my hard work training for the marathon was fully exposed. My pink tank top was just a regular arms-out affair. Josh's words, though, made me feel like I was in some skimpy lingerie. I didn't hate it.

Guilt sloshed up the sides of my neck. Here was my hot husband, turning those heated eyes on me, and I had been ushering him out the door because he couldn't handle what was happening with me yet.

Josh's fingertips skated across my shoulder, dancing down my arm to the simple drugstore lily tattooed on my forearm. A mother-daughter tattoo. Mom had a brilliant, colorful Stargazer lily. I went for black-and-gray alstroemeria. Pinpricks and goose bumps followed his touch.

A gentle *rap rap rap* resounded from the front door. The glass panes in the door rattled a bit. They hadn't selected the door for how it held up to the randos who tried to sell fictitious magazine subscriptions. Soliciting wasn't a problem when you were miles and miles from town. We had different problems. Like a barn that stalked me. And the farmhand who had committed crimes inside it.

Now that I thought about it, I missed the magazine guys. And the security systems dudes.

Josh released me and opened the door for Ray.

"Come on in. Can I get you a cup of coffee?" I offered, hoping the pot I'd made earlier hadn't turned bitter.

"I appreciate the offer, Mrs. Hauk, but I'm good." The farmer didn't enter. The porch creaked beneath his shifting weight, but he kept his boots on the other side of the threshold.

"Call me Emily." I used my winningest smile. Or at least I thought it was. It didn't melt any of the tension wafting off the man.

He shuffled. "Sure. We need to get going, Josh."

No formalities for my husband. Of course not. Josh waved an arm toward the man in a "just a second" fashion. "I need to grab one more thing, and I'll be ready."

My husband disappeared into our bedroom.

Ray inspected the eaves of my house, the bolts securing the porch swing, looking anywhere but at me. But this was an opportunity, and I was quickly learning I had to take them when they *poof*-ed into my path.

"Since I have you here," I said, waiting for Ray to look at me. His attention flitted over my face and then past my shoulder. Josh hadn't returned yet.

He cleared his throat. "Yeah?"

"I wanted to thank one of your guys, but I can't remember his name for the life of me."

"Oh, I'm sure whatever was no bother."

"Still, I just feel terrible not knowing their names. I was raised to believe knowing first and last names is important."

He made a thick sound of agreement deep in his throat. "Who is it you're asking after?"

The creepy guy who is in the barn all the time? I couldn't say that.

"Younger guy," I started, fumbling for a good way to describe the young man I'd seen with the pickup, with the tarp. "I usually see him driving that red pickup?"

Ray's eyes narrowed, lines deepening at the corners. "Those boys bothering you? The deputies came by—"

"Oh," I fumbled. *Shit shit shit.* Thinking quickly, I went with a half-truth. "I wanted to thank them for hauling some trash for me."

Ray lifted his chin in acknowledgment, though skepticism never left his hardened gaze. "Few of my guys use the pickup." He rattled off a few men's names with a clear expectation that they'd click for me.

"Nick maybe? He was driving a whole bunch of young boys into the field the other morning."

Ray chuckled. "Our detasselers." His stance loosened. This was safe territory for him. "Hope none of them gave you trouble. They're hard workers, but young boys are young boys, if you catch my drift."

I didn't think poor choices had anything to do with gender, but I suspected he wasn't up for a gender studies conversation. Though with how hard he leaned on the *Mrs.* when he talked to me, he could use it.

"Everyone was polite. You can be proud."

"Good, good. The two guys who handle that crew are Nick Ditmer and Tyler Jorgensen."

"I'd ask which one wears the Huskers cap—"

"That's all of us, Mrs. Hauk." Ray adjusted the brim of his own hat.
I laughed because it was expected and not a frustrating data point on my journey to answers.

"Before I forget," Ray said, brightening. "One of the guys tagged a nice early-season buck the other weekend. Tyler will drop by some venison jerky for you later this week, if you want it."

I said yes with more enthusiasm than the offer warranted. *Was that what had been in the back of the truck the other night?* I thumbed the ring in my pocket and thought about what I'd said to the police. *"Deer don't have fingers."*

The wheels on Josh's suitcase clacked over the hardwood to join us. His hand pressed against my lower back before he was even in line with me.

He stepped around to face me. "You sure you're going to be good while I'm gone?"

"I'm good. I've got work, the hens, *Love Island*." All the playfulness in my tone earned me a flash of his dimple.

"Keep the phone handy though? Gotta see my girl somehow." There was a prurient undercurrent that had Ray shuffling his way down the steps toward his truck. A black quad cab.

I dropped my voice to a whisper. "You're going to scandalize the farmer."

"I want to scandalize *you*." Where was this intensity coming from? Why had Josh held this back until right before he left?

I planted a kiss on his cheek. "You should have taken me up on driving you."

"I'll tell Ray to leave." His breath was hot against my neck.

"You will do no such thing!" I slapped his arm. "That guy is already grumpy with me. I can't have the farmers hate me."

"They can't hate you."

Because they don't know me. The implication was clear. Josh had kept the farm and the house separate in his mind. Only the knot in my chest said the two were tangled. What had happened here was tied to out there. Now and in the past. The barn demanded my attention. It taunted me. And each time I'd entered its eerie walls, I'd come away with an aching sense of dread and the knowledge that darkness lived there.

Josh kissed me in a way that Ray would be thankful to have not seen. Heat, need, and a promise filled that kiss. I stood at the front door, fingers against my mouth, breathless.

Josh was my best ally. He'd back me once he understood what had truly happened here, what was still happening. He'd see the danger we were in, this place was in, and he'd help me turn this farm into the haven it was promised to be.

The stippled petals on my forearm caught my attention. Simple, clean, beautiful. My mom had not been great about keeping fresh flowers in the house. We'd pick them up every time we walked to a market, but they'd languish in the vase unattended for weeks until the water was mostly gone, the stems were brittle, and crunchy petals littered the table. Her follow-through came through where it mattered most. She never missed a parent-teacher conference. She'd dragged her friends to my art shows in my junior and senior years. She'd loudly praise my work, usually at the expense of everything around it. Once a critic, always a critic, I supposed.

Her priorities had always been ensuring I knew I was loved and valued, and then music, career, and everything else after. Flowers fell *way* after. But it was why she'd suggested we get a bloom on our bodies. "No work after it heals. No watering, no trimming. Just beauty that we can enjoy and share."

Mom would have believed me. She would have heard that first song and known it was real. Tiny fires lit behind my eyes, tightening everything. I pressed a hand to my chest, as though I could pack the emptiness within.

The dust kicked up by Ray's tires had long settled by the time my tears fell. Anger rode on the back of them.

Mom's voice—a memory—resounded in my mind. *"Emmy Bear, you do what you need to do. Get answers and make them believe."*

I tapped the two men's names Ray had provided into the notes app on my phone. If the library could tell me the Belkins' secrets, maybe it could also reveal a truth or two about Nick Ditmer and Tyler Jorgensen.

Emily's Running Log:

11 minutes, 45 seconds to the barn—2,115 steps
16 minutes, 16 seconds to the barn—2,925 steps—It just keeps getting farther from my house. Is that a good thing?
14.2 mile run—Only 20% red heart rate. Improvement, I guess.
Didn't run into the farmhands today, but I swear they were in the field next to me.

CHAPTER 23

MY DRIVE INTO HASTINGS WAS QUICK AND QUIET. I'D LET Spotify play DJ and ignored whatever it cultivated. My mind whipped a whirlwind of teenagers' names.

Bridget Belkin.

Tyler Jorgensen.

Nick Ditmer.

How was it I'd moved to the middle of nowhere and fallen into this mess? I'd driven away from the gossip that was perpetually active over on Haight. Away from the technology sector and its eighteen-dollar drinks. Away from the judgment in every gym I'd ever visited in the Bay Area. I'd left all those eyes, and yet now I was seeking drama. I was looking into *kids*. I mean, sure, the farmhands were definitely this side of legal, but there was technically an adult and *actually* an adult. One doesn't see the difference until they cross the line into the latter. There was a time I'd believed paying for my own health insurance made me an adult. Then my mom got sick, and I realized I was going to be alone. Like, run my life with no parent to phone for help. That was being an adult, and it was garbage.

Making sense of what was happening on my farm, of the screams, of the people, it sure felt like that kind of alone. That kind of adulting level.

Were the farmhands still kids? I hoped so. But I thought about the way I'd seen them stare into that pickup. I thought about the way the tall one—Tyler, I thought—talked to whatever lay beneath that tarp the other night. He was no child. Was that his fault?

Hell if I knew. Blame didn't matter now. My goal was to understand what had happened at my house. Why the barn crept closer some days and farther on others. Whose voice spoke to me when the room went cold? And why was she there?

My mind was solid, reliable. I trusted what I'd experienced and what my gut said. Something terrible had happened in that barn, was *still* happening in that barn. And the family who lived here first had to be the place to start.

And that meant I needed to know more about the Belkins.

Librarians are the best people. This is not an opinion, but a fact. I met Courtney at the front desk of the Hastings Public Library, and she was more than happy to leave her post to help me set up in their materials archive room.

Courtney was probably five years younger than me, but with

infinitely more style. Her brown hair was pinned back with a rainbow barrette. Her tapered black pants made the cherry-red Mary Janes on her feet pop.

"It's usually the high schoolers dominating the newspaper archive. We've been trying to digitize everything, but archival funding only goes so far." She led me to a machine that she cued up with the local paper from the years I'd asked for and then walked me through using the machine.

"You sure you don't want help looking?" she offered, not for the first time. I couldn't tell if Courtney was nosy or bored, but I wasn't ready to take her up on the invite. If I wasn't able to tell my husband what I was doing, I didn't think it was fair to divulge it to a random cool lady I met at the library.

"I don't need help yet, but maybe after I get a little deeper into things," I said.

Her shoulders slumped. "Of course." She started to leave but turned back for a moment. "Make sure to keep your coffee close. It spills, and it'll be a whole thing."

She didn't tap the No FOOD OR DRINK sign, but the message was received.

I threw back the last few sips of my Starbucks and then tossed the cup. "Better safe than sorry."

Her smile was kind.

I had an idea. "Actually, Courtney?"

She perked. Eyes wide, hopeful. "Yeah?"

"Are you from around here?"

Her face brightened when she smiled. "Most everyone is."

"Not me." I punched as much self-deprecation into the comeback as I could.

She slipped down in the chair next to me without invitation. "I put that together."

"Because only high schoolers come to the library to look at the archives?"

"It's good for year-end papers and true-crime reports. Ohmigod, are you like a podcaster?"

I really wished I were the celebrity she saw. "Nope. I don't even listen to podcasts. Though my husband blasts through *Armchair Expert* like it's necessary for his health."

We bantered for a bit. She'd grown up in a small town—her words—outside of Hastings, but moved to the city—again, her words—for college and never left. She'd visited California when she was eleven in the name of Mickey Mouse and Sleeping Beauty's castle and was disheartened to hear how long of a drive it was from my mom's house to Disney.

People always forget that California is huge.

"I can't believe you just picked up and moved thousands of miles." Courtney eased back in her chair but made even a slouch seem poised.

"Sometimes I can't either." I stretched my legs forward, crossing them at the ankles. "This place is magical though."

"Is it?" She was awful disbelieving for a woman who had chosen to stay in the beauty of the Heartland.

"The air, the sunrises, the quiet? Epic." This was why I needed to find answers. Yes, I needed to stop whatever might be happening on my farm, but I also needed to reclaim this parcel of peace I'd made mine.

"You seem outdoorsy." Courtney made this sound like a condition that was untreatable.

Perhaps it was. "And?"

"And I'm wondering what you could be looking for here that was worth being inside."

Was I so transparent?

"I like inside too." My chill couch time was not to be discounted. "But I'm looking into the people who used to own my home."

"Why?" Courtney did not hide her judgment.

Luckily, I'd grown up in a house where the only thing filtered was the coffee. "Someone died there."

"Some of the houses around here are more than a hundred years old. Not sure that is unusual." Courtney pursed her lips, like another thought was forming behind them. "Who died in your house?"

"I don't know," I hedged.

"Then how do you know they died?" As soon as she asked the questions, her eyes flared white. "Is your place, like, haunted?"

"I'm not saying that." Because doing so would make this all too real.

"What are you saying?" Did she realize she was leaning toward me now, like a few inches would make me spill my secrets?

"I live on a farm. The wife of the couple who owned it last died falling from the hayloft. Not in my house. But I don't think it stops there." I paused, waiting to be dismissed, but Courtney simply listened. I continued. "There are men walking around my property all the time, and I don't know them at all. I don't know what happened to the people who lived in the house before me, and I don't know if those guys in my field"—in my barn—"are related."

"Oh, man. So the family still farms the land, but you live there? I didn't know farm gentrification was even possible."

I tried not to flinch but failed. "Ouch. I moved in, but didn't displace anyone. Not the same."

She held up her hands in surrender. "Poor choice of words. It would be hard to work the land you no longer own. That's all."

"The land is theirs to use. I just wanted the house."

Courtney's eyebrows pinched, but even hardened, she held a friendly tone. "I can tell you're here because you care about them."

I care about who they might hurt. "I just want to know what happened. When you buy a house from across the country, the Realtor isn't going to tell you everything. I'm trying to do right."

The tension in the room ebbed.

"You are." Courtney nodded once, a decision clearly made. "And you are in luck. In addition to hooking you up with old newspapers, I am your go-to person for genealogy. If you're living on a farm, then it probably passed from brother to brother or father to son."

"Until it passed to me and my husband."

She shrugged, that earlier judgey-ness blunted. "Farming is a hard business. Sometimes people just want out."

Minutes and hours ticked by in the library. On Courtney's recommendation, I tried the nearby Runza restaurant for lunch. Sated by the local chain's signature beef-and-cabbage pocket sandwich and the crispiest fries of my life, I returned to reading all the small-town gossip I could. Drinking was prevalent in the incidents reported. Underage parties. Drunk driving where cars were towed from ditches. DUIs and DWIs—the difference I couldn't suss, but the impact was the same regardless. Sprinkled between the alcohol and narcotic lines were domestic "incidents" and public disturbances.

The noise complaints had at first made me think of my least favorite neighbor in our old building. That woman would complain about anything if she had the chance, but never to our faces. She'd call the super. She'd file a complaint with the admin office. She'd even slipped a note into our mailbox after I'd played music during a 5 a.m. workout.

But after scrolling through several years of the "Smoke & Sirens" stories in the local paper, it was clear those complaints held greater implications than the charges listed. One person calling to get help for a friend, a sister, another loved one. Because these people didn't live stacked on top of one another. There was no one fifteen steps from your front door to ask for help in rural Nebraska.

My home had frequently been the destination of these disturbance complaints. The local authorities had been checking in at my house for years. My new librarian friend, Courtney, helped me pull an older set of papers. Before Bridget Belkin had even been born, the sheriff's department had been making regular journeys to the farmhouse. Deeper dives only brought dead ends with "both parties refused to press charges."

Both parties. As if there was equity in abuse. Herb and Alice, Bridget's parents, weren't the only ones. Walter and Mary Belkin had the same story a generation earlier. What was it about this place that wrecked people? Had another woman's pain—multiple other women's pain—saturated my walls? The flooring had been replaced and the drywall painted, but had we painted over something horrible?

I shivered against the hard plastic chair. Its unforgiving bite bringing focus. No, this wasn't on me. None of this had happened because of Josh and me. These were stories about the old Belkin farm. Not my farm. Only it was the same acreage that held Cluckingham Palace and the windowsill I was totally going to let pies cool on. What made me so different from the Belkin women? I'd already experienced the seventeen-minute wait for deputies to come help me. What had they seen from my kitchen window?

Courtney dropped into the chair next to me. Her stainless-steel water bottle clanked against the tabletop. "How's it going?"

I wasn't sure how to reply. I'd discovered that violence had been commonplace at my farm for generations. Was that what I'd needed?

I scratched a phantom itch on my elbow. I didn't want to lie. Instead I told her what I needed next. "I wish I could find out why the family sold their farm."

Courtney straightened.

I tried to suck back in the statement, certain I was asking too much. "Sorry. My brain's going a mile a minute over here. It looks like there was a lot of friction on that farm over the years."

I gestured toward the screen. I'd highlighted a 9-1-1 call from the farmstead from the 1980s.

"How much do you know about modern agriculture?" Courtney

said this with the smoothness of requesting your usual coffee order from a barista you'd seen every morning for years.

I fumbled. I had not forgotten her comment from when she'd heard we'd leased the land back to actual farmers. "Not a lot. I mean, I certainly see everyone working and machines and whatnot, but farming isn't my..."

"Yeah, I got that you're not a farmer. That's fine." She fluttered her fingers toward me in some dismissive spirit-fingers move. "I'm not either. I don't even want to live over ten minutes from a grocery store, but you do you."

"You get used to it." I shrugged. I'd had groceries delivered in California. Now I just planned further out. I hadn't ventured inside a grocery store back home—my old home—in years.

"I'm sure you do." She waved off the comment. "I asked about farming because you want to know why they'd sell. The modernization of farming has cut back the work available, but also it's a *hard* business."

That was obvious within the first week in Nebraska. "The guys who work the land at our acreage are on site twelve hours a day, easily."

"Exhausting just to think about." Courtney slouched in her seat. Zero judgment on her face. Thank God.

"Are you implying that the people who had the farm before us bailed because it was hard?" I arched a brow. "I get the impression most people go down with the ship, and we didn't buy under foreclosure." They might not have disclosed a death on the property, but they would have told us *that*.

"Let's see where they moved then." Courtney popped up to her feet like we'd made a decision. I got the distinct impression that she liked having a project and I was clearly today's task.

Fair enough because I needed the help. Why hadn't I thought to look up where Herb Belkin was now?

Courtney moved to sit at a computer on the other side of the room. She asked for the names again but was already typing before I finished talking. "Huh."

"That's not a helpful noise," I hedged.

"Well, the guy Herb bought a house up in York." She tapped a bit more. "Right next to one of his brother's houses."

I didn't bother asking where York was. I'd heard the name, and I could look it up later. Another city. "You know who his brothers are?"

Pink dappled her cheeks. "Digging into it this morning was more interesting than the other tasks on my desk."

"Why did you ask for their names then?" I appreciated her helpfulness, but did she already know the Belkin family drama? Was it dangerous to tell this woman I was looking into the past? Haunted looks had stolen all joy from the faces of the VFW set from the truck stop breakfast place when I mentioned where I lived, when Bridget came up. Was Courtney young enough to have known her?

"It makes people feel better when I ask questions while I work." She was still clicking around on the page, but there was a waver in her words. "People don't like when you dig into their lives without permission."

Someone had told her that. A bunch. "Well, I asked," I reminded her. "But I'm having you look into other people's lives. Is that better or worse?"

"As long as someone is making the request, my guilt is mitigated." There was a wryness that made me believe guilt had not been in the cards before the permission either.

"Okay. Then tell me how you know about his brother," I prompted.

"Did I mention I'm a genealogy expert?" She tapped the Enter key hard and then pushed the keyboard forward across the table like a mic drop. "There it is."

I stared at the property tax details on the page. Herb Belkin owned a house in York, Nebraska. I could plug it into my Maps app later and see how far away he was.

"What am I missing?" I asked, because it was clear Courtney saw something far more interesting on the screen.

"No wife."

"Ah, yeah, she's the one who had the accident."

Courtney puckered her lips, wagging the pout from side to side. Then toggled to another tab. Three taps later. "Oh wow. I remember this story."

Courtney leaned to the side to show me the full screen. The newspaper headline read: "Mother of Missing Girl Found Dead."

All the warmth in my body drained. My face froze, my fingertips tingled, my chest ached.

A photo of a slender woman with dark brown hair teased enough to create the illusion of height filled the right side of the screen. Beside her was the beaming teen face of her daughter. I recognized them both. Bridget from my earlier investigation, but Alice... She'd been in the photos I'd found in the barn—the ones mottled with black mold.

And she'd stood behind me. In my house. A terrifying visage reflected in my windows.

Alice Belkin was dead, but she wasn't gone.

CHAPTER 24

I CUT COLD BUTTER INTO SMALL CUBES AND MUSHED IT INTO my flour-salt combination with a fork. The stabbing motion made for a lot of clinking of metal against my glass mixing bowl. Really putting the Pyrex to the test.

I switched to squeezing the pastry dough between my fingers. The food blogger I'd found said a food processor was easiest, but she liked to use her hands. I needed to touch something tangible. Alice had died on my farm. I'd known that, but the truth that she'd never left? That she'd loomed in our house? That she was the one whispering warnings about Josh? The pie was supposed to be my reward for finding answers at the library. *Ding ding ding.* Lucky me. Now making pie felt like my only chance at getting out of my head. Baking was methodical. Perform each step correctly, and you get the correct result. I deserved *something* to work out correctly. And so I squished that butter into the flour until I had a ball worthy of rolling out. I popped the base into the oven for a partial bake.

The raspberries I'd collected over the last few days filled another bowl. There was no uniformity in the container. Light mauves to rich purples. Petite berries the size of the end of my pinky finger were nestled beside bold plump ones that were wider than my thumb.

Had Alice Belkin planted that bush? Were these the fruits of her labor? Literally? My hands trembled, but I dumped the berries into a saucepan with sugar. The emptied bowl knocked against the counter. The harsh bite against my ears also ignited an ache in my chest.

"Why would you plant a bush on the other side of the barn?" I asked, like the dead woman stood here with me.

I stared out the window over the sink. Blue skies faded into dusty pinks and oranges as the day was winding down. The barn was stalwart. Looming in its dingy red. Heat from the pan warmed my fingers. Right. Pie filling. I broke my attention away from the barn and returned to the task at hand. Brilliant warmth burst from the fresh fruit. I stirred and tried to focus on the steps of making a pie.

Beyond the window a farmhand lingered beside the barn door. My mixing slowed, and I turned fully toward the glass. The guy's attention turned to my house, to me. His lip curled in a sneer I hadn't seen before.

I blinked and he was gone. I waited, my shallow breathing and the bubbling of berries on the stove filled the room, but no one emerged from the barn.

I refocused on the pie.

I was going to eat this whole dessert in the next twenty-four hours. It probably wasn't great for my blood sugar, but then my cortisol levels had to be bonkers anyway. Switching to two-a-day runs while Josh was gone was tempting. It would let me clear my head.

I picked up my phone, flipping from the baking blog article in the browser over to my thread with Josh. I'd sent him a pic of my latte this morning and he'd replied with his "boring hotel drip" in a paper cup. The normal playfulness of the exchange eased the weight of the day enough to want to talk to him. Josh liked a playful smirk. I snapped a quick selfie and sent it to him.

> **Emily**: Miss you. 😘
>
> **Emily**: Baking a pie now. LMK when your meetings are done today
>
> **Josh**: Love that face
>
> **Josh**: There's a dinner thing 2nite will call after
>
> **Emily**: I'll wait up.
>
> **Josh**: LOL We both know u were going 2 b up anyway

The trilling *beep beep beep* of the oven timer jerked my attention back. I turned, readying to nix the sound and get my crust from the oven.

Everything stopped.

The barn was outside my window. Not looming in the distance. The haggard wood walls, the peeling paint, they were pressed against the glass pane above my kitchen sink. There was no sky. There was no garden. No sunlight. Only the decrepit edifice.

Silence squeezed my skull. Fire lit my fingertips. A steady throb at the back of my neck was out of sync with my racing heartbeat. Darkness swallowed the room. The crinkle of fracturing glass shot through my mind.

Denial roared in my chest, but I still tried to scream. Sound was swallowed by the shadow of the barn, now fallen over my kitchen, my body. A panicked look at the door proved it was closed and I was sealed in. The oven indicator light remained illuminated. A blue flame rose from a burner, licking out toward me in a shot of orange. My gaze flicked from one corner of the room to the next, though my body refused to so much as flinch. Shadows stretched around me. Inky blackness. Charcoal.

Minutes ticked by. Hours. Days? The peeling paint of the barn wall curled against the pane of glass between us. Beckoning me? Pushing me? Sickness splashed the back of my throat, but I couldn't muster up the strength to swallow. The acrid bite lingering, welling tears.

I waited for the voice.

For her.

For a warning. Or instructions.

But no one spoke. I shut my eyes as tightly as I could. Was this house meant to swallow women? Alice had died here. Her daughter had gone missing. What about the women before that? What did they have to do with this barn now pressing against my home as if only the solid wood framing kept it from crushing me too.

The window whined. An aching groan that reverberated in my sternum. The heavy heartbeat in my ears turned sluggish. Sweat slicked my back, and if fear weren't holding me upright, I would have melted right into the floor.

The men who had lived here, who worked here now, never hesitated around this barn. They flitted in and out of that building like nothing nefarious had ever occurred there—as though they knew they were never in danger.

Or perhaps because they *were* the danger.

Sound rebounded, a rubber band of noise snapping against my very soul. The incessant cry of the timer. The softer call of cicadas chattering in the late afternoon. The buzz of my phone against the floor tile, its vibration cascading against my foot. The double-timed late verse in the Flobots song playing from the Bluetooth speaker on the counter.

I peeked through squinted eyes, as though my lashes could guard me. The barn was back by the fields, boring and unassuming. I skittered toward the sink, grasping the counter to keep from tumbling to the floor. Beyond the glass, my garden was a patchwork of greens and reds. The hens, though, were all inside the roost at Cluckingham Palace. Beyond both, back near the edge of the southern crops rose the barn. The interior lights were off, but the broken windowpane at the top of the loft seemed to wink at me. The prickle of adrenaline continued to zap my fingers. I gulped down air like I'd sprinted to the barn and back instead of standing alone in my kitchen.

My phone rattled against the floor, and the oven timer beeped, but the thought of breaking eye contact with the worn walls of the barn sent my tummy tumbling. I squeezed the counter as if it were my anchor, but after counting to one hundred and still standing alone in the silence, I began to let go.

"What am I supposed to make of this?" I said to no one, probably. Fear loosened my lips. "You've warned me before. You must have advice now."

But there was no voice. No woman with a warning.

Just me. Standing alone in my kitchen. Waiting.

A fleck of gray paint clung to my window. The only hint this had truly happened.

Move, Emily. You can do this. I refocused myself. I quieted the timer, pulled my piecrust from the oven, and tried to pretend I hadn't just seen the barn wall's peeling paint pressed to my window like it was spying on me. Josh thought I was hallucinating. He believed everything with the barn was in my mind.

"Maybe he's right." I sighed. I focused on filling the pie and adding a lattice to the top. My hands shook, but the movement steadied my heart.

Focus on the pie. Focus on what's real.

Only, the women who lived here before had been real.

Their deaths were real.

The bloody hand in the back of that pickup had been real.

"Watch the boys." I jerked at the ghastly woman's scratchy voice.

"Alice?" It had to be her. The picture, her death, it all made me believe she was with me.

"Watch the boys." The ghost's message carried an amused lilt. Did that mean I was right?

"Who?" I asked, not daring to move.

A cold knuckle nudged me toward the window. Toward the pane that separated me from the barn. The farmhands drove past the barn and my house and off to the highway. The truck bed filled with dusty, sweaty preteens.

"Which one?" I asked, but Alice didn't reply. I turned slowly, but no one was in the kitchen with me—human or apparition.

I put the pie in the oven.

"Am I losing it? What if this is all in my head?" I could very well be the type of person not built for solitude. Or grief. My mom had lived her life surrounded by boisterous bands, and I'd gone the opposite. Quiet one-on-ones made me happiest. Maybe I was missing something in my DNA. Mom would know. If I could call her, tell her what was happening, she'd have answers.

She'd believe me. She always believed me.

"Just because someone else's truth is different from yours, it doesn't invalidate how you feel, Emmy Bear. We can only trust ourselves, and if I have to believe anyone other than myself, it's going to be my daughter." Her voice was still rich in my mind. How long would that last? How long would I hear her? How long until the voice I remembered was an echo, a best guess?

"Mom," I said like she was here and not ashes scattered in Golden Gate Bay. "How can I explain a barn moving?"

She didn't answer, but then what had I expected?

Talking to her eased the tension around my heart though. "You were the one who taught me about braving anything on my own. You were never scared to go to a new place, to try a new food, a new dance, a new life. But the longer I live here, the more I feel like I can't live up to that."

Not that she'd ever asked that of me. Josh's parents hated that he hadn't gone into programming, but my mom had been chill about me not even wanting to so much as play an instrument.

Her voice, from a memory, caught me now. *"Your ability to bring colors together, to structure a room, a page, an art installation, it's a gift."* She saw art in everything. At least I got that from her. This farm could be a masterpiece. But the balance was off. The risk that came with that barn, with whatever that guy—Tyler Jorgensen—had done there before, was doing now. It was more than killing the vibe; it was stealing life. The barn was dangerous, and there was no way that day with the shovel and the person beneath a tarp in his truck was an isolated event.

The newspaper had said Alice Belkin's death had been a tragic accident. A loose floorboard. A fall in the wrong direction. Bad timing. Wrong place, wrong time. All the phrases people used to absolve themselves of the truth: Alice had been in danger long before she'd died.

Why didn't the police look at the barn? Had they even considered that she'd been killed? The number of dropped domestic complaints against Herb should have at least made them ask questions. Had Tyler been here then? I'd let him drive off with blood seeping from beneath the tarp in the back of his truck. What else had he gotten away with? Alice had died just outside the barn. Had Tyler hurt Alice? Bridget? Both of them?

What could I do to get the police to take this seriously? To get Josh to believe me? I'd found the ring, but there had to be more in the truck. The deputy said they'd checked it out, but they'd also thought I could confuse fingers with hooves.

I needed to see his pickup. Find more proof they couldn't deny.

When the pie was safely on the counter cooling—no way was I opening that kitchen window just for farmhouse vibes—I snapped a picture for Josh.

A notification descended from the top of the screen.

> **Courtney**: Hi it's Courtney. From the library. I know we exchanged numbers, but I should have texted right away.

I had to shake my head. I'd given her my number because I was hurting for local contacts, but also she'd said she was going to look into Tyler and Nick with her genealogy research.

> **Emily**: It hasn't even been a day. This counts as fast.
> **Courtney**: Cool cool.
> **Courtney**: I found info for you.
> **Emily**: Damn. You're fast!
> **Courtney**: I should have found it before you left TBH
> **Courtney**: They're all related.
> **Emily**: Who?
> **Courtney**: Everyone.

What did this woman mean? Was this an "everything is intertwined" conspiracy thing? Courtney had told me she listened to a metric ton of true-crime podcasts.

Emily: When you say everyone...

I wasn't trying to be purposefully dense, but these were men who worked on the farm beyond my windows. They didn't act like I lived in what was once their family home. Or did they? The guys were polite to me, but they kept their distance. But Ray had told them to stay away. Josh too, maybe.

Courtney: Does 'everyone' mean something different in California?
Emily: Har har. Just didn't realize.
Courtney: Obviously.
Emily: Thanks.
Courtney: There's some more here. Want me to send it to you?

She started dropping links and screenshots before I could reply. Who else was related? Ray was an in-law relation to Herb, but did he consider himself a Belkin too? If not, why would he hire guys who were? Did that add a layer of friction or offense for Nick and Tyler?

Emily: Thank you! I'll probably be messaging you later with questions.

Hopefully she'd be willing to answer. Was it risky to bring her into this? We were talking about probable killers here.

Emily: Unless you want to be done with my silly project.

Courtney: Nothing silly about trying to find answers for people.

This woman barely knew me, and she believed me. Hell, she had helped. Why couldn't Josh have immediately backed me too? I may not have mentioned the barn to Courtney, but when I said I thought something had happened on my farm, that someone might have died here, she had no problem helping me get answers.

Emily: Thank you. Really. I need to figure out what happened to these Belkin women.

Understatement. I wasn't going to find any calm in my house until I'd gotten answers. It wasn't safe here otherwise.

Courtney: I'll send more if I find more, but you have to tell me what you learn!

Courtney: I love a good mystery.

Me too, but only the ones where riddles get solved. Where people are safe and the bad guys get theirs. I was still in the thick of it and the malevolence beyond my walls kept growing. Ignoring it only put others in danger.

Emily's Running Log:

14.4 miles—Cows mooed for the teal sports bra. Leg cramps. Try coconut water?
0 seconds to the barn—0 steps—WTF

CHAPTER 25

JOSH RETURNED TO THE FARMHOUSE, AND MOST DAYS WE'D eat lunch together on the porch and share a bottle of wine in the evening. The farmhands' truck would rumble past, laugher pealing from open windows. Each night, Josh would shuffle to bed, and I'd wait for the barn, for Alice, for *something*.

The barn light came on more nights than not, but now I watched for movement below. Night smudged the view around the barn, but the doors opened and closed in the wee hours. Someone was inside that barn. Not a single person or creature tripped the floodlights tucked in the eaves of the farmhouse, but I heard footsteps and the rustling of my chickens. When I'd look outside though, there was no one.

Days went by, and I didn't bother sleeping. A perpetual headache had blossomed at the base of my skull. Every time I dozed, memories of my mother rose vividly in my mind, and then I'd wake and they'd slip back into that ethereal place where memory goes squishy and hopeful.

Last night's dream had been a highlights reel from a trip we'd taken to Coronado when I was fifteen. It'd been the apex of July, all blazing sunshine making the Pacific glisten. Mom and I had set up under a giant umbrella with sodas, snacks, and sunscreen. The ocean was a violent beauty my mother had admired. The riptide would make a harrowing song, she'd said back then. In the dream, I heard the screams of children playing and my mother and me losing it in a giggle fit. There was no barn, no haunting figures, no fear for missing women.

I'd woken around three again. As was my habit, I drank a cup of coffee, but this time with a slice of berry pie on the side. I pumped one of Mom's rainy-day favorites into my headphones and listened to Elliott Smith sing about his heavy metal mouth while I let my mind settle back into the now.

By the time Josh was up, I was still *off.* I'd put in nearly twenty miles this morning, but my attention kept flitting to my soft notebook on the counter and the distance to the barn logged within it. It'd been inching farther away the last week. It was 472 steps from the farmhouse today. What did it know that I didn't? Was it done haunting me?

I heard Josh rustling in the bedroom and started on a batch of pancakes.

The hens had our egg carton overflowing. I grabbed a light brown one from the top and cracked it on the counter, but when I poured its contents into the mixing bowl, vivid red stared back at me. I staggered back, blinking. Was this like everything else and going to flash back to normal in a moment? I blinked again. Blood pooled in the bottom of the heavy ceramic mixing bowl, garish against the pristine white.

The buzz of Josh's electric razor simmered on the air. Should I show him this? *No*, I chided myself. This was an egg. A fluke. I dumped the contents down the sink and grabbed a fresh egg.

Blood swirled in deep yellow yolk.

The next egg was pure red, thickened to a custard consistency.

Again and again I broke the eggs open, and they bled into my bowl.

A low breeze slipped through the open kitchen window. Honeysuckle and morning sunshine on the air. The barn waited in the distance, dull and unassuming.

The grating whine of the coffee grinder made me jump.

"Sorry, babe." Josh's hair was still wet. The corner of his mouth quirked. "Didn't meant to startle you when you were readying to be very domestic."

I swallowed, staring down into the mixing bowl. The pool of eggs and blood daring me to say something. I should. This was strange. Josh would have to agree, but would he blame my hens?

My mouth went dry, but I tried to wet my lips regardless. "So something strange is happening—"

"If this is about the barn again, babe, I've already talked to the guys. No one is messing around out there."

"It's not about the barn," I snapped. Although it somehow felt like it was.

The espresso machine hummed, and he poured the drink into his mug. Josh glanced at it, but when his attention returned to me, tension sharpened his features. "Emily, you didn't sleep again last night. Did you even wait for the sunrise to go running?"

"What does that have to do with anything?" My stomach twisted. Somehow I knew that even blood in the eggs wouldn't be enough for him to see anything was wrong. Not enough to make him listen.

"You're pushing yourself too hard, babe. You need rest." He picked up his coffee and began frothing milk to make a cappuccino. "Maybe skip the breakfast and go lie down?"

That was his answer to everything. Sleep. Rest. Ignore.

Okay. I could pretend this was normal. So the eggs had blood in them. I'm sure that was fine too. I didn't have the energy to bother the hens for another batch. I poured in the flour and milk, and then I threw a handful of berries into the pancake batter. Raspberries from the bush by the barn and blackberries that I'd grown myself. Josh loved seeing me use the garden; I loved not having to argue about my chickens and whether their bloody yolks were somehow the result of me getting in over my head. *No, Josh, I watched over them every bit as dotingly as any chicken mama influencer on Instagram did.*

I lit the burner and placed the griddle on the stove to heat.

"You've been baking a lot lately. I owe you a good meal." Humor made his dimples surface. "How about I cook steak tonight?"

My biceps ached with how hard I stirred the batter. It shifted to a rosy color. "I could let you do that." I might make him cook it well done for the first time in my life.

"Then I'm going to need to drive into town today. Meat market is open on Tuesdays, and I'm bringing home the best New York strips you've ever had."

I folded my arms, jutting my chin up. "We'll see."

Excitement sparked in Josh's eyes. My husband loved a challenge. "We're going to have to eat dessert first because you're going to be so enamored with dinner, you're not going to have room for anything else."

I shifted my stance. Red streaked my elbow and any humor in my body sank. Just pulp from the fruit, I reminded myself, but my fingers froze at the splashes of red. I reached for a kitchen towel, but the white and yellow daisy patterned cloth fluttered to the floor in slow motion.

Falling petals, dripping blood flashed in my mind. *Love me. Love me not.*

There was no frigid breath on my neck, but the singsong taunt vibrated in my molars. I gnashed my teeth and yanked the towel from the floor.

Josh was staring at me. Hard. That worrying crease between his brow telling me he saw too much—not that he'd do anything other than place another pill on my bedside table. A not-so-subtle nightly nudge.

"You're assuming you're getting dessert?" I choked on the words, but I got them out.

"Pancakes and dessert are a lot in one day, I bet. Sorry, I didn't mean to—"

"I'll make a pie." I said quickly and gave him my back. I flipped his pancakes in the skillet. "But I used most of my berries in this."

His arms came around my waist. I jerked forward, slamming my hip into the knob for the oven. I swore and Josh staggered back like he'd been the one who'd been poked with an appliance.

"Jeez, Emily!" His hands were up in supplication, but a sneer contorted his face into pure judgment. As though I'd somehow hurt him by not wanting to be groped at the stove.

Was he kidding? "I'm *cooking.*"

All the humor, the softness, the hope fizzled into disdain. "You used to like when I touched you."

"What the fuck? I'm *cooking*, Josh. Hot pan in front of me. Trying not to burn me or your food."

He backed away, not hiding his offense. "I just wanted to touch my wife, but yeah. Whatever."

"We had sex *last night.*" It was a miracle I didn't roll my eyes.

"Touching and sex aren't always linked, Emily." He threw this at me like my desire to sleep with my husband was an egregious sin.

No. I wasn't doing this. "Your pancakes are ready."

He lowered his hands slowly. "Em—"

"Bring your plate over," I directed. We were moving on. He made me do it all the time. Today was his turn.

He parted his lips but decided against whatever argument he was about to test.

I placed three pink pancakes on his plate. "Do you want powdered sugar?"

Before he could answer, I moved to the cabinet and pulled the canister with the confectioner's sugar down. I placed it on the table.

Josh took his seat. "I don't think I've ever put powdered sugar on pancakes. Isn't that a waffle thing?"

He asked this like he wasn't already sprinkling the white stuff on top of his blood-and-berry cakes. I hoped they tasted good.

"You can—and maybe should—put powdered sugar on any baked treat," I said, because fighting was more effort than it was worth.

"That sounds like a Penelope tip." He took a bite and made a rumble of deep satisfaction. "Lord. This is good. Better than hotel fare by far, babe."

And like that, grief gripped my chest all over again. Josh invoked her name and memories flooded my mind. My mom had not been a remarkable chef, but there were four things she made epic versions of:

French toast—with a metric ton of powdered sugar.

A tres leches cake that she made for her own birthday every year.

A beef bourguignon she'd learned from her mom, who I'd never met. We weren't French, but my mother swore it was a family recipe. I'd put all my chips on it being in some *Intro to French Cuisine* cookbook by Julia Child, but whatever. We both hated mushrooms, but she'd use them every time because *flavor*, and then I'd be tasked with plucking them all out when it was done cooking.

Finally, her pièce de résistance, chocolate crinkle cookies. Again, with a liberal coating of confectioner's sugar. I tightened my grip on the spatula in my hand, but even its solid state couldn't pull me from sinking into the intrusive thoughts. The baking. My mom. The loss.

We made those cookies every Christmas Eve from as young as I could remember. Even if she was in the studio or on the road, we'd find a kitchen and they would happen. Our last year together, I'd done all the mixing of the tough dough, but Mom had sat at my side on a counter-height chair. She'd been in those chartreuse silk pajamas. Thinning hair pinned up with a loose headband. Thick globs of grief gelled down my throat, plunking into my belly. I'd have to make them myself this year. Alone. Or with Josh. He'd help, right?

Tears welled, and I turned toward the window. For once staring at the barn for an escape.

"Watching the morning sun?" Josh asked like he didn't know the kitchen window faced south.

I bit my lip, the skin pulling away a bit. I needed to drink more water. Oh well. "Barn's been busy." I said. A tear tracked down my cheek. I'd let the sunshine dry it.

"*People* have been busy at the barn?" He corrected me in a way that reminded me so much of that teacher in elementary school who would always reply to bathroom requests with "I don't know, *can* you?"

"Lights were on again last night." Surely he only needed another opening to hear me out. Courtney from the library had jumped on the investigation train with me without question. Josh, who knew all my deepest darkest secrets, should be able to do the same.

Not that he did. "Hmph. Ray said the guys come with the detasselers around four thirty."

"It was earlier," I said before I realized I'd slipped. Now I'd confirmed I hadn't slept much. Shit.

"Em." Josh could squish my name to make me feel special or small. Today was firmly the latter.

I wasn't letting it go. "Do you think Ray knows that Tyler kid is in and out of the barn so much?"

He sighed in that way that said I was the problem. I always was these days. "If he is, then it's fine. Ray trusts his guys."

He shouldn't. "But we don't know what he's doing out there. I saw him with that shovel and the—"

"Emily." There was my name again. Full. Patronizing. "We don't know what they're doing in the fields either. The whole point is to let Ray run the farm side of things. His business."

"But—"

"No. It's really okay. The sheriff's office confirmed that kid did nothing wrong. You made a mistake, and that's okay. Look, if they come up to the house or there's a real threat, let me know. But some guys dicking around in an old barn isn't really an emergency." Josh shoved a too-big bite of the tainted pancakes into his mouth. Conversation over, I guess.

What would be enough for Josh to believe me? What would make this serious for him? Would I survive crossing that threshold?

Emily's Running Log:

2 minutes, 37 seconds to the barn—472 steps

16.0 miles—New record! No cramps today. Queasy at 13 miles but held steady. Actually cleared my head.

CHAPTER 26

MEMORIES OF MY MOTHER WERE BRIGHTEST IN MY DREAMS.
And yet there was this ethereal distance when I relived the past while asleep. I don't know how or when I'd fallen asleep. I'd been half watching a reality show and half doomscrolling social media, and the next thing, I knew I was inside Amoeba Music, thumbing through vinyl with my mom.

Visits to the record shop were holy experiences with my mother—or at least she'd treated them like our version of church.

"Oh, Emmy Bear!" my mom exclaimed, holding the signature pink and green lettering on the cover of London Calling aloft. "This was the first record I bought for you."

My delight was solid enough that my chest must have rumbled in the waking world. "As you love to remind me quite loudly in this store every other week."

Mom sidled next to me, all conspiracy theory–like. "If we can't influence others around us to make better decisions, why did we come here?"

I gave her the side-eye. I was twenty and still an expert in the look. "I was told we were looking for 'the best damn thing to listen to during dinner.'"

It was the goal Mom set every trip. We'd find a record we didn't own—or at least a special edition of something we did—and play it that night while we ate the best dim sum in the city.

"We can both find the perfect music for us and introduce others to better taste." Her fingers danced over the spines of the albums.

"Spoken like an influencer." It'd been a running joke that her impulse to recommend new bands to every person she met could make her internet famous.

Mom dropped her head back, as if her lament needed to be spoken to the rafters. "Can we not use that word?"

"It's what you do." I didn't bother trying to hide my smirk.

"Tastemaker." She teased the word out like she wanted me to see fancy sprinkles on top. "If we're going to call me anything other than a music lover, it's that."

"Mom," I'd groaned. "You know YouTube star is like a career now."

"I already have a career. Plus, I don't want to be on my phone." Her dismissive wave carried the air of a middle finger. Penelope Wagers had never been one to hide her opinion.

It was for the best. The last thing I needed was my mom videoing her song recs. I'd watched her write up her column for the local alt weekly. She was always three tokes in and never wearing a bra.

I pulled a Knocked Loose record from the bin. "How about a metalcore dinner?"

Mom's trilling laughter stretched to the triple-height ceiling. It danced with the clean guitars of whatever indie rock was pumping through the store's speakers. Mom would have recognized it.

Slowly she turned toward me, her head tilted to the side. "The screams are more than screams."

Was this right? My memory was muddled. "They're the vocals," I said, wariness stretching my words thin.

"You have to listen closely." She took a step closer to me as though she was imparting a secret. "It's more than hearing the sound; it's everything beneath."

I parted my lips to try to pry into my mother's suddenly philosophical thoughts of cookie-monster vocals, but the dream glitched. Like someone paused and rewound an old VHS. The image jerking forward and back for a hiccup of a moment. When my mind smoothed out, Mom was scurrying off toward the electronica and dance records. I trudged behind her, but I never made it to the section.

A high-pitched, terrified wailing woke me.

I jerked upright on the couch. The air was stagnant. Darkness ensconced the living room. A small halo of yellow light from a lamp curled around the end table, illuminating my water bottle and the remote. A muted glow from the television told me the pained cries weren't fiction.

"Are you still watching?" it asked.

I rose, but my knees went liquid. The scream had sliced through the farmhouse. Scraping the walls, stabbing fear directly into my sternum.

Is that a fox? Doubt dug into me, dulling my motions. Josh wasn't sprinting from the bedroom. But then he could sleep through most any natural disaster. I suspected he had started taking Ambien again simply to not deal with me in the middle of the night.

The modern silver numbers on the clock across the room said it was edging toward sunrise. I focused on those numbers. Three forty-two.

Another tiny sharp scream pierced the house, my heart. I pushed to my feet again, legs holding me this time. I staggered toward the front door. Moonlight stretched its pale fingers through the sheer curtain of the big window. My palm was slick against the doorknob.

What am I going to do out there? Hesitation gnawed at my nerves. If someone was in danger, how was I to help them? I should call the police. The sheriff could be out here in...twenty minutes?

Twenty minutes and we'd be dead. She'd be dead.

Frost formed on my fingernails. Tiny white lattice, hardening my grip.

"Open the door. You must see." That voice. Her voice. Alice Belkin, the surety of it rang in my breastbone.

Fear raked my very soul, but I obeyed. If she could freeze my fingers, then she could certainly do more.

"Alice?" The screaming outside escalated at my invocation of the former homeowner's name.

I ripped the door open, half hoping I'd see some red fur scuttling along the porch. This could be a fox. Josh would tell me it was just some animal. The Belkin relations who ran my farm would promise it was a creature.

They would all be lying to me.

The soil and stone of our drive were black in the shadow of night. The cornstalks had taken on the bleached gray tone of black-and-white photos. The moon hung low and huge.

Creaaaaaak. Yip yip yip. Eeeeeeeeeeeeeee.

Salty sorrow permeated the air, as though painful tears had become palpable. I swallowed, someone else's hurt snaring my throat and shredding my insides all the way down. A hard thwack walloped the center of my back, like a shove, like a command, like a sacrifice.

I staggered forward, ready to run out there again. Ready to ruin my bare feet. Ready to save this woman, whoever she was, from terrible men.

The light was on in the barn's loft. The glow yanked my gaze there. Demanded I watch as it did every time. The noose swayed like a pendulum. The looped cord empty. A guttural cry emanated from the direction of the barn, more melodic, like a heavy metal singer. Panic slicked my palms. I rushed forward.

Sharpness bit into my foot. I scooched backward onto my butt. The thump of my fall not stopping the music now playing across the air. I turned to the barn.

"Why are you fucking with me?" I shouted.

In the noose I saw a body. Purple and black face. Blood seeping from blue lips. Her eyes milky white and staring at me.

"Loooooook," the voice rattled.

Was it the woman in the barn? Was it Alice Belkin? Her daughter? Another woman who had experienced hell on this farm? I shook myself. How could this even be real?

Covering my face with both hands had to make this go away. Could I conceal myself long enough to let daylight dispel this? Josh was right. I was losing it. Because I couldn't have this happen. I'd called 9-1-1 before, and it had helped no one. Not whoever had been in that truck and certainly not me. I couldn't do it all over again.

"Look!" The voice sharpened the more she repeated the words. As if she sought to break down a wall with her voice alone. Hoarseness coated that rasp.

"Emily." My name stretched, brittle in the air.

I opened my eyes. Expecting I don't know what. The barn loft remained aglow. The noose still swaying. Body gone. Music rattling the early-morning stillness. The side of my foot was still stinging. I dared a look. I'd been able to play off my previous injuries around my husband for some time, but blood on the porch was going to be another "discussion" topic. That wouldn't help me. Wouldn't help the girls who might be targeted next.

Scattered on the whitewashed planks of my porch were human teeth.

Adult teeth.

One molar clung to the ball of my foot. The screaming stopped, but I replaced it with my own shout. I slapped the offending tooth from my flesh and scrabbled backward until my spine knocked the side of the house.

Why the hell were there teeth outside my front door?

I spared a glance at the barn. Still and dark now. Without the light it felt farther away. Or maybe it fled this too.

Josh had to believe me now. I couldn't make up fucking teeth. Whoever left them for me was either determined to unnerve the shit out of me—and holy hell did it—or wanted me to have proof.

I leaned forward slowly, as though moving too quickly could make the offending bone bits attack me. Given my experience with the goddamned barn, I wasn't about to rule it out. There were five teeth in total. Two incisors and three molars. Dark brown marred the sides of most of them.

The churning disgust in my stomach was certain they were from five different people. Prizes. My stomach roiled. Who would relinquish them to my porch? Had the voice conjured this for me? Did she know I needed Josh on board? This had to be real evidence something terrible had happened here. More than my gut and a malevolent barn. My husband could help now. This was the type of puzzle he was good at. He'd know how to make the police investigate. They'd find answers. They'd arrest people. Maybe they'd even find Bridget Belkin. I stared at the teeth and wondered which one was hers.

Whatever tragic event had occurred in my fields, in my barn couldn't happen again.

I took a picture of the teeth with my phone, which had miraculously stayed in my joggers pocket through everything. Documenting the evidence allowed for distance, like this was me solving a crime and not being involved in one. Okay, and I wanted to capture the proof without touching the *teeth*. A full-body shudder overtook me, but I steadied myself and went to wake my husband.

CHAPTER 27

JOSH STAGGERED FROM OUR BEDROOM. RED RINGED HIS eyes, but he snatched the emergency bat, and his shoulders flexed as he shifted his grip. Menace emanated from his body, but the grogginess of sleep had not fully left his limbs. I'd flipped up each light switch as I'd sprinted to the bedroom, but now I followed him closely, determined to be his shadow.

"I don't think anyone is out there right now," I whispered like my fears were secrets and, if I kept them small, they'd be innocuous.

"You said someone was hurt. I don't know who is messing with us, but I will stop them." His gait steadied with each protective word.

Only I hadn't said anyone was hurt. I'd said I'd heard something outside and found a terrible sight on our porch. Had I said teeth? Had I said more? It'd been only moments ago, but my brain was already muddled, like the highs of adrenaline and caffeine were battling at the end of each of my nerves.

"Those teeth had to come from somewhere." My lips barely moved, but there was no avoiding what was happening now.

Josh swung an arm behind him, like he'd make a barricade with the move. "Babe, stay here."

We stood before our front door. I'd closed it for obvious reasons, but the porch light glowed sickly and yellow through the new glass pane. I'd been out there already. Faced the darkness. Witnessed the lonely teeth. But I didn't argue. I'd come to Josh for help; he was ready. My husband hadn't questioned me for a second when I shook him awake, when I'd urged him to rush to the porch. It wasn't like with the barn light. There was no "Are you sure, Emily?" Not a single "have you slept?" worried look. Just straight out of bed, to the bat, and now readying to bolt outside to fix the problem. *That* was my Josh.

The screen door clapped hard against the side of the house. It, too, needed to throw a punch. The shot rang out into the emptiness of night. There was no echo from the field. Josh stepped onto the porch.

"Careful!" I shouted, like that one word had the power to protect anyone.

He hushed me and peered from one end of the porch to the other. But there was no one standing near enough to be seen.

"The teeth are on the porch. Watch where you're stepping." As if having a molar jammed between his toes was the biggest problem. I tried to shake sense into my fear-addled brain.

"Hey!" Josh shouted, like anyone skulking around the farmhouse would simply reply. Crickets and the thick wool of summer air were the only things surrounding us.

He stepped to the edge of the porch and leaned forward, like he'd find some kid crouching behind the steps ready to shout *gotcha*. This was never going to be that simple.

He hadn't stepped on a tooth.

After a long moment, he asked, "Where exactly are they?"

"Directly in front of you." Frustration oozed from my pores. Proof was literally at his feet, and he still needed to be directed where to look. For real?

I hustled forward, nudging him to the side.

The white of the porch had gone sallow beneath the bulb by the door. Clouds covered the pristine moonlight.

There were no teeth.

I rushed out onto the porch, my bare feet slapping the planks like they were at fault. "They were here."

Spinning in circles, running my fingers across the wood, none of it returned the cluster of human teeth to our porch.

The patronizing "babe" from my husband unleashed a scream from deep within my chest, maybe from within my soul. I swore louder and louder. This was unfair. All of it.

"They. Were. Here." I dropped to my knees. "Get me your flashlight."

"Emily." He softened my name like I was fragile in this moment. Fragile like a bomb. "Get the flashlight, Josh."

He flinched but trudged into the house and returned with the Maglite. Under its glow there were no teeth on the porch. I looked in every corner. I tried to look in the dirt surrounding the house; even with the flashlight, night hindered me.

I crumpled onto our couch twenty minutes later. "They were there, Josh. And this house..."

What I'd learned about the Belkin family, the constant police calls, Alice's suspicious death, the missing daughter, everything that told me our home had seen horrible things came pouring out.

Josh's hand made small circles on my back, shushing me like I was some injured kid and not his traumatized wife who had unveiled the truth about evil in our home.

"I'm not saying that bad shit didn't happen before we lived here, but domestic violence isn't communicable. We aren't in danger by simply living in a place where it happened."

"This is more than that." I bit my tongue to keep from underscoring how significant violence in a marriage was. How often women were killed by the men they loved. He hadn't memorized those statistics because it'd never been necessary, but I wasn't here to educate him on female fear. "Those men are up to something out there."

"They're farming, Emily. Doing their jobs." His hand pressed more firmly against my spine.

It only incensed me. I pivoted out of his touch, making him look me in the face. "And what else?"

"Nothing." He shrugged like he truly believed that. "They work hard, and then they go home to their families."

"Their families that used to live here?"

Josh tossed his arms up like I was the one being stubborn. "And? That was the whole point!"

"Excuse me?"

"We wanted the farmers to keep the income from their crops. Those who already worked here were supposed to benefit from the land." He spoke slowly and softly. Ugh. I understood the plan. I'd explained it to enough people that the little loop of explanation had become routine for me.

It was different now. Being here. I hadn't thought it'd be some legacy I was usurping. Our leasing back to the farmers was supposed help people keep their jobs when the original owners left—only the Belkin family was always here. And at least one of them was dangerous.

I took a deep breath before I replied, hoping Josh would actually listen. "But it's strange to take the family home and leave them the land."

"Unless they don't want to live on the farm," he countered.

Heat scraped the sides of my neck. "Right. Because horrible shit happened here."

"Probably." At least he didn't deny it.

"They're fine visiting the place of family trauma on the daily, but not spending the night? Think it through, Josh. No one wanted to give up this house. They had to. We're the assholes from California who took their family home." The guilt sifted like filthy sand in my gut. I didn't need another reason for that farmhand to take interest in me.

"We're not assholes." He sighed, his steam fading. "And they sold us their home. Even if it was about an infusion of cash instead of whatever, how does that mean there's a criminal on the loose? Do you think they're coming for you?"

"I don't know anymore." Had those teeth belonged to women like me? How did I explain this? "I think this farm is where they get rid of bodies."

"You said there were teeth on our porch."

"Don't make me sound like I'm crazy."

"There aren't teeth on our porch." He was emphatic.

I swiped open my phone and held the lit screen high for him to stare at the picture. "Those are human teeth. On our porch. And I saw that Tyler kid putting a tarp over a bleeding body in the barn."

"No, you *thought* you did. It was a deer." He wasn't even looking at the picture. Clearly too busy checking my shoulders for the sprouting of a second head.

"Are you kidding me? Are you...?" I stared at my husband like I was seeing him for the first time. There was a hardness in the set of his jaw, disappointment swirling in his eyes. I'd come to him with actual proof, asked for his help in stopping a killer and keeping us safe, and he only saw a nuisance. My vehemence congealed into resignation. "You don't want to believe me, do you?"

"It's not a question of want. The deputies investigated and found nothing. The farm crew brought us *venison* jerky," he hedged. "None of this makes sense. That kid you called a killer? You just said he's related to the missing girl. It doesn't track, Em. Besides, there aren't tons of missing persons here. Someone else—like the sheriff— would have noticed if a handful of women up and disappeared."

Only they wouldn't. People left town all the time. They left dangerous home lives, they ran for freedom and opportunity, and they had to because no one believed them. My fingers itched for the ring

I'd found, the band that had belonged to whoever had been beneath that tarp. I'd placed it in my bedside drawer, but now missed the touchstone. But it wouldn't have convinced Josh. I'd told him about the hair clip, the ring, the goddamned blood, and he still watched me with only pity and worry.

The next words out of his mouth proved that. "I think you need a break from Nebraska, babe."

Emily's Running Log:

1 minute, 51 seconds to the barn—333 steps

CHAPTER 28

CALIFORNIA HAD BEEN MY HOME FOR DECADES. SAN
Francisco's unique atmosphere wrapped around me the moment
I stepped off the plane at SFO. It was a warmth that pressed down
upon you in the summer, but I was a short drive from the breeze
of the ocean licking my skin. I'd spent the few hours on the plane
letting my skin prickle and squeeze like it'd been wrapped around a
body that wasn't my own.

Maybe that was because this trip wasn't my own either.

Josh had rubbed my back, he'd paced the floor, he'd spoken
to me like I was a wayward child. All of it had been because he
didn't believe me. There were no teeth. He hadn't seen a single
one on the porch. The photo on my phone "could be anything."
Why the fuck did I pay for the fancy upgraded phone if he could
call my photos blurry? My husband's panic made me agree. He
wrung his hands, worry splattering my feet. He said I needed time
with friends, but he'd meant I needed time away from the farm.
Like a weekend in the buzz of San Francisco would jump-start my

brain, like those paddles they use on every TV emergency room drama. Like the barn wouldn't move anymore, I wouldn't hear Alice Belkin's words again, and I sure as shit wouldn't step on molars on our front porch.

But I knew what I'd seen. Those teeth weren't the end of anything for me. Whether I came back on Sunday or in a month, I would find out what happened to the Belkin family. I'd find out why the barn made my stomach flip. And I'd get answers about what the farmhands did behind the barn walls.

But I'd agreed to the trip. It was better than fighting, and coming back to the Bay Area was necessary. I'd put off the estate details long enough. I needed to let my mother's house go. The keepsakes stashed in its nooks had no place in my new life. I simply wished the attorney had handled it for me. He'd given me a lecture about living trusts and how if my mother had moved her assets into one before she'd died, blah blah blah. The worst time to lecture a person is when they are beneath an avalanche of grief. I'd snapped with a reminder about how quickly her cancer progressed, and the guy stopped with the upsell.

Had Alice Belkin needed a trust settled? No, Nebraska was a community property state. Her possessions would have gone to her husband, but this picturesque view remained. It was the one thing that truly belonged to us both. The idyllic home hadn't spared her a tragic end. The newspaper said she'd killed herself. What had Alice seen? What had it done to her? Whatever had happened on my farm, it'd tainted the air.

I tried to shake off my thoughts of the late Alice Belkin. I hopped into my rental car and headed toward the hotel Josh had booked for me—I would not be staying in the house we needed to sell. I had been immersed with other people's ghosts in Nebraska. I didn't need to invite my own to haunt me now.

Josh had booked my hotel because he was *helping*. What had once felt like kindness now carried this tinge of control. He'd dismissed my proof about what was happening at our farm. He tried to *delete* the photo of the teeth because he claimed they didn't look real and it was *upsetting* me.

"That asshole," I muttered under my breath, as if talking to the postcard-perfect San Francisco view beyond the hotel room's balcony. Choppy deep blue waters, Golden Gate Bridge disappearing at the peaks into fog, expansive hills with homes for days. It was beautiful, but it wasn't my home. Not anymore.

How could a handful of months in the center of the country change that? The pang of loss in my chest had nothing to do with letting San Francisco go and everything to do with the truth that this was my mom's home. Nomadic as my mom could be, she always returned to her home base. This city. Its culture. Its life. It was hers. My mom was the proto-Californian from the bare feet whenever possible, to the eclectic style, to the music turned to eleven, to the communal mindset. She thrived in the collective energy that surrounded the Queen Anne house I'd grown up in.

But I hadn't.

The Bay Area hadn't been built for me. It might have helped raise me, but I'd found roots in the rich soil and piercing blue skies of Nebraska. The sway of crops along the side of the road there—home—might make me carsick if I wasn't driving, but it also steadied something in my soul.

Josh had wanted me to come here to seek sense. Like he thought the solitude of the farm was ruining the woman he married. But in reality, it was freeing me. I did the things I loved. I ran, used my body, and did so without concern for anyone else stopping me. The farmhouse was my fresh start. It was my first true home. A place where I could explore who I wanted to be. It was me outside of my mother's shadow. It was me beyond grief. It was Josh and me starting anew. Or it should have been.

It wasn't fair that past tragedy haunted the barn. That darkness continued to flit beyond the walls of my home. Until I stopped it, I didn't truly have the home I deserved.

Josh said the Belkin family history didn't impact our future. He was wrong, but it gave me an idea. I needed to quit looking into the past and instead do what the deputies wouldn't: investigate now. Were there girls missing from the area that could have been in the back of that pickup? Who were Nick and Tyler? I had the internet and time to kill here in between obligations. If I knew who was on my farm—and who that slim ring belonged to—it could change everything. It'd keep me safe, it'd make the farmhouse mine, and it'd give a voice to the Belkin women, I suspected. Josh might not care about them, but every word I'd read strengthened the kinship I felt toward them.

Plus, Josh needed a couple days alone with the farm to feel the dread of the barn coming for him, to witness Tyler Jorgensen stealing in and out of the barn, maybe with another body. He'd promised to "keep an eye out" in the way you promised your parents to "be good" while they were gone even when you were grown and living on your own. But the cocoon of loneliness Josh wore when he was solo made me think he'd follow through. If only to prove me wrong.

My watch did that incessant tapping of an incoming call. I dug through my travel backpack to find the phone. My hands ached. How long had I been clenching them? I found the device in time to answer.

"Heyo!" my longtime friend Serena sang across the line.

"Am I already late?" I bit back a flash of panic. Serena only used the talk functionality of her phone when I hadn't arrived to spin class, the bar, or coffee shop within five minutes of the promised time.

"What? No." It sounded like she was in a car. "We aren't meeting for like an hour. Actually, that's why I'm calling."

"You're canceling?" The only other acceptable reason to call instead of text.

"You're making a lot of assumptions there, Emily." She punctuated the admonishment with a fake laugh, which made it sting all the worse.

"Sorry." I started over, putting on a show. "Hi, Serena, I've made it to my hotel."

Her snicker was effervescent even over the phone. "We all lose track of time on travel days," she said, like this was a fact.

I'd checked the clock every ten minutes until I had boarded the plane. We were different fliers, apparently. I muttered an almost agreement and then asked, "What's up?"

"So Rick got pulled into a last-minute meeting. He can't take the baby until four thirty. Mind meeting at five?" Her car's turn signal *tink tink tinked* in the background, like it too was very busy.

"Sure," I said slowly, still unsure why this warranted a call. "Gives me time to take a shower and wash the plane off me."

There had been so many bodies in the airport. The cacophony of voices still echoing in my mind. I shuffled my sneaker back and forth on the thin carpeting, the hotel version of touching grass.

"Oh." Serena's disappointment at my hygiene stilled my motion. Tension ratcheting with every second of her long pause. "I thought you were seeing that guy about your mom's estate today."

"That's tomorrow." She'd been talking to Josh. We'd barely exchanged a meme in DMs in the last six months, but she was clearly taking my husband's calls.

"Hopefully it won't eat up your whole day. I'm crossing fingers you'll get enough time in the city to get homesick."

I needed to shut that door quickly. "It better be quick. The guy is getting a cut, and I'd like to see him do all the work to earn it."

Serena was one of those people who liked to tell you how much every item in their house cost, along with the discount they'd managed. Her strategic shopping was a point of pride. So I was hopeful the money would distract her from this homesick business.

She soundly agreed and then dropped the call with a promise to be at the tapas place on time.

I took a long shower and tried to relish in the double shower heads and endless supply of hot water. When I got out, Josh had texted. I'd been so caught up that I'd forgotten to let him know I'd landed.

Josh: You make it ok?

Emily: Ack! Yes. I went into autopilot when I got here.

Josh: Returning home can do that

Josh: Happens every time I'm down at my parents'

Josh: I mean when I make the drive without u

Oh, I was well aware. He'd also slip back into a shyer version of himself. It was a defensive mechanism, but he swore those trips were better when I was there. Would this journey have been better with him? Maybe, but I wanted him alone on our farm. Was that petty? My husband wasn't in danger. The men there had been nothing but deferential to him. And there weren't a lot of missing thirtysomething men in rural Nebraska.

Emily: You're home. I'm in a fancy hotel. Thanks, by the way.

Josh sent a series of kissy emojis.

Josh: The spa is supposed to be bonkers

Josh: if u have time

This was my Josh. Distance could be good for us. When I was the one out and about anyway. He had time to sit and think about me, think about what I'd told him. And I guess I could let some nice person dig their elbows in my back before flying home. If everything stayed on track with this trip.

He wanted to keep chatting. We switched to FaceTime while I put on my makeup. I hadn't worn much of the stuff since moving to the farm, but aside from the eyeliner, it was like riding a bike. And, honestly, if Serena noticed the uneven line around my eye, she wouldn't say shit.

Josh sat in our kitchen while we talked. He was determined to try working in rooms other than his office today and tomorrow. He said it was good to experience all the views. I took this as the concession that he needed to get a feel for what it was like to be me in our house. I could not see the barn out the window behind him. For the best.

I asked him to send pictures of the hens.

"What, you need proof of life?" He faked clutching pearls.

"I want to show Serena." Because I'd need something to show her after she went through a zillion photos of her growing family.

He laughed, calling me out on having plenty of photos of my Cluckingham Palace girls. But he promised to send a picture when he checked the coop door before going to bed.

We had a two-hour time difference, and we both pretended I'd still be out partying it up with Serena when that happened.

———

Seeing Serena lit an echo of joy in my chest. She'd already snagged a table when I walked into the tapas place she'd selected.

"A few picks are already on the way," she said as a way of greeting.

And like that we slipped back into the people we were years ago. We talked about people we'd both been friends with before and the "did you see" updates from social media. She shared stories of her mom life with me, and it comforted me to see her so happy.

"So you are really all in on this farm life?" Serena's skepticism was blatant.

"The air is so clean, I'm pretty sure I'm running the best I have in my life." Though my running log had become a barn tracking journal.

She smirked. "I'd rather hit an oxygen bar, but I'm happy for you."

I laughed because the old me would have found it funny, but not in the same way.

"How are things with Josh?" Her careful tone needled me.

I waved off her question. "Good. He's gone all Mr. Fix It."

"I can picture that, actually, but I meant between you two. It's just the two of you all the time now. Is he helping you?" Hell, she was looking at me like she knew. All sympathy and knowledge.

I should tell her. He'd *sent* me here because he thought I was delusional, but then what would I have thought if he'd told me there were teeth outside our house but they were gone when I arrived? And yet Josh had dismissed actual proof. I was starting to realize he'd only return to the supporting husband I knew when he saw the evidence firsthand. Why was my word not enough for him?

"He thinks he is?" I shouldn't have made it a question.

Serena didn't miss a beat. She propped her elbow on the table, her chin resting on her hand. "What did he do?"

"Nothing—" I tried to dismiss it, but with my friend's raised eyebrows and hardened gaze I relented. "He sent me here because he thinks the isolation of the farm isn't great for me."

"But everything you've told me said you absolutely love it there. Running with cows like the weirdo you are." Humor and alcohol rosied her cheeks.

"I do love it there. It feels like there's a history at that place, like something I need to understand, but when I try to explain it to him, he shuts me down."

"What kind of history?" Serena was already conjuring the kind of friendship backup that meant she'd take out her earrings at any minute. I loved her so much.

"It's nothing." It was everything, but the threat of yet another beloved person throwing more doubt my way was more than I could take. "I just want to know about who lived there before."

"And he thinks that's a reason to come back home? Well, I don't hate him setting up this visit, but maybe dude needs to look *inward*." She took a long drink from her margarita.

"Facts." I laughed. Genuinely. "On the whole though, he's great. Really. He made sure I got to spend time with you this weekend, didn't he?" I hated deflecting, but having my friend hate on him didn't change anything. I wanted Josh to trust me, but another part of me understood he was a data guy. He hadn't seen the things I had, but he'd cared for me through the days after my mom died. He was trying in his own way. I wanted to believe that after a few days solo at the farm, he'd be more open to hearing me out.

After two margaritas and as many hours rehashing friendship highlights with Serena, I walked back to my hotel. The streets were loud. The open patios of the nearby restaurants were packed. Serena had offered to drive me, but she'd needed to get home. She wanted to pump and get some sleep before her baby inevitably woke hungry for his mom. Our lives had diverged sharply in the last few years, but when I spoke of marathon training in the fields and adopting the hens, she'd been supportive.

"I guess Nebraska really suits you," she'd said, awed. "I'm going to have to come visit."

I was imagining her reaction to the cozy guest room when Josh texted me the image of my hens. They were inside the coop, in full roost mode. I smiled at the picture as I bustled toward the hotel. Only another block away. I booped Rose's nose on the screen and the image zoomed in. A few kernels of seed remained on the floor of the coop alongside the bedding that needed to be cleared out. I was readying to switch apps to remind Josh to clean tomorrow when I realized one kernel was cast in a creamy tone.

I stopped in the middle of the sidewalk and enlarged the photo again.

Was that a tooth?

Was there a fucking tooth in my chicken coop?

CHAPTER 29

MY MARATHON TRAINING WAS THE ONLY REASON I MADE IT
to the hotel without passing out. My heart throttled against my ribs.
The damned organ was determined to slam through my chest wall
and flee my body. Fair enough. I didn't want to drown in the deluge
of dread overwhelming my limbs.

I pressed the elevator call button over and over. I clutched my
phone like it was a towline and I was beyond the breaks in the bay.
The single speck of white in the dim photograph became a beacon
pulling me forward.

How did my hens have a human tooth in their pen? In the actual
coop? Was this one of the teeth from the other night? The molar
that had stuck its ridges into my foot?

An older couple in Hawaiian-style button-down shirts stepped
into the elevator car with me. I ignored them, stewing in the silent
ride upward. The tourists were having a different Bay Area experience today.

What if that was a *new* tooth? Was someone threatening Josh, and he didn't even know it? Had it been a warning for me, and they didn't know I was tucked away drinking overpriced margaritas with Serena?

By the time I reached my hotel room, my heart had accepted its confinement. Dread weighted my feet. I shuffled to the bed and opened my laptop.

I called Josh. He didn't answer.

I called again. No answer.

My repeated attempts didn't earn me anything. I flipped back to our text thread. "Josh has notifications silenced."

The hell? How did he not have me opted out from his Do Not Disturb settings? The text I sent asked this exact thing.

Panic collared my throat. What if he wasn't asleep? What if something had happened? I'd been lured out to the barn in the darkness, to the teeth, to the screams. Was Josh in danger?

What could I do about it? I was thousands of miles away in a fancy hotel while my husband was alone—God, I hoped he was alone—on our farm. I'd wanted this for him. For him to experience the isolation tainted by whatever was happening at night in our barn, whatever *had* happened that continued to mar the air, the soil, and the soul of our farm.

Was I getting what I asked for?

"Be real nice if my ghost friend could whisper a bit of advice now," I grumbled. An icy breath with proof of life would be helpful. But Alice Belkin was dead, and if she truly was the woman speaking to me on the farm, she wasn't here. She stayed where the secrets slept.

I cradled my face in my hands. The amber and cayenne scent of the lotion from the tapas bar's bathroom shunted itself into my sinuses.

I shook my head, attention catching on the pale pink of my toiletry bag. A Valentine's Day gift from Josh a few years back. He'd had my name embroidered on the side. Just the first name, because he knew I hated my initials. He'd slipped a bottle of his Ambien into the bag. My husband should have been in pharmaceutical sales with the way he pushed drugs on me.

But maybe that was my answer. Self-disgust at considering taking one and the resignation that it might be the only way I made it to morning took turns raking my brain until the headache blossoming at my temples pushed me to my feet.

I couldn't fly home right now. There were only two direct flights to Nebraska a day. I could try to zip through Denver or Minneapolis or Kansas City, but there weren't flights leaving here until after sunrise.

I could call Ray and make him go check on my husband, but we'd involved him enough. If I was wrong, everyone would lose their shit on me. That'd been made quite clear. Besides, Tyler was *his* person. He might well know what the kid was up to. He never wanted to come into our home. Could he feel Alice watching him? Had he seen the violence in the house before?

Fuck. My head was pounding. Ray wasn't my answer.

I needed to *do* something. I typed the first two letters of the *Hebron-Journal Register* into the search bar and the web address autofilled. The sheriff's deputies had told me there was no body, no one harmed. But a family would plead for help; they'd demand the authorities find their daughter. I clicked into the advanced search, and after a few attempts at various combinations of *missing* and *girl*, I landed on a list of names. Short articles, sometimes only two or three paragraphs long. The sheriff's comments in each dismissed the worries. "We have no reason to believe anything has happened to..." "At sixteen, Miss Wright could choose to leave her home." It was all versions of runaways and "I'm sure she'll come back soon."

It wasn't all ignored though. An article dated just yesterday came with a picture. I clicked it, and an image of a cute teenage girl filled my screen. Her hair was wrapped in a high bun. A temporary tattoo featuring a knight or warrior caricature was on her cheek. Like she'd been at a sporting event for a team I'd never heard of.

Something about her stilled my rampant heart; she looked so familiar. It might as well have punched me back to a few weeks ago when I stood in the shadows in my barn and watched Tyler Jorgensen grouse at the back of his pickup.

MISSING TEEN: 15-YEAR-OLD KINSEY MCALLEN
LAST SEEN AT FAIRBURY WALMART

I tapped my phone screen to keep the chicken coop image live. As if seeing a goddamned tooth was a centering stone. Definitely not the healthiest way to remain focused.

I should have been home tonight. I could have walked down to the barn, looked Tyler in the face, and asked about this girl. A chill settled in my bones. But I was here, more than a thousand

miles away, with a headline and a shitty photo of the chicken coop.
I couldn't call the cops with that. If my own husband was shunting
me off, I could only imagine how that phone call would go. There
had to be a way to help. Even if this tooth wasn't Kinsey's. *God,
please don't let it be this girl's.*

Josh could have witnessed something and not realized it. He
brushed off the farmhands moving around the barn, but maybe if I
told him there was a missing girl in the area, he'd take it seriously. All
night Josh's texts had been placid, teasing...generic. Had he so much
as looked out the windows, peered at the barn? If so, would he have
seen this girl? If she'd even been there. I swiped my forehead, but
the skin remained damp. I was connecting loose bits of information.
There wasn't any reason to think Tyler was behind this. At least not
anything more than a sourness in my stomach that nullified any
remaining alcohol.

I read each line of the article carefully. Kinsey had disappeared
nearly three weeks ago. Her parents only now were reporting it. The
local police had found footage at a Walmart at that time. She'd been
seen leaving the store with a white male, early twenties. Store sur-
veillance was grainy, but from the still captured for the newspaper, it
appeared the guy kept his ball cap tugged down. He had a mustache.
Had Tyler grown one since I'd last seen him? Facial hair changed
nothing about my certainty that he was dangerous.

If Kinsey had been missing that long, could she have been in my
barn with Tyler? I racked my brain to recall details. *The Polaroid.*
Was Kinsey the girl I'd seen in that instant camera image? The girl
who had been crying? How old was that image? My stomach sank.

I tried calling Josh again. I tried pacing around the room. Staring at the image of the tooth on the floor of the coop didn't help either.

Screw it. I couldn't leave now. I couldn't talk to Josh. I stalked over to the bathroom counter and snagged the pills Josh had snuck in the bag. I popped the cap on the prescription sleeping aid while my mind whirred. Was the reason Ray didn't repair the barn because he wasn't willing to go in there either?

Maybe I should have been talking to him this whole time. I swallowed the pill.

I would sleep tonight. Force myself to get pulled under, because otherwise I would tear myself apart in my inability to fix anything.

I pulled a tiny bottle of vodka from the mini fridge. In for a penny, as they say...

"Josh, you better be fine," I muttered before throwing back a shot. "And you better apologize like you accidentally wrecked the car."

My husband had been trying to get me to take drugs before bed for months on end. Maybe even a year. Tonight I took them so I wouldn't languish worrying about him. The unfairness of that was the last thought I had before the booze and snooze pills took me under.

———

The steady *buzz buzz buzz* of my alarm pierced the thick fog enveloping my head. I couldn't remember the last time I'd needed an alarm to wake me, but it sure wasn't with this kind of sleep stickiness. Grogginess wasn't purely in my mind; the fatigue lingered in my limbs. My breaths were slow and heaving. I rolled to the side and tapped my phone screen to make the sound stop. Warm light pooled at the edges of the thick curtains over the balcony window. Morning then.

Josh.

His name in my mind sent a surge of adrenaline down my veins, shoving whatever medicinal lag was holding me down right out of the way. I pushed upright and snatched my phone from the nightstand.

Seven missed calls.

Josh: Emily?

Josh: r u ok?

Josh: Em?

Josh: Should I call Serena?

Josh: Call me pls

Air flowed a little easier seeing his fretting. He was safe. I was safe. The time stamps were only fifteen minutes ago. So he'd slept through my panic. Well, I guess I had too. But that was his fault as well.

I pulled my laptop close. We both needed to see each other, I suspected. A quick video chat would soothe my hackles and hopefully ease his worry.

I tucked my hair behind my ears, like it made me look like I had my shit together. As if Josh hadn't seen me first thing in the morning for years. I called him.

He answered before the little song Apple played could even get two notes out.

"Emily?" His eyes were wild, his hair mussed.

I inclined my head in his direction. "Good morning," I hedged.

"Are you okay? Did something happen?" His questions blended together.

"I'm fine, but, babe, can you tell me why you blocked calls from me with Do Not Disturb?" It wasn't my biggest concern last night, but in the haze of morning—and an Ambien hangover—the loneliness creeped in. I wrapped my arms around myself.

"What?" His surprise was genuine.

I leaned forward, closer to the camera, but also more into a self-cuddle. "When I called last night and texted, you'd turned off notifications."

"I know, I saw them this morning..." He rocked back, letting me see the old Metallica shirt he swore he'd thrown away. There were holes in the armpits. Problems for another day.

Heat licked the side of my throat. "I'm your wife. I'm supposed to be able to get past."

He rasped his fingers over his stubble. "I didn't bother setting up any of that when I got the new phone."

Come on. "You spent like half a day curating all the different workflows."

Josh leaned in, getting his face close to the camera. Like he wanted me to see how truthful this conversation was, like he knew this was a little thing about a much bigger issue. "We are together all the time. I only changed the settings to make sure my boss gets through."

"What if you were traveling?"

His reply was automatic. Fast. The thing he should have said first. "I'm sorry. Truly. I'll fix it now."

His phone was in his hands, and his fingers tapped rapid-fire.

"Thanks." *I guess?* I shouldn't have had to ask. "Have you already been out to check on the chickens?"

He arched a brow. "Were the many calls last night about the Golden Girls?"

He didn't answer my question. Maybe it was the lingering medicine head or the headache that hadn't disappeared, or just that I hated to start my day with us at odds, but tears welled.

"I'm sorry." His swallow was audible. "Babe, I didn't mean—I'm sorry. I just freaked out when I saw all the missed calls. You said you're okay, but something scared you last night. Did something happen with Serena?"

I reached for my water bottle before I realized I'd left it across the room and only had a tiny half-empty bottle of vodka on the nightstand. Thankfully out of camera view. "Hold on," I told him as I went for the water. Once I was back, I said, "Serena is fine. Dinner and drinks were like you'd expect. Old times, but with a lot more pictures of kids and such."

"Did you show her pictures of your feathered ladies?" There was no teasing in his voice. Just support. This was my Josh.

"I did." The memory of the photo he'd sent me made me choke on my next words.

"Babe?" he urged.

"The picture you sent me...on the coop floor..." Could I do this? Could I bring up the teeth again? Last night I'd been ready to confront and check, and now with the distance of hours and miles, I wondered if I was in for another chiding from a disbelieving spouse.

"It's a total mess, right?" He laughed, like the mood had instantly brightened. He was sitting in our kitchen again. Honeyed light cut through the air behind him. He lifted a coffee mug to his mouth. It was the textured cream mug debossed with the word *mine* in a looping cursive punctuated with a little red heart. Josh wasn't a guy who cared about his beverage vessel, but picking a lovey one had to have been a conscious choice.

"Have you already been out there?" Had he seen the tooth? Had he tossed it without even noticing?

Sheepishness crept from beneath his shorn beard. "I know you like to get it all done before six, but it's hard to sleep here without you." He licked his lips, like he was buying time, like there was more. Like he'd heard music last night or a voice or *something*, but then he revealed nothing. "I took the Ambien early, which is why I missed your calls."

"So you haven't been out there yet?" And the tooth was just *waiting*?

"No, but the chickens are quiet. I'll go out there once we're done. You look like you got some sleep too."

"Thanks for packing the sleeping pills." I sipped more water, trying to wash the taste of too much rest from my mouth.

"It's hard to sleep when we aren't together." Affection poured from him.

I didn't correct him. "The picture you sent of the hens last night—"

"I swear they're fine, Em." He jumped on it. As though I was disappointed in him and he needed to defend himself.

"It's not that." I needed him on my side. He was supposed to be on my side. That's what this whole thing was about. "You're doing great with them, and I appreciated the picture. It's just I saw something on the floor of the coop that I want you to check on."

He held his mug in front of his mouth like he was drinking, but his throat didn't move. Finally he lowered it and said, "What exactly?"

"A white chunk. I don't know if it's plastic or a piece of wood off the coop somewhere, but it's not something we want the girls eating." Why was I lying to him? It was a tooth.

But he needed to see it himself. Let him make the discovery, and then tell *me* about finding freaking teeth on the farm. Then we could be in it together.

One more night alone there, and he'd understand. I'd come home and we could work together to stop whatever tragedy was tainting our farm. Josh would help me stop Tyler. He'd help me quell Alice's rage.

Josh would help me.

He had to. He was my husband.

CHAPTER 30

I'D HONESTLY EXPECTED JOSH TO CALL ME BACK IN A PANIC within a half hour. It'd been seventy-two minutes since we hung up—not that I was counting—and nothing. It's not like he had to shower and shave to go muck a chicken coop. It was a pull-on-shoes-and-grab-the-gear kind of thing. While he hadn't done the task before, it was not like I was asking him to calculate the trajectory of a surface mission to the moon. I'd lamented the process to him enough times that he'd know the steps. And I'd left a to-do list on the counter. I'd originally thought it was overkill and accidentally condescending, but now as time ticked by, perhaps I should have been more detailed.

I spritzed a setting spray over my makeup. My eyeliner was significantly smoother today. My mother would have been proud of that. I tucked my dull hair behind my ears, wishing I could exude her level of cool.

My phone display still had zero notifications from my spouse, but the time kept increasing. I needed to leave in five minutes to meet the estate attorney. I paid him in fifteen-minute intervals, which meant my ass was not going to be late. I also hoped it meant we could be efficient. Talking to a lawyer was low on my list of good times, but doing it in the home I grew up in surrounded by some of my dead mother's favorite possessions was possibly an unwritten circle of hell.

My palms itched with the need to grip the phone, to grasp control. He hated being rushed, but one little text wouldn't hurt.

Emily: Those girls aren't giving you trouble, are they?

There. That was cheeky enough.

I pulled a pair of cat-eye sunglasses from my purse and perched them atop my head. I toed my feet into black knit ballet flats, five seasons out of style. I hadn't cared about such things in so long. Hadn't needed to. I loved pulling together colors, aesthetics, tones. I wanted rooms to carry ambiance, and I wanted images and pages to carry a balance. But I'd settled into clothes that catered to comfort and colors that made me smile. I'd restocked sports bras and leggings like I'd been doing two-a-days for years, but the dress I wore today was legit a decade old.

Focusing on fashion couldn't quell my obsession with the coop. I should have won a shiny award for not opening the picture of the henhouse again this morning. I looked at zero teeth that weren't my own this morning. Who has those kinds of thoughts? What if this was all in my head? Normal people did not praise themselves for that kind of thing. My brain was on the same track as a demented dentist from a B horror movie. Josh still didn't reply. Had he found the tooth, and he was trying to decide how to admit he was wrong? Was he sussing the best way to admit he'd believed it was all in my head? He didn't need to say it. I was very much aware of the words he refused to speak. You couldn't be married to a person for years and not read between the lines.

I tucked the phone in my purse like a totally logical woman and headed for my rental car.

Josh messaged before I'd exited the parking garage. I wanted to have the restraint to wait until I arrived at Mom's house to read it. But I pulled to the side of the exit lane and swiped open my phone.

Josh: all clean!

He included a picture of the inside of the coop. Fresh bedding, clear floor, the brightness of sunlight through the open door. Was he seriously not going to comment on the fucking tooth?

I couldn't show him my panic.

Emily: Great! Mother Clucker looks cozy!

She was the only hen in the picture.

I started to type more but saw the telling triple dots of more from my husband. I waited.

Another image came through. Chicken feed on the plate and scattered around the ground. The warm glow of the sun above the blurred green of cornstalks in the background. How long ago did he take this? The sun should be high now. It was 10 a.m. here, which meant noon at the farm. I didn't have to be good at math to put that together.

It took me half a dozen attempts to reply with a message that wouldn't make me look insane out of context.

Emily: The girls look happy. Thanks for cleaning the coop. Did you find out what that white thing was?

That felt safe. Complimentary. Like a normal question a person would ask. I did not use the word *tooth*, which had to help keep me off some NSA list.

Josh: it was nothing

Nothing? It was a fucking tooth, Josh.

Emily: Huh. Ok. I'm heading out to meet the lawyer.

I couldn't do this now. I'd find that tooth when I got back tomorrow. Had he not looked for it? Had one of the hens eaten it? Could chickens even eat teeth? Their beaks were strong, but why would they peck at it if they had delicious snacks provided?

For the first time *ever*, I wanted to see Winston Lanford, Esquire.

It wasn't his fault that I'd avoided his calls for the last several weeks. It wasn't even one of those weird "no one likes lawyers" things. I loved people who liked details and kept others to their words. I hadn't wanted to be around Mr. Lanford because it meant dealing with my mom's death. While I loved dipping into memories with her, divesting myself of her actual possessions was a special kind of gross.

I'd moved to the middle of the country, started my life over. Sure, I was having to reclaim the farmhouse and battle whatever darkness had set up shop in my barn, but it was a bright space that was clean of all the remembering, the grief, the regret, the longing, the tears, the emptiness. My new house was filled with sunshine and fresh pies and the freedom to be wholly myself with no outside judgment. No asshole neighbors. No interruptions with sales guys at my door. (If we didn't count the one I lived with.)

I found street parking in front of my late mom's place. The Queen Anne–style house rose from the angled concrete sidewalk with all the presence of a rock queen. The paint had faded, but it carried the charm of experience instead of the graying of a withered plant.

Winston Lanford waited for me outside the front door. We'd met in person once before, but as I approached the stairs, I was again struck by how normal he looked. For a man who spent his days dealing with dead people's things—like some sort of legal grave robber—he sure looked friendly. He was nearly as tall as the front door. His lean frame was made more slender by his black suit in front of the dark wood behind him. He was in his early forties and offered an affable smile, like he didn't know I'd been dodging him.

He shook my hand. "Mrs. Hauk, I'm so glad you could meet me to today. I appreciate you making the trip."

Okay. So he was fully aware I'd been avoiding him. "Thanks for your patience."

He unlocked the door like this was the house he'd grown up in instead of one steeped in my childhood. "I don't expect this to take too long."

Easy for him to say. I stepped over the threshold and inhaled my mother's memory. Patchouli and amber saturated every surface. It wasn't merely her clothes that carried the musky aroma. It was the wallpaper. It was the curtains. It was the wood beneath my feet. I let out a shaky breath, as though it would flush the heady connection from my system.

I reached automatically for the light switch. Mom had replaced the original entryway dome light with an avant-garde chandelier. Rungs from a playground ladder had been fused together to mimic a massive jack. Like the child's toy could be a weapon. The end of each rung was capped with a small Edison bulb. It was one of those pieces that added warmth and fear to the room, which was exactly what Mom had been going for.

Natural warmth filled my home back in Nebraska. The morning sun stretching through the windows and dappling the hardwoods. It was a different kind of cozy, and I'd cultivated it for myself.

"Your mother certainly had an eclectic style," Mr. Lanford said, sauntering through the house like he'd seen it all.

I guessed he had. I'd given him the key to the house before we moved. His team had been cataloging my mother's belongings and preparing for a sale. Because I didn't want any of it.

"My mom loved a vibe." I didn't say more. He needed my

signature on paperwork, and he needed me to identify a few items for him, but he did not need me to crack open a vein and bleed all over this house.

I snickered to myself. I had 100 percent bled all over the kitchen, which is where he led me. I'd been determined to make a gumbo after seeing it on a television show. I'd been eleven or twelve. Prepping veggies with the knife skills of a pro chef was not in my wheelhouse now, much less in my tween days. I ran my thumb against the pale white scar on the inside of my index finger. Three stitches, a kitchen splattered red, and a mom who had sworn the whole way to the emergency room that she wouldn't let me lose a finger. I did not, in fact, lose a finger. It'd kept me out of the kitchen for four months though. Who had bled in my farmhouse? The thought chilled my core.

I hurried across the room like I could escape the intrusive thought. The white and red page of our favorite Chinese food take-out place's menu peeked from a drawer across the room.

"You didn't clear these out?" I pulled the drawer open, and the stack of menus billowed forward as if they had been reproducing while we weren't looking.

He cleared his throat, clearly not expecting to be chided. "We didn't remove anything from the home."

"You're allowed to toss garbage. No one wants to keep takeout menus." I took a handful and put them in the trash can. Not like they'd do me any good halfway across the country where the only deliveries that made it to our door were from the USPS.

"You'd be surprised." He laughed at some joke I didn't catch. Quickly, he sobered. "That's the goal today."

"To rid ourselves of garbage?" Cool. My mood was solidly trashed too.

"Poor choice of words on my part, ma'am. Today I need your approval to place certain items up for sale, for donation, or for removal from the estate."

That was the fanciest way to say, "Pitch it in the trash," I'd ever heard. Guess we'd picked a good estate guy. Even if he needed me to tell him to throw away old menus.

My mom had created this bohemian den that was more historic Bohemia and less peace-and-love. Dark walls, heavy velvet curtains, warm but dim lights. I'd grown up in this cocoon of darkness and energy. Music lit the walls, even in silence. I could hear the high-hat *tink tink tink* of the indie rock band Mom had worked with in the late aughts in the dining room. The tiny oval scuffs in the mahogany table compliments of the drummer's writing process. A steel guitar was mounted above the bed in Mom's room. The stairwell had a gallery wall. My childhood friends' homes would have the same. Theirs had pictures from family photo shoots and vacations to Disneyland. Ours were recording booth snapshots signed by famous people.

I told him to donate those to a museum.

Mom had treasured them all, but they had no place in my life now. I had the music and that connection to who I'd been with my mom. The farmhouse, though, was a rebirth of sorts. I'd grown up in this plush, decadent darkness, but I'd found freedom in my open bright house. White and yellow paint, open windows, and all the fresh air I can handle were what I needed now. Even if there was a darkness encroaching at night back home, it was worth it to carve out my own haven.

Admittedly though, I'd never found a tooth that wasn't my own in this house. So one up on Mom's place.

We trudged through the house, a sluggish pulse pushing us from one set of memories to another. I nodded absently at every question Mr. Lanford asked. I signed papers with a half-hearted scribble. I was no longer in a shadow, and I wouldn't let grief or any other useless feeling ruin me. Each room we moved through was another collection of memories that weren't me any longer. I was no longer the same person I'd been when my mother was alive. Even this home that once left me cozy, conjured claustrophobic vibes now. I longed for the bright walls and big windows of my farmhouse. Even with the barn, it was made for me. I just had to help the farm find peace and get Tyler off the property to fully claim it.

We designated the donations and the estate sale items. The lawyer promised to keep me apprised—as if I wanted to know more than the dollar figure hitting my bank account. I nodded like it all mattered, and then got in my little rental car and drove straight to the airport.

The ticketing agent bumped me onto an earlier flight. I texted Josh and gave him my updated arrival time. He asked no questions, but he also didn't say a word about the chicken coop.

In five hours, I'd be home.

In five hours, I was going to find that tooth.

In five hours, I would have proof that Josh couldn't deny, and then he would help me reclaim our piece of rural paradise.

CHAPTER 31

CLUCKINGHAM PALACE WAS AS SPOTLESS AS ITS NAME-
sake when I returned to the farm. Josh had picked me up at the
airport in Omaha with zero questions about my early arrival.
We'd autobahn-ed it home on I-80 in record time. There was
enough traffic on the interstate to make me feel like an event was
underway, but the only thing I cared about was getting to my slice
of Americana. To my chickens. To the farmhouse. Hell, to watch
that damned barn.

Why was I trying to fool myself? I wanted to find that tooth.
Getting home meant getting my hands on those molars and making
Josh believe me. Seeing the house and the hens was a start, but
finding that bit of proof would change everything. I could open an
investigation. The sooner that happened, the sooner my farm could
be the respite it'd promised on the Realtor site.

Would there be another tooth left for us tonight? Would the
barn be close to the house today or tucked back by the field? It'd
been only a couple days since I'd last marked the distance, but

knowing where it was in relation to the house could clue me in to how bad things had truly gotten. I bit my tongue to keep from asking Josh if he'd seen the farmhands go into the barn. He hadn't been watching it, just like he hadn't bothered to look at what was on the coop floor. Oblivious husband was oblivious.

Did Tyler know I'd been watching him? Would he have bothered Josh in the first place? Had anyone told the farmers I'd left? What disasters could have occurred while I was stewing in memories in California?

No, Tyler flitted in and out of the barn, grabbing tools, canvas bags, bodies, whatever. He wouldn't do that if he'd knew my eyes were on him. A criminal who knew they were being watched wouldn't flaunt it. Not that I could really say I was some sort of expert in the minds of maybe murderers. I had tried listening to the *Crime Junkie* podcast on my flight home. The host's charisma made me want to keep listening, but the unnerving sense that I was living in an episode had me tapping out after the first ad.

If a cruel man—like the young one I'd heard speaking to whomever or whatever was beneath that tarp in the barn—had been aware I was watching, I wasn't safe.

I took hold of Josh's hand over the center console. He squeezed my fingers, again rejoicing in me being home.

"I was tempted to start up some kissing game show at night." Humor splashed Josh's face. He moved his hand back to the steering wheel as we bounced onto the gravel drive to our house.

"Kissing game show?" His word choice pulled me from my dread spiral, if only briefly.

"Yeah. That's what it is." He paused, flattening his mouth like he was searching for the right words. "The one where they have all the make-out games?"

"You mean *Love Island*?" I put emphasis on the show's title. It absolutely was the kind of television that could rot a brain, but he knew the name.

"Probably. I just know every time I walk in the room, there are a dozen half-naked people around a firepit daring each other into three-way kisses."

He had a point there. "They don't win cash for kisses though."

"Wait, *is* there a big check at the end? How do you win money on a dating show?" His chortle burned a little, but as usual he wasn't off base.

I swallowed the urge to defend the show I loved. "It's like any other reality show where people get voted off. You win by staying until the end."

"So it's like *Highlander* with copious kissing? There can only be one couple?"

Actually, now that he mentioned it, the whole thing was more confusing. "You have to make it to the end and get voted the favorite couple by the viewers."

"I'm so glad I don't have to date now. I wouldn't know where to start. Apps. Swiping. Getting millions of viewers like you to say they like watching me make out with my partner."

I fake slugged him, but it was light and playful. "That's the only reason you are glad you're not in the dating game?"

"Well, I supposed there'd be a bitch of a drive for dates now that I live in the sticks."

I laughed until tears ran down my cheeks.

Josh's smile dimmed the longer my chuckle fit went. "It wasn't that funny."

"You. Saying. *Sticks.*" I gasped for breath between each word.

"What?" Josh grimaced in a clear attempt to be cool when he was feeling anything but.

Familiarity suffused my muscles. This banter I could do. "It's like you learned how to talk by watching Nick at Nite or some horribly dated movie from the seventies."

He sputtered. "Wait, so the idea of me seeking love isn't the problem? It's the way I said it?"

I got out of the car. The sun had already set, but I beelined it for the chicken coop. Josh followed.

"Emily?" The harshness in his voice slowed my steps.

When he caught up to me, his cheeks were blotchy. It wasn't the slow rising of blush of amour, but the punched dots of ire. He was honestly mad? We poked at each other like this all the time. Had keeping secrets made us strangers?

"You weren't serious," I said with all the softness I could muster. One long step forward, and I was up against him, hip to hip, hand cradling his jaw. "We are a pair."

"We're a package deal," he agreed.

My lips pressed firm to his, reassurance, promise, and hope that it wasn't a lie shot along my nerves at the contact.

"Endgame," he whispered. A slow summer breeze tried to snatch the promise, but I caught it.

He might not have seen the teeth. He might not have been able to align his brain to the danger around us. But he was mine.

I'd find that tooth. If I could make him see it, I could make anyone. His embrace was tight enough that my ribs whined under the pressure.

Beyond his shoulder, the barn loomed. It was two stories as ever, but the weathered boards had stretched to make the building rise higher overhead. Not that a building could grow. I was simply closer to the house, which altered the perspective, right?

A shadow flitted past the hayloft window. I jerked, but Josh didn't notice. Or chose not to acknowledge the sudden stiffness in my body against his. I watched for a light, a noose, another peek at a person, but the shadow remained elusive.

When Josh finally released me, he was steadier on his feet. The heat on his cheeks faded. That boyish grin that always conjured a matching one on my face appeared. The twist of muscle in my cheeks lighting in response wasn't as immediate as usual.

Josh didn't notice. "I put that white wine you like in the fridge before I left. Want me to open it?"

His hands still held mine, like we were about to make out after a first date and not as though we'd just been throwing verbal jabs because we joked about breaking up. *What kinds of dumbasses joke about finding new lovers with their partners?* This was the kind of thing old me might have talked about with Serena or, after enough wine, with my mom. But I had neither now.

"That would be great." I pressed a quick kiss to his shoulder. "Let me feed the girls real quick, and then I'll be ready to couch snuggle."

He shook his head. "I promise I took care of your chickens, babe." His tone remained this side of saccharine.

"Oh, I'm sure they're not hungry, but I bet they missed their mama." I missed the birds but wanted their henhouse's secrets more.

His laugh was loud enough that it should have echoed back from against our house, the barn, and maybe even a crop sprinkler parked a mile out. "Fine. Chicks before dicks."

I rolled my eyes. "Yes, those chicken hussies."

Josh jutted his chin out like he could command the universe. *Men.* "If you're not inside in five, I'm coming to get you."

"To do what?" His take-charge tone was so at war with his relaxed posture. What was this husband of mine up to?

Had he seen the tooth and was trying to distract us both? It was mostly working.

"Throw you over my shoulder." He slapped my butt and walked toward the house. "I saw that in a movie too."

I shook my head and hurried to the hens. Dorothy and Sophia brushed my ankles and gladly took the food. Blanche lifted her head inside the coop, but didn't deign to come out to say hello. Probably full from yet another fruit foray. No teeth on the floor, and I even ran my fingers through the straw to make sure. Josh had cleaned it up. In the dark, I couldn't go searching for wherever he'd dropped the muck. I latched the gate. Huh. There were scratch marks on the outside of the enclosure's door. A shadow obscured my fingers on the wood. I spun. Alone again.

The pale glow of artificial light stretched from the kitchen window. It'd be safer there, with my husband. I pretended not to hear the rumble of a truck in the fields. *Welcome home, I guess.*

Once inside, I found a half-full glass of sauv blanc waiting for me and a reality show Josh actually liked on the TV. A sputter and pop of exhaust stilled me.

"You going to sit?" Josh gestured beside him, like unveiling a new plush seat on the couch.

The old red pickup pulled up beyond the bay window at the front of the house. Tyler was on my farm at night. Did he have a girl with him? Would I see her picture on the newspaper website next week? The truck parked. Headlights dying slowly. Dripping fear down my neck that a killer was walking up to my doorstep.

CHAPTER 32

I NEEDED WINE FOR THIS. LIKE A WHOLE BOTTLE. GRAVEL crunched outside, crescendoing with increasing closeness until the sound shifted to the creak of a wooden step, the clunk of boots on the planks outside the door. I picked up the stemless wineglass Josh had filled generously and drank it like a frat boy with a pen and a PBR.

Gulped and gone.

It did exactly shit for my nerves because it's not like my body metabolized alcohol fast enough to keep pace with my fears clomping up to the front door.

Josh was already pulling the door open when our visitor knocked. The full glass of the front door, the wide window beside it, meant one couldn't hide outside the front of my house. We'd have seen them coming. We saw the fields swaying beneath the moon. We saw the sun stretch sleepy and then sharp each morning. We saw the dust scattered from nearby movement but would have to guess if it was a truck, a person, or an animal. None of which mattered during the day. Because none of it came to the door.

Except whatever had left teeth on the porch. It'd come right up when I was zonked out. It'd used the night and my fatigue to get close. To get right where my husband now stood. To where a farm-hand now stood.

Josh shifted his weight onto one side, and the casual stance let him fill the doorway. He wasn't so broad as to actually graze the frame, but he leveraged his body like he was.

"Hi, Mr. Hauk." The smooth masculine voice hiccuped on our last name.

"Nick." Josh's acknowledgment was sharp, rude, not the way my husband usually spoke to anyone.

Wait. *Nick?* I approached my husband's back, letting my palm rest on his shoulder. Was Tyler waiting in the truck? The vehicle wasn't idling.

Nick had never approached me. In fact, I'd never seen him alone on the farm. He was always arms-deep in a project. Cleaning out the pallets, loading fertilizer, hauling whatever needed to be shuffled around. He was every bit as old as Tyler—at least nineteen—but the bulldozer way he attacked all farmwork made me view him as younger. Even from my worn running paths, his need to seek guidance and praise from others had been apparent. The one time we'd spoken, he'd been deferential. Respectful. Ray had told him to leave the lady from California to her business—likely in kinder terms—and he'd taken it to heart. Nick didn't want to be seen talking to me. Didn't want to stop his work and fall behind. He was the Huckleberry Finn to Tyler's Tom Sawyer. So why was he at our house?

"Can I help you with something, Nick?" Josh pushed. That cold bite to the kid's name sent a shiver down *my* spine.

Nick stuttered through a few attempts before finally settling on, "Sorry for knocking so late."

Josh pounced. "It *is* late."

Jeez. Asshole much? I stepped in, slipping under Josh's arm. "Is everything okay, Nick?"

Nick's eyes flared white. His attention flitted to my chest, and I pretended not to notice. "Yes, ma'am."

Josh's hand found my waist, yanked me closer. "Ray didn't say anything about you needing to speak with me." Josh said this like there was a standing agreement. Like a rule had been broken. A big one.

How were there rules on this farm I didn't know about? What more did he know about the truth here? *Did* he know about the teeth?

"Yeah. Sorry. Ray tried to come by earlier, but you weren't here..."

Nick focused on my husband, all attention on the menace radiating from him. I scoped out the truck. The windows were dark. The aging red paint took on the tone of rust in the low light. It matched the barn in that way. Tinged with age and secrets.

And probably blood.

My stomach soured. Probably the nine ounces of wine I'd thrown into it like I was lobbing laundry into the dryer.

But unless Tyler was lying on the bench in the cab or flattened in the bed, he wasn't out there. If he felt the need to lie where the dead had been, under a tarp too, then good for everyone, I guess.

"I just needed to tell you about the barn, sir," Nick continued. *The barn.* I swayed on liquid legs. The place was supposed to be *barely* used. Josh had told me so. Said it was strange that I saw anyone going in and out on the regular. But then he also told me I hadn't seen a light on in the loft, that music hadn't played, and that the building didn't move all over the goddamned place. I had the logs in my running journal to prove it shifted. I'd get new numbers tomorrow. It had appeared to loom closer today, but I'd have the steps to show it tomorrow. Now this kid was on our doorstep saying he had information? This wasn't in my head.

"What about the barn?" I prompted, because there was no way I was letting Josh scare this kid off.

My husband scowled. Any other time I'd joke about how he looked like that old-man-yells-at-cloud meme from *The Simpsons*, but right now I was pissed that he was trying to put the kibosh on this.

Nick lowered his gaze but answered, "We had to move equipment around inside, ma'am."

"Oh?" What did that mean? Why would we care? "Like what?"

Josh jumped in before Nick could answer. "Thanks for letting us know. It's not a problem."

The farmhand nodded like a bobblehead. Like he was the kind of kid who agreed to anything. "Of course. I just know you store some things in there, and I didn't want us to be in the way if you needed access."

Josh lifted a hand, like it would stop the guy from talking.

Nerves had the better of Nick though, and his politeness

continued. The guy's hands were clasped together in front of him. He wrung his fingers but kept eye contact with the grumpy man at my side. "I just know you've called the sheriff before, and I didn't want to scare you or anything."

If Nick knew, they all did. Did they know it was me? Had they been watching me as much as I'd been watching them? "Oh."

Josh leapt on my loss of words. "That was all a misunderstanding."

Nick nodded, but his attention kept flicking to me like he was waiting for an apology or for me to accept one. The whole interaction set my nerves on edge.

"Right." Nick said quickly. "If you need us to clear space or move anything, just give a holler."

"We've been parking the car next to the house." Josh lifted his chin toward the sedan.

"What about those—" the farmhand started.

"We're good," Josh shut down the conversation. His arm tightened around my waist, pulling me against his side in a move that might have been sexy if we didn't have a teenager standing in front of us.

"Okay then. Really sorry to bother you." Nick tucked his hands in his pockets, turned, and trudged down toward the truck.

I should have let him go. I should have let this end. I wasn't good at *should haves*. I called after him, "Thanks, Nick. Were you working alone today?"

He opened the driver's door and then looked back toward our house. A Polaroid camera sat on the dash. The corner of Nick's mouth pulled up in a wry little grin. "I'm never alone on the farm, ma'am." Light reflected off something in the truck cab, but Nick was inside and firing the engine before I could consider it further. He waved goodbye and kicked up clouds of dirt as he peeled toward the highway.

"What was that?" Josh asked, already trying to tug me back into the house.

My legs locked. I stared at the plumes of dust, wishing they'd at least Rorschach out some hint of what was happening. "Right? Isn't that the other guy's truck?"

"What?" Josh stilled. "You're worried about their truck?"

"Not worried," I corrected him, as though that was the silly part of this conversation. "Just I've never seen anyone but Tyler drive that truck. And those two are always together."

And one of them had the kind of camera that had taken that picture I'd found in the barn. The one I needed to compare to Kinsey McAllen.

"I think the truck belongs to Ray." Josh dropped his hand from my waist, but quickly took my hand instead. "C'mon. I know you're my hot farm wife, but can we get back to sexy couch wife?"

I laughed, temporarily disarmed. "Sexy couch wife? What even is that?"

"Come to the couch and we'll find out." He waggled his eyebrows, and while objectively not sexy, it was certainly endearing. And 100 percent my Josh.

How could he flip so quickly from being a total jerk to a teenager, to being Mr. Playful with me?

"Why did he think we'd care if they rearranged the barn?" There would be no avoiding this conversation. Whether it was the secrets, the time away, or the wine, I was ready to ask him questions.

"Because it's our barn?" Josh stretched his legs out, crossing them at the ankles. Peak comfort on the couch.

"But they know we don't use it. He said we did."

"He's practically a high schooler, Em, you're overthinking this." That was me. The problem. "I don't think I am. He said we store things in there, that Ray wanted you to know."

They knew I'd called the authorities on them.

Josh leaned forward, no longer faking ease. He planted his elbows on his knees like he was going to give me a sportsball coaching. "Why are you so set on the barn being something terrible?"

"I'm not!" I choked on the retort.

"I thought we were past you being convinced someone was fucking with you from the barn. But I didn't think that mean you'd start thinking I was to blame."

I hadn't brought up the lights or the music in weeks. I hadn't told him about the voice or the mold or the photos. I hadn't even shown him the steps I'd logged proving the place was shifting on our property. But the pity in his gaze said he knew. He'd watched it all and pretended it wasn't real.

Must be nice.

"What was in the chicken coop?" I swallowed any emotion, inflection gone.

"What?" he sputtered. "What are you even asking?"

"I asked you to clean the coop while I was gone. I told you there was something on the floor of their house. What was it?" I locked my muscles, hoping hardening my body would somehow strengthen my point.

"There was nothing there!" Josh shot to his feet, storming straight for me.

"*Don't let him touch you.*" The words were freezing, but my feet moved anyway. She was here. Alice. She knew the truth, and she wanted me away from Josh.

He stilled when I backpedaled. "Emily." Sorrow filled his throat. He coughed, clearing whatever regret lodged there.

I kept my voice even. "Tell me what was in the coop, Josh."

"Nothing." He threw his hands in the air like I was being the frustrating one. "There was nothing but dirty straw and chicken shit."

I pulled my phone from my back pocket. Showed him the picture he'd sent me. I zoomed in on the tooth. "What does that look like to you?"

He was quiet for a long moment. The only sound in the living room was the heavy breaths of agitated people.

I expected him to lie, but there was only astonishment. "A tooth."

"Exactly."

"The...the...teeth were..."

"Real? Not in my head? Yeah. I didn't lie to you, and I'm not losing my shit." I shouldn't have had to say it.

His skepticism didn't dissipate. Josh shook his head. "I honestly didn't see it. There was nothing there."

"Well, it's here." I pointed at the picture again, like he might have missed it.

He nodded a few times, gaze fixed to the floor instead of the proof in my hand.

"Em?" He waited for me to acknowledge him. When I did, he continued. "What does that have to do with the barn and that kid?"

"I don't know," I said honestly. "But I know that you lied about both, and I really hate it."

"Don't tell him. Don't tell him. Don't tell him." The voice grew louder and louder the closer I got to asking what else he could be hiding from me.

"Why were you so cold with Nick?" I asked, hoping it would stop the litany of warnings from the frigid voice. Alice might not trust Josh, but I did. He wasn't a bad person; he was my husband. I needed to give him a chance.

His shoulders slumped. Josh rocked back on his heels but didn't back away. "Because I wanted to have a nice night with my wife. I missed you so much these last days. I don't want to live on a farm alone. I want to be here with you."

"You're mad because he interrupted couch time?" I didn't hide my disbelief.

"I also didn't much like that he ignored Ray's rules. They aren't supposed to come to the house unless it's an emergency." He cupped both my biceps in his palms, holding me steady. "And before you think it's some weird classist move or because you called the cops on the workers, it's about making sure everyone understands that Ray runs the farm, not us. We aren't in charge of any of that. They can do whatever they want out in those fields. But this house is ours."

"I called in an emergency," I reminded him.

"What you *thought* was an emergency. Nothing happened, and that's going to make them wary of us." He pulled me to the couch.

I looked toward the window, not willing to face him now. "I found a ring. The one I saw on that hand in the barn."

"A ring?" His skepticism was bitterer than I'd ever tasted it.

I snapped back to face him, the ghost's chill kissing my nape. "Yes. This farm is littered with proof of what I saw."

His hand found my thigh and squeezed, like it was all that kept him from throwing it in the air. "Then show me."

I'd wanted this, but now the weight of it all crashed into my chest. "What's the point, Josh?"

"To make you feel safe," he muttered.

"No. Me showing you actual proof—photos and jewelry and my own firsthand account of seeing *blood*—isn't enough for you. If I bring it out here, you're going to tell me there's some logical reason I didn't consider. Like how the reason you want to keep the farmers separate is this reasonable request for boundaries."

CHAPTER 33

"IT'S NOT THAT I DON'T BELIEVE YOU, EM. I WANT YOU TO show me all of it. I want to hear what you're thinking." He sighed so heavily I felt it in *my* lungs. "But I also saw you through the last year. Memories of your mom can send you spiraling."

"They don't anymore."

"No," he admitted, "not now. But they did. You can see how I might think—especially after police were involved and cleared the farmers of any wrongdoing—that perhaps not sleeping and your grief might be a factor here."

I locked my jaw, teeth gnashing. I wasn't making this up. The ring was real. The Polaroid was real. The teeth were real. Shit. Alice's death was real. But he made so much sense. He could say this same thing to anyone else, and they'd nod and agree. So why did disgust churn in my gut when I lifted my chin in agreement? "I can see that."

"My choices here are about building our life, babe." Josh pulled me close, resting his chin on the top of my head. My body instantly relaxed into his. This spot—the wife spot—was my safe place. My happy place. And yet my mind rebelled as though his cradling me were infantilizing.

"This farmhouse is our fresh start."

"Free from nosy neighbors and toxic memories," he agreed.

Only toxicity had followed us. The darkness beyond these walls practically proved my soul sought sadness. I'd left my mom's possessions in California, now on their way to new homes where they'd be appreciated. She hadn't left me though. Not the heart of her. Even now, with Josh swaying our bodies in tandem, it was her voice in my head. Alice's ghastly chill replaced by the familiar focus of my mom at her best. I imagined her asking, "Are you seriously going to let him ignore the fucking teeth outside?"

Grasping this new life was proving more challenging than it should be.

Sweat slicked the small of my back. Did Josh notice my shirt sticking? I tilted my chin up, forcing space between us and bringing that roguish smile into view. The one that had a way of making me go gooey even after seven years. But not today.

I wet my lips. Josh clocked the movement, eyes hungry.

"It's supposed to be us versus the world," I started.

He jumped in immediately. "Always, babe."

"But there are human teeth outside our home. Like outside-of-mouth teeth." A full-body gag could not express how ick the whole thing was. "And you saw them. I *know* you saw them and then you just pretended not to. You stood there and looked at me with all that pity on your face and *lied*. So when did you decide not to trust me? You owe me an explanation, Josh, because I got nothing."

Josh's humor faded, sharpening his features. "I didn't lie to you."

"Hard disagree." My full-body shudder did not go unnoticed.

"I'm doing my best here with what I have, but I'm on your side. I'm *always* on your side." He leaned in, all earnest and direct, but the tilt in his chin was enough for me to know he was offended.

Join the club.

I couldn't look at him. "It doesn't feel like it right now."

"I was there every night during hospice. Every morning the days and weeks after your mom's funeral. I am never abandoning you."

"Interesting word choice." I sucked my teeth like it'd clear my distaste for *abandoning.*

"I'm not saying the photo couldn't have been a tooth, but I didn't see anything when I went out there."

The barn had moved on me. The lights would be on, then in a flash they were off. The screams suddenly went silent when I sought help. Could the teeth have been stolen away before Josh saw them? Why was he not seeing any of this?

I wouldn't lose my courage. "There is something *off* here, Josh."

"We should look for it." His attention danced around our living room, like the molars were going to be on a shelf next to an African violet.

"Them," I corrected, getting my phone screen back in his face. This time I swiped over to the blurry image of the teeth on our porch.

"Those look even less like teeth than the other picture." His grumble was punctuated with a longing look at the bottle of wine.

I hadn't kept a single damn secret from him until my mom had died, until he'd looked at me like I was the ghost, like I wasn't still the same woman he'd married. "Do you think I would lie to you?"

His answer was immediate. "Never."

"I'm telling you there were teeth on the porch. How are you not freaking out now?" Because if he believed me, he'd be scared too.

Josh staggered backward, hand gripping the back of his head like I was bringing on a migraine. *Tough, buddy.* "I am freaking out, Em. It's just..."

"Just what?" No more hiding. He needed to say it.

"You also think the barn is moving. A barn that was built decades ago. And then the things with the farmhands." There it was. His face curdled with pity. "I don't think they're out to get you."

"I never said they were after me, but..." Was it worth showing him anything? Was it worth telling anyone what I'd found? My own husband thought I was making it up. My proof should have scared the shit out of him. My hands shook. Every piece I'd gathered had been for nothing.

"It just isn't logical, Emily." He invoked my whole name like it made him the adult in the room and not the one running from what he didn't understand.

"Give me a logical answer for teeth on our porch and in the henhouse, Joshua." I could throw around accusatory full names too.

He stumbled over to the wine. Poured himself a glass and downed it like I had when the headlights hit the front window. His cheeks lit with a ruddiness of uncorked emotion. "I can't think of a good reason for there to be teeth on the porch."

"People have died here." There. I said it.

"No, Em, no one has died." Exhaustion throttled his reply, despite his regular nine hours of sleep.

However, one of us was accustomed to functioning without a reserve of energy. I didn't hold back. I reminded him about Alice Belkin's death, her daughter's missing-but-presumed-dead status. I showed him the links on my laptop. Missing girls. Kinsey McAllen and the description of the guy she was last seen with. I pulled out the Polaroid and held it next to the girl's face. Made him look at the same girl in both. It was one degree milder than presenting a PowerPoint presentation. I gave him the information about how everyone on the farm is linked back to this family and tragedy.

Josh melted on the sofa.

"But we don't know that anything happened to Bridget, right?" he asked. He had to hear that he was reaching.

"I suspect very few people know what happened to her, but I have a good guess." And it involved that red pickup truck that had pulled up to our house tonight.

Josh blanched. Agog, he made the leap. "You think she was murdered, and her teeth were thrown on our porch a few years after?"

When he said it like that, I sounded like I was losing it.

I held a hand up, like it could stop him from looking at me like I was wearing crazy pants. "After what I saw in the barn..."

"If this is about it playing your mom's favorite songs in the middle of the night again, we've been over this. It's not possible. That's grief in action. You're taking the anti-anxiety pills at least, right?"

"I'm doing all the promised things, Josh." I was not. "This isn't about the music or the barn moving."

My running journal was proof of it shifting locations, but if my husband didn't trust me, there was no way he'd accept my numbers either. I'd hold it for now.

I continued before we could crack open the "Emily and her medication" conversation again. "It's about watching one of the farmhands drive away with a body in the back of his truck. It's about the way he spoke, like whoever was bleeding beneath that tarp had inconvenienced him."

Josh lowered his head but then nodded for me to continue. It looked like he was listening, like he wanted to hear what I had to say. This was going to be it.

"Anyone who could do that, could come for us. I don't know how teeth ended up on our porch or where they went, but I wouldn't have dreamt there could be a killer on our farm either." God, I couldn't look at him. The ceiling fan whirred softly overhead.

"I—I—I don't know what to say." His nostrils flared, face tightening like he could smell the threat of death beyond our door.

"Say you believe me." Hope was a lure in the distance. Sticky, sweet, and so bright. I wanted to swallow it whole and let it light me from within.

Josh took my hands in his. Warmth enveloped me. Instantly I was less alone. "I always have your back, Em."

"That's not quite an agreement," I hedged.

"I believe you." He said the words with all the earnestness of a vow at the altar.

"What do we do now?" Because that was the point of telling

him. We were a team. He could help me solve this, save our farm, stop other girls from being taken.

"Right now? My God, we drink this wine." He inclined his head toward the chilled bottle sweating on the coffee table.

I yanked my hands from his.

He reached for me again. "It's too dark out to look around, but I'll get up early. Let's try to find the teeth in the morning."

"That's where we start?" Not calling the cops? Because if Josh believed me, they'd believe us together.

"I know you're right, but we need more than loose connections to take any action. The locals probably know all the stuff you do about the family who lived here before, and the deputies were already out here once." He was so practical.

"Fair enough." Alice Belkin's death had been ruled a suicide after all.

"If there are teeth, that changes everything." His confidence was a brick wall, and I bolstered my own on its foundation.

Josh set the alarm on his phone for fifteen minutes before sunrise. I tried not to think too hard about how he'd said "if" we found the teeth. Did that mean they might be gone? Did that mean he didn't think they existed and was merely placating me? Did we have to worry that whoever left them for us was different from who took them away? Who else knew what was happening here beyond me, likely Tyler, and now Josh?

Could I make it until morning without knowing?

Emily's Running Log:

2 minutes, 31 seconds to the barn—453 steps

CHAPTER 34

EVEN BY MY GARBAGE SLEEP STANDARDS, I SLEPT POORLY that night. Josh went to bed following his usual routine. He brought me the chill-and-sleep pill he very much wanted me to take before going to bed. I told him I wanted to drink water between it and all the wine but would be in soon. I threw the pill down the sink, which was probably horrible for turtles somewhere, but I couldn't very well leave it in the trash, and taking it now was laughable.

I stared at the barn as though I could will the light to come on. But there was only darkness and silence beyond the walls of my house. Josh and I had quickly annihilated that bottle of sauv blanc and opened a second. There were still at least two more glasses waiting to be poured. Picking my own tunes might help keep Mom's music at bay, right? A normal night, and then in the morning we could search our grounds for teeth. A shudder rattled my bones.

I pulled on headphones, connected the Bluetooth, and started my "Big Thoughts" playlist. How had this become my life? We'd moved here for a fresh start. Nebraska was clear skies, freedom, independence. And it was those things, but it'd also become a den for isolating secrets and crimes I couldn't have imagined happening in such a beautiful and safe place.

I propped my laptop on my folded legs, set up on the couch in peak work-from-home form: blanket draped over my shoulders, popcorn bowl wedged at one side, wineglass full, headphones bumping, and a search engine open before me.

What would it take to open a murder investigation? Who was the sheriff? I dug through all the possible next steps as if there was no question we'd find those teeth tomorrow. Who was going to collect them? Should we touch them? We had a fresh set of dish gloves. I could wear those. And just pretend it was gravel and not enamel and bone that had once been inside a person's mouth. My stomach clenched, and I sipped more wine like alcohol was an antinausea medication. My head hit that mush level where I could squish my forehead and the room took on the haze of a default Instagram filter.

My playlist flipped over to a Lady Gaga track and next thing I knew, I was sofa dancing while checking property records to see who my neighbors were. Shouldn't I have met them? I waved to them when they drove past while I jogged the dirt roads leading to our respective homes. The closest one was about a twenty-minute run away. The Colemans. They'd owned their acreage for 113 years. I mean, the family had; the current residents were the grandkids of the original farmer and his wife.

How did that work? I'd never considered following in my

mother's path. I loved music—who didn't?—but I wanted to dance to it and not dissect it. My mom loved every element.

"A song is like a puzzle, Emmy Bear," she'd told me.

"Can't it just be a moment for fun?"

"It's that too. But to make that perfect three minutes where you can feel every beat in your body and move without thought? Each layer needs to be in sync." She'd swayed like she heard notes beneath the buzz of the television playing in the next room.

I was seventeen and in my collage-art era. "So you're trying to balance the song."

"Exactly!" she'd beamed with pride.

"I want the eye to start here." I held up my latest piece, mapping the journey I wanted a viewer to go on. The plump lips to a pool of oil to the pom-poms to the splashes of pink and green.

"I can hear that song." Awe filled my mother in that moment. As if she saw me as the same kind of artist she was.

Was that how farmers were with their kids? Everyone here carried the mantle of the fields and the farm animals and the fourteen-hour days. What happened if you weren't willing to be the next generation of farmers? What if you swapped crops? What if you hired out all the work and acted as a manager?

Is that what Herb Belkin had done? He'd had no heir. Had he offered this property to his brothers? Their kids? Had Tyler

Jorgensen wanted this farm? If so, why wasn't it his? Why was he working for Ray and allowing the Californians to come claim the house?

I shook my head, sending my brain swimming. Too much wine then. I giggled. Okay, definitely too much wine. I pulled off the headphones, shut the laptop, and tottered on liquid legs to the bathroom to wash my face and consider going to bed like a healthy person.

Foam covered my face when I heard the first scream. Sharp, shrill, and directly in my ears. I spun to my right, but opening my eyes only put soap in them. My world blurred beneath burning bubbles. I clapped my hands to my face on instinct, but that only upped the firestorm at my eyes.

Another scream. I slapped my palm against the counter, feeling for the washcloth that should have been directly in front of me. The counter was too close, the cloth too far away, my eyes turning into charcoal pits. My wrist collided with the edge of a jar. Pain sang up my forearm. The ceramic of what I assumed was my moisturizer clacked then crashed on the floor. The wet splat of forty-dollar lotion on the tile was nothing compared to the screeching scraping the walls.

I fumbled the faucet on and dunked my face as best I could. The cold water cooled the ire in my eyes, but when I lifted my chin, my vision remained blurred.

The hazy halo beside me in the mirror was familiar regardless. The woman's face was missing—it was always missing, in the photos in the barn, in the momentary glimpses in glass—but I recognized her all the same. The teased ring of dark-brown hair, a lion's mane for a woman who had likely been brave for decades before she died.

"Alice?" Her name slid from my mouth like a promise. Though I had nothing I could assure her of. I'd barely convinced my husband to *consider* tragedy continued here.

The woman in the glass did not speak. There was no cold wind, but as she lifted her arm, goose bumps marched across my whole body. Her hand came into focus. Square nails, white tips, slender gold band on her ring finger. My chest ached. Even in death, the only part of her that could be seen was the symbol of her marriage, not her face. Not her.

I parted my lips like I would tell her these things. Tell her I saw her. Tell her I believed her. Tell her I was going to bring the truth to light. Even if that last part was wishful thinking.

I would try. For her. For her daughter. For—

A shriek erupted in the direction she pointed.

The barn.

It was always the barn.

God damn it.

This was an opportunity. Here it was. The screaming was happening. The barn was the source. A dead woman was sending me there. Josh could see it. He could experience it with me. We could do this together. Save someone. Save me.

I toed around the broken glass on the floor, rushing to the bed. My brain sloshed in a sea of white wine. Every motion was too big, too much. *Story of my life these days.*

I said Josh's name, but he didn't stir. The screams turned piercing.

How was he sleeping through this? My foot caught on the thick pile rug beneath our bed and pitched me right onto Josh's legs.

He didn't move.

He didn't groan.

Oh, God. Oh, God. Oh, God.

"Josh!" Now I was yelling. My voice punching straight to the exposed beams overhead. Concealing the shrieks from beyond our house.

Was he...? I slid my palm up his stomach to his chest. His heartbeat was relaxed and steady. Air, warmed by his body, brushed my skin. Josh was fine, if completely knocked out.

The apparition in the mirror remained in focus. Her hand emphatically gesturing toward the sound. Those manicured fingers said I was an asshole. Maybe I was. What kind of person ignored an obvious emergency, obvious distress to wake their partner?

My legs remained rubbery, but I could walk. I used Josh's nightstand to stabilize myself. His pill bottles toppled to the floor. How much of this was he taking? The pills rattled, but hadn't we just refilled? Whatever. I didn't want to math anyone's medicine, and I had bigger problems.

The bedroom door slammed open, bouncing against the doorstop to make it beat against the wall several times. No one stood there. No wind rushed in. The implication was clear though. Get the fuck outside and help her.

The screaming redoubled as I moved through my house. I shoved my feet into the slip-on shoes I'd left beside the back door—not planning to get caught unaware en route to the barn again—and booked it outside.

The floodlights set into the eaves of the farmhouse erupted white light around me. Cold, brilliant, and helpful. That light proved this time was different.

I ran toward the barn without question. The loft was illuminated, but a sickly yellow glow also stretched out from the barn doors to the east. The screams wrecked the air. I rushed past Cluckingham Palace. The girls flapped and nickered inside. *Same, hens.*

Yesterday morning it had taken me two minutes and thirty-one seconds to reach the barn. But time lengthened now. Even the thump of my pulse in my ears slipped into slo-mo. One beat for every eight steps, or was it nine? Each step on the uneven road mattered. If I bit it out here, I couldn't help anyone. And I couldn't get justice if I was dead too. My mushy muscles protested every move, and adrenaline thickened my throat. I clenched my jaw and told myself to keep breathing, keep moving, keep quiet.

As I approached the decrepit building, ice clamped around my forearm. The skin puckered and turned pink in a small band. The invisible hand yanked me toward the back of the barn. I was out here with no idea what I was doing; I would 100 percent take the guidance. *Ah, the back door.*

What was the point of tiptoeing into this building? What was I about to witness? How was I going to stop it? I should have brought a weapon. It was too late now. Where were the farm tools in the barn? Maybe I could find a big knife or a scythe. I'm pretty sure the grim reaper didn't wear joggers and an oversized pink tee, but he sure as shit carried a scary blade. Maybe I could fake the scary part.

It felt like a plan: find a tool I could turn into a weapon. Even if

I didn't know how to be menacing, I was strong, and the woman in that barn needed me. There wasn't another person to call for miles. If we didn't count Josh, and his numb and knocked-out status benched him.

I could do this. I swallowed my nerves and ignored the sourness in my stomach. Fear sobered me. My vision steady, my movements more precise.

I slipped through the door, clinging to the back wall. The lamplight didn't stretch here. A large tractor blocked my view both of the light source and of the people on the other side of the room.

Okay, Emily, you made it in here. You're inside and you are hidden. I coached myself like this was another round of marathon training, and I was just going to convince my core that it wasn't screaming for rest. Only there was an actual person weeping on the other side of this vehicle. She had been screaming for real. If I fucked up my workout regimen, I puked a bit. If I fucked this up, a living, breathing person would die. Was I already too late? Had taking the time to try to wake Josh risked her life? Had my stupid boozy night made me the worst person to rescue her?

"You don't get to leave," a masculine voice purred.

CHAPTER 35

MY STOMACH HOLLOWED AS THE TAUNTING THREAT stretched toward the rafters.

"But you knew you weren't going anywhere," the man continued.

I trembled, though the words weren't meant for me. I edged around the tractor, hand in contact with the metal for stability. The walls were as dilapidated inside as they were out. The roughened material sure to splinter under my touch. The wall in front of the tractor, though, had some rusted tools. Shadows hung over them, but around the front of the tractor, sepia lighting spilled forward.

Music played softly. I stopped. My heart stuttered. My lungs stilled.

Stevie Nicks's resonant vocals slipped over the air, filled every crevice of the barn.

"This one was her favorite, right?" He was taunting her. At least he was talking instead of whatever he'd been doing before that had such terrible sounds coming from the woman he spoke to on the other side of the room.

"Like you would know." There was a wheeze and hiss wrapped around the reply, but this girl was fighting. The voice was youthful, high, and determined to screw with the guy.

Bless her.

Thwack. A heavy thump on the other side of the tractor might as well have smacked my sternum. A scraping echoed through the room. The sound cut off with a soft grunt.

His grunt was wet and followed by the distinct sound of spit. "She destroyed this farm. You know that?"

"Fuck the farm." The disgust in the girl's voice was palpable. Thick enough that it made me want to spit too.

Slap. "Shut your mouth." Heavy footfalls clomped across the room, as though he were pacing.

"You don't have to do this. Any of it. They don't need me." The girl's wheezing grew more pronounced with each sentence.

The volume on Fleetwood Mac's "Landslide" was cranked loud enough that all I had was Stevie and my heartbeat in my ears. If the girl was still speaking, I didn't know.

I needed to do something. Standing here behind farming equipment wasn't saving anyone. I patted my pocket for my phone because I could absolutely call the cops now. This wasn't me showing evidence and asking them to investigate. This was about saving lives. Except my pocket was empty. Stupid fucking charging pad. It had to be sitting back in the house.

The girl yipped like a wounded animal, and adrenaline flooded my body. Even my fingertips lit ablaze.

She didn't have time for me to get the phone, didn't have

time for the sheriff to trek out here. I couldn't let Tyler do this to her.

The tools weren't too far away. I took my first tentative step forward. The old hay on the worn wood made the floors slippery. I shuffled another inch until I was in front of the tractor. The jaundiced light to my left pulled my attention. Like it could pull my life too. The warmth in the air, the treacle tainting everything in the barn, it enveloped me. The sweet sickness coating my throat.

I choked on it.

At the center of the grisly golden light was a blue tarp like the one I'd seen in the back of Tyler's pickup. The one with bloody fingers stretching from beneath it. His truck was backed through the barn's main door now, its tailgate lowered. The tarp had to be ten feet wide in both directions, and it stretched open in the center of the room. *Was this why they'd been "rearranging" in the barn?* Tears formed in the corners of my eyes, waiting there on my lids as though they were too fearful to fall. The room brightened through the glistening prisms.

Atop the ocean of plastic, a petite brunette woman sat bound to a metal chair with zip ties. Beneath mottled splotches on her cheek, her split lip, and the blood and sweat smeared across her brow, she was still Bridget Belkin. Her cherubic face was twisted into a sneer. Was her bravado running on fumes, or was that terror curling her features? Her black leggings were torn at the knees, the skin beneath raspberry and shouting in its own way. Her puffy eye narrowed toward the truck, where a small Bluetooth speaker sat on the edge of the bed. The pill-shaped device pumped out pop hits of the 1970s. Everything was wrong.

The lighting.

The sound.

The fact that Bridget Belkin was here. Back on the farm she grew up on. Bound. Injured. Where had she been? How was she back here? Why now?

I readied to run to the wall of tools. I scanned the items on the wall. Pliers, rusted saws, bridles for horses that hadn't lived on this estate in at least a decade. What could I use to save her? A small sickle-shaped blade was closest to me. It only had a trio of dots of rust on its edge. The handle was the length of my forearm, but I could manage lifting that. To save Bridget, I could heft it, swing it.

A shadow peeled forward from the side of the truck. His thumb pressing a button on the top of the speaker. Gone was Stevie's serene voice. The air crackled as though a storm was imminent. I shuffled forward, focused on keeping my motions as quiet as I could. I felt my way across the pegboard with the tools, never taking my gaze off the truck, off Bridget, off that shadow.

"You know this place is a legacy." The masculine voice was familiar but missing the sting of Tyler's ego. "We can't opt out of fate, Bridge."

"Please. Just let me go. What's the difference? Me leaving or you doing this?"

"What am I doing?" He preened, like they both knew the plan and he was getting off on making her say it back to him.

"Nick. We're family. Just don't."

Nick? I staggered, heel slipping against the slick straw. I banged my back against the wall laden with tools. Nothing fell. I expected the two teens to turn toward me, but they continued to glower at one another.

"You're choosing to leave the family, Bridget." Nick sauntered forward. His silver belt buckle shimmered in the light. He made a fist and struck the lip of the truck bed. A panel fell open, like a built-in toolbox. He pulled a ball-peen hammer from the interior, and let it dangle at his side. His fingers loose on the light wooden handle.

"This farm is toxic." Her vehemence rattled the walls. "Everything about this place screws with your head. Look at you, Nick. You have your own cousin tied up. We don't need to be this way."

"You think I want to do this?" Nick's nostrils flared. Pain made him look even younger. As though I were looking at a too-young-to-drive version of the farmhand. "It's not up to me."

"That's what I'm saying. It is, cuz. You don't have to be who they say you are. You don't have to haul feed and work twelve-hour days and see the same twenty people for the rest of your life."

Nick shook his head. "Your problem is loyalty."

I wrapped my fingers around the small scythe's handle and lifted it from the wall. Bridget might think she could get this guy to let her go, but the way he looked at her—like she was an obstacle to his goal—said he'd fully made up his mind. He might be scared to hurt her, but he'd already hit her. The whitening of his knuckles around the hammer handle said he was preparing to do it again.

I tightened my grip on my tool turned weapon. Icy cold gripped my shoulder.

"Be still," the voice said.

"This is your daughter," I whispered so softly even I could barely hear my words.

"*She was.*"

"Alice." My body trembled, but the ghost couldn't miss my words. "Let me save her."

"*Save yourself.*"

What kind of fucked-up family was this? Nick had kidnapped and injured his cousin because of "loyalty"? He was readying to do something far worse, and a dead woman was speaking into my ear, telling me to let him?

"I won't let him do this." The tears I'd stockpiled fell in earnest.

Nick trudged toward Bridget, like he was moving toward yet another chore. To Bridget, he said, "You could stay, you know. Make the choice."

"We both know I can't." She slumped against her bindings. "My parents are hammered half the time..." She sputtered, a fit of hysterics racking her body.

"A little booze isn't a reason to run."

Her chin rested on her chest, but Bridget's voice reached for the rafters. "That house is violence. I need a place I can dance without stepping on glass, where I can sing without worrying a fist is going to knock one of my teeth out again for being too loud."

Nick shuffled back a step. Had she gotten to him? "You just gotta listen to your parents. Your dad works hard here. This place needs its men in the fields, and its women keeping the home."

"I'm not some farmer's wife, Nick," Bridget sputtered. "I'm fifteen. I do 4-H. I'm a *cheerleader.*"

Wait. Fifteen? Didn't she disappear at fifteen? That was three years ago. She would be eighteen now. I narrowed my gaze at the horror show in front of me. I'd misheard her.

Maybe Nick had too. His attention slid to his truck, to his hammer, to the tarp beneath the girl's feet. Everywhere but at his cousin, bound and bleeding. Finally, he lifted his chin toward her. The move was so much like a dare that I lifted my makeshift weapon like I knew how to swing it.

"Your mom isn't well. Uncle Herb needs you to can food and cook and keep it together here." He said it all like he believed this was a reasonable ask of a teenage girl. As if it were totally normal for her to have to take care of her father because men couldn't clean their own clothes or make their own meals.

How had I thought he was the safe one?

Scratch tap scratch tap. The unnerving sensation of tiny feet at my back was unrelenting. I clenched my jaw, tightened my grip, and moved.

Or tried to.

Again cold embraced me. I twisted and jerked, but it was as though frigid metal bands had locked around my upper body. A chill bit my skin, though the barn should be sweltering.

"*You need to run.*" Alice rasped against my ear. I squeezed the sickle handle. Maybe if I twisted enough, I could get free. Black mold oozed from the wood between my fingers.

"*Run!*" Alice's voice had gone ragged. From distance or pain, I didn't know. Could the dead feel agony? It sounded like they could.

I couldn't leave Bridget though. Shouldn't leave her. Her mother shouldn't be telling me to flee.

The wall behind me, the door maybe, rattled. It was the sucking push-pull of heavy wind hitting the side of the building. Or an angry mother?

Mine? Bridget's? The sound of Fleetwood Mac suffused the air. The room. The bucking boards on the surrounding walls.

"Run. Now. Run run run!" Each plea connected with my back as though it sought to flay me.

I stepped toward the frightened girl and the boy who loomed before her. His back was to me now. Did he weep for what he was about to do? Did he smile? Did he feel anything when he stared into her doe eyes?

Bridget's lower lip trembled. Her earlier bravado exchanged for resignation. The latter was far more terrifying. My heart tripped in my chest, like I hadn't been training it for exertion.

"Runrunrunrunrunrunrunrunrunrunrunrun."

The frigid litany reached a fever pitch, the urgency cutting into me. The rasping scream slipped beneath my skin, shaking and slicing until I should have been shreds. Sludgy mold squished between my fingers. The hand scythe slipped from my grip. Its clatter broke me. I dropped to my knees. The ground sticky and dark.

My name surged overhead. Not Mrs. Hauk. *"Emily."*

I turned away from Bridget and Nick. My fingers fumbling over the filthy floor. The tool couldn't have melted into the goddamned wood, but the harder I sought it, the less my touch found.

As soft and as cold as the ghastly voice urging me to flee, Nick whispered, "I really am sorry."

The wet *thwack* that followed crushed my soul.

Fuck the tool. I rocketed to my feet and sprinted past the nose of the tractor.

Bridget's head lolled forward. Gore splattered the tarp, her clothes, her body.

Nick's hammer.

He swung again. *Crack. Squelch. Crack.*

"There is no leaving," he said through gritted teeth. Did he believe himself? Did Nick want to leave too?

I could help with that. I'd tackle his ass and figure out a way to get the cops here later. I lurched forward, but warm hands caught my hips.

I screamed.

Nick turned slowly toward me. That unnervingly slow shift that only had a place in creepy dolls in blockbuster horror flicks. But he looked *through* me. Nick didn't acknowledge me or anyone. Relief washed over his blood-speckled face.

Bridget's chest no longer lifted with breath. Nick swung again anyway.

"Emily!" The hands on my hips jerked me backward against a hard body. "What are you doing?"

That voice. Familiar. Safe. Mine. I pivoted to face my husband. He was in pajama pants and flip-flops, like he'd run from the house. The screams had finally pierced his veil of sleep. Thank the Lord.

"Do you have your phone? Call 9-1-1." Panic thickened my tongue, bumbling the words.

"Babe. Calm down." He hunched down, like he was checking my pupils for sign of a head injury. "What are you talking about? Are you hurt?"

What was wrong with him? He was being too loud. Nick would hear him. I looked back at the crime happening less than a dozen feet away, but Nick was diligently cleaning up a fucking murder like no one was watching.

I pointed toward the horror show, as if my husband couldn't recognize a fucking crime in progress.

He stared past me, brow furrowed, like he was trying to solve a tricky sudoku.

"He can't see it. He wouldn't have helped her." The ghastly voice didn't hide its disdain for my spouse.

"He would help," I said back to the ghost. He loved with his whole heart, and he trusted, and he defended. Would a man who had held me up through Mom's hospice not have a heart?

"What?" Josh shook me a little, like he was at a loss to what was going on.

Same, man, but I was starting to understand.

He'd never looked out the window and seen a light. He never heard the music. He had no sense of foreboding with this ugly, falling-apart barn. He couldn't see Nick wiping his hammer on Bridget's shirt and then stuffing it back in the toolbox. Because it wasn't happening.

Not now. But this *had been* real. Back when Bridget was fifteen.

Alice had chosen to show me this. She'd planted those screams in my mind or resurrected the memory in reality. Had she heard her daughter's pleas from bed that night? Had Herb? Had they both been too drunk to wake? Bridget had been killed here. In this barn. By a boy who still worked on the farm. Who believed loyalty to the family, to the farm, to knowing your place was most important. He'd come to my door this very night. He'd told us they'd rearranged the barn. Why? Was he planning more? I'd come to this farm with the intention of making it mine. If this horror show Alice had made me witness said anything, it was that Nick would do anything to keep this farm in the family.

So why hadn't he? How had they let it go?

This was a mindfuck I wasn't prepared for. Where was Bridget now? Who else had met terror in the barn? Was I next?

And yet Josh had seen none of it. No blood. No Nick. No Bridget or her broken body. Because Alice didn't trust him, now I was alone in this knowledge. As I had been since we'd arrived in Nebraska. For my husband there had been no lights, no music, no murder.

I pressed my palms to my face, surprised to find smooth, dry skin. Even my body was gaslighting me.

Understanding how much danger was real—in the now—and why Alice chose to haunt *me* was a problem I had to tackle after I convinced my husband I had not completely lost my shit. My insides quaked. I'd known there'd been danger, but it was one thing to sense it and another to see it. My hands shook, and I pressed them together to hide the adrenaline rush.

"Sorry, I got spun around—"

"What are you doing out in the barn this early?" As if the hour was the real problem.

"I heard that screaming...fox again." Now I was a liar too.

"I heard it too." He loosened his grip on me but didn't let go. "I actually thought it was you. Scared the shit out of me."

"I tried to wake you." The fear, the regret, the loneliness in my words were real even if the reason required squinting at the truth.

His hands left my sides and went directly into his pockets. "Sorry about that. I accidentally double dosed tonight."

Was he lying to me or to himself? He'd been going hard on the Ambien the last couple weeks. Guess he was picking up my pill-popping slack.

"We're both okay now," I said, trying to convince myself. "Can we get out of here?"

"Of course." He took a couple long steps to the doorway and pushed it wide.

I picked up the hand scythe from the floor and placed it back on the rack. The urge to bring it with me left my palm itchy. I spared a long look back toward Bridget's body and Nick, but the echo of trauma had evaporated. The room was dim, but the cleared space was empty save a few fertilizer bags stacked against the wall.

"Did you find the missing chicken?" Josh asked as we stepped out of the barn.

Only the dread dripping down my spine stopped me from screeching. Bile coated my throat. I swallowed like it could clear the taste of sick from my mouth. Like I could forget what I'd just witnessed so easily.

"I went after the fox's screams," I said, continuing with my half-truth. There *had* been screams. "Who is missing?"

"Blanche. Again. Probably off scavenging." He shrugged like this was no big deal. "That bird is a big DIYer."

I tried to focus on his words. To find normalcy. To buy myself time to figure this out.

"She's self-sufficient." I wished I believed that. Blanche snuck off in the sunshine for berries, but that bird nestled down in the dark. She was a cozy girl at heart. Had Nick taken her? Where was he, and why had he said anything about the barn—was he taunting me?

"We should look for her again at sunrise." Josh took my hand and led me back toward our house. Like this was a romantic stroll in the dark and not a night that sent us both running toward screams.

I'd been trying to stay quiet in the barn, to protect Bridget. When I took my first sip of coffee, my throat practically sizzled. How long had I been screaming? What good had it done? Why hadn't Bridget's parents come to her aid? If Josh could find me, why hadn't Alice found Bridget?

Was that why Alice was dead too? Had failure pulled her under? I wouldn't let that be me.

The ghost's conviction as she vowed that Josh wouldn't have helped her daughter, wedged fresh worry between my ribs. Each inhale pushing on my certainty that we could still do the right thing.

I just had to find where Nick had taken Bridget's body. Or find that hammer.

Whatever I did next, I sure as hell was avoiding Nick Ditmer.

CHAPTER 36

JOSH LACED HIS SNEAKERS AND WENT ON THE MORNING RUN
with me. He said he was watching for Blanche. We'd already scoured
around the house for both her and the teeth before the sun had fully
crested the horizon. See, he was on my side. He was the one who
brought up the need to discover that molar again.

But after an hour digging through the muck bucket from the
chicken coop, poking our heads into the crawl space beneath the
front porch, and walking a lap around the barn, Josh suggested we
try a run and then look again.

Blanche wasn't found beneath her favorite berry bush. I'd been
trying to pick only from the top because I figured if my chicken
could snatch the bottom berries, other critters could too.

Purple pulp squished into the soil beneath the plant, but there
was no sign of the ambitious hen. My attention strayed to the haggard barn door nearby. The one I'd entered last night. The one
Alice had directed me to, that had left me alone in that barn with
the ghost of what had happened three years earlier. My shoulders

ached from carrying the weight of what I'd seen. So I agreed to run, because it centered me. A flush of endorphins could cure the cortisol eating away at my muscles now. Then I'd be clearheaded enough to figure this out: how to protect my farm and how to expose what had happened in that barn.

Josh and I took a loping pace—more a jog than a run—out toward the highway. The slower cadence was easier on Josh's medicine headache and kinder to my dehydrated quads. It did, however, mean we moved at a slow enough pace that my mind refused to clear and Josh had breath to talk.

"Blanche probably didn't come this far, right? What kind of distance can a chicken cover?" he asked as we turned on to the well-graveled road.

I stayed on the grassy shoulder of the path. Even in trail-running shoes, I hated the sensation of running on rocks.

"We could Google it when we get back, but Blanche has to be closer to the house." Because I didn't want to think about where else she might be.

The sun was that perfect clementine hue that made for a ripe day. Yet my insides withered with rot. I needed to talk to someone, and I needed it to be Josh. I let the breeze and the soft slap of my sneakers against the silt fill the emptiness for as long as I could.

Finally, I asked, "What do you think of Nick Ditmer?"

Josh's toe caught on the ground, and he stumbled forward. He caught himself before he could fall. "I don't think about him."

"Um, okay, weirdo." I had not expected that.

He tried to recover, taking a couple high steps. "He works for

Ray. I'm sure he's fine. I just try not to interact much with the kids on the farm."

"Boundaries, I remember." Had the answer been so shaky last time?

"Yeah. Boundaries." Distance had crept into the conversation despite our shoulders bumping against one another's every so often.

If he shut that down, now wasn't the time to ask about Bridget, but my mind churned with possibilities. She'd been killed on our farm. In our barn. What had they done with her body? Was she in our fields? Had she been taken far away? How many places would someone who grew up in the country know to hide a body?

I couldn't very well go to the cops with what I had. Seeing a murder from three years ago was less likely to impress them than the bloody body I'd seen before—only had that been a memory too? Maybe if I had one of those teeth. Maybe if one belonged to Bridget. But where would I even look now?

The answer was obvious: I had to go back into the barn.

This hadn't ended with two teenagers and a hammer. Nor with Alice's death the following year. The history haunted me for a reason. I could help; I had to help.

Only my husband was glued to my hip, and he hadn't seen so much as a fleck of mold or a spot of blood or an eerie glow. Made it hard to bring him on board—but then Alice's ghost never wanted that.

"Why don't you shower first?" I offered when we got back into the house. "I'm going to check on the hens. Mother Clucker gets worked up when Blanche is gone."

Josh linked his fingers with mine. "Or you could come shower with me?"

Three hours of small touches, little pats, and bumping ankles made it clear Josh needed the contact to know I was here. Whether he believed I'd truly gone to the barn in search of a fox didn't matter. I'd scared him last night. If he only understood how much danger we could be in...

My soul remained in tatters. I'd heard Nick's determination, Bridget's acceptance, and the wet sounds of his hammer connecting; it all continued to reverberate in my skull. Like it too wanted to shatter to release the pain. Unshed tears burned my eyes, but I demurred with a rain check that I hoped wouldn't put Josh back into unhelpful mode.

He said he'd hold me to that "later," but went to shower alone. All I could think about was that barn. What I'd seen. What I could find.

God, I wished I could tell him and be believed. To have an ally would change everything. But I was alone. Like Bridget had been. Like Alice. Maybe that was part of being a woman on this farm.

Why I'd thought I could dart to the barn and back before Josh finished his shower, I don't know. Ambition? Delusion? Hope?

As soon as the water kicked on, humming softly through the kitchen wall, I booked it out the door. I tapped on the step counter and the stopwatch apps on my watch, and focused on taking my usual path down the dirt drive toward the barn. Rose and Sophia preened in the chicken pen. The hens would be fine until I got back.

My lungs expanded in the fresh air. I could taste the petrichor around me, though it'd been hours since the rain had saturated the soil. The sunlight overhead was hazy behind streaky white clouds. This was everything that I'd wanted. This place appeared perfect. Gorgeous views, clean air, space to exist unjudged, a place to build a new life.

But the old lives. The lost ones. They never left. Bridget's memory deserved honor, and I deserved peace. The Belkin family was beyond broken, but how far did it go? Was it only Nick? Had someone put him up to it? He'd been a kid himself. Hell, he still *was* a kid.

Had he stopped with Bridget? Why did I see that pickup at my barn more often than not? What did the others know? Were more girls in danger? Was Tyler involved too?

The headlines I'd scoured surfaced in my mind as my legs maintained a pounding pace. *The barn is farther today. I should be there already.* I sprinted harder, making my legs burn as though a little lactic acid could counter the cold knowledge that women died and disappeared too often. Runaways didn't make the paper. Domestic violence survivors didn't get a front-page splash when they disappeared. Their husbands didn't report them missing.

At least Herb Belkin had called the cops when his wife died. I slowed, as though the thought was going to conjure Alice. But I was alone with sweat shimmering on my arms and an ugly destination rising before me.

I stared at the pedometer reading: 3,132 steps. The barn had never been so far from my house. Did it want space after divulging its darkest secret? Was that even the worst of it? I thought about the mold, the broken boards, the noose.

We should tear the damned building down. Not the safest thought to fill me as I shouldered open the door, but I'd left security behind long ago. The only way back to peace, to the future I deserved here on my farm, was to get justice.

The thick heat of the barn swallowed me before I stepped fully inside, but I didn't have time to hesitate.

Dude showers ran all of five minutes. I expected he'd shave too, which would buy me time, but I wasn't about to have him come find me in the barn again.

The interior was disorienting. The treacle of mildewy hay hit me, but nothing was where it should be. Nick had told us they had rearranged, but this was more.

The open space where Bridget had been killed was clear, as it had been a few hours ago—a few years ago?—when I'd hidden behind the tractor. It was the other side that threw me. A dirt-laden blue tarp had been spread on the floor next to where the ladder to the loft was mounted to the wall. The bottom rungs were broken now, the wood dangling at ninety degrees.

Pallets had been stacked next to the two tractors, which were the cleanest I'd ever seen them. The wooden containers were wrapped in plastic, but wouldn't I have seen that delivery?

Focus, Emily, I chided myself. I moved to where the teenage girl in the memory had raised her chin in challenge to her cousin. But the dusty floor was bare. Of course it was. It'd been years.

That didn't stop me from going on hands and knees and checking closer. There were gaps and grooves in the flooring. Pebbles. A small blue bead, like from a friendship bracelet.

My watch buzzed on my wrist. I peeked to see a message from Josh. "Your turn, gorgeous."

How could he just flip to flirty after everything? He hadn't seen the past, but he knew about the teeth. We'd looked for them. He'd vowed to protect me, to love me, to trust me. He should be unnerved as shit about human teeth just *showing up* at our doorstep.

Why wasn't he?

I crawled closer to the wall. It might have been decades since anyone had swept this floor for the filth rolling around me. But there was no blood. So the teeth would have landed on the tarp too? But then how did they end up on my porch? In my chickens' coop?

Another buzz at my wrist. "Where are you?"

Doing what you should be doing, Josh. Looking for proof of a crime. I grumbled and ran my finger along the ragged joint of the wall and the floor. Black mold sprouted another foot away. As though even the barn walls were decaying. Everything in here was rotten.

My fingertip caught on something hard. It could be a pebble, right? I dug my nail into the gap and pried a tooth free. It had been one of her front teeth. I knew it. I choked on a sob.

None of this was fair. But this would help. This would be proof I could approach the sheriff with. I didn't know how I'd tie it to Nick yet, but the evidence existed. He would not get away with this.

I put the tooth in my pocket, because keeping it on my person was the safest option even if it was gross as all get-out. I pushed up from the floor, dusted my palms against my bare thighs as if that somehow would reduce the ick.

Once outside the barn, I exhaled until my chest screamed. I

wanted every particle of the past horror that resided in that barn air out of my body.

I reset my running metrics and sprinted back toward real life. The farmhouse was the bastion of white and sunlight on the top of the hill. Absorbing the postcard-perfect view couldn't flush the fear and anxiety from my body though.

What was I going to do with this tooth? Should I put it somewhere for Josh to find? Like set it next to the henhouse and then bring him outside to see it? No, what kind of dumb idea was that? I couldn't just *leave* the proof of what had happened here unattended. I needed to show it to my husband, to see him believe me.

What if it's not Bridget's tooth? The thought shivered through my skull. Clenching my jaw wouldn't protect my teeth, but I sure did it anyway.

The cornstalks rustled in the breeze. I couldn't see any of the farm crew, but then they'd been working for hours now. Could be deep in the fields. Could be...anywhere.

I needed to find the red pickup truck. Did they still have that hammer? A tooth and a hammer. Cops couldn't ignore that. No one would.

How close was Nick to the rest of the farmworkers? The librarian had given me genealogy notes on the Belkins. Nick and Tyler were Bridget's cousins, and Ray had been related to Alice. Did that make him more likely to keep the boy's secret or less?

I approached Cluckingham Palace, poking in to check on the girls and giving them a few gentle pats. They'd believe me. Blanche's empty spot made my burning muscles soften. I crouched inside the pen.

"We're looking for her," I told the chickens of their sister. But also maybe telling the ghost of Bridget's mother.

Dorothy stretched her head high, looking past me to Josh at the door of the house. He'd braced his hands on either side of the frame and leaned out. Clean-shaven, damp hair, no shirt. It was textbook hotness, but I couldn't force a smile.

Not now. Not with what had happened in this place.

I pulled the tooth from my pocket and held it aloft.

"I found one of the teeth." My tone dared him to tell me this wasn't real now.

Emily's Running Log:

17 minutes, 17 seconds—3,132 steps—to the barn.
12.5 miles run today. Heart rate is orange and red zones constantly,
but given everything else, I don't care.

CHAPTER 37

JOSH URGED ME TO COME INSIDE AND EXPLAIN. HE SAT, steepling his fingers as though he was prepared to rationalize away proof. I stormed into the house, straight toward him, and dropped the tooth onto our kitchen table. It skittered forward, tapping Josh's empty coffee mug. My husband scrabbled backward so fast, the kitchen chair toppled with a crash onto the tile.

"The fuck?" was all he could say as he backed away until his butt collided with the side of the sofa.

"I found one of the teeth." My shock was finally wearing off, and panic tried to weasel in. Squeezing my joints, curling around my throat, pinching my nerves. But I forced a rebar through my words. Because this mattered.

"There's a tooth on our table." Josh's lips remained parted, aghast.

This was how he should have looked that first night. This was the horror he should have shared with me when I saw the teeth on our porch, when there was one in our chicken coop, when I *showed him freaking photos* of them. A needle pierced my focus, tugging a thread of doubt through my overwhelm.

"I know," I bit out.

He freed his widened gaze from the enameled tooth and met my eyes. "I...I... Where did you find it?"

The slackened jaw, the white flare of his eyes. For real? It was obvious now: he'd never believed me. Josh had been certain I'd never find proof. I stared at him, letting the pain pour over me. My knees burned from the rough barn floor, but that fire was nothing compared to the blaze erupting at the base of my skull. Every flicker of understanding on my husband's face laid another tinder on the bonfire.

I lowered myself into a chair to keep from hurling myself toward him in anger. "There are human teeth on the farm, and '*Where?*' is your question?"

Josh rushed forward, practically shoving the sofa away behind him. He kept an arm's length from the table but rounded the kitchen to be closer to me. "I'm trying to figure out how I didn't see it. We looked, Em."

Not in the barn, where a girl who had lived here was murdered. I didn't say that. I loved Josh. Deeply. But he'd proven he couldn't bear this weight. Maybe that strength had been worn down by Mom's illness and then my grief. I'd put so much on him, but had I taken the time to see the toll it'd taken on him? The weight of his wife's grief, of losing a mother-in-law, of worrying over me... He hadn't built himself back up. Had I helped him regain his footing? Was that my job? I'd planned meals and cuddled and laughed with him, but what had I missed?

"We looked a handful of places. I looked elsewhere, and even though the tooth is little, I found it." I pointed at the tooth like he should see how much the discovery explained.

He shook his head. "We have to call the cops."

Finally. That was the right next step. I nodded with a firm "no shit" expression tightening my face.

I tried to stand, but my legs gave out. Josh hurried forward, catching me and guiding me back into my seat.

"Babe?" His hands were in my hair, his face close to mine, nostrils flaring and cool mint riding his exhale.

"I'm fine." I pushed his hands away. "Freaking out, but fine."

Understatement. I stared at the off-white piece of another person lying all neutral on the oak table. Sunlight from the kitchen window slipped over the tooth. A spotlight, a softening, but also adding a sallow tinge that made it clear that tooth had no place in a peaceful home.

Where was Bridget now? She deserved peace. Her family did too. It was too late for that though. Her mother had killed herself. Her father moved away. Her cousin had been the one to kill her. Would knowing what had happened to her offer succor to anyone? Maybe Herb. Maybe Tyler. Maybe her friends from high school.

But I knew one thing for sure. It mattered to me.

———

The sheriff parked his car under the big tree in the front yard like it was his designated spot. He was a short stout man clad in head-to-toe khaki. He pulled his brown belt up after exiting his cruiser.

He adjusted his equipment—radio, cuffs, gun—while he sauntered toward our front door.

Josh had made me a cup of tea and cuddled me on the couch while we waited the forty-five minutes for Sheriff Randy Wilson to arrive. I hadn't even remembered that we had tea in the cabinet. Had the Belkins left it for us? It was an herbal green blend that left a film on the roof of my mouth. I pressed my tongue to my palate and made myself stay on the sofa while Josh approached the door. He let the sheriff knock once before opening it.

At least Josh was finally as scared as I was. And he didn't know everything I did. He hadn't stepped into the past to see how Bridget Belkin died. If he had, he'd be truly terrified.

The country cop tapped the toes of his boots against the door-jamb before walking in. "Mr. Hauk, Mrs. Hauk." He removed his hat and inclined his head toward each of us. "Sherry tells me you found something I need to see."

That wasn't quite the language Josh had used when he'd called the nonemergency line. My body shouted it was an emergency, but I kept my mouth closed.

"We appreciate you coming out so quickly, Sheriff Wilson," I said, already rising from the couch.

"Please, call me Randy."

Relief trickled over my shoulders. I'd called an emergency number before, and had two deputies come to the farm and dismiss what I'd seen, but the sheriff was here and focused. Worry pulled at the corners of his eyes. I hadn't told him anything yet, but the wariness was there. Like his law enforcement senses picked up on what I'd been feeling too.

Josh shook his hand first, but I reached out as well. Having the authorities here, people who could actually change things, fix things, save lives, bolstered my confidence more than Josh's acknowledgment that I wasn't making shit up. And certainly more than the weak tea.

This was my chance to save the farm. To get justice for the dead. To make sure Nick didn't place me in his sights.

"I don't know that there's a good way to say this, but we've been finding teeth on our property." I led him to the kitchen and gestured toward the evidence still waiting for someone to touch it again.

"And this isn't yours?" He cast a long look at Josh, like he'd be the most knowledgeable person in the room.

"Excuse me?" I sputtered. What, did he want us to have dental exams?

"You said teeth, ma'am. Where are the others?" He sighed like I was wasting his time. Like he was too busy to solve serious crime.

No. No no no not this again.

"We don't know," Josh replied for us both.

Randy's eyebrows rose. For a cop, this guy had a garbage poker face. "Mr. Hauk—"

"Josh."

Randy nodded, and it was the most bro move I'd ever seen of a man in uniform. The sheriff was about a decade older than us, but not too old to look at Josh like they should be friends. Like he didn't care that there was a fucking tooth on the table.

"Josh, did you see all these teeth?" he asked.

It was like I wasn't even in the room. The scream that sliced at my insides, fighting for release, locked my neck. I tightened my fists at my sides so much that my nails had to be carving sickles into the pads.

Josh hesitated. *Are you fucking kidding me?* His attention flitted to me, to the small piece of another person lying on our table, and then finally back to the sheriff.

Finally Josh nodded. "There were four of them, but it was late at night. We've got chickens, you know?"

"Chickens don't have teeth." Randy pulled a little notebook from a pocket. "Where were these teeth?"

Anger simmered beneath my breastbone. He'd dismissed me like I wasn't someone who *raised* chickens and obviously knew they didn't have teeth. I bit the inside of my cheek and let Josh talk, because clearly that's what Sheriff Wilson wanted. I needed this man to listen to us.

Josh gestured toward the farm with a simple wave. "We spotted the teeth on the front porch and the chicken coop, but it was late. We locked the house until we could search during the day. That's when we found this tooth in the barn and called you."

Randy glanced at me, sucked his teeth, and then returned his attention to my husband. "You get a lot of animals about here, I'm sure."

The sheriff made it sound almost plausible.

"We do." Josh replied too quickly. "Foxes have been worked up lately." Was he still believing that bit about foxes?

Randy nodded. Josh couldn't stand still; his heel bounced throughout the conversation, but Randy didn't mark it. My husband and I were both rattled, but it was clear Randy only saw the stress in the lady.

"Now this one, can you show me where you found it?" He collected the tooth in a small baggie, much like what I kept in a drawer next to the refrigerator.

I swallowed hard enough that both men cast me hard looks, as if being freaked out was out of place now. This was normal. Healthy. I was going to cling to the truth being bagged up right in front of me.

"I found the tooth out in the barn. I can show you where." I lifted my chin because I didn't have shit to be ashamed of. I was helping solve a crime.

Josh mouthed, "You're going to the barn?" at me and I pretended not to notice.

"You spend a lot of time in the barn, Mrs. Hauk?" Randy took in my running shorts and tank top in a way that made me think he called this place the old Belkin farm and thought it still should be.

"Not often. One of my hens is missing. I thought she might have found her way in there. The guys just rearranged the equipment in the barn, and I was worried about her." Half-truths were all this man deserved.

Josh quickly appended, "The barn is technically ours, but the team that runs the farm uses it for storage."

Randy ignored him. Did it bother Josh the way it dug at me? "Did you find your chicken?"

"She's still missing," I admitted, "but she's our escape artist. I've found her before. I'm sure she'll turn up."

Randy made a rumble deep in his throat. "I see. Well, I can assure you a tooth on its own isn't a sign of anything terrible."

"A tooth isn't a problem?" I might have screeched. He deserved some hawklike responses.

"This is an old farm, Mrs. Hauk." He said my name like I was some child he could placate with a pat on the head.

I straightened. "Old or not, teeth don't just show up on people's porches."

"But you found this in the barn," he countered.

Like that was better? "That barn is for storing tractors and fertilizer. Maybe someone kept animals in it before. None of that is cause for human teeth to be on its floor."

"Of course not." Randy rested his right hand on his service piece. Like touching a weapon calmed him.

It did not soothe me in the least. I'd had limited interactions with cops in the past. I'd met the stoic ones stationed at street fairs. I'd run into a few backstage at concerts when I was a kid or when things grew rowdy on tour. But none had ever dismissed me so blatantly. And I'd honestly thought they would want to help with something like this.

Why didn't Randy Wilson?

Josh must have had caught a similar vibe because he asked, "You're really not worried about there being a tooth here? Because I have a problem with how it showed up here and how it ended up outside of someone's mouth."

"We'll investigate," the sheriff was quick to say. "I only meant that whatever happened could have been from long ago. Decades. You aren't in any danger."

We hadn't said we were yet, but he was hitting exactly what was churning in my brain. This sheriff wasn't a mind reader. So why was he going there? The man who had knocked that tooth out of a mouth could be on my farm right now. Everyone knew I'd called in the deputies before. That mean a killer knew I was watching. So yes, Randy, I was in danger. I stuffed down my outrage and tried to play his game. "What if it is recent though?"

"The tooth looks like it'd been in the dirt for a bit, ma'am."

I couldn't take this. "What about Bridget Belkin?"

He had the good sense to blanch. "Where'd you hear that name?"

"We live here. Of course we know about her." I held back from commenting on his intelligence.

He shook his head like this was simply a sad story. "That girl had a lot of problems. It broke the community's heart when she went missing."

"What if she's not missing though?" I had to push. I knew the truth. And my gut said Randy Wilson did too.

The sheriff didn't meet my gaze. He peered over my shoulder, and I wished Alice Belkin's face would appear, so he'd have to look her in the eyes when he pretended her kid was a runaway. Finally, he said, "Bridget's case is still open. We have her dental records. If this is her tooth, we'll know."

"Good." I edged closer to my husband, who had folded his arms across his chest and was watching this exchange with growing concern tightening his jaw.

Josh volunteered to take him to the barn, but he didn't know where I'd found the tooth. I needed to watch the sheriff do his job. I hoped Alice could see this now. See the police searching for evidence of Bridget's murder. Once the sheriff matched that tooth to Bridget, there'd be no question about an investigation. They could stop Nick. They'd have to revisit my complaint before about the other crime. They'd search for real and find evidence. They'd do their job. They'd arrest Nick. This could be over.

The goose bumps that marched over my body when I stepped into the barn weren't preternatural. No flashes of the past rose around us; no icy breath chilled my nape. Success was within my reach. Vindication. Answers. It was all on the horizon.

The sheriff found nothing new in the barn. Not a surprise.

"You should treat that mold though," he said, pointing to the sticky black climbing the wall. "Especially with your garden up the way."

Josh nodded like he was the one who managed the crops—both the corn and my burgeoning garden. "Will do. I'm planning to head to Farm Supply this weekend."

"Well, I'll let you two be on with your day. If I have any further questions, I know where to find you."

Why did that feel like a threat? What did this guy know that I didn't?

———

Emily: Hi, Courtney. It's Emily Hauk. The not-a-podcaster you were helping.

Before I would type the next text, a reply pinged through.

Courtney: It's been like no time. I know who you are. What's up?

Emily: Could you look up a couple more names for me?

Courtney: Of course.

Courtney: What do we want to know about these people?

Emily: Same as the others. Are they connected to the Belkin family? Property records, etc.

Courtney: Are we looking for crime records too?

Emily: Why do I picture you doing a Mr. Burns' style "excellent" move when you ask that?

Courtney: It's good to love your job. Do you want to come into Hastings for lunch tomorrow? I can pull this stuff in the morning.

Did I want to get off this farm for a few hours? Yes. Did I want to do that in a way that wouldn't raise flags with Josh? Also yes. Had I told him about Courtney at all? I couldn't remember. I'd kept so much of that trip to the library a secret. Could I tell him now? Now that we had the tooth in the open?

Emily: Meet you at the library at 12:30 tomorrow.

I sent Courtney, librarian extraordinaire, two more names: Randy Wilson and Ray Clausen. I asked her if there was a way to see if anyone had tried to buy the farm before us.

I was determined to find out how many men were connected to this farm. How many could have known this place was breaking down its women, and let it happen?

The realization that I was the only woman within miles shouldn't have conjured dread. But knowing a young woman had been killed in my barn. That her mother had died falling from its loft. That the man who had done the former still trod this land. Another man had fled the farm for another life. My own man hadn't wanted to hear any of it.

That night, while Josh and I made pizza from scratch like we were having some normal date night and not striving to stuff our sorrow away until it composted itself, I turned on a "Best of the Eagles" playlist and let my mother join us for dinner.

Josh and I both leaped to skip "Hotel California" in her honor. She'd hated the track—which always felt like shunning popularity to me—but also the last thing we needed was the reminder that some places and states are inescapable. As the person who was haunted by both a barn and her own past, this felt especially ominous.

I took the Valium that night.

I shouldn't have.

CHAPTER 38

COFFEE CALLED TO ME BEFORE SUNRISE. THE ANTI-ANXIETY pill didn't linger in my body, but a fatigue had settled in my limbs. The weight of yesterday, the exertion of trying so hard, settled in the muscles in a way that had me lumbering into the kitchen.

The big wall clock announced it was 4 a.m. Early but not terribly so. A round of coffee, and I could be sprinting soon. I swiped my hair back and held it off my neck. The air-conditioning had kept pace last night, but humidity cared not.

I only made it two steps into the kitchen before my legs threatened to give out.

Jet black was garish against the white countertop. Pulp texturized each smear.

I took a single half step closer.

HE WAS HERE.

Three simple words in blocky letters. I wanted to believe it was the berries on my counter encased in shadows, but the longer I stood there, the more clearly I tasted rotting earth in the air.

"Alice?" I whispered the name, my whole body quaking.

"You didn't watch, but they were here. He was here." The whole room dropped ten degrees in an instant.

"Did Nick do this?" A sudden weight pressed down on my sternum, holding my breath hostage. I gasped.

"Outside," was all she said. The temperature returned to normal.

I pleaded and paced and stared at the fucking black mold spelling out words on my kitchen counter, but Alice would say no more.

The more I paced, the more useless energy made me twitchy. Should I wake Josh? If he came out here and there was no mold, there would be no coming back to him trusting me. Believing me.

Shit. I was going to have to touch it. I tiptoed closer to the counter, my stomach straight-up doing backflips. My jittery hand reached forward and dipped my fingertip in the mold. It was gooey and cold and smudged beneath my touch.

Real. I exhaled hard.

I spun, ready to dart into the bedroom and get my husband. Only when I looked down at my hand, there were no remnants on my fingers.

"Alice, you have to help me. I know what happened was real, but giving me proof that makes me look like I'm losing it is not helpful." I spoke to the ceiling like ghosts lived in the attic.

I scrubbed the counter four times. The mold disappeared. I made coffee for the sake of a clear head.

And searched my brain for an answer. Alice said he'd been here.

She said he'd been outside. But was she talking about then or now? Maybe I could find out.

The chicken coop camera was on overnight. I grabbed the small device we used to monitor the girls from the living room. I tapped backward to see the last motion detected.

Nick and Tyler had been outside at 2:07 a.m. Both of them. Nick opened the coop door, like he meant to let my chickens run free. Tyler closed it back up. There was no audio, but I wanted to know what they said.

They skulked around on and off camera. The path leading to the back door of the house was on the edge of the screen. The two boys argued there. Tyler threw a clump of mud toward the house. Nick laughed and opted for throwing double middle fingers near his groin.

He was nothing like the kid I'd met. It'd been a show. If I hadn't known Nick had killed Bridget, would I think this was a prank? Would Josh? The farmhands had been outside our house, and Alice wanted me to know.

When a ghost tells me I'm in danger, I sure as hell listen.

When the sun rose, I checked outside. No new teeth, but mud smudged the handle to the door. I'd started locking it the night before.

CHAPTER 39

THE BARN SHOULDN'T HAVE BEEN MOVING ANY LONGER. I'D done my job. I'd witnessed its secrets and called in reinforcements. If we could call Sheriff Randy that. But the farmhands were still a problem, and Alice wanted to protect me.

So I still logged the time and steps to the barn, and it was still changing. If I'd told Josh, I'm sure he would have said I was merely getting faster and joke about some personal record. Only it wasn't that. We weren't talking seconds here; it was minutes.

Courtney had rescheduled on me. Flu struck the library, which she pointed out was not unheard of because of "all the people."

Was that one of the perks of the farm? No flu? I would trade an occasional bout of fever and congestion for the worry welling in my insides. Nick was still on my farm.

I'd brought my coffee and laptop out to the front porch this morning. Needing fresh air and to soak in the view. The mornings were when I loved the farm the most. Sunlight had a thickness here, like it could wrap me in comfort and soothe my soul. Songbirds called to one another; occasionally my chickens clucked in the background. All of them carrying on a conversation I wasn't privy to but loved hearing regardless.

Blanche was still missing. Part of me had truly believed she'd wander back to the coop, but we were still at four chickens. Despite the farmhand trying to free them the other night. Maybe that's what the girls were twittering about now. Their monitor was next to me on the bench seat. The screen showed the inside of their pen, where just three of the four girls were walking around and Mother Clucker ignored them from inside the henhouse. If we were giving out performance bonuses for eggs, she'd get a very fancy plaque.

Dust billowed in the distance. A few minutes later, the red pickup came into view. Tyler and Nick waved at me. Were they making eye contact today? Were they staring? Did Nick catch the recognition on my face? I did my best to return the greeting. Friendly. Neighborly. Distant. Like I didn't see a boy who had killed his cousin riding in that truck. As if I didn't know they'd tried to come inside my house.

Tyler jerked his chin up, which I think was meant as a hello or acknowledgment, but only made me think he knew. He knew that his cousin was a killer, and yet he worked side by side with the guy. How would someone forgive that?

No matter how much I tried to put myself in their shoes, I could only see cruelty that deserved consequences.

I toggled up the "Nebraska" playlist that I'd created when we'd bought this place. Back when moving to a farm was only an idea. Music played from the stereo in the living room. I'd opened the windows to let the sound drift out. Josh wore his noise-canceling headphones in his office at the end of the hallway. So he couldn't complain. Well, I'm sure he *could*, but he wouldn't.

A Tilly and the Wall track came on. Soft, slow, soothing. Mom loved this one.

I could imagine her looking out at this farm, surveying my new home. "You need to make it yours," she'd say.

"It is mine," I said softly.

"Not as long as they are here," she'd say. I wouldn't have to ask her who she meant. Nick. Tyler.

"I called the sheriff," I told myself, my mom's memory, probably my subconscious.

"Great. Way to catch a killer." That wry twist to the voice wasn't quite right for my mom. She'd tease and taunt, but was I remembering her or making it all up? Was Alice seeping into my thoughts?

I took a drink of my coffee and scrolled my email like mundane tasks could help me forget about Bridget and the fact that Nick was still here when she was not.

The coffee curdled in my stomach. A man—or boy—who could beat his cousin to death without help? He wouldn't do it just the once. I flipped from my work email to the *Hebron Journal-Register*'s digital front page. No updates about the missing girl Kinsey and nothing about a new missing girl, but then people didn't always talk about them, did they?

I emailed the sheriff from my personal account asking him to update me, but it didn't soothe a single frayed nerve.

The dust in the air had settled, even in the distance. So Tyler and Nick must have stopped the pickup. They couldn't be too far out. I checked my work calendar. I had one hour until the weekly department check-in call. I marked myself as "in a meeting" on Slack, turned off the tunes, and peeked inside the house to make sure Josh wasn't rummaging in the kitchen for a snack. His office door was closed still.

Good.

I stepped off the porch, reset my timer for a fresh barn measurement, and then took off toward where I suspected they'd parked their truck. If I could get in the back and find that hammer, then I could give the sheriff more evidence. He could do something, stop them. And I could go on with the life I was supposed to live out here.

Unfortunately, the sunshine cocoon I'd loved while sitting on the porch swing slapped me like a wet blanket when I went for a full sprint. There was a reason I didn't train at midday, and it wasn't because of work. One of those remote-job perks was the ability to block out an hour for workouts. Only the humidity did more than clog my pores. It required double the effort on every inhale. Like I was sucking down a post-gym sauna. Barf.

I checked my tracker as I sprinted past the barn. It was close to the house again. Three hundred and seventy-eight steps. Two minutes, fifteen seconds.

If only the truck could be so close. I sprinted down the packed earth. This was my least favorite of the jogging paths. Not because of the barn—I clocked that part of the run at least once a day—but because this route through the southern fields rarely brought a crosswind and never resulted in animal sightings. *Maybe Blanche went this way. Not a people person, that hen.*

I charged through the sea of green. The stalks had a full head on me, and as I ran deeper along this road, it was easy to lose sight of where I'd come from. Not only the farmhouse, but California. Grasshoppers bounded before me in the path. Other insects hummed in the fields. Me? I just ran. The road forked. I headed into the southern fields. It was where the youngest crops had been planted. Made sense they'd be driving out there now. Young plants needed more attention. Or perhaps I just felt that way with my garden because I'd been so determined to make life grow. A twinge shot through my hamstring. My gait wobbled and forced me to slow. Stretching while running was, I'll admit, not the healthiest choice. Sane people stretch before and after their runs. Not me. I was the asshole out here beating her body into submission because answers surely were parked around the next turn.

I couldn't bear to think about what I'd do if I was wrong. Josh had seen nothing I had. He'd stood in our barn, next to me, and saw none of the cruelty of the past. My husband might have his own delusions, but his love for me was unwavering.

Hell. If this run took too long, he'd come out of his office and freak out when he saw that I was gone. I should have told him. Should have let him know I was leaving for a run. We'd just had the cops here because I was convinced a murder had happened and—oh, God, was I the asshole? If he stepped out and I was missing, would he think Nick had done something? Would he call the cops instead of Ray this time?

Ray. The memory of that man at our doorstep the first night I'd seen Alice's face in the window rose in my mind. He'd looked in our home like he saw her too. Because he knew. How could he not? Everyone, it seemed, had been aware of the hotbed of domestic violence that was the farmhouse. The same place I'd selected as "destination: marital bliss" had been one of destruction.

My thigh whined, slowing me yet again. I flexed and pushed on. Ray was a good guy. He drove my husband hours to get to the airport. He'd checked on me, real concern twisting him.

And yet he'd never warned us. Never warned me.

The path between the crops was worn from both vehicles and runoff from the irrigation. It split ahead. I heard voices, the rumble of men at work, off to the right. My sprint had already eased from the griping of my leg, but I slowed. Approaching the corner with caution was almost silly. My cornfield runs were far from a secret. The neighbors whose names I didn't know, the cows, and most certainly the farmhands expected to see me in my bright sports bra hoofing it through the fields. And yet, this was different. I didn't want to be seen. I peered around the corner.

The truck waited, unassuming, twenty feet ahead. The engine was silent, the lights off, and yet the headlamps stared me down nonetheless. I edged closer.

"Three more," a voice called from beyond my view. Ray. He was here too.

It should have been comforting. Extra eyes, extra hands, extra person who my husband trusted. Only I was no longer willing to trust anyone on this farm. I padded closer. The cab was empty. Crouching down twinged that strained muscle in my thigh but didn't stop me from scuttling along the side of the pickup. Up close, the truck wasn't as beat-up as I'd built it up in my mind. It was older, absolutely, but it'd been well maintained. Paint covered the holes where the weather had tried to rust. Did they pay this much attention to everything? Why had the barn been allowed to slip into its dangerous level of disrepair?

Because they knew.

I peered over the edge of the bed. Ball caps bobbed on the other side, moving into the field. Tyler, Nick, and Ray were doing whatever it was farmers did, and it took them away from this path. My chance was now. I hurried toward the back of the truck. I'd like to say climbing into it was natural, but I'd never actually hopped in the bed of a pickup before. I stared at the latch on the tailgate. Did I drop it down to get in? No, that might make too much noise. The men weren't far away.

"Keep it moving, boys. We've got two more of these to replace," Ray grumbled from beyond the corn.

A bead of sweat slipped over my shoulder blade and down my back. A shiver that had nothing to do with the temperature rocked me. Time was running out. I grabbed ahold of the bed gate, lifted my aching leg to plant my foot on the rail, and launched myself into the truck. There was no grace in this movement. The tires groaned as they shifted beneath me. I yanked myself up and slipped over the gate and onto the floor of the truck bed. I crouched there, refusing to lie down in the same spot I'd watched blood seep from. There was no tarp covering the ribbed metal, only a smattering of dirt. Bags of pesticide were stacked at the back of the truck, but none of that mattered. Inside the bed of the truck, there had been a panel that popped open. A cubby where Nick had put his hammer. The guy was too practical to toss the hammer, right? Why would he? No one ever came after him for Bridget's death. No one even called her disappearance a murder.

Nick had thwacked the edge of the truck with a fist to open the panel when I'd watched him store the weapon there, but the latch for the storage bin was obvious. I flipped it open, hinges whining. I winced, but the hammer was there. Worn wooden handle. Mottled metal on the rounded head. Whatever blood had splattered there years ago was gone, at least to the naked eye. But that's why they had scientists at police departments. A crime scene unit could descend on this truck and—

"You need to get out now." Ray's sharp tone yanked me from my reverie.

I jerked my chin up. The older farmer stood next to the truck, his face mere inches from mine.

"It's not what it looks like," I sputtered automatically, even though it was likely *exactly* what it looked like.

He pressed a blue bandanna against his sweaty cheek. "Doesn't matter what I think, Mrs. Hauk. You need to get out of that truck now. Before those boys come back over here."

Those boys. That glimmer in his eye was more than knowledge.

It was fear. It'd flared when he'd come to my house that night. Did the barn haunt him too? I almost asked.

"Now, Mrs. Hauk. Run before he sees you. *Go.*"

The young men's voices approached. Tyler cracked a joke about how only the strong can stay in Nebraska.

"The weak ones always run. Better without them, I suppose," Nick agreed. I'd only heard that tone from him once before—in the barn, in a memory from three years ago, when he'd killed Bridget Belkin.

I clambered out of the truck. It wasn't quiet or smooth. I smashed my shin against the hitch, but didn't have time to worry about it. The cornstalks were rustling. Flashes of blue and red shirts catching through the thick green growth.

Ray moved toward the rear of the truck, giving his back to me. Providing me cover? Neither of us wanted me to be a target, though my galloping heart said I'd already been marked as a problem. After all, only the weak run, and I did it every day.

I hurried down the path, around the corner, and didn't stop running until Cluckingham Palace was firmly in my sights. My thigh screamed, my shin whined, but my heart? It had sunken into my gut. I'd been right about it all. The hammer was there. Nick had done this. Ray knew.

When I got home, I had a voicemail from Sheriff Wilson. The tooth I'd found had been Bridget's. "But please don't be alarmed, ma'am. As I said on your property, it could be very old. It may not mean anything."

The hell it didn't. We'd see what he had to say when I told him where to find a hammer, when I told him to talk to Ray. I'd make him stop Nick Ditmer.

Emily's Running Log:

2 minutes, 15 seconds to the barn—378 steps

19.7 miles!—Josh finally let me run alone! Fifteenth-mile weakness solved with a good glucose chew.

CHAPTER 40

I CALLED THE NUMBER SHERIFF WILSON HAD LEFT WITH HIS voicemail. It rang and rang. How could one protect and serve if they didn't answer the damned phone? It clicked over to voicemail. I hung up and tried the main line for the sheriff's office. The kind receptionist said he was unavailable and if it wasn't "a life-threatening emergency" she'd be happy to take a message.

A message? What was I supposed to tell this woman? I couldn't very well have her jot down that a ghost had shown me Nick Ditmer killing his cousin.

"Ma'am?" she prompted.

"Can you let him know that Emily Hauk called, please?" I asked, as if this was my first time talking to anyone's assistant.

"Sure thing, hun."

Before I could think better of it, I blurted, "It's about Bridget Belkin."

The phone went so silent I thought we'd been disconnected.

"Hello?" I tried.

"Yes, ah, I'll pass that right along." If one could transfer ill ease over cell phone towers, I would have been doubled over with nausea based on this woman's apprehension.

She hung up first.

I tucked my phone in my pocket and hurried down the hallway to Josh's office. He had his big headset on and the ring light ablaze. I waved from the door, not concealing even a hint of my panic.

He held up two fingers toward his screen and then turned his attention to me. "Babe?"

"It isn't safe here." Those four words encompassed all my fear, my realizations, the past and the future.

Josh's face scrunched like I'd fed him spoiled sausage. "What are you talking about?"

"I was out in the field and..." I let it all tumble out. The truck, the hammer, the fact I was certain it had been used to kill Bridget.

Josh's lips thinned with each passing sentence. His jaw hardened. His nostrils flared. But he remained silent.

"I know how it sounds, but Ray told me to run. It's not just me. He knows. Ray said I needed to run before they saw me. Why would he do that if he wasn't afraid of them?"

"Maybe to make sure those young guys aren't scared of you?"

"What?"

"You were climbing around in their truck, Em. Can you imagine if you had to worry that your landlord would just randomly snoop in your belongings?"

"That is not the same!"

"Isn't it?"

"They were outside our house the other night," I blurted.

"What do you mean? Why didn't you say anything?"

I stalked toward the window in his office. "Because every time I tell you something, you blow me off. I have video of them outside the house. They opened the coop door. They flipped off our house. You'd tell me it was boys being boys."

"They may have been blowing off steam, but I would have said something to Ray."

"He told me to run today, Josh. It's dangerous." There had been a real warning in Ray's voice earlier.

"I'll talk to him." Defeat laced Josh's words.

"The tooth belonged to Bridget!" I shouted like it should make it all click in his brain.

Ice chilled my shoulder. *He was never going to believe you. They never believe us.*

Now was not the time for Alice Belkin to chime in. I focused on Josh. "You were freaked out by the tooth."

"Because it's a tooth. Of course I was!"

"So trust me here."

He stepped around from his desk, approaching me with hands out, but mouth still flattened in that disappointed-dad look. "I always trust you," he said, taking my hands in his.

"Then—"

"Then let me help. I'll call the sheriff. See what we can do about investigating. I'll talk to Ray too."

"What's Ray going to do? He's scared too." If he hadn't stopped them by now, what made Josh think he could help?

"He can keep them away from the house, the barn, while we sort this out. Give them things to do far away from us. And you can skip running the next few days while we get the sheriff to look into it." I hated that he sounded so rational. His palms skimmed up and down my forearms like he was trying to infuse his calm into my pores.

It didn't work, but I nodded anyway. I could give him a day. "You're home for the next week, right?"

"Even if I wasn't, I'd cancel trips. Or we could both leave? Do you want to spend a week in Omaha?"

That would have been the smart thing to do, right? What I thought I'd wanted? Get out of here while the cops sorted it out. Only every bone in my body said the second I left this farm, it was lost. No one else would push for answers about Bridget if I left.

As if she read my mind—could ghosts read minds?—Alice said, *"None of those men will come in this house."*

If I'd been alone, I would have asked her why. The mud on the door handle said they'd tried to come inside my home. Maybe the boys feared the farmhouse when she was alive, but I doubted that was still true.

"It's his house. They won't disrespect it."

If only I could be so sure.

———

I ate half a berry compote pie by myself that evening. Josh had the good sense to not ask me to share, but stayed at my side. I watched the day fade beyond my windows. The red pickup didn't drive up

to the barn or pass my house. There was another path that led out
to a state highway at the far end of the property. Clearly they'd left
that way.

Josh's call with Ray had lasted nearly a half hour, which was
eons in guy time. Perhaps that's why Nick and Tyler had taken the
long way off the farm. Josh had made it clear this was our space. I
helped Josh down two bottles of wine, because I had little else to
do but drink and worry. At least the former helped numb the latter.
I trusted Josh to protect me. I trusted this house to be safe. Even
Alice had said it was.

But then night fell. My husband and I stumbled into bed,
crashed in a literal way. The screams returned that night. Sharper.
More piercing. I shoved Josh. He groaned but didn't wake.

"Hurry." I heard Alice before I felt her this time. Her hazy apparition formed near the doorway. Dark hair teased high, face a shadow.

Intelligible cries for help carried over the land and directly to
my window. The words were garbled, but there was no question
this was human. I slammed my feet into shoes at the side of the
bed and hurried out through the kitchen door. The floodlights
next to the barn had flared on, but no one emerged onto the gravel
driveway. The sky was dark. Too early even for the young detasselers then.

I sprinted past the barn in record time. Almost like it wanted
me to get to the fields faster. The cries were coming from within
the corn. This wasn't a threat from the hayloft. It remained dim.
There was no eerie throwback jam carrying on the air tonight. The
humidity clung instead to a throaty plea. I charged forward. I'd find

the woman who was screaming. Kinsey? Another girl? Whoever was out there, I was coming.

Everyone had failed Bridget, but I could save this girl. I just had to find her.

I blasted past the berry bush, past row after row of corn. The stalks slapped me, the hard bodies of cobs thunking against my bones, the sticky sides scratching and clawing my skin. I kept running. Faster than I'd run home when I heard Mom was sick, faster than when Josh had promised a surprise the night he'd proposed, faster than my heart could take. I ran and let the stalks swallow me.

Light glowed ahead between the dense stalks, like a headlight positioned two feet too high. The soil was near black at my feet and flecked with yellow and white. I shielded my eyes from the glow, called out.

The screaming stopped, but a muffled plea came from near my feet. I shuffled, turning in a circle. The corn crushed against me. The soil stuck to my soles.

"*Find her,*" Alice's voice was an echo. Reedy and cold.

"I'm trying," I muttered. Then louder, "I'm here. Where are you?"

Garbled versions of *help* erupted beneath me, around me. I squinted but could only catch glimpses of white in the fertilized soil. I dropped to my knees, and the voice grew louder. I sank my fingers into the soil. I dug with my hands, razing the earth the way this place had stripped me. Teeth, both old and rotted, and new and tiny, tumbled over the backs of my hands. The shudder that rattled my spine settled into a heavy dread. It weighed down my belly, pushed my knees deeper into the dirt. I couldn't let myself leave, couldn't look up. I could only dig and dig until the only body lying in the earth was my own.

The cries stopped. I flopped into the hole I'd made. Me, the dirt, and more than a mouthful of teeth.

"*Keep trying,*" Alice said right before I passed out.

CHAPTER 41

A FOURTEEN-YEAR-OLD FOUND ME THERE. YELLOW POLLEN stained my shirt where he had shaken me. Moldy red raspberries and broken teeth littered the ground around me. The sun was hazy orange on the horizon. Josh loomed over me, an EMT holding an emergency kit standing at his side.

I tried to tell them about the screams, but my own throat was raw. My voice diminished to a painful whisper.

Josh shushed me, hand on my forehead. "They're going to get you up to the hospital. You're going to be okay."

Hours passed. First bumping along the road into Hastings, then in the emergency room. I was prodded and poked and asked questions for hours. And then they let me rest.

The hospital was cold. I had buzzed my nurse too many times, begging for another warm blanket.

She entered the room this time already holding the blanket. "They pumped your stomach, sweetie. You don't need to apologize for needing a blanket. Can I get you more ice chips?"

My belly rioted at the thought. The muscles still screaming from the final round of heaving. I'd been in the hospital now for nearly fourteen hours. There'd been blood taken and scans processed and a whole lot of me puking. The mental health team had been in twice, but both times left without much concern. I was too tired to revel in that. Josh remained stalwart at my side, rubbing my back and answering questions for me until the nurse told him to knock it off.

No one asked about the teeth aerated into the ground where they'd found me. I tried to bring it up, but Josh would shush me, and I was too exhausted to fight.

Finally a doctor came into the room. He was tall, with dark skin, and wore blue scrubs beneath his white lab coat. The stethoscope around his neck more an accessory as he thumbed through pages pinned to the clipboard.

"Mrs. Hauk," he said without looking up from the page. "Or would you prefer Emily?"

"Emily is fine," I rasped.

He nodded and then continued with a steady, smooth confidence, like I wasn't a mess lying under a mountain of blankets in the hospital bed. "Well, Emily, how are you feeling?"

"Like I just barfed more than a frat house on a Saturday night."

His mouth twitched like he was fighting a smile. "Sense of humor means you're probably going to be fine."

"So can I go?"

"I have a couple questions." Was there intrigue or excitement in his eyes?

At least someone wanted to hear what I had to say. "Okay."

He asked about the berries. About what I'd been eating and drinking. He asked for a way to contact our farmers.

"Why do you need to call the farm?" Josh was wary.

"Just give him Ray's number," I pleaded. The sooner we were done, the sooner this could be over.

"Between your blood work and everything our team here has heard…" He hesitated. "I need a little more information, and then I hope I can give you answers."

Twenty minutes later the doctor returned.

"The berries you've been eating are next to your barn?" He posed it like a question.

"That's what I've said. I mean, I also grew some blackberries in the garden by my house, but they didn't fare as well."

He nodded sagely. "Your farmers store insecticides in that barn and use a significant amount on the crops."

"You're saying all of this is because of bug spray?" Josh's eyebrows were practically in his hairline.

"Corn earworms are plaguing crops this year. We rarely see anyone hit a toxicity level with pyrethroids or organophosphates, but your farmers are using both this year. I am wondering if your contact with them has to do with a potential leak in the storage. Either way, have you been washing all your produce with a vinegar bath?"

No, I had not. Water apparently wasn't enough? "Hold up, what are you saying is happening here?"

"When a person comes into contact with these particular insecticides, there are side effects. Pyrethroid poisoning results in convulsions and auditory hallucinations."

Josh pounced. "Like hearing music?"

"Sure, music or people talking." The doctor ignored the pointed look my husband gave me and continued on. "The organophosphate poisoning tends to have a host of neurological symptoms like memory loss, confusion, or unstable emotions."

"And you think I'm suffering from this?"

"I do. The good news is this doesn't require an antidote."

"She's just going to hallucinate forever?" Josh gripped the arms of his chair, like he was alone in this.

Wonder what that's like.

"No, of course not. It'll flush out your system in time." He listed off instructions that sounded a lot like recovery from the flu—and I wondered how much of it was just repairing myself from them pumping my stomach.

"Did we have to make me puke?" I blurted.

"Given the information we had when you arrived from your husband and where he found you in that field, we needed to be sure you didn't ingest anything lethal." That was a no.

I nodded and thanked the doctor for his insight.

"I did instruct your farmers to review their storage of pesticides and insecticides, but I'd just nix that bush altogether. This kind of poisoning is incredibly uncommon, but you definitely don't want it happening again."

Eventually we were discharged. Josh was comforted to learn the screams I'd heard were hallucinations. That the moving barn was as well. I was supposed to believe Alice Belkin was in my head.

But no one could explain the teeth. Not the one I'd handed over to the sheriff or the several they'd found beside my unconscious body.

CHAPTER 42

TIME MARCHED FORWARD. WE RETURNED TO THE FARM, AND Ray vowed that they'd changed their storage for all the chemicals in the barn. His apologies were profuse, but he also still wouldn't step inside our home. I lounged on the couch and drank lots of water and ate nothing that came from our farm for three weeks. I used the time to think about Bridget Belkin. Even if the rest of it had been in my head, I'd found her tooth in the barn. That was real, and that girl—and her mother—deserved justice.

Josh canceled work travel for the whole month. We'd been running together each morning, because now I wasn't supposed to be scared anymore.

"Did you get good sleep last night?" he asked over our coffee that morning. There was only adoration in his tone. He no longer worried about me and my 3 a.m. coffee habit.

"Good enough," I said, like I believed two hours of sleep was all my body needed.

I continued to log the distance from the farmhouse to the

beat-down barn, but waited until Josh had ducked into the bathroom to shower before I wrote it down. I'd felt it looming behind me on our first run back. And sure enough the distance changed daily. I kept the haunting a private secret. If Josh knew, he'd say I was still sick. He'd take me to specialists, start pushing medicines again. He'd have a new reason not to believe me.

And so I'd stayed up most of the night watching the barn. Because no matter what the doctors said about the berries from the bush by the barn and the vegetables in my garden being tainted by the insecticides used on the farm, the barn was still moving. The light still flicked on every few nights. I'd been told the "symptoms" would abate after seventy-two hours, a week at the worst. It'd been nearly a month, and they still continued.

Because it had never been a hallucination.

"Are you ready to dive into DIY mode today, babe?" Josh asked, already chipper. He had his tool belt on the counter and was ready to unleash his inner Property Brother again.

"I'm ready to see something beautiful outside that kitchen window." I mustered enthusiasm, but even the brightest paint wouldn't hide what had happened inside that barn.

Alice's voice had stopped after I'd stopped eating the pesticide-riddled foods. But that didn't change the fact the tooth had been real; it'd belonged to Bridget Belkin.

But I couldn't let the barn stand untouched. It'd housed so much trauma, it was time to give it some renovation therapy.

That Josh took it as me being healthy again was a bonus.

Josh and I walked to the barn, and I tried not to note the steps this time.

He surveyed the array of supplies we'd stacked. "You did amazing, babe. I bet all the neighbors are going to want to renovate their barns after they see ours." Josh said this like it was a real thing. Like people would somehow see the barn from the distance and go, "I'll take one."

"Crisp white and cornflower blue are classic colors, but our barn will be the only one like it for miles." I needed to force a bright spot in my life, but I also liked that giving it a feminine touch was the kind of middle finger that I gathered Alice would appreciate.

Josh had stacked the painting supplies inside the barn. Stepping inside those doors twisted my insides. No matter the amount of puking I did at the hospital or the long talks from medical staff about the impacts of the chemicals I'd accidentally ingested, I couldn't forget what I'd seen in here. Even if I had been sick, my imagination simply wasn't that good. Or that dark.

My shorts and sports bra were the same blue as the accent paint I'd picked out. We'd coat the doors and shutters in that color, and I hoped it'd quell the tide of worry rising in my chest. We took our little spatula scrapers and headed outside to the back of the barn. Josh had power washed the walls earlier, but there were still small pieces of the old ugly paint that had refused to come free. We went to work removing the last vestiges of the rusted red from the sickly gray wood.

We worked up a decent sweat. Josh had already ditched his shirt. So when he paused, hands on his hips, I hoped it was time for a water break.

"You good?" I asked.

His mouth tightened, but finally he said, "Well, that's going to be a problem."

I walked closer to him. He was next to where we'd ripped out Blanche's berry bush, as I'd taken to thinking of it. He was near the back entrance to the barn. I'd avoided both. "Did we miss some of the roots? Is it in the way of painting?" I guessed.

"No, it's not that. There's mold," he said as though this was a shock.

I'd reminded him about the mold inside the barn more than once. Even the sheriff had called it out to us. "You did hit all the spots inside with the mold-mildew primer, right?"

"I told you I would," he snapped.

Not enough, apparently. "Guess there was more than we realized."

I pushed open the barn door. The whine of the hinges scraping nails across my spine. I leaned in to look at the inside of the same patch of wall. "It's moldy here too."

Josh followed me in, swearing. "I sprayed here." He pointed at the fresh white paint on the wall.

The mold had crawled over the crispness. How could it creep so quickly? *Alice?* I thought, like the ghost was still here and she could read my mind.

"There's a hole there." I pointed to a broken board with frayed edges.

"Probably a fox's work." His answer was automatic. *Because those screams have always been animals, Emily.*

"We haven't heard foxes on the farm in weeks." There had been no screams since the night I went into the cornfield.

"Maybe he hasn't needed to announce himself?" Josh winced at his poor excuse of a joke.

I ignored him and crouched near the hole.

Josh's hand clamped on my shoulder. "Em, you don't want your face down there without a mask."

Like looking at the mold was going to smack me with a toxic reaction. I shook my head but stepped back.

We both put on masks, because I refused to be left out of this. The mold was back. The same black growth I'd seen on the photos of Alice, the fuzz I'd seen on the floorboards next to Bridget's tooth, the black mold that said, "This isn't in your head."

We began prying away the wooden planks on the inside of the barn wall. Whatever was causing the blackened growth was inside, and these boards couldn't be painted over. We needed to replace them. We had new wood waiting at the other end of the barn. *No big deal*, I told myself as my heart galloped like I was forty-five seconds into a sprint.

A board popped off with a crack. I jerked backward.

"Babe, don't look," Josh said quickly.

But not fast enough. Feathers, sticky and flat, were matted to the floor. Blanche. I knew it immediately. Her neck had been snapped; her body, though, was... Well, it *wasn't* a body anymore. My sweet chicken was now a husk of a corpse crammed in this small space.

I clamped a hand over my mouth and willed the vomit rising in my throat back down. The tears, though, I couldn't stop. Josh had been right about a fox.

Another animal had stolen my hen. The fox had shoved her in here like the barn was a disgusting, forgotten pantry. I couldn't stop staring at what remained of my hen.

"Emily, really, go back to the house. I can handle this." Josh was pleading. He stepped forward to block my view of the new hole.

But it was too late. I'd seen the interior of that wall. Along the back, next to a supporting wall was something light, like a cream bolt behind my chicken's body.

I moved around him. "No, Josh, look."

He wasn't looking at the interior of the barn wall. My husband was staring at me, bewildered.

"There's more in there. More than Blanche." I took his hand and tried to turn him. The more I stared past him, the more clearly I understood what I was seeing. When he didn't budge, I added, "That looks like a bone."

Doubt clouded his eyes. That familiar hardness overtook his jaw. He was going to placate me and try to prove me wrong. "I can look. You go."

"I'm not going anywhere." I stepped around him, gripped the bottom board, and yanked. It came free too easily, sending me onto my ass.

It was worth it. The stretch of bone continued upward. And there was another, near parallel in the alcove.

I leaned forward, blasted with a wave of rot. I tucked my masked nose in the crook of my arm. "What is going on here?"

I hadn't really been asking Josh, but he replied, "Doesn't matter. Let's call the sheriff."

Oh, so now we should believe me? I grasped the next plank and ripped it from the wall. "Those are legs."

My announcement was met with silence. I turned back to my husband. Sweat gathered on his quickly paling cheeks. "We don't know what that is."

Snap. Crash. I threw the next board on the floor. "We're finding out what's in this wall."

Josh reached for my arm, tried to still me. "We need help."

"I did before, but I can pull these boards off just fine." I ripped another away, making sure to step aside so Josh could see the pelvis in the wall as well as I could.

Later I might be horrified, there would be tears, but right now anger lit my nerves. There'd been a body in the wall of my barn this whole time. Someone locked here, left to die. Was this why Alice kept bringing me here?

To her, I said, "I wish I'd understood."

"Understood what?" Josh asked. "There's no way anyone could have guessed there was a... You know what, no, I'm calling the cops."

He fumbled with his phone, like he'd forgotten how to unlock the screen.

"Josh." I waited for him to look at me. "I told you a girl was murdered here. I told you the farmhands had done horrible things here. I told you Ray was scared. Shit, I told you *I* was scared. And you didn't believe me."

"It was never that, babe," he said, his thumb hovering over the Send button.

Giving him my back, I ripped another board and another from the wall. I pointed at the corpse within. Textured with age and heat, sad and screaming. The body was small and still clad in ragged clothes.

Tears welled, fell. My lack of crying quickly switched to hyperventilating. This poor girl. Dead and hidden in a wall. Bridget had wanted to leave here more than anything, and they'd put her body in the fucking barn.

Josh shouted a curse word I hadn't thought he even knew. He called 9-1-1, voice steadier than it had been moments earlier.

I yanked off another board despite Josh's demands I stop and wait for the cops. I needed to see. With each plank removed, more of the corpse came into view.

I'd known. This whole time.

I scanned the other walls. Were there more? Josh stopped me from demolishing the barn before the authorities could investigate.

Sheriff Wilson arrived with a whole team this time. Corpses will do that, I suppose. His team extracted it from the wall after taking lots of photos and collecting Blanche's remains too. Evidence (of what, I wasn't entirely certain).

The body had been mummified by years of blistering sun against the wall of the barn, but from the short stature, the long hair, and the small gold cross around the neck, the truth was obvious.

We'd found Bridget Belkin.

Emily's Running Log:

2 minutes, 18 seconds to the barn—411 steps

5 minutes, 38 seconds to the barn—994 steps

1 minute, 9 seconds to the barn—207 steps

8 minutes, 12 seconds to the barn—1,476 steps

CHAPTER 43

THE SHERIFF CALLED IN A FULL FORENSICS TEAM. THEY WERE looking beyond the barn, beyond Bridget's body. They were in the fields, in the equipment, in my house. Everywhere. This is what should have happened the first time I'd called. We could have found her so much sooner.

They brought out a team to remove more walls within the barn.

Josh was nursing a glass of water at the kitchen table. A deputy was asking him questions, but the sheriff finally saw the truth.

"Have you seen anything unusual, Mrs. Hauk?" Sheriff Wilson finally asked the question that he should have asked the first time he'd come here. I had his attention now.

"You mean other than teeth showing up on my farm?" I couldn't resist the dig.

He lowered his head in acknowledgment. "I only had the one to test, Mrs. Hauk, but I'm here. I'm listening."

It was as close to a mea culpa as I expected. I wasn't having this conversation to make myself feel better. This was about

Bridget and any other girl that Nick might go after. And so I was honest. We were beyond me getting the crazy-lady looks. No one mentioned my hospital stint or the night I was found in the dirt. Alice had wanted me there; her ghost had wanted these secrets out.

Sheriff Wilson jotted careful notes as I recounted the night I'd seen a hand reaching out beneath a tarp. The night his deputies said it was nothing. Whether it had happened weeks or years ago didn't matter. It'd happened, and they needed to do something.

"But then he also gave Josh venison jerky," I hedged, internal doubt creeping in.

"Could have been a deer, but it's worth checking out. Anything else?"

"There was a hammer in the back of the truck," I blurted. If it was even still there.

"I'd suspect there are more tools than that in the back of a farm truck." His cheeks tightened like he was swallowing a laugh.

"You should look for the hammer," I snarled with the undercurrent of a woman they'd ignored before.

He nodded and wrote it down. "I will. What else have you seen from that kitchen window?" The way he asked it made it clear he knew the vantage point well.

"What makes you think it's always from the kitchen window?"

"People have watched the world through that window for years." Regret tinged our conversation. Was he thinking of Alice?

"Everyone on this farm wanted me to stay away from that barn. They avoid my farmhouse."

"They're respectful folk, ma'am." It's like the sheriff had been talking to my husband.

"They're a family who keeps secrets."

"You're saying I should investigate the farmers?"

"I'm saying that you need to look at Bridget's family. We both know Alice killed herself in that barn too."

Sheriff Wilson reeled back. "What do you know about Alice?"

"I know women on this farm have been ignored. Don't let it continue." With that, I stood up, got myself a cup of coffee, and went to sit on my porch.

The police hadn't protected Bridget. Sheriff Wilson hadn't advocated for Alice. It was time for people to do the right thing, and I would watch them do their jobs from my porch swing with a fourth cup of coffee and zero shame.

They found more teeth—more than could have fit in Bridget's mouth. The bodies came later. In my fields. Buried beneath the corn. Sheriff Wilson had followed through on the hammer, and with it came blood from more girls.

Bridget Belkin.

Kinsey McAllen.

Adeline Wallace.

Maryanne Parde.

Both Tyler and Nick were arrested. The latter confessed first, apparently. He claimed his uncle and his dad told him to stop Bridget from leaving. He'd been told to make her stay at any cost. He said he'd had to do it. For the farm. But the other girls Tyler picked out. They'd also wanted to leave town, leave the state, like they could forgo their roots. And he said it all with conviction, as if a woman choosing to live her life in a way that made her happy was abhorrent.

All of it hurt my heart, but I continued to watch. To witness.

CHAPTER 44

FREQUENT FLIERS HAVE A SYSTEM FOR TRAVELING. THEY know exactly how to roll their clothes to fit into their overhead-bin-friendly carry-on bag. They slip their laptops out of their backpacks or totes before they're even fully to the conveyor belt at the airport security checkpoint. Josh's job meant he was one of these people. He could gather his things and be ready to leave for a week in under thirty minutes.

He'd canceled the trip he'd had scheduled the week we found Bridget's body. No need for me to be alone while the deputies roved the farm, while they upturned the soil and found more girls. But while I watched it all, my husband pulled deeper into the house. As if he were safer at the center of it.

"Get away from the window, Em," he started, but then his demand would become a plea. "Sit with me. Let's forget about all of *that*."

Were we supposed to forget about the dead girls? Did he want me to ignore their loss like everyone else had? Or was his dismissal here bigger? It sure felt like he was going to pretend the last several months of me seeing, hearing, *knowing* had not happened.

"I don't want to forget," I muttered.

"How can you not? This place..." He trailed off, shaking his head like it'd dispel some intrusive thought.

"Is ours," I said firmly.

Josh slid down on the couch, resting his head on the back of the sofa. "But do we want it anymore? This place frightened you. Those guys—Nick, Tyler—they were dangerous, Emily."

I remained at the big bay window. It was late afternoon, and streaks of orange punched through the dusty sky. "I'm well aware."

"It's okay to admit that this place isn't right for us." He continued like he hadn't heard me.

I turned from the window, stalking toward him.

"Do you think moving back to San Francisco is a good idea?" I sure as hell didn't.

Josh rose from the couch, like this was a standing-up type of talk. "I know there are too many memories there for you, but we could pick a new place."

He reached for my hands. His warm grip had gotten me through the worst of it with my mom's death, but he'd done the same since we moved here. Those gentle squeezes whenever I shared a worry or exposed a threat. I'd thought it was understanding, but it was placation. He hadn't believed me this whole time. He'd sided with the strangers on our farm—the ones who were killers.

I pulled my hands away. "Did you ever believe me when I told you about the lights or the tooth?"

"The tooth was real." He was adamant.

"It all was." Even if he couldn't see some it. It'd been real.

Josh nodded emphatically and tried to take my hands again.

I stepped backward. "Why weren't you scared?"

"Excuse me?" It was his turn to stagger away.

"You were freaked out when I showed you the tooth—"

His brow pinched, worry seeping in. "Of course I was. Anyone would be."

Exactly my point. "But then after the sheriff was here, you were fine."

"He told us it likely wasn't a big deal."

Fucking A, Josh. "But I told you it was. Why was his word believable and mine wasn't?"

"Oh, baby, it's not like that at all."

I shrugged. "But it was."

Josh sat and dropped his elbows against his knees. Hunched over, he spoke to the coffee table instead of to me. "Emily, you've got to see it from my side. None of what you said made sense. There was no sign of anything nefarious happening, and you weren't taking any of your medication. Why wouldn't I believe that you were just struggling? Moving here didn't wipe away everything from before."

"I would have told you if it was grief, if a new wave was hitting." Or at least the old me would have. I shook my head. "Besides, my doctor gave me the 'as needed' talk on the meds."

His sharp exhale of derision didn't help us. "Well, you needed it."

Had I though? Seeing Bridget get her justice, knowing Alice had witnessed it, giving them both peace? That was...a relief. Who knows how many other girls Nick and Tyler would have gone after? I'd done a good thing here, and still my husband wouldn't just say I was right. It's not that I wanted to play an "I told you so" game—that was toxic—but where was the confidence in me?

"I'm good, Josh," I said coolly.

The fan whirred overhead, cicadas chirped outside, and Josh and I pointedly avoided eye contact for long moments.

Josh sucked his teeth, but it was another minute until he spoke. "I've got a meeting in Boston tomorrow. I'm taking the evening flight."

He never took the overnight flights like that, and it was already edging toward dusk. I should have asked him to postpone until the morning. *Cancel the red-eye and stay with me. Talk about how we bridge this gap.* Only I didn't know if I could sit on that couch next to him with the knowledge that he still thought he'd done right by me.

"How long is the trip?" I walked back to the window. A deputy drove past, kicking up a cloud that matched his uniform.

"Depends on how the meetings go. Probably two days."

Josh left the room to go pack, and a weight lifted from my chest. I had a slice of pie—coconut cream this time—while I waited for him to finish with his bag.

I was placing the dishes in the washer when Josh rolled his suitcase into the living room. It was the large hard-sided one we used for international trips. It could hold more than a week's worth of clothes. Not a two-day-work-trip bag.

I stared at the black bag and then at Josh. His tight jaw and ruddy cheeks said everything. Reality had set in—what had happened here, both on the farm and between us—and he was running.

Who knew when it came to fear that I was the one who leaned into fight and he was ready for flight?

"If you change your mind, I can fly you to Boston tomorrow. We could stay longer and explore the city." The offer fell too quickly from his lips, like he'd tumble over the lies if he didn't barrel through them.

I nodded, but Josh was looking over my shoulder to the barn beyond the window. Fear bloomed red up the sides of his neck; the resonance of what had happened finally connecting in his body. I understood the feeling, but this place was mine, and I wasn't going to bail.

Josh's nostrils flared; his jaw flexed. "I love you, Em. Get some rest. I'll call in the morning."

My husband pressed a kiss to my forehead and wheeled his bag out the door.

CHAPTER 45

THE FARMHOUSE WAS SUPPOSED TO BE MY REFUGE. THE place my marriage grew stronger. The place free of my mother's memory. A sanctuary from grief. No matter how hard I tried, it'd been none of those. But I never saw Alice's ghost again. The barn stopped shifting locations after Bridget's body was removed.

My husband, however, couldn't stand still. Josh couldn't stand the farm anymore. He called it too hard, too traumatic. He asked how I could want to stay in a place that had made him question me. I asked why he could have questioned me in the first place. That's how we landed on him moving to Omaha. Alone. Our divorce was in progress, but it felt like freedom for us both, I suspected.

I remained on the farm. I bought goats and another four hens. I broke the farming lease with Ray, and let new farmers take over the land. Not a one was related to the Belkin family. I couldn't erase the blood from the soil here, but I would keep new trauma from seeping in.

The farmhouse finally became my solace. The air was no longer still and quiet. I put on a Selena Gomez track, tended to my animals, and then ran in my fields. Safe for the first time in too long.

Emily's Running Log:

26.4 miles on dirt and gravel—Order a new pair of shoes after you
ace this marathon

ACKNOWLEDGMENTS

Whenever someone talks about how solitary writing is, I think about how my writing family continues to grow. I'm not alone, and the people who listened to me talk about *The Farmhouse*—from the eerie barn to the gaslighting to the teeth—made sure I was never alone with this book. Which is probably good because it's creepy, right?

I am immensely grateful to have worked with editor Rachel Gilmer on this book. She understood what I wanted to say with *The Farmhouse* and made that vision happen. Her insights were spot on, and working with her was a dream. (Who gets to say that about edits?! Please nominate her for awards.)

The team at Sourcebooks and Poisoned Pen Press are wizards, y'all. Immense thank-yous to Emily Engwall, Aimee Alker, Jessica Thelander, Laura Boren, Erin Fitzsimmons, Stephanie Rocha, and Dominique Raccah. To Simon Mendez, thank you for your amazing artwork for the interior of this book. Thank you for bringing Emily and the farm to life in your illustrations.

Thank you to Naomi Davis, whose unwavering enthusiasm for this book from concept to pitch to novel to sold was everything. And to my agent, Cheyenne Faircloth, thank you for championing this book and the next and the next.

I am incredibly lucky to have talented writer friends who will read my work and give valuable feedback. To Lish McBride, Kristen Simmons, Amanda Bonilla, Jaye Wells, Cathlin Shahriary, Molly Harper, Jeanette Battista, Carina Bissett, and Rachel Fikes, thank you for making time to read my spooky thriller.

And, of course, no acknowledgments are complete without giving love to my family, especially Matt and Simon. Special bonus appreciation to my mom, Marcia, and my stepmom, Dodie, who both will love me even if this book keeps them up at night.

Finally, thank you, Nebraska, for being beautiful, resilient, and forever feeling like home.

ABOUT THE AUTHOR

Chelsea Conradt (she/her) writes twisty speculative thrillers. Her books are packed with both murder and kindness, because we can be more than one thing. When not writing stories that make you question what's real, she is likely watching a baking show or a true-crime documentary. She is nothing if not on-brand. Chelsea lives in Texas with her husband, son, and two big dogs.

Website: chelseaconradt.com

Facebook: /ChelseaConradt

Instagram: @authorchelseaconradt

TikTok: @chelseaconradt